ISBN 978-1-331-47864-5
PIBN 10195708

This book is a reproduction of an important historical work. Forgotten Books uses
state-of-the-art technology to digitally reconstruct the work, preserving the original format
whilst repairing imperfections present in the aged copy. In rare cases, an imperfection in
the original, such as a blemish or missing page, may be replicated in our edition. We do,
however, repair the vast majority of imperfections successfully; any imperfections that
remain are intentionally left to preserve the state of such historical works.

1 MONTH OF
FREE
READING

at
www.ForgottenBooks.com

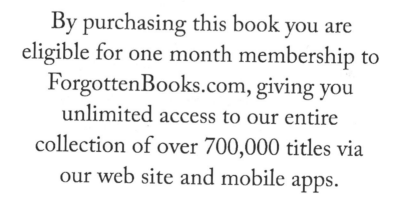

By purchasing this book you are
eligible for one month membership to
ForgottenBooks.com, giving you
unlimited access to our entire
collection of over 700,000 titles via
our web site and mobile apps.

To claim your free month visit:
www.forgottenbooks.com/free195708

English
Français
Deutsche
Italiano
Español
Português

www.forgottenbooks.com

Mythology Photography **Fiction**
Fishing Christianity **Art** Cooking
Essays Buddhism Freemasonry
Medicine **Biology** Music **Ancient**
Egypt Evolution Carpentry Physics
Dance Geology **Mathematics** Fitness
Shakespeare **Folklore** Yoga Marketing
Confidence Immortality Biographies
Poetry **Psychology** Witchcraft
Electronics Chemistry History **Law**
Accounting **Philosophy** Anthropology
Alchemy Drama Quantum Mechanics
Atheism Sexual Health **Ancient History**
Entrepreneurship Languages Sport
Paleontology Needlework Islam
Metaphysics Investment Archaeology
Parenting Statistics Criminology
Motivational

THE SILVER BRACELET, WALPI.

Frontispiece

WESTWARD HOBOES

UPS AND DOWNS
OF FRONTIER MOTORING

BY

WINIFRED HAWKRIDGE DIXON

PHOTOGRAPHS BY
KATHERINE THAXTER AND ROLLIN LESTER DIXON

NEW YORK
CHARLES SCRIBNER'S SONS
1921

WESTWARD HOBOES

UPS AND DOWNS
OF FRONTIER MOTORING

BY

WINIFRED HAWKRIDGE DIXON

PHOTOGRAPHS BY
KATHERINE THAXTER AND ROLLIN LESTER DIXON

NEW YORK
CHARLES SCRIBNER'S SONS
1921

OCT 19 1921

THE SCRIBNER PRESS

©Cl. A624860

CONTENTS

CHAPTER   PAGE

    I. WESTWARD HO! . . . .

   II. FROM NEW YORK TO ANTOINE'S . . . .

  III. A LONG WAYS FROM HOME 15

  IV. CHIVALRY VS. GUMBO 25

   V. NIBBLING AT THE MAP OF TEXAS 35

  VI. "DOWN BY THE RIO GRANDE" 47

 VII. SANDSTORMS, BANDITS AND DEAD SOLDIERS 60

VIII. TUCSON 74

  IX. TWENTY PER CENT GRADES, FORTY PER CENT
      VANILLA 82

   X. THE APACHE TRAIL AND TONTO VALLEY . . 98

  XI. FRIDAY THE THIRTEENTH 121

 XII. WHY ISLETA'S CHURCH HAS A WOODEN FLOOR . 148

XIII. SANTE FÉ AND THE VALLEY OF THE RIO
      GRANDE 160

XIV. SAYING GOOD-BY TO BILL 190

 XV. LAGUNA AND ACOMA 204

XVI. THE GRAND CANYON AND THE HAVASUPAI
      CANYON 220

CONTENTS

CHAPTER   PAGE

XVII.   FROM WILLIAMS TO FORT APACHE 234

XVIII.   THE LAND OF THE HOPIS 244

XIX.   THE FOUR CORNERS 258

XX.   RAINBOW BRIDGE 270

XXI.   THE CANYON DE CHELLEY 296

XXII.   NORTH OF GALLUP 308

XXIII.   ON NATIONAL PARKS AND GUIDES 326

XXIV.   THE NAIL-FILE AND THE CHIPPEWA . . . 346

XXV.   HOMEWARD HOBOES 358

ILLUSTRATIONS

The silver bracelet, Walpi . . . . *Frontispiece*

FACING PAGE

Our first camp, Texas 52

San Xavier Del Bac, Tucson, and the Rapago Indian village 76

Doorway of San Xavier Del Bac, Tucson 78

Great rocks seem to float on the stream, mysteriously
 lighted, like Böcklin's isle of the dead 116

Natural bridge, Pine, Arizona 118

The church at Isleta 152

Her bread was baked, delicious and crusty, in the round outdoor ovens her grandmothers used as far back as B. C.
 or so 154

Against a shady wall, all but too lazy to light the inevitable
 cigarette, slouches, wherever one turns, a Mexican 164

A Mexican morado, New Mexico 166

The museum of Santa Fé 166

Santa Domingo woman 176

Taos woman 176

Koshari: rain dance: San Yldefonso 176

Rain dance, San Yldefonso 178

Cave dwellings in the pumice walls of Canyon de Los Frijoles, Santa Fé 182

Artist's studio in Taos, New Mexico 188

vii

ILLUSTRATIONS

FACING PAGE

Coronado was the first white man to visit this ancient pueblo at Taos, New Mexico 188

The car sagged drunkenly on one side 200

Fording a river near Santa Fé 200

On the way to Gallup 200

Pueblo women grinding corn in metate bins 206

Pueblo woman wrapping deer-skin leggins 206

Acoma, New Mexico 212

Burros laden with fire-wood, Santa Fé, New Mexico 212

At the foot of the trail, Acoma 214

The enchanted mesa, Acoma, New Mexico 214

A street in Acoma, New Mexico 218

The Acoma Mission, New Mexico 218

In the Grand Canyon of the Colorado 222

A Navajo maid on a painted pony 222

The land of the sky-blue water, Havasupai Canyon, Arizona 224

Horseman in Havasupai Canyon, Arizona 226

Panorama of Havasupai Canyon, Arizona 228

Mooney's Fall, Havasupai Canyon, Arizona 232

A trout stream in the White Mountains, Arizona 240

The village of Walpi 250

Oldest house in Walpi 250

Young eaglet captured for use in the Hopi snake-dance ceremonies 254

Second mesa, Hopi Reservation 256

A Hotavilla Sybil 256

ILLUSTRATIONS

FACING PAGE

Navajo Mountain from the mouth of Segi Canyon   278

Rainbow Bridge Trail near Navajo Mountain   .   .   .   282

Crossing Bald Rock, on Rainbow Bridge Trail   284

Rainbow Bridge, Utah   286

Monument country, Rainbow Trail   294

Rainbow Bridge Trail   294

Entrance to the Canyon de Chelley   298

Quicksand; Canyon de Chelley   300

Near the entrance of Canyon de Chelley, Arizona   302

Cliff-dwellings, Canyon de Chelley, Arizona   .   .   .   304

Casa Blanca, Canyon de Chelley, Arizona   306

Navajo sheep-dipping at Shiprock   312

Cliff-dwellings, Mesa Verde Park, Colorado   .   .   .   316

Shoshones at sun dance, Fort Hall, Idaho   322

A Shoshone teepee, Fort Hall, Idaho   324

Camping near Yellowstone Park   328

Grand Canyon, Yellowstone Park   330

Glacier Park, Montana   332

Blackfeet Indians at Glacier Park, Montana .   .   .   336

Two Medicine Lake, Glacier Park, Montana .   .   .   344

Wrangling horses, Glacier Park, Montana   344

A Mormon irrigated village   354

The "Million Dollar" Mormon Temple at Cardston, Alberta,. Canada   354

WESTWARD HOBOES

CHAPTER I

"WESTWARD HO!"

TOBY'S real name is Katharine. Her grandmother was a poet, her father is a scientist, and she is an artist. She is called Toby for Uncle Jonas' dog, who had the habit, on being kicked out of the door, of running down the steps with a cheerful bark and a wagging tail, as if he had left entirely of his own accord. There is no fact, however circumstantially incriminating, which this young doctrinaire cannot turn into the most potent justification for what she has done or wishes to do, and when she gets to the tail wagging stage, regardless of how recently the bang of the front door has echoed in our ears, she wags with the charm of the artist, the logical precision of the scientist, and the ardor of the poet. Even when she ran the car into the creek at Nambe——

At the outset we did not plan to make the journey by automobile. Our destination was uncertain. We planned to drift, to sketch and write when the spirit moved. But drifting by railroad in the West implies time-tables, crowded trains, boudoir-capped matrons, crying babies and the smell of bananas, long waits and anxiety over reservations. Traveling by auto seemed luxurious in comparison and would save railroad fares, annoyance

and time.   We pictured ourselves bowling smoothly along
in the open air, in contrast with the stifling train; we previsioned no delays, no breakdowns, no dangers; we saw
New Mexico and Arizona a motorist's Heaven, paved
with asphalt and running streams of gasoline.   An optimist is always like that, and two are twenty times so.   I
was half-owner of a Cadillac Eight, with a rakish
hood and a matronly tonneau; its front was intimidating,
its rear reassuring.   The owner of the other half was
safely in France.   At the time, which half belonged to
which had not been discussed.   It is now a burning question.   I figure that the springs, the dust-pan, the paint,
mud-guards and tires constituted her share, with a few
bushings and nuts thrown in for good measure, but having acquired a mercenary disposition in France, she differs from me.

What I knew of the bowels of a car had been gained,
not from systematic research, but bitter experience with
mutinous parts, in ten years' progress through two, four,
six and finally eight-cylinder motors of widely varying
temperaments.   I had taken no course in mechanics, and
had, and still have, a way of confusing the differential
with the transmission.   But I love to tinker!   In the old
two-cylinder days, when the carburetor flooded I would
weigh it down with a few pebbles and a hairpin, and
when the feed became too scanty, I would take the hairpin out and leave the pebbles in.   I had a smattering
knowledge of all the deviltry defective batteries, leaky
radiators, frozen steering-wheels, cranky generators,
wrongly-hung springs, stripped gears and slipping clutches
can perpetrate, but those parts which commonly behaved
themselves I left severely alone.   Toby could not drive,

but a few lessons made her an apt pupil. She paid her money to the Commonwealth of Massachusetts for a license, and one sparkling evening in early February we started for Springfield. We were to cover thirteen thousand miles before we saw Boston again,—eleven thousand by motor and the rest by steamship and horseback.

As I threw in the clutch, we heard a woman's voice calling after us. It was Toby's mother, and what she said was, "Don't drive at night!"

In New York we made the acquaintance of a map—which later was to become thumbed, torn and soiled. A delightful map it was, furnished by the A.A.A., with an index specially prepared for us of every Indian reservation, natural marvel, scenic and historical spot along the ridgepole of the Rockies, from Mexico, to Canada. Who could read the intriguing list of names,—Needles, Flagstaff, Moab, Skull Valley, Keams Canyon, Fort Apache, Tombstone, Rodeo, Kalispell, Lost Cabin, Hatchita, Rosebud, Roundup, Buckeye, Ten Sleep, Bowie and Bluff Winnemucca,—and stop at home in Boston? We were bent on discovering whether they lived up to their names, whether Skull Valley was a scattered outpost of the desert with mysterious night-riders, stampeding steer, gold-seekers, cattle thieves and painted ladies, or had achieved virtue in a Rexall drugstore, a Harvey lunchroom, a jazz parlor, a Chamber of Commerce, an Elks' Hall, and a three story granite postoffice donated by a grateful administration? Which glory is now Skull Valley's we do not yet know, but depend on it, it is either one or the other. The old movie life of the frontier is not obsolete, only obsolescent, provided one knows where to look. But the day after it vanishes a thriving city has arrived at adolescence and "Frank's" and "Bill's" have placed a liveried black at their doors, and provided the ladies' parlor upstairs with three kinds of rouge.

It was love at first sight—our map and us. Pima and Maricopa Indians, Zuni and Laguna pueblos, the Rainbow Bridge and Havasupai Canyon beckoned to us and hinted their mysteries; our itinerary widened until it included vaguely everything there was to see. We made only one reservation—we would *not* visit California. California was the West, dehorned; it possessed climate, boulevards and conveniences; but it also possessed sand fleas and native sons. It was a little thing which caused us to make this decision, but epochal. At the San Francisco Exposition, I had seen a long procession of Native Sons, dressed in their native gold—a procession thousands strong. Knowing what one native son can do when he begins on his favorite topic of conversation, we dared not trust ourselves to an army of them, an army militant.

What we planned to do was harder and less usual. We would follow the old trails, immigrant trails, cattle trails, traders' routes,—mountain roads which a long procession of cliff dwellers, Spanish friars, gold seekers, Apache marauders, prospectors, Mormons and scouts had trod in five centuries, and left as they found them, mere footprints in the dust. The Southwest has been explored afoot and on horse, by prairie schooners, burro, and locomotive; the modern pioneer rattles his weather beaten flivver on business between Gallup and Santa Fe, Tucson and El Paso, and thinks nothing of it, but the country is still new to the motoring tourist. Because a car must have the attributes of a hurdler and a tight-rope walker, be amphibious and fool-proof, have a bea-gle's nose for half-obliterated tracks, thrill to the tug of sand and mud, and own a constitution strong enough to withstand all experiments of provincial garage-men, few merciful car owners will put it through the supreme agony. Had not the roads looked so smooth on the map we wouldn't have tried them ourselves.

And then, in New York, we met another optimist, and two and one make three. It was not until long afterward, when we met the roads he described as passable, that we discovered he was an optimist. He had motored through every section of the West, and paid us the compliment of believing we could do the same. When he presented us with our elaborate and beautiful itinerary he asked no questions about our skill and courage. He told us to buy an axe and a shovel, and carry a rope. A tent he advised as well, and such babes in the woods were we, the idea had not occurred to us.

"And carry a pistol?" asked Toby, eagerly.

"Never! You will be as safe—or safer than you are in New York City." Toby was disappointed, but I heard him with relief. By nature gun-shy, I have seen too many war-dramas not to know that a pistol never shoots the person originally aimed at. The procedure never varies. A pulls a gun, points it at B. B, unflinching, engages A in light conversation. Diverted, A absent-mindedly puts down the gun, which B picks up, shooting to kill. I realized that as B my chances were better than as A, for while I would surely fall under the spell of a western outlaw's quaint humor and racy diction and thus hand over the weapon into his keeping, the chances were that he might be equally undermined by our Boston r's, and

the appeal to his rough Western chivalry which we intended to make. Toby held out for an ammonia pistol.
We did debate this for a while, but in the excitement of
buying our tent we forgot the pistol entirely.

Our Optimist directed us to a nearby sports'-goods
shop, recommending us to the care of a certain "Reggi,"
who, he guaranteed, would not try to sell us the entire
store. Confidently we sought the place,—a paradise
where elk-skin boots, fleecy mufflers, sleeping bags, leather
coats, pink hunting habits and folding stoves lure the
very pocketbooks out of one's hands. We asked for
Mr. Reggi, who did not look as Italian as his name. He
proved a sympathetic guide, steering us to the camping
department. He restrained himself from selling the most
expensive outfits he had. At the price of a fascinating
morning and fifty-odd dollars, we parted from him, owners of a silk tent, mosquito and snake proof, which folded
into an infinitesimal canvas bag, a tin lantern, which
folded flat, a tin biscuit baker which collapsed into nothing, a nest of cooking and eating utensils, which folded
and fitted into one two-gallon pail, a can opener, a hunting knife, doomed to be our most cherished treasure, a
flashlight, six giant safety-pins, and a folding stove. The
charm of an article which collapses and becomes something else than it seems I cannot analyze nor resist.
Others feel it too; I know a man who once stopped a
South American revolution by stepping into the Plaza and
opening and shutting his opera hat.

Only one incident marred our satisfaction with the
morning's work; we discovered, on saying farewell to
Reggi, that we had been calling him by his first name!

CHAPTER II

THERE were, we found, three ways to transport an automobile from New York to Texas; to drive it ourselves, and become mired in Southern "gumbo," to ship it by rail, and become bankrupt while waiting weeks for delivery, or, cheaper and altogether more satisfactory, to send it by freight steamer to Galveston. By this means we avoided the need of crating our lumbering vehicle; we also could calculate definitely its date of arrival, and by taking a passenger boat to New Orleans, and going thence by rail, be at the port to meet it.

Our baggage we stowed in a peculiarly shaped auto trunk containing five peculiarly shaped suitcases, trapezoids all,—not a parallelepiped among them. Made to fit an earlier car, in its day it had been the laughing stock of all the porters in Europe. Too bulky to be strapped outside, it was to become a mysterious occupant of the tonneau, exciting much speculation and comment. It was to be the means of our being taken for Salvation lassies with a parlor organ, bootleggers, Spiritualists with the omnipresent cabinet, show-girls or lady shirt-waist drummers, according to the imagination of the beholder; but it never was aught but a nuisance. Whatever we needed always reposed in the bottom-most suitcase, and rather than dig down, we did without. Next time, I shall know better. A three-piece khaki suit, composed of breeches, short skirt split front and back, and many-pocketed Norfolk coat, worn with knee-high elk boots, does for daily wear in camping, riding or driving. It sheds rain, heat and cold, does not wrinkle when slept in, and only mellows with successive accumulations of dirt. For dress occasions, a dark jersey coat and skirt, wool stockings and low oxfords is magnificence itself. A heavy and a light sweater, two flannel and a half dozen cotton or linen shirts, and sufficient plain underwear suffice for a year's knocking about. Add to this a simple afternoon frock of non-wrinkling material, preferably black, and no event finds you unprepared.

Our trunk made us trouble from the start. The administration had given us to understand we might ship it with the car, but at the last moment this was prevented by a constitutional amendment. Accordingly, an hour before our boat left, we took the trunk to the line on which we were to travel, and shipped it as personal baggage. It was only the first of many experiences which persuaded us to adopt the frontiersman's motto, "Pack light."

Every true yarn of adventure should begin with a sea voyage. The wharves with their heaped cargoes tying together the four ends of the world, the hoisting of the gang-plank, the steamer flirtations, the daily soundings, the eternal schools of porpoises, the menus with their ensuing disillusionments, and above all, the funny, funny passengers, each a drollery to all the others,—all these commonplaces of voyage are invested by the mighty sea with its own importance and mystery.

On board, besides ourselves, were some very funny people, and some merely funny. A swarthy family of Spaniards next us passed through all the successive shades of yellow and green, but throughout they were gay, eating oranges and chanting pretty little Castilian folk-songs. At table sat a man wearing a black and white striped shirt, of the variety known as "boiled," a black and white striped collar of a different pattern, and a bright blue necktie thickly studded with daisies and asterisks. He looked, otherwise, like a burglar without his jimmy, especially when we saw him by moonlight glowering prognathously through a porthole. He turned out to be only a playwright and journalist, with a specialty for handing out misinformation on a different subject each meal.

The stout lady, the flirtatious purser—why is he of all classes of men the most amorous?—the bounder, the bride and groom, the flappers of both sexes, the drummer, the motherly stewardess and the sardonic steward were all present. And why does the sight of digestive anguish bring out the maternal in the female, and only profanity in the male? Our plump English stewardess cooed over us, helpless in upper and lower berths; our steward always rocked with silent mirth, and muttered, "My God!"

Our own stout lady was particularly rare. She appeared coquettishly the first calm day off Florida, in a pink gingham dress, a large black rosary draped prominently upon her,—which did not much heighten her resemblance to a Mother Superior, owing to her wearing an embroidered Chinese kimona and a monkey coat over it, and flirting so gayly with the boys. On the Galveston train later, we heard her say helplessly, "Porter, my trunk is follering me to Galveston. How shall I stop it?" She could have stopped an express van merely by standing in front of it, but we did not suggest this remedy. The picture of a docile Saratoga lumbering doggedly at her rear was too much for words.

As to the purser, we left him severely alone. We did not feel we could flirt with him in the style to which he had been accustomed.

The last night of the voyage, when the clear bright green of the Gulf of Mexico gave place to the turbulent coffee color of the Mississippi, our stewardess knocked.

"On account of the river, miss, we don't bathe to-night." It was a small tragedy for us. Earlier in the voyage we could not bear to see the water sliding up and down in the tub,—so much else was sliding up and down. It was on one of those days that the stewardess informed us that there were "twenty-seven ladies sick on this deck, to say nothing of twenty-four below," and asked us how we would like a little piece of bacon. We firmly refused the bacon, but the Gilbertian lilt of her remark inspired us to composing a ballad with the refrain, "Twenty-seven sea-sick ladies we."

The river which deprived us of our baths presented at five next morning a bleak and sluggish appearance. I missed Simon Legree and the niggers singing plantation melodies, but it may have been too early in the day. Most picturesque, busy, low-lying river it was, nevertheless, banked with shipyards, newly built wharves, coaling stations, elevators, steamship docks—evidences to a provincial Northerner that the South, wakened perhaps by the Great War, has waited for none, but has forged ahead bent on her own development, achieving her independence —this time an economic independence. To the insular Manhattanite, who thinks of New York as the Eastern gate of this country, and San Francisco as the Western, the self-sufficiency, the bustle and the cosmopolitanism of the Mississippi's delta land, even seen through a six A.M. drizzle, gives a surprising jolt.

Six months later we were to cross the Mississippi near the headwaters not many miles from Canada. More lovely, there at the North, its broad, clear placid waters shadowed by green forests and high bluffs, it invites for a voyage of discovery.

On both banks of the river, whose forgotten raft and steamboat life Mark Twain made famous, are now being built concrete boulevards, designed to bisect the country from Canada to the Gulf. Huck Finns of the near future will be able to explore this great artery through what is now perhaps the least known and least accessible region of the country.

New Orleans, those who knew it twenty or forty years ago will tell you, has become modern and ugly, has lost its atmosphere. Drive through the newer and more pretentious outskirts, and you will believe all you are told. You will see the usual Southwestern broad boulevard, pointed with staccato palmettos, but otherwise arid of verdure, bordered with large, hideous mansions which completely overpower an occasional gem of low-verandahed loveliness, relic of happier days. For such grandeur the driver of our jitney,—undoubtedly the one used by Gen. Jackson during his defence of the city,—had an infallible instinct. I don't think he missed one atrocity during the whole morning's drive. Yet we passed one quite charming "colored" dwelling,—a low rambling cottage covered with vines, proudly made of glittering, silvery tin!

But in the old French or Creole quarters you find all

the storied charm of the city intact,—a bit of Italy, of
Old Spain, of the milder and sunnier parts of France,
jumbled together with the romance of the West Indies.
In the cobbled narrow pavements, down which mule teams
still clatter more often than motors, the mellow old
houses, with iron balconies beautifully wrought, broad
verandahs, pink, green or orange plastered walls, peeling
to show the red brick underneath,—shady courtyards,
high-walled with fountains and stone Cupids, glimpsed
through low arched doorways, markets like those of
Cannes and Avignon, piled with luscious fruits, crawfish,
crates of live hens, strings of onions, and barrels of huge
oysters,—oh, the oysters of New Orleans,—here lies the
fascination of the town.

Set down close to the wharves is this jumble of old
streets, so close that the funnels of docked tramps mingle
with the shop chimneys. From the wharves drift smells
of the sea and sea-commerce, to join the smells of the old
town. It is a subtle blend of peanuts, coffee, cooked food,
garlic, poultry,—a raw, pungent, bracing odor, inclining
one to thoughts of eating. And just around the corner is
Antoine's.

Eating? There should be a word coined to distinguish
ordinary eating from eating at Antoine's. The building
is modest and the lettering plain, as befits the dignity of
the place. The interior, plainly finished and lined with
mirrors, resembles any one of five hundred un-noteworthy
restaurants where business New York eats to get filled.
There the resemblance stops. A sparkle, restrained and
sober withal, rests on the mirrors, the glasses and the
silver. The floors and woodwork have a well scrubbed
look. The linen is carefully looked after, the china busi-

ness-like; everything decent, adequate, spotless,—nothing
to catch the eye.   It is not visual aestheticism which lures
us here, or causes the millionaire Manhattanite to order
his private car to take him to Antoine's for one hour of
bliss.   Antoine is an interior decorator of subtler but
more potent distinction.   And I would go even farther
than that New York multi-millionaire whose name spells
Aladdin to Americans; for such a meal as Antoine served
us that morning, I would travel the same distance in one
of those wife-killing contrivances which are the bane of
every self-respecting motorist.

The waiters at Antoine's are not hit-or-miss riff-raff
sent up by a waiters' employment bureau.   They are
grandfatherly courtiers who make you feel that the responsibility for your digestion lies in their hands, and for
the good name of the house in yours.   Old New Orleans
knows them by name, and recognizes the special dignity
of their priesthood, with the air of saluting equals.   Their
lifework is your pleasure,—the procuring of your inner
contentment.   You could trust your family's honor to
them, or the ordering of your meal.   Only at Antoine's
and in the pages of Leonard Merrick does one find such
servitors.

We accepted our Joseph's suggestion that we allow
him to bring us some of the specialties of the house.   It
was a wise decision,—from the prelude of oysters
Rockefeller,—seared in a hot oven with a sauce of chives,
butter and crumbs,—to the benediction of café brulôt.
Between came a marvel of a fish, covered with Creole
sauce, a sublimated chicken *a la King,* a salad and a
sweet, all nicely proportioned to each other, but their
memory was crowned by the café brulôt.   In came Joseph,

like all three Kings of Egypt, bearing a tall silver dish on a silver platter. The platter contained blazing brandy, the dish orange peel, lemon peel, cloves, cinnamon stick, four lumps of sugar, and two spoonfuls of brandy. Joseph stirred them into a melted nectar, then with a long silver ladle and the manner of a vestal virgin, swept the blazing brandy into the mixture above, and stood like a benevolent demon over the flame. An underling brought a pot of black coffee, which was added little by little to the fiery mixture, and stirred. Finally it was ladled into two small glasses. We swam in Swinburnian bliss. We paid our bill, and departed to a new New Orleans, where the secondhand stores were filled with genuine, priceless antiques, the pavings easy on our weary feet, the skies, as the meteorologist in the popular song observed, raining violets and daffodils. Mr. Volstead never tasted café brulôt.

CHAPTER III

A LONG WAYS FROM HOME

TWO days of downpour greeted us at Galveston while we waited for our car to arrive. It was the climax of three months of rain which had followed three drouthy years. The storm swept waves and spray over the breakwater toward the frame town which has sprung up hopefully after twice being devoured by the sea monster. A city of khaki tents dripped mournfully under the drenching; wet sentries paced the coast-line, and looked suspiciously at two ladies—all women are ladies in Texas —who cared to fight their way along the sea-wall against such a gale. Toby and I were bored, when we were not eating Galveston's oysters.

The city, pleasant enough under the sun, had its usual allotment of boulevards, bronze monuments, drug stores, bungalows of the modest and mansions of the local pluto-crats, but it had not the atmosphere of New Orleans. We were soon to learn that regardless of size, beauty or history, some towns have personality, others have about as much personality as a reception room in a Methodist dormitory.

Next day, news came that our boat had docked, and telephoning revealed that the car was safely landed. There are joys to telephoning in the South. Central is courteous and eager to please, and the voices of strangers with whom one does curt business at home become here so soft and winning that old friendships are immediately cemented, repartee indulged in, and the receiver hung up with a feeling of regret. That is the kind of voice the agent for the Mallory Line had. To be sure, it took us a day to get the car from the dock to the street, when it would have taken half an hour at home, but it was a day devoted to the finer shades of intercourse and good fellowship. I reached the dock half an hour before lunch time.

"Yes'm, the office is open, but I reckon yo' won't find any hands to move yo' car," was the accurate prediction of the official to whom I applied. "Pretty nearly lunch time, yo' know."

So I waited, filling in time by answering the guarded questions the watchman put to me. I was almost as fascinating an object of attention to him as his Bull Durham, though I must admit that when there was a conflict between us, I never won, except once, when he asked where the car and I came from.

"Massachusetts?" Bull Durham lost.

A great idea struggled for expression. I could see him searching for the right, the inevitable word. I could see it born, as triumph and amusement played over his features. Then caution—should he spring it all at once or save it for a climax? Nonchalantly, as if such epigrams were likely to occur to him any time, he got it off.

"You're a long ways from *home,* ain't yo'?"

With the air of saying something equally witty, I replied, "I surely am."

Like "When did you stop beating your wife," his question was one of those which has all the repartee its own way. For six months, we were to hear it several times daily, but it always came as a shock, and as if hypnotized, we were never to alter our response. And it was so true! We *were* a long ways from home, further than we then realized. At times we seemed so long that we wondered if we should ever see home again. But we were never too far to meet some man, wittier than his fellows, who defined our location accurately.

After his diagnosis and my acceptance of it, further conversation became anticlimactic. The "hands" were still absent at lunch, so I followed their example, and returning at two, found them still at lunch. But at last the agent drifted in, and three or four interested and willing colored boys. Everybody was pleasant, nobody was hurried, we exchanged courtesies, and signed papers, and after we really got down to business, in a surprisingly few minutes the car was rolled across the street by five-man power, while I lolled behind the steering wheel like Cleopatra in her galley. At the doorway the agent halted me.

"Massachusetts car?" he asked.

"Yes, sir," said I. Were there to be complications? In a flash he countered.

"Yo' surely *are* a long ways from home."

I laughed heartily, and with rapier speed replied, "I surely *am*."

They told us the road from Gal*ves*ton to Houston (Hewston) was good—none better.

"Good shell road all the way. You'll make *time* on that road." This is the distinction between a Southerner and a Westerner. When the former tells you a road is good, he means that it once was good. When a West-

erner tells you the same thing, he means that it is going
to be good at some happy future date.   In Texas the
West and South meet.

We crossed the three-mile causeway which Galveston
built at an expense of two million dollars, to connect
her island town with her mainland.   On all sides of us
flatness like the flatness of the sea stretched to the horizon, and but for the horizon would have continued still
further.   The air was balmy as springtime in Italy.
Meadow larks perched fat and puffy on fenceposts, dripping abrupt melodies which began and ended nowhere.
The sky, washed with weeks of rain, had been dipped in
blueing and hung over the earth to dry.   After enduring
gray northern skies, we were intoxicated with happiness.

The happier I am, the faster I drive.   The road of
hard oyster shell we knew was good.   They had told us
we could make time on it, in so many words.   Forty-
eight miles an hour is not technically fast, but seems fast
when you suddenly descend into a hard-edged hole a foot
and a half deep.

When we had separated ourselves from our baggage,
we examined the springs.   By a miracle they were intact.
In first gear, the car took a standing jump, and emerged
from the hole.   For one of her staid matronly build, she
did very well at her first attempt.   Later she learned to
leap boulders, and skip lightly from precipice to precipice and if we could have kept her in training six months
longer, she could have walked out halfway on a tight-
rope, turned around and got back safely to land.

The holes increased rapidly until there was no spot in
the road free from them.   Our course resembled an

earthworm's. Except for the holes, the road was all its sympathizers claimed for it. We maneuvered two partly washed away bridges, and came to a halt.

Airplanes were soaring above us in every direction. We were passing Ellington Field. But the immediate cause of our halt was two soldiers, who begged a lift to Houston. We were glad to oblige them, but after a hopeless glance at the tonneau piled high with baggage, they decided to ride on the running board. If the doughboy on the left had only been the doughboy on the right running board, this chapter would have been two days shorter. It was Friday, and we had thirteen miles to go, and Friday and thirteen make a bad combination.

Toby chatted with her soldier and I with mine, who was a mechanician at the flying field. It was a disappointment not to have him an aviator, though he admitted a mechanician's was a far weightier responsibility. Before the war, he had been a professional racer, had come in second in a championship race between San Francisco and Los Angeles, and gave such good reasons why he hadn't come in first that he seemed to have taken a mean advantage of the champion.

"Sixty-three miles is about as fast as I've ever driven," I said in an off-hand way.

"Sixty-three? That's not fast. When you get going ninety-five to a hundred, that's something like driving."

"This car," I explained, "won't make more than fifty. At fifty she vibrates till she rocks from side to side."

He looked at the wheel hungrily. "Huh! I bet I could bring her up to seventy-five."

Stung, I put my foot on the gas, and the speedometer needle swung to the right. As we merged with the traffic of Houston, shell-holes were left behind us, and passing cars were taking advantage of a perfect concrete road.   A Hudson with a Texas number passed us with a too insistent horn, the driver smiled scornfully and looked back, and his three children leaned out from the back to grin.   And they were only going a miserable thirty. The near-champion looked impotently at the steering wheel, and in agonized tones commanded, "Step on it!"

The Hudson showed signs of fight, and lured us through the traffic at a lively pace.   My companion on the running board was dying of mortification.   I knew how he itched to seize the wheel, and for his sake I re-doubled my efforts.   In a moment the impudent Hudson children ceased to leer from the back of their car, and were pretending to admire the scenery on the other side. Then suddenly the Hudson lost all interest in the race.

"Turn down the side street," yelled my passenger, frantically.   I tried to turn, wondering, but the carbure-tor sputtered and died.

I will say that it is almost a pleasure to be arrested in Texas.   Two merry motor-cops smiled at us winsomely. There was sympathy, understanding and good fellow-ship in their manner,—no malice, yet firmness withal, which is the way I prefer to be handled by the police. As officers they had to do their duty.   As gentlemen, they regretted it.

Toby, chatting about aviation with the man on her run-ning-board, was completely taken by surprise to hear "Ah'm sahry, lady, but we'll jest have to ask you-all to come along with us."

What an embarrassing position for our passengers! They had accepted our hospitality, egged us on to un-

lawful speed, and landed us in the court-house,—with
pay-day weeks behind. Their chagrin deepened as their
efforts to free us unlawfully went for naught. Our indulgent captors could not have regretted it more if we
had been their own sisters, but they made it clear we must
follow them.

"You go ahead, and I'll show her the way," suggested my tempter. That he had traveled the same road
many, many times became evident to us. In fact, he confided that he had been arrested in every state in the
Union, and his face was so well known in the Houston
court that the judge had wearied of fining him, and now
merely let him off with a rebuke. So hoping our faces
would have the same effect on the judge, we trustingly
following his directions into town, our khaki-clad friends
leading.

"Turn off to the right here," said my guide. I turned,
and in a flash, the motor-cycles wheeled back to us.

Smiling as ever, our captors shook their heads warn-
ingly.

"Now, lady, none of that! You follow right after
us."

Profusely my guide protested he had merely medi-
tated a short cut to the station house. Elaborately he
explained the route he had intended to take. Poor chap,
D'Artagnan himself could not have schemed more nimbly
to rescue a lady from the Bastille. I saw how his mad-
cap mind had visioned the quiet turn down the side street,
the doubling on our tracks, the lightning change of himself into the driver's seat, a gray Cadillac streaking ninety
miles an hour past the scattering populace of Houston,

then breathless miles on into the safety of the plains—
the ladies rescued, himself a hero——

Instead, we tamely drew up before a little brick sta-
tion-house two blocks beyond. He did all he could, even
offering to appear in court the next day and plead for us,
but from what we now knew of his local record, it seemed
wiser to meet the judge on our own merits.

Our arrival caused a sensation. The police circles of
Houston evidently did not every day see a Massachusetts
car piled high with baggage driven by two women,
flanked by a soldier on each running board. When we
entered the sheriff's office, every man in the room turned
his back for a moment and shook with mirth. They led
me to a wicket window with Toby staunchly behind. The
sheriff, in shirt sleeves and suspenders, amiably pushed a
bag of Bull Durham toward me. I started back at this
unusual method of exchanging formalities. A policeman,
also in shirt sleeves and suspenders, a twinkle concealed
in his sweet Southern drawl, explained,

"The lady 'thawt yo' meant them fixin's for her,
Charley, instead of fo' that mean speed-catcher."

The sheriff took my name and address.

"Massachusetts?" he exclaimed. Then, all of a sudden, he shot back at me. "Yo're a lawng ways from
home!"

"I wish I were longer," I said.

"Never mind, lady," he said, soothingly and caress-
ingly. "Yo' give me twenty dollars now, and tell the
jedge your story tomorrow, an' seein' as how you're a
stranger and a lady, he'll give it all back to you."

On that understanding, I paid him twenty dollars.

At three next afternoon, Toby and I sought the court-house to get our twenty dollars back, as agreed. The ante-room was filled with smoke from a group of Houstonians whose lurking smiles seemed to promise indulgence. The judge was old and impassive, filmed with an absent-mindedness hard to penetrate. Yet he, too, had a lurking grin which he bit off when he spoke.

"Yo' are charged with exceeding the speed limit at a rate of fo'ty-five miles an hour."

"Your Honor, this was my first day in the State, and I hadn't learned your traffic laws.

He looked up over his spectacles. "Yo're from Massachusetts?"

"Yes, sir!"

Toby and I waited in suspense. We saw a faint spark light the cold, filmed blue eye, spread to the corner of his grim mouth, while a look of benevolent anticipation rippled over his set countenance. It was coming! I got ready to say with a spontaneous laugh "We surely *are*."

And then he bit it off!

"Yo' know speeding is a very serious offense——"

"I wouldn't have done it for worlds, your Honor, if I hadn't seen all the Texas cars going quite fast, so I thought you wouldn't mind if I did the same. I only arrived yesterday from Massachusetts."

"Thet's so. Yo're from Massachusetts?"

We waited hopefully. But again he bit it off.

"It's a mighty serious offense. But, seein' as yo're a stranger and a lady at that——"

His voice became indulgently reassuring. We felt we had done well to wait over a day, and trust to Southern chivalry.

"Considering everything, I'll be easy on you.   Twenty dollars."

His tone was so fatherly that I knew only gratitude for being saved from two months in a Texas dungeon.

"Thank you, your Honor," I faltered.

Outside, Toby looked at me in scorn.

"What did you thank him for?" she asked.

Whether it be contempt of court or no, I wish to state that subsequent inquiry among the hairdressers, hotel clerks, and garage men of Houston, revealed that a fine of such magnitude had never been imposed in the annals of the town.   The usual sentence was a rebuke for first offenses, two dollars for the second and so on. The judge was right.   I *was* a stranger——

But what could you expect from a soul of granite who could resist such a mellowing, opportune, side-splitting bon mot?—could swallow it unsaid?

I hope it choked him.

CHAPTER IV

CHIVALRY VS. GUMBO

A GUIDE, who at the age of twelve had in disgust left his native state, once epitomized it to me.

"Texas is a hell of a state. Chock full of socialists, horse-thieves and Baptists."

Socialists and horse-thieves we did not encounter; it must have been the Baptists, then, who were responsible for the law putting citizens who purchase gasoline on Sunday in the criminal class. Unluckily the easy-going garage man who obligingly gave us all other possible information neglected to tell us of this restriction on Saturday night. Accordingly, when we started on Sunday morning, we had only five gallons and a hundred odd miles to go. We had no desire to meet Houston's judiciary again.

A little group of advisers gathered to discuss our problem. The road our New York optimist had routed for us as "splendid going all the way" was a sea of mud. Four mule teams could not pull us out, we were told. Three months of steady rain had reduced the State of Texas to a state of "gumbo." Each man had a tale of encounter and defeat for each road suggested. Each declared the alternatives suggested by the others impossible. But, at last, came one who had "got through" by the Sugarland road the day before. He voiced the definition of a good road in Texas, a definition which we frequently encountered afterward.

25

"The road's all right, ef yo' don't boag, otherwise you'll find it kinder rough."

With this dubious encouragement we started, at nine in the morning, hoping the Baptists further out in the country would grow lenient in the matter of gasoline, as the square of their distance from Houston.

It was a heavenly day, the sun hot and the vibrant blue sky belying the sodden fields and brimming ditches. The country, brown and faintly rolling, under the warmth of the Southern springtime was reminiscent of the Roman Campagna. Song sparrows filled the air with abrupt showers of music, and now and then a bald and black-winged buzzard thudded down into a nearby field. For miles on both sides of the road we saw only black soil soaked and muddy, with rivers for furrows, and only a few brown stalks standing from last year's cotton or rice crop. The eternal flatness of the country suggested a reason for the astounding height of the loose-jointed Texans we had seen; they had to be tall to make any impression on the landscape. It accounted, too, for their mild, easy-going, unhurried and unhurriable ways. What is the use of haste, when as much landscape as ever still stretches out before one?

Before we reached Sugarland, a lonesome group of houses on what had once been a huge sugar plantation, our misgivings began. Mud in Texas has a different meaning from mud in Massachusetts; it means gumbo, morasses, Sargasso Seas, broken axles, abandoned cars. From the reiteration of the words, "Yo' may git through, but I think yo'll boag" we began to realize that it was easier to get into Texas, even through the eye of the police court, than to get out of it.

At Sugarland we took on illicit gasoline and a passenger. He was bound for a barbecue, but volunteered to steer us through a particularly bad spot a mile further. We roused his gloom by a reference to the Blue Laws of Texas.

"Ef this legislatin' keeps on," he said, "a man'll have to git a permit to live with his wife. Texas aint what it used to be. This yere's a dry, non-gambling county, but this yere town's the best town in the state."

We followed his gesture wonderingly toward the lonely cluster of houses, a warehouse, a store, an ex-saloon with the sign badly painted out, and "refreshments" painted in, and the usual group of busy loafers at the store.

"Yes ma'am. It's a good town. Twice a year on Gawge Washin'ton's birthday and the Fo'th we hold a barbecue an' everyone in the county comes. I'm right sorry I cain't take yo' ladies along; I'm sure I could show yo' a good time. Whiskey flows like water, we roast a dozen oxen, and sometimes as much as fifteen thousand dollars will change hands at one crap game. We whoop it up for a week, and then we settle down, and mind the law again."

Under the guidance of our kindly passenger, we learned a new technique in driving. In first gear, avoiding the deceptively smooth but slimy roadside, we made for the deepest ruts, racing the engine till it left a trail of thick white smoke behind, clinging to the steering wheel, while the heavy car rocked and creaked in the tyrannical grip of the ruts like a ship in the trough of the waves. Without our friend, we never should have got through. He walked ahead, selected the impassable places from those which merely looked so, and beamed, when rocked and bruised from the wheel I steered the good car to comparatively dry land. A little further, where the barbecue began, he bade us a regretful fare-well, and requested us to look him up when next we came to Texas.

"I sure would 'a liked to have went to Boston," he added, "but I aint sure ef I had 'a went theah, whetheh I could 'a understood their brogue."

Since Houston we had learned the full meaning of Texas optimism. "Roads are splendid, ma'am. I think you'll git through," we mentally labeled as "probably passable." But when we heard, in the same soft, gentle monotone, "Pretty poor roads, ma'am; I think yo'll boag," we knew we should "hoag"—bog to the hubs in a plaster of Paris cast. At Richmond, where they told us that the roads which Houston had described as "splen-did" were quite impassable, we sadly learned that to a Texan, any road twenty miles away is a "splendid road," ten miles away is "pretty fair," but at five, "you'll sure boag."

Again we faced the probability of progressing only a few miles further on Texas soil, but the town flocked to our aid, told us of two alternate roads, and promptly split into two factions, each claiming we should "hoag" if we took the road advised by the other. A friendly soda clerk gained our confidence by asserting he never advised any road he had not traveled personally. He was such a unique change from the rest of Texas that we took his advice and the East Bernard road to Eagle Lake. It was only the fourth change from our original route planned when overlooking the asphalt of New

York, and each detour decreased our chances of getting back to the highways. But there was no alternative. The soda clerk as he served us diluted ginger ale, reassured us "It's a pretty good road, and ef yo' don't boag, I think yo'll git through."

We bogged. We came, quite suddenly to a tell-tale stretch of black, spotting the red-brown road, and knew we were in for it. At each foot, we wondered if we should bog in the next. Eliza must have felt the same way, crossing the ice, especially when a cake slipped from under her. As directed, I kept to the ruts. Sometimes they expanded to a three-foot hole, into which the car descended with a heart-rending thump. Once in a rut, it was impossible to get out. The mud, of the consistency of modeling clay, would have made the fortune of a dealer in art supplies. At last, a wrong choice of ruts pulled us into this stiff mass to our hubs, almost wrenching the differential from the car, and we found ourselves stopping. As soon as we stopped, we were done for. We sank deeper and deeper.

We got out, sinking ourselves halfway to the knees in gumbo. We were on a lonely road in an absolutely flat country, with not a house on the horizon. We had no ropes, and no shovel. We looked at the poor car, foundered to her knees in sculptor's clay, and wondered how many dismal days we must wait before the morass dried.

And then came the first manifestation of a peculiar luck which followed us on our entire trip. Never saving us from catastrophe, it rescued us in the most unlikely fashion, soon after disaster.

Along rode a boy—on horseback—the first person we had seen for hours. We stopped him, and inquired where we could find a mule, a rope and a man. Having started out to make the trip without masculine aid, it chagrined us to have to resort to it at our first difficulty, but we were not foolish enough to believe we could extricate the car unaided from its bed of sticky clay. The boy looked at us, looked at the imprisoned machine, and silently spat. Texas must have a law requiring that rite, with penalties for infringement thereof. We never saw it broken.

The formality over, he replied, "I don't know." We suggested planks,—he knew of none. We put him down, bitterly, as an ill-natured dolt. But, as we learned later, Texans move slowly, but their hearts are in the right place. He was only warming up. Finally he spat again, lighted a cigarette, got off his horse, silently untied a rope from his saddle, and bound it about our back wheel, disregarding calmly the mire sucking at his boots. I started the engine. No results. All three watched the fettered Gulliver helplessly. Then, while Toby and I lifted out heavy suitcases and boxes from the seat which held the chains, he watched us, with the mild patience of an ox.

Reinforcements came, a moment later, from a decrepit buggy, containing a boy and two girls. They consulted, on seeing our plight, and the girls, hearty country lasses in bare feet and sunbonnets, urged their escort, apparently to his relief, to stay the Sunday courtship and give us aid. Of more agile fettle than our first knight, he galvanized him into a semblance of motion. Together they gathered brush, and, denuding their horses for the purpose, tied bits of rope to the rear wheels. The engine started, stalled, and started again a dozen times.

At last the car stirred a bit from her lethargy, the two boys put their country strength against her broad back and pushed; the engine roared like a man-eating tiger— and we got out.

But we still had to conquer a black stretch of about one hundred yards, in which one of our rescuers had broken an axle, so he cheerfully told us, only yesterday. We were faced with the problem to advance or retreat? Either way was mud. We might get caught between two morasses, and starve to death before the sun dried the roads. We might turn back, but why return to conditions we had worked two hours to escape? We decided to advance boldly, and, if need be, gloriously break an axle. "Race her for all she's worth," counseled the livelier of our rescuers, from the running board where he acted as pilot. I raced her, though it nearly broke my heart to mistreat the engine so cruelly. We wavered, struck a rut, and were gripped in it, as in the bonds of matrimony, for better or worse. It led us to a gruesome mass of "soup," with a yawning hole at the bottom.

"Here's where I broke my axle," shouted my pilot. To break the shock meant to stick; to race ahead might mean a shattered car. There was no time to think it over. I pushed down on the gas. A fearful bump, and we went on, the mud sucking at the tires with every inch we advanced. Cheering, the others picked their way to us. Our friends piled our baggage into the tonneau. Toby and I looked at each other, worried by the same problem,—the problem that never ceased to bother us until we reached Chicago;—to tip or not to tip?

They were such nice lads; we already seemed like old friends. Yet they were strangers who had scratched their hands and muddied their clothes, and relinquished cheerfully the Sunday society of their ladies on our behalf. Too much to offer pay for, it seemed too much to accept without offering to pay. We learned then that such an offer outrages neither Western independence nor Southern chivalry when made in frank gratitude and good-fellowship. The first suggestion of payment invariably meets an off-hand but polite refusal, which tact may sometimes change to acceptance. If accepted, it is never as a tip, but as a return for services; offer it as a tip, and you offer an insult to a friend. We found it a good rule, as Americans dealing with Americans, to be graceful enough to play the more difficult role of recipient when we decently could, and in the spirit of the West, "pass it on to the next fellow."

Eagle Lake seemed as difficult to attain as the treasure beyond seven rivers of fire and seven mountains of glass. An hour's clear sailing over roads no worse than ploughed fields brought it nearly in sight,—seven miles to go, under a pink sky lighted by a silver crescent. And then Toby, seeing a grassy lake on the side of the road, forsook two tried and trusty mud-holes for it, and ditched us again!

Nearby was a farmhouse, with two men and a Ford standing in the driveway. Hardly had we "boaged," our wheels churning a pool deep enough to bathe in, when we saw them loading shovels and tools into the car, and driving to our aid. They came with boreboding haste. They greeted us cheerfully—too cheerfully, we thought; joked about the hole, and admitted they spent most of their time shovelling people out. They knew their job—we had to admit that. They wrestled with the jack, setting it on a shovel to keep it from sinking in the swamp; profanely cheerful, fussed over the chains, which we later guiltily discovered were too short for our over-sized tires, backed their car to ours, tied a rope to it, and pulled. We sank deeper. They shoveled, jacked, chopped sage-brush, and commandeered every passing man and car. The leader of the wreckers was a Mr. Poole, a typical Westerner of the old school,—long, flowing gray whiskers, sombrero, and keen watchful face. He had also a delightful sense of humor,—was in fact so cheerful that we became more and more gloomy as we noted the array of Fords and men clustered about. It looked to us like a professional mud-hole.

They hitched two Fords to the car, while eight men pushed from the back, but nothing came of the effort. A fine looking man named Sinclair, with gentle manners, was elected by the crowd to go for his mule team, "the finest pair in the county." An hour later he came back. He had gone two miles, changed to overalls, and hitched up his mules in the meantime, returning astride the off beast.

At sight of the fallen car, the mules gave a gently ironic side-glance, stepped into place, waited quietly, and at the word of command, stepped forward nonchalantly, while I started the car simultaneously. It took them exactly five minutes to do what eight men, two women, two Fords and a Cadillac had failed to do in two hours' hard work. For days. after, when we passed a mule, we offered him silent homage.

While Toby, looking and acting like a guilty wretch piled the baggage into the car, I approached Mr. Sinclair and Mr. Poole, who stood watching the rescued leviathan with eyes gleaming satisfaction, and put the usual timid question.

"Will you tell me what I can offer all these people for helping us out?"

Mr. Sinclair, owner of the stalwart mules, smiled and said: "I shouldn't offer them a thing. We all get into trouble one time or another, and have to be helped out. Just you tell them 'thank you' and I reckon that'll be all the pay they want."

And before we could turn around to carry out his injunction, half the crowd had melted away!

To all motorists who become "boaged," I beg to recommend the mud-hole of my friends, Mr. Poole and Mr. Sinclair, of Lissie, Texas.

CHAPTER V

NIBBLING AT THE MAP OF TEXAS

VISITING an ostrich farm is as thrilling as going in wading, but to be thorough, we did our duty by San Antonio's plumed and gawky giants before starting again on our well-nigh hopeless task of making an impression on the State of Texas.

When we looked at our mileage record we were encouraged, only to be cast down again by a glance at the map, whose south-west corner we had only begun to nibble at in six days' faithful plodding. It was an incentive to an early start. We filled our tank with gas at the tiled station near the Alamo, rejoicing in the moderate price. In one respect, at least, Texas is the motorists's paradise. Gasoline is cheap, oil is cheap, storage for the night ranges from "two bits" to half a dollar, while clear weather and local honesty make it possible to avoid even that expense by leaving the car overnight in the Garage of the Blue Sky. Tires are mended and changed for a quarter, and in some places for nothing. And garage-keepers are honest,—except when, yielding to local patriotism, they describe the state of the roads.

For three miles we meandered through San Antonio's "Cabbage Patch," steering around tin cans, Mexican babies, and goats taking the freedom of the city, until we came to a fine broad macadam in good repair,—our first real road since the ill-fated stretch outside Houston.

Mexicans hung outside their little shops, whose festoons of onions and peppers painted Italy into the landscape. Overhead, we counted dozens of airplanes, some from the government school, others from Katharine Stinson's modest hangars, making the most of the weather. One coquetted with us, following us for several miles. We leaned out and waved, but at that, it was a most impersonal form of flirtation. Not a quiver of the great wings, not a swoop through the blue, rewarded our abandon. I wish I might record otherwise, for a moment later a rusty nail had flattened our back tire, and we were left alone on the prairie to solve the problem of changing the heavy rims, which our combined strength could hardly lift. How romantic and happy a touch could be added to this narrative if at this point I could state that the airman fluttered to our feet, saluted, changed the tire, and then circled back to the blue. But, doubtless himself from Boston, he did no such thing. He kept steadily on his course, till he was only a speck in our lives. If the cautious man reads this, let him know he is forgiven the tire, but not the climax.

We had been airy, at home, when they mentioned the tires. There were, nevertheless, internal doubts. Massachusetts is too crowded with garages to furnish much practice in wayside repairing, and I had been lucky. But now came the test. Theoretically, we understood the process, but jacks go up when they should go down, nuts rust, and rims warp. We searched the horizon for help, found none, pulled out the tools, and got down in the mud.

Our jack was the kind whose advertisements show an immaculate young lady in white daintily propelling a handle at arm's length, while the car rises easily in the air. Admitting she has the patience of Job, the strength of Samson, and the ingenuity of the devil, I should like to meet her just long enough to ask her if she stood off at arm's length while she put the jack in place, rescued it as it toppled over, searched vainly for a solid spot in which the jack would not sink, pulled it out of the mud again, pushed the car off as it rolled back on her, hunted for stones to prop it up, and a place in the axles where the arm would fit, and then had the latch give way and be obliged to do it all over again. And, with no reflections on the veracity of the lady or her inspired advertiser, I should demand the address of her pastor and her laundress.

We worked half an hour jacking up the car. No sooner had we got it where it should be, than the car's weight sank it in the mud, and we had to begin again our snail process. To my delight, Toby was fascinated by the thing, and from that hour claimed it as her own. We mutually divided the labor as our tastes and talents dictated. It seemed that Toby revelled in handling tools, which dropped from my inept grasp, while my sense of mechanics and experience surpassed hers. I was to be the diagnostician, she the surgeon. In other words, I bossed the job, while she did the work.

While Toby struggled with the jack a Mexican on a flea-bitten cayuse slouched on the horizon. He was black and hairy, and one "six-gun" in his teeth would have signed his portrait as Captain of the Bandits. I stopped him and asked him to lend us his brute strength, which he smilingly did, pleased as a child at being initiated into the sacred mysteries of motoring. When I allowed him to propel the socket-wrench his cup ran over. He did everything backward, but he furnished horse-sense, which we lacked, and when we attempted to lift heavy weights, he courteously supplanted us. The three of us invented a lingua franca in Mexican, Italian, French and musical terms.

"Tire,—avanti!" Gesture of lifting. Groan,—signifying great weight.

"Troppo,—troppo! Largo, largo! Ne faites pas ça! Ah-h, si, si,—bono hombre, multo, multo bono hombre!"

Thus encouraged, he worked willingly and faithfully, and at the end of a half hour's toil, waved aside our thanks, untied his weary cayuse, and raised his sombrero. He had not robbed us nor beaten us, but had acted as one Christian to another. I ran after him saying fluently, as if I had known the language all my life, "Multo, multo, beaucoup bono hombre." He showed his brilliant teeth. I offered him money, which he at first refused. "Bono hombre," I insisted, "Cigarettos!" And so he took it, much pleased. He thoroughly enjoyed the episode. I hope his boss did, when he arrived an hour late. Toby enjoyed the episode, too, and persisted in sending home postcards, on which she spoke of being rescued by a Mexican bandit.

During the morning several little towns,—all alike, flitted by us,—Sabinal, Hondo, Dunlay. At Hondo, where the mud was thickest, we stopped at a little general store for lunch. The proprietor, a tall, vague man, discussed earnestly, as one connoisseur to another, the merits of the various tinned goods he submitted, and after a leisurely chat and several purchases, in which the matter of trade became secondary, he urged on us several painted

sticks of candy, a new kind which he said he enjoyed sucking during his solitary guard at the store. After the
customary, "You're a long ways from home," he bade us
goodbye, hopefully but sadly, as one would a consumptive
great-aunt about to take a trip to the North Pole, and
watched us bump out of sight.

We had twenty miles of such luxuriant mud that we
stopped to photograph it. It is only slight exaggeration
to say that the ruts came to the camera's level. Then
we forded the Neuces River, a stream woven into early
Texan history, and began to climb out of the land of
cotton into the grazing country. The herds and herds
of sheep and white angora goats we now encountered
made a charming landscape but an irritating episode. A
large flock of silly sheep rambled halfway to our car,
then, frightened, fled in the other direction, turning again
with those they met, who also faced and fled, baa-ing;
no militia could clear the traffic they disorganized. Each
herd we met meant a wasted half hour. Their herders
sat their horses in grim patience, with the infinite contempt shepherds get for their charges and for life in
general. Out here, "being the goat" takes a new and
dignified meaning—for a goat is placed with each hundred sheep to steer the brainless mass, act as leaders in
danger, and furnish the one brain of the herd.

These pastoral happenings delayed us, until toward
night we climbed dark dunes into a clear golden sunset.
Through a gate we entered what seemed to be a cattle
track through a large ranch, but was in fact the main
highway to El Paso. The roads in this part of the
country cut through large holdings, and the pestiferous
cattle gate begins to bar the road, necessitating stopping,

crossing, shutting the gate again, several times a mile. And let me warn the traveling Easterner that not to leave a gate as you find it is in truth a crime against hospitality, for one is often on private property.

Queer blunt mesas rose on all sides of us, and when dark came upon us we had entered a small canyon, and were winding to the top and down again out of the hills. The cattlegates and rocky road made going slow, and as Venus, frosty and brilliant, came out, we were imprisoned in this weirdly gloomy spot, on the top of the world. A quaver in Toby's usually stalwart voice made me wonder if she were remembering her mother's last words,—"Don't drive at night." This is no reflection on Toby's staunchness; the immensity of the West, after dark, when first it looms above one used to the coziness of ordered streets, must always seem portentous and awful. We hastened on, winding down through one enchanting glade after another, till we met the highway again. Toby took the wheel, and we hummed along. Suddenly a stone struck the engine, and a deafening roar like that of an express train frightened us. Something vital, by its clatter, had been shattered, and we again faced the possibility of delay and frustration—even retreat. We got out and searched for the trouble. Luckily we had that day unpacked our flash-light, for Venus, though she looked near enough to pick out of the sky, furnished poor illumination for engine troubles. Search revealed an important looking pipe beneath the car broken in two, with a jagged fracture. Should we chance driving on, or camp till morning?

We were tired and our pick-up lunch of deviled ham and crackers seemed long ago. After a hard day's run, the difficulties of making camp in the dark, with our equipment still unpacked, and going cold and supperless to bed loomed large. Besides, there could not have been worse camping ground in the world. Soggy cotton fields under water on both sides gave us the choice of sleeping in the middle of the road or on the back seat piled high with baggage. The engine, though roaring like a wounded lioness, still ran steadily. I knew just enough to realize we had broken the exhaust pipe, but hardly enough to know whether running the car under such conditions would maim it for life. But though hunger won out, the real mechanic's love for his engine was born in us, and feeling like parents who submit their only child to a major operation, we drove painfully at eight miles an hour the ten miles into B—, the town echoing to our coming.

The village was a mere cross-roads, a most unlikely place for a night's stop, picturesque and Mexican, with low 'dobe houses, yellow and pink, the noise of a phonograph from each corner, and lighted doorways filled with slouching Mexicans and trig American doughboys from a nearby camp,—and everywhere else, Rembrantian gloom. At a new tin garage with the universal Henry's name over the door we were relieved to learn we had done no damage. Most of the cars in town had, in fact, broken their exhaust pipes on loose stones, and ran chugging, as we had.

It is not usual for garage helpers to aid strange ladies in hunting a night's lodging, but ours willingly let themselves be commandeered for the purpose, and the chase began. The town had a "hotel";—which, in the South, may be a one-story café, or something less ambitious.

This one, kept by a negro woman, was more than dubious looking, but when the proprietor said it was "full up," our hearts sank.   We wearily made the rounds of the village, guided by rumors of a vacant room here or there, only to find the houses, four-roomed cottages at best, filled with army wives.   Our needs reduced us to Bolshevism.   Passing an imposing white house, neat as wax, and two stories high, we sent our cicerone to demand for us lodging for the night.   Had it been the official White House we should have done no less, and as the residence of the owner of the garage where our cripple was stored it gave us a claim on his hospitality no right-minded citizen could deny.   Alas, we learned that Mr. V's eleven hostages to fortune, rather than civic pride, accounted for the size of his house.   The owner sent us a cordially regretful message that his bedrooms teemed with little V's, but thought his brother's daughter might take the strangers in, as her parents were away and their room vacant.

A little figure in a nightgown opened the door a crack when we knocked at their cottage.

"Who is it?" asked a Southern voice, timidly.

"Two ladies from Boston, who would like a room for the night."   We threw as much respectable matronliness as possible into our own voices.   The magic word "Boston" reassured.   Boston may be a dishonored prophet in Cambridge and Brookline, but to the South and West it remains autocrat of the breakfast table.   I know our prospective hostess, from the respect and relief in her tones, visualized Louisa May Alcott and Julia Ward Howe waiting on her doorstep, and she hastened to throw open the door to what we saw was her bedroom, saying "Come in! You're a long ways———"

Boston, your stay-at-homes never realize how distant, how remote and fabulous your rock-bound shores seem to the Other Half west of the Mississippi!

It was a German Lutheran household into which we stepped. Two little tow-headed boys were curled up asleep in their sister's room, and we tip-toed past to the parents' vacated bedroom, ours for the night, with its mottoes, its lithographed Christ on the wall, its stove and tightly shut windows. This German family had brought over old-world peasant habits, and curiously contrasted against its bareness, promiscuity and not over scrupulous cleanliness was the American daughter who needed but a little more polish to be ready for any rung in the social ladder. She was a real little lady, as hospitable as though we had been really invited.

Supperless, footsore and weary, we tumbled into the sheets vacated by the elder V's that morning, too grateful for shelter and the softness of the feather bed to feel squeamish. We waked in the sunshine of next morning to smell coffee brewing on our bedroom stove, and hear cautious whispers of two sturdy little Deutschers tip-toeing back and forth through our room to the wash-shed beyond, stealing awed glances at the Boston ladies in their mother's bed. In a stage whisper one called to his sister to learn where "the comb" was. She answered that Pa had taken it to San Anton', but after some search found them "the brush" hidden near father's notary stamp, on the bureau,—for the father was the local judge and a man much respected in the community.

When the little boys departed for school, she brought

us coffee in the best china, apologizing for not offering us breakfast. She explained that she was to be married in three days, and was following her family to San Anton' for the wedding. She showed us her ring, and her trousseau, all in pink, to her joy, and told us of her fiancé, who had been a second lieutenant in France. Though she seemed a child, she had refused to marry him when he left, because she believed haste at such times imprudent. And now she was all excitement over the great event, yet not too much to show a welcome as simple as it was beautiful to the midnight intruders from Boston.

As usual, our desire to pay for our lodging met a firm, almost shocked refusal. We only felt more nearly even when at El Paso we sent her something deliciously pink for her trousseau.

In Texas, overnight promises are to be discounted. Or is it not, perhaps, a universal law of the "night man" to pass on no information to the "day man?" Has the order taken a vow of silence more binding and terrible than the Dominican friars? It must be so, for never in ten years' experience with night men, have I known one to break the seal of secrecy which prevents them letting your confidence in the matter of flat tires and empty tanks go any further. Their delicacy in keeping all news of such infirmities from the ears of the day man is universal. Nor was there any exception next morning, when we visited our garage, hopeful of an early start. The exhaust pipe was still unwelded, and our spare tire still flat. Furthermore, we were half an hour in the garage before anyone thought to mention that the resources of the place were inadequate to mend the pipe. They had trusted to **our** divining the fact, as the **day** wore **on,**—a more tactful way of breaking the news than coming out bluntly with the truth.

At last, a passing stranger suggested we take the car to the nearby Fort, where a new welding machine had recently been installed. We chugged up the hill, attracting the notice of several soldiers from East Boston, on whom our Massachusetts number produced a wave of nostalgia. By this time, so used were we to being beneficiaries of entire strangers that before hailing anyone likely to offer to do us a favor, we fixed smiles fairly dripping with saccharine on our faces.

A sergeant, hearing sympathetically our story, sent us to a lieutenant. He wavered.

"I hate not to oblige a lady, ma'am, but this is government property, and we aint allowed to do outside work."

Looking at his stern face, we decided it would take at least an hour to win him over. Without moving a muscle he continued——

"But, seein' as you're a lady and a long ways from home, and can't git accommodated otherwise, you run your car back to the garage and I'll send a sergeant down to get the part, and he'll have it welded for you in a couple of hours."

Two hours later not only the sergeant but the lieutenant were at the garage to see that the part went back properly into the engine. Meanwhile, doubting the ethics of letting Uncle Sam be our mechanic, we had provided two boxes of Camels for our benefactors, having learned that cigarettes will often be acceptable where money will not. The part was perfectly welded, the sergeant replaced it with military efficiency, and then we exchanged confidences. The lieutenant told us he was a "long-horn," but had been, before the war, a foreman in the very factory which had built our car. Which explained his cordiality, if explanation were needed in a land where everyone is cordial. We found that respect for the sterling worth of our car helped us along our way appreciably,— people everywhere approved it as "a good car," and extended their approval to its inmates. The lieutenant nonplused us by refusing both pay and tobacco, but indicated that we might bestow both on the sergeant. He asked us to let him know when we came again to Texas, and we promised willingly, thanked Uncle Sam for his chivalry by proxy, and were quickly on our way to Del Rio. Texas had not yet failed us.

CHAPTER VI

"DOWN BY THE RIO GRANDE"

EVERY thriving Western town, if its politics are right, looks down on its hotels and up to its post-office. Del Rio was no exception; her granite post-office, imposing enough for three towns of its size, suggested Congressional sensitiveness to fences, while down street a block or two, the weather-beaten boards of "Frank's," with its creaking verandahs and uncarpeted lobby, printed the earlier pages of the little settlement, which, straddling the river from Mexico, had become the nucleus for frontier trade eddying to its banks.

It is true that other hotels, of the spick and span brick ugliness the New West delights in, flanked the motion picture houses and drug-stores, but we chose Frank's, the oldest inhabitant,—a type of hotel fast becoming extinct. Downstairs, plain sheathing; upstairs the same. Our bedroom opened on a veranda which we had to traverse to reach the bath. It was a novelty to us, but the traveling salesman next door took it casually enough, —or else he had forgotten to pack his bath-robe.

Our hostess was the first of a long list of ladies young and old we were to meet, who knew well the gentle art of twirling a toothpick while she talked. Perhaps it is the badge of a waitress in these parts, like a fresh bush over ancient wine-houses, a silent, but eloquent testimonial to the gustatory treats of the hotel. I think we

never met, from now on, a waitress in Texas, Arizona
or New Mexico, who was not thus equipped. Ours did
not flourish hers in vain. The flakiness of the biscuits,
the fragrance of the wild honey, and the melting de-
liciousness of the river fish, caught fresh in the Rio
Grande an hour before, caused us to see Del Rio with
happy eyes. To this day, Toby speaks of it as if it were
the third finest metropolis of the West, which must be
attributed entirely to the seven biscuits which floated to
her hungry mouth. I might as well admit at once our
tendency, which I suspect other travelers share, to grade
a town by the food it served.

I suspect that Del Rio, to one unfed, would seem a
commonplace hamlet, save for its interest as a border
settlement. Mexico, three miles away, held out the
charm of a forbidden land. We circled next morning to
its border, past thatched shanties of Mexicans and
negroes, and took a glance at the desolate land beyond, barren, thorny, rolling away to faint blue hills. A
camp of United States soldiers lay athwart our path, and
two alert soldiers with a grin and a rifle apiece barred
our progress.

Toby had been keen to cross the line, but when she
saw them she said characteristically, "Mexico seems to
me vastly overrated." So ignoring the khaki, of our own
free will and choice we turned back. I confess I was
relieved. Toby has the post card habit to such an extent
that I was prepared to have to fight our way across the
border, dodging bullets and bandits, so that she might
mail nonchalant cards to her friends, beginning, "We
have just dropped into Mexico."

Our curiosity as to Mexico gave us an early start.

Soon we were on a high plateau, all the world rolling below us. Soft brown hills led out to faint blue mountains outlined on the horizon. With a thrill we realized we were viewing the beginnings of the Rockies. For the first time in my life, I felt I had all the room I wanted. We basked in the hot sun, expanding physically and spiritually in the immensity of the uncrowded landscape. The air in this high altitude was bracing, but not cold. From time to time we passed prosperous flocks of sheep, spotted with lively black goats. Occasionally a lonely group of steers held out against the encroaching mutton. We shared with them the state of Texas. At Comstock, a flat and uninteresting one-street town, we lunched, forgetting entirely to make a four-mile detour to view the highest bridge in the world. All day, we bent our energies to covering another half inch on the interminable map of Texas. We passed our last stopping place for the night. There was too much outdoors to waste; we decided to make our first camp in a live-oak grove somebody had described to us.

With a sense of adventure, we purchased supplies for our supper and breakfast at a little town we reached at glowing sundown. The grocery was closed, but the amiable proprietor left his house and opened his store for us. Rumors of deep sand ahead disturbed us, and against the emergency we purchased for "seven bits" a shovel which came jointed, so that it could be kept in the tool box under the seat. The fact that it was so short that it could easily repose there at full length did not mar our delight at this novel trick. It had the elemental charm for us of a toy which will do two things at once,—a charm which in other eras accounted for the vogue of poison rings, folding beds, celluloid collars and divided skirts. It was a perfectly useless little shovel, which made us happy whenever we looked at it, and swear whenever we used it.

Thus fortified we sped on, and it soon became pitch dark, and a windy night. The country suddenly stood on end, and we coasted down a surprising little canyon, to emerge into a long black road tangled with mesquite on both sides. When we almost despaired of finding a suitable camp, we came casually on a snug little grove, and heard nearby the rush of a stream. The black sky was radiant with stars. Orion stood on his head, and so did the dipper, surrounded by constellations unfamiliar to our Northern eyes.

In the chill dark we felt for a spot to pitch our tent. Spiky mesquite caught and tore our hair nets. Texas' millions of untenanted acres brooded over our human unimportance, till a charred stick or empty tin can, stumbled over in the dark, became as welcome a signal as Friday's footprint to Crusoe. Jointing our useless little spade, we dug a trench in the soft sand for our hips to rest in, hoisted our tent-rope over a thorny branch, folded blanket-wise our auto robes, undressed and crept inside our house. The lamps of the car gave us light to stow away our belongings, and its lumbering sides screened us from the road. With a sense of elation we looked at the circling stars through our tent windows, and heard the wind rise in gusts through the bare branches. The world becomes less fearsome with a roof over one's head.

Dawn is the camper's hour of trial. I woke from a

dream that a mountain lion had entered our shelter, when Toby sat up excitedly.

"I just dreamed a bear was trying to get in," she said. The coincidence was forboding, yet no menagerie appeared. Our aching hips, tumbled bedding and chilled bodies made us dread the long hours to breakfast. Toby hinted I had my share and more of the blanket. I had long entertained a similar suspicion of her, but was too noble to mention it. We portioned out the bedding afresh, vowed we never again would camp out, and in a moment it was eight o'clock of a cold, foggy morning.

Yesterday the sun had been hot enough to blister Toby's cheek. Today was like a nor'-easter off Labrador. We were too cold to get up, and too cold to stay shivering in the tent. It seemed a stalemate which might last a life-time, when suddenly indecision crystallized, exploded, and we found ourselves on the verge of the ice-cold stream compromising cleanliness with comfort.

How different seems the same folding stove viewed on the fifth floor of a sporting goods store in New York, and in the windy open. Piffling and futile it appeared to us, its natural inadequacy increased by our discovery that our fuel cans were locked in our trunk, and the lock had become twisted. It further appeared that most of our cooking outfit was interned in the same trunk. Accordingly I tried to build a fire, while Toby took down the tent. Camp cooking is an art which I shall not profane by describing our attempts to get breakfast that bleak morning. The fire smouldered, but refused to break into the bright cheery crackle one hears about, and finally, untempted by the logs of green mesquite we hopefully fed it, went out entirely. We breakfasted on the remains of last night's supper, washed down with a curious sticky mixture made of some labor-saving coffee preparation. Realizing that it took more than the outfit to make good campers, we went our subdued way. Our water bag bumped on the running-board, falling off frequently, and once we retraced ten muddy miles to retrieve it.

It was not a lucky day. Our scant breakfast, lost waterbag and an unhappy lunch, our locked trunk and all, were but the precursors of a worse afternoon. The air was thick with yellow dust, and the western sky, sickly green, showed columns of whirling, eddying sand to right or left of us. Though we followed the Southern Pacific with dog-like devotion we lost our way once in a crooked maze of wagon tracks which led us to a swamp, and had to drive back ten miles to the nearest house to ask directions. To make up for lost time, in the bitter, reckless mood every driver knows, when nobody in the car dare speak to him, I raced for two hours at forty-five, through sandy, twisting tracks, with the car rocking like a London bus, and Toby clinging to the side, not daring to remonstrate, for it was she who had lost us our way. Each turn was a gamble, but the curves were just gentle enough to hold us to our course.

We had every chance of making our night's stop before dark, when the air oozed gently out of the rear tire. Behind us a sandstorm rising in a shifting golden haze lifted twisted columns against the vivid green sky, over which dramatic dark clouds drove, while a spectacular sunset lighted the chains of cold dark blue and transparent mauve mountains on both sides. It was a glorious but ominous sight, and the tire meant delay. A flat

OUR FIRST CAMP TEXAS

tire, however, acts on Toby like a bath on a canary. The jack holds no mysteries for her, and tire rims click into place at sound of her voice. And our peculiar luck had halted us within a few yards of the only house we had passed all afternoon. Having learned that frail woman-hood need neither toil nor spin in Texas, I was for seeking aid, but Toby scorned help, and so painted the joys of independence that though it was hot and dusty and the sand storm threatened, I bent to her will. And the next moment, the key which locked engine, tool-box and spare tire, broke off in the padlock. As I had with unprecedented prudence bought a duplicate in New York, we were not completely stranded, but that, I mentioned bitterly to Toby, was no fault of hers. Only a cold chisel could release the spare tire, and we found we had none.

"I will now go for help," I said to Toby who was defiantly pretending to do something to the locked tire with a hammer, "as I should have at first but for your foolish pride."

As stately as I might with hair blown by the wind, yellow goggles, leather coat and a purple muffler tied over my hat, I retreated toward the ranch-house. In the kitchen I startled a grizzled old couple sitting near the fire. When I explained our predicament, and begged the loan of a cold chisel the old man asked, "You two girls all alone?"

When I admitted we were, he called to his son in the next room, "Horace, go see what you can do for the ladies."

More bashful than most Texans, the lank Horace fol-lowed me in painful silence for a few yards. Then in a burst of confidence, he said, "When you come in just now, I thought it was maw dressed up to fool us. Yes, sir, I sure did."

My glimpse of his septuagenarian parent would not have led me to suspect her of such prankishness, but appearances are often deceitful. For all I knew she may have been just the life of the family, doubling up Horace and his paw in long writhes of helpless mirth at her impersonations. So I accepted the compliment silently and led our rescuer to the car.

Once more I triumphed unworthily over Toby. For she had hinted that my fast driving had flattened the tire, but investigation revealed a crooked nail,—the bane of motoring in a cattle country. Horace proved most business-like in handling tools. In less than half an hour, bashfully spurred on by our admiration, he had cut the lock and helped us change the tire. Then he saw our sign,—and said it. As if it were a thought new-born to the ages, he smiled at his own conceit, and remarked, "You're a lawng ways from home!"

As Horace did not smoke, we drove away from the ranch-house eternally in his debt. We put him down to the credit of Texas, however, where he helped off-set sand-storms and mud holes, and added him to the fast growing list of cavaliers who had rescued us from our folly. The storm had died, and with it our bad luck had apparently departed, but when a day begins badly, it is never safe to predict until the car is bedded down for the night. According to a bad habit she has, Toby tele-scoped two paragraphs of the route card, skipping the middle entirely. Consequently we turned left when we should have gone right,—and found our front wheels banked where a road had been playfully altered by the wind to a mountain of sand. On all sides were waist-high drifts of fine white sea sand, from which the tops of mesquite bushes showed. We could not turn, so we tried running straight ahead,—and stuck. Twilight had fallen, and if there were a way out, it was no longer discernible. At what seemed a short half mile, a light gleamed from a house. Once more, I cravenly went for help, while the optimistic Toby began to shovel sand with our toy shovel. The half mile trebled itself, and still the house was no nearer. At last I came to the end, only to find that a wide canal separated us and the car from the road. I shouted across to two men in a corral, and at last they heard and came to the edge of the canal while I asked to borrow a rope. They debated a while, perhaps doubting my intentions, but finally threw a rope in the back of a little car, cranked it and, coming to the bank of the canal, helped me across. Unlike a Westerner who when he leaves a spot never fails to orient himself, I had not noticed in which direction I had struck out from the car. I fear my deliverers thought me a mild kind of incompetent when I confessed I had no idea where to find it: darkness and sand dunes completely hid it from sight. But after some skirmishing about canal beds and bridges, we reached the broad shape looming up in the dark, and found that Toby had dug the car out, wrapped an old tire about the spinning back wheel, and driven it on firm ground.

Our rescuers put us on the road to our night's objective, and with mild patience told us we could hardly miss it, it being a straight road all the way. They did not compliment us too highly, for by the time Venus had risen we reached the hotel, kept by a sad, distrustful one-eyed man from Maine, who in spite of twenty years' residence still abhorred Texas as a desert. He fed us liberally with baked beans and apple pie before showing us to a bare, clean little room furnished with a tin basin and a patchwork quilt.

We were nearly dead. We had much with which to reproach luck and each other, but by mutual consent postponed it and sank into peaceful sleep in the lumpy bed.

As somebody said, luck is a fickle dame. Having flouted us to her heart's content, she tagged docilely at our heels as we started for El Paso next morning. Two hundred miles away, the average run was ten hour's time, but we made it in eight and a half. The garage-man's wife's cousin was a dentist on Huntington Avenue, and the extraordinary coincidence drew her to us almost as by the bonds of kinship. She hurried her spouse into mending our tires promptly, and speeding us on our way with valuable directions. It was ten when we left, but moving westward into Rocky Mountain time saved us an hour.

Once out of the village we encountered the enveloping desert again. Driving in those sandy tracks became a new sport,—we learned to make the sand skid us around corners without decreasing our speed; we could calculate with nicety when a perceptible drag on the wheels warned us to shift gears. And then they must be shifted instantly, for at a moment's delay the car sank deep, and mischief was done which only shoveling could undo. Once we found ourselves facing another car blocking the road, and sunk in thick, unpacked sand. We could not turn out, and the instant's stop put us in a like predicament.

They wistfully asked us to pull them out, but as we were heavier than they, and would have made two obstacles instead of one in the road, we had to refuse the only help asked of us, who had so many times been the beneficiaries. We left them to an approaching mule team, after they had returned good for evil by pushing us out of the sand. For twenty miles we had hard going, but by spinning through the sand in low gear we escaped trouble.

We were still in the desert, but serrated peaks with lovely outlines and stormy, snowy tops marched beside us the entire day. The aspect of the country became semi-tropical. The single varieties of cactus and century plants were increased to dozens. The ocotillo, sometimes wrongly called octopus cactus, waved slender green fingers, on which a red bud showed like a rosy fingernail. The landscape warmed from lifeless gray to gold, mauve, blue and deep purple, and always on our left were the benign outlines of the blue Davis Mountains. We mounted higher and higher on a smooth orange road cut through the mountains and came out on a broad open highway with wide vistas. Close by, the mountains looked like huge heaps of black cinder and silt, but distance thinned them, as if cut from paper, into translucent lavender and blue, the edges luminous from the setting sun.

Thirty miles out of El Paso we were astonished to find ourselves on a concrete road in perfect museum condition, on which in dismal file many cars crept city-ward at the discreet pace of fifteen miles an hour. It was the first bit of good road Toby had encountered for days but an uncanny something in the self-restraint of the El

Pasans on the only good road in Texas recalled Houston to us. We joined the funereal procession and arrived in the city without official escort.

Mexico in this southwest corner is merged with Texas, making gay its vast grayness with bright spots of color and slouching figures, and suggesting other-world civilization by its Spanish street signs, and the frankness with which the Latin welcomes the world to the details of his daily life. The outskirts of the town were lined with one story 'dobe huts, and even more fragile shelters made of wattled reeds and mud. Forlorn little Mexican cafés, with temperance signs brazening it out above older and more convivial invitations, failed of their purpose; their purple and blue doors were empty as the be-Sundayed crowds swarmed the streets.

El Paso has its charms, but to us it was too modern and too large to mean more than a convenient place to sleep, shop and have the car overhauled, and the gumbo of Texas, now caked until it had to be chipped off with a chisel, washed from its surface. "The old lady," as Toby nick-named the car, was to leave Texas as she had entered it,—with clean skirts. Once more we viewed her gray paint, which we had not seen for many a long day. She seemed to feel the difference from her former draggle-tailed state; she pranced a bit, and lightened by several hundred-weight of mud, shied around corners. We gave her her head as we passed the great smelters on the western edge of the town, whose smoke stacks cloud the rims of the mountains they are attacking, and slowly, slowly eating into. A smooth macadam road led us,—at last!—out of Texas. We were not sorry to leave, hospitably as we had been treated. Ahead lay greater miracles of nature than Texas could offer, and adventure no less. The great prairie of which in two weeks we had only nibbled one corner was behind us. We were fairly embarked on the main objectives of our journey.

CHAPTER VII

SANDSTORMS, BANDITS AND DEAD SOLDIERS

ALONG a macadam road fringed with bright painted little Mexican taverns and shops, toward mid-afternoon we threaded our way, still defenseless "ladies," tempting fate. I mention what might seem an obvious fact, because the continuance of our unprotected state required strong powers of resistance against the offers of itinerant chauffeurs, anxious to get from somewhere to anywhere, filled like ourselves with spring stirrings toward Vagabondia, and seeing in our Red Duchess inconsequence an opportunity to get their itching hands on the wheel of a car which made of driving not a chore but an art. Even garage helpers, who now humbly washed wheels and handed tools to mechanics, hoping to end their apprenticeship by a bold stroke, besieged us with offers to chauffeur us for their expenses.

As we were leaving El Paso, I returned to the car to find Toby conversing with a likely looking lad. This did not surprise me, for whenever I came back to Toby after five minutes' absence, I found her incurable friendliness had collected from one to half a dozen strangers with whom she seemed on intimate terms. But I was surprised to hear this lad urging us to take him as chauffeur as far as Tucson. His frank face and pleasant manner and an army wound seemed as good references as his offer of a bank president's guarantee. He wanted to go so badly!

I have a failing,—one, at least,—of wanting to live up to what is expected of me. If a stranger with an expensive gold brick shows any real determination to bestow it on me for a consideration, he always finds me eager to cooperate, not because I do not know I am being gulled, but that I hate to cross him when his heart is set on it. Even in dour Boston it is congenitally hard for me to say "No," but in Texas where people smile painlessly and the skies are molten turquoise, it is next to impossible. Of course, we might take him as far as Tucson. We would have to give up driving, which we both loved. And pay his expenses. One of us would have to sit in the back seat, and be pulverized by jolting baggage. Still, it didn't seem right to leave our new friend at El Paso, which of all places bored him most. Would Toby be fair, and sit among the baggage half the time?

Toby, I saw, was wondering the same of me. That decided it. Toby loves her comfort. I started to say, "I suppose we might," when she countered, "But we don't want any chauffeur."

He looked hopefully at me, recognizing the weaker will.

"No," I said, glad to agree with Toby, "that is perfectly true. In fact the whole point of our trip is to see if we can get along without a chauffeur."

It was the point; his wistful smile had been so persuasive that I had almost forgotten it. Fortunately this reason convinced him without further arguing. He gave us directions about our route, and we left him, hat off, smiling and waving us bon voyage.

Crossing a state line is an adventure in itself. Even

with no apparent difference of landscape there seems inevitably a change, if only the slight psychological variance reflected by any country whose people are marked off from their neighbors by differences however slight. The universe reflects many distinctions, I firmly believe, so subtle as to be undefined by our five senses, which we note with that sixth sense finer than any. Their intangible flavor piques the analyst to the nice game of description. Hardly had we crossed the political line dividing sand and sage brush from sage brush and sand before we sensed New Mexico;—a new wildness, a hint of lawlessness, a decade nearer the frontier, Old Spain enameled on the wilderness.

Or perhaps it was only Mrs. Flanagan, with her Mexican face and Irish brogue, when we stopped to buy gas, whose longing to have us for guests at her hotel made her paint the dangers of New Mexico with Hibernian fluency and Iberian guile. She thickened the coming twilight with sand storms, bandit shapes and murders.

"Do ye know what a sandstor'rm is in these parts? Ye do not! I thought not! Last month a car left here to cross the desert to Deming, as ye're doing. Late afternoon it was,—just this hour, the wind in the same place. I war'rned thim to stay, but they w'd be gettin' along,—like yourselves."

"And what became of them?"

She gave us a look that froze the blood in our veins, despite the scorching wind from the edge of the desert.

"Yes, what did become av thim? That's what many would like to know. *They have not been heard of since!*"

"You would advise us to stay here for the night, then?"

"Suit yourselves, suit yourselves. I see your rad-ay-tor's leakin'. 'Tis a serious thing to get out in that desert, miles fr'm anywhere wid an impty rad-ayator. What could ye do, an' night comin' on? Ye're hilpless! An' suppose ye get lost? The road's not marked. 'Tis a mass of criss-cross tracks leadin' iverywhere. At best, ye'd have to stop where ye are till mornin', if ye don't git too far lost ever t' find y'rselves again."

Here entered a Gentleman from Philadelphia, a traveler for Quaker Oats, who listened to our debate with great interest. He was a brisk and businesslike young man, with a friendly brown eye and a brotherly manner.

"If you ask *me*, Mrs. Flanagan," he began diplomatically, "I'd advise the young ladies to take a chance. I think they can make it."

Something in this advice, slightly stressed, implied a warning. Mrs. Flanagan with her swarthy Mexican features was not the most prepossessing landlady in the world, nor did a lonely roadhouse on the edge of the desert, with no other guests than ourselves, promise complete security. Tales of Swiss inns, and trap-doors yawning at midnight came to me, faintly conveyed by the young man's tones. She turned on him with ill-concealed anger.

"It's nothin' to *me,* go or stay. But here's a good hotel,—with a bath-room, even,—and there's night, and sandy roads, and a stor'rm comin'. If ye had a man wid ye, I'd say 'go on,' though it's not safe, even f'r a man. But bein' two ladies, I say stop here."

We wavered, anxious to get on, but not to meet a

violent end. On the pretext of filling our water-bag, the Gentleman from Philadelphia took us aside.

"Don't let Mrs. Flanagan fool you," he advised. "She only wants customers. I stayed here once," he twitched nervously,—"and I'd rather run the chance of being robbed and murdered. Not that I think that will happen to you."

So we thanked him, nice brisk, friendly young man that he was, taking care not to incriminate him before the watchful Mrs. Flanagan, and bade that lady adieu. She gloomily wished us good luck, but it was apparently more than she dared hope.

"Only last week, two men were held up and murdered by the Mexicans," she called after us. "Watch out for thim Mexicans,—they're a wicked bad lot."

With the sky yellow-green from the gathering sand-storm, night coming on fast and her warning in our ears we struck out into our first desert with a sense of uneasiness, exhilarated a little by the warm beauty of the evening. We seemed to have left all civilization behind, although after passing the last hamlet about nightfall, we had only forty-odd miles more to go. Never shall I forget the eerie charm of that drive. We saw not a soul. Occasionally a jack rabbit, startled as ourselves, leaped athwart the gleam of our lamps. Sometimes we wandered, in the pitchy black, from the guiding Southern Pacific into a maze of twisting trails. Sometimes we dived into a sudden arroyo, wrenching the car about just in time to stay with the road as it serpentined out again. When, now and again, a lonely light far off suggested a lurking bandit, we remembered with a homesick twinge the last words of Toby's mother, and wondered when we should get a chance to obey them. At four cross roads, the only guide post lay flat midway between the roads. We were obliged to guess at the most likely route. At last we came on the lights of Deming, five miles away, in the valley. We sighed with relief and moved toward them rapidly.

And then a figure stepped out from a truck blocked beside the road, and a deep voice called "Stop a moment, please!"

At that moment we sincerely wished ourselves back in Mrs. Flanagan's road house. Then, before Toby could get out the monkey wrench which was our sole weapon of defense, the voice changed shrilly on a high note, and we saw our bandit was a fourteen year old boy. He hopped aboard, never dreaming of the panic he had caused our bandit-beset minds, explaining that his batteries were out of order, and he must return to Deming. He added, naïvely, that his father owned the second best hotel in town, which he recommended if we failed to find a room in the best hotel. Then he swung off the car, and we went on to the Mecca of all Western voyagers,—a clean room, a hot bath, and a Harvey eating house.

Like all of the Southwest, Deming was in the midst of an oil boom. Beneath the arid sand and cactus of long unwanted acreage, rich sluggish pools were in hiding, arousing the old gambling spirit of the West. It was a timid soul indeed who had not invested in at least one well. In newspaper offices we saw the day's quotations chalked on blackboards, and in the windows of real estate agents were greeted by imposing sketches of Deming Twenty Years from Now; no longer half a dozen streets completely surrounded by whirling sand, but a city of oil shafts and sky scrapers. We dropped into a hairdresser's to be rid of the desert dust, and found a group of ladies as busily discussing oil as were their husbands at the barber's.

"Jim and I had five hundred dollars saved toward a house," confided one gray-haired gambler, "so we bought Bear Cat at a cent a share. If it goes to a dollar, like the land next it, we've got fifty thousand. If it don't, why, what can you get with five hundred anyway, these days?"

"Way I do is to buy some of everything," said the hairdresser, rubbing the lather into my scalp. "Then you're sure to hit it right. I got a claim out to Stein's, and they're striking oil all around. When they find it on my claim,"—(it is always "when," never "if")—I'm going to have a rope of pearls to my waist, and a Colonial Adobe house,—twenty rooms and a dance hall."

We left the little town, hideous in its barrenness and dreaming of its future, the waitresses chewing the inevitable toothpick, the two motion picture houses, the sandstorms, and the railway with its transcontinental standards, and hastened through to Arizona, leaving a more thorough inspection of New Mexico for spring. At the garage, we had one word of advice from a weather beaten old-timer, of whom we inquired as to roads.

"The w'ust trouble ye'll have in a prohibition state is tire trouble."

"Why should prohibition affect our tires?"

"Dead soldiers."

"Dead soldiers?"

"Empty whiskey bottles."

When we looked back half a mile down the road, he was still laughing at his wit. What would have happened if the really good one about our being a long way from home had occurred to him I cannot picture.

Two routes offered for Tucson; the short cut through Lordsburg and Willcox, and the longer way by Douglas and the Mexican border. When we inquired which route would have more interesting scenery, we had met invariably with a stare and a laugh.

"Not much *scenery*, wherever you go,—sand and cactus! Just as much on one road as another."

We therefore chose the shorter way, to learn later that the Douglas-Bisbee route which we discarded was one of the most beautiful drives in the country. Yet we ourselves moved into a theater of loveliness. Saw-toothed ranges, high and stormy, snow-topped, shadowed our trail. The wide amphitheater of our golden valley was encircled with mountains of every size and color; blue, rosy, purple, and at sunset pure gold and transparently radiant. The gray sage turned at sun-down to lavender; mauve shadows lengthened on the desert floor; gorges of angry orange and red cliffs gave savage contrast to the delicate Alpine glow lighting white peaks; a cold, pastel sky framed a solitary star, and frosty air, thinned in its half-mile height to a stimulating sharpness, woke us keenly to life. We felt the enchantment that Arizona weaves from her gray cocoon toward sunset, and wondered at eyes which could look on it all, and see only sand and cactus. Show them the unaccustomed, and they would doubtless have been appreciative enough. A green New England farm with running brooks and blossoming orchards would have spelled Paradise to them, as this Persian pattern of desert did to us; beauty to the parched native of Arizona is an irrigation ditch, bordered by emerald cottonwoods.

If I tint these pages with too many sunsets, it is not from unawareness of my weakness, but because without them a description of Arizona does not describe. In the afternoon hours, between four and eight, the country wakes and glows, and has its moment, like a woman whose youth was plain but whom middle age has touched with charm and mystery. Not to speak of the sunsets of Arizona, till the reader is as saturated with their glory as is the traveler, is to leave the heart of the country unrevealed.

From Willcox to Lordsburg we realized there was more than jest in the remark of our old-timer concerning "dead soldiers." All the way through that uninhabited desert, we picked our road through avenues of discarded flat bottles of familiar shape, turning all shades of amethyst under the burning rays of the sun. It is an odd effect of the sun on glass here in the desert that it slowly turns a deeper and deeper violet. The desert-wise can tell the date a bottle was discarded from its hue. I was told that one man made a fortune by ripening window-glass in this manner, and selling it to opticians at a fancy price. It may have been a similar industry which lined our path with empty bottles. It must have been so, for Arizona had been "dry" for three years.

Even the lakes were dry. When we met with the term "dry lake" in the guide book, we set it down as another flight of the fanciful creature who had composed its pages, but soon we came upon it. Four miles and more we drove over the bottom of a lake now not even damp, making deep tracks in the white sand. Dry rivers were later to become commonplace, but we were children of Israel but this once. Suddenly beyond us in the distance, through a heat where no drop of water could live, we saw a sparkle and a shimmer of cool blue, and cottonwoods reflected in wet, wavering lines. Our dry lake had turned wet! Mountain peaks rose and floated on its surface,—and not till they melted and skipped about could I believe Toby's assertion that we were gazing on a mirage. When she focussed her camera upon the mirage I scoffed loudly. Tales of travelers in the desert had early rooted in my none too scientific mind the idea that a mirage is a subconscious desire visually projected, like the rootless vines which climb the air at the command of Hindu fakirs. When our finished print showed a definite, if faint, outline of non-existent hills, my little world was slightly less shaken than if Toby had produced a photograph of an astral wanderer from the spirit world. I do not like to look at it. It seems like black magic.

The desert, bleached dazzling white under an afternoon sun, seemed shorn of all the mysteries and apprehensions with which the previous night and Mrs. Flanagan had enveloped it. Now it lay stark and unromantic, colorless in a blare of heat. We were only a few miles from Tucson, when we mounted a hill, and poised a second, looking down on a horseshoe canyon. Our road, narrow and stony, threaded the edge of it,—a sharp down grade, a quick curve at the base, and a steady climb up. As we turned the brow of the hill and passed a clump of trees hiding the view of the bottom, ahead,

directly across the road and blocking all passage stood
a car. I put on the brakes sharply, and our car veered
toward the edge and wavered. How stupid to leave a
car directly across a dangerous road on a down grade!
This was my first reaction. Then we saw two men, with
the slouch that marks the Westerner, step from behind
their car, and await our approach. Even while I concentrated on avoiding turning into the ditch, their very
quiet manner as they awaited us arrested attention. It
was not stupidity which made them choose to alight at
that spot. It was an ideally clever place for a hold-up!
Concealed itself, it commanded a view of the entire
canyon, and would catch a car coming from either direction at lowered speed. These men were not waiting our
approach for any casual purpose; something too guarded
and watchful, too tensely alert, lay taut beneath their
easy slouch. The elder, a bearded thick-set man, carelessly held his hand on his hip pocket, as they do in all
Western novels. The taller and younger man stepped
into the middle of the road, and raised a hand to stop us.

"Toby," I said in a low voice, "this looks serious."

"Bandits!" said Toby, her tone confirming my suspicions.

"Get out the monkey wrench, and point it as if it were
a gun. I'll try to crowd past the car and up the hill."

"If we only had the ammonia pistol," sighed Toby,
murderously, getting the wrench and cocking it.

A gentle voice tinged with the sharp edge of command came from the younger man. "Better stop a
minute, lady!"

We stopped, entirely contrary to our hastily made
plans. Something in his level tone, and in a quick little

gesture the man behind him made, changed our minds.

Without removing his hand from his hip the other man, who I quickly decided was the more desperate character of the two, strolled about our car with an appraising and well satisfied look. At that moment we felt we were indeed a long, long ways from home. I began to calculate the time it would take to walk to Tucson,—hampered, possibly, by a bullet wound. Then he pulled open his coat, and a gleam of metal caught the sunlight.

"I'm the sheriff of Pima County," he said, briefly.

I did not believe him. I put my foot on the gas, and tightened my grip on the wheel, measuring the road ahead and calculating the slight chance of crowding past his car and up the steep hill ahead.

"Please show us your badge again, if you don't mind."

He gave us a full view of it this time. It looked genuine enough,—a silver star, not quite so large as the planet Jupiter, with rays darting therefrom, and Pima printed on it in bold letters,—a staggering affair, calculated to inspire respect for law and order.

"Were we speeding?" Toby faltered, remembering Houston.

"We're making a little search," he replied very crisply.

"Search,—for what?"

"Booze, for one thing," said the lank young man. The other did not waste words.

It was evident from their manner they expected to find what they were hunting for. They walked about and punched our tires, darkly suspicious. We could not have felt more guilty if we had been concealing the entire annual output of Peoria. I heard Toby gasp, and knew she was wondering what Brattle St. would say.

"Where did you come from?" asked the sheriff.

"Benson," we replied, mentioning the last town we had passed through.

"Ah!" Evidently a highly incriminating place to come from. They proceeded to examine our suit-cases thoroughly.

"I hate to search ladies," said the sheriff, in brief apology, "but if ladies *will* smuggle booze into Pima County, it has to be done."

At that moment his assistant caught sight of our knobby looking auto trunk.

"Ah!" Such a queer shaped trunk was beyond explanation. I handed over the keys in silence. They made a grim search, with no sign of unbending until they came to our funny little folding stove. Then the sheriff permitted a short smile to decorate his official expression, and I knew the worst was over. A moment later, the lank young man discovered our number-plate.

"Say! Are you from Massachusetts, lady?"

"Boston."

I pass over his next remark. The reader has heard it before, and so had we. The air was cleared, and so were we. To the sheriff of Pima County and his deputy, Boston meant only Susan B. Anthony and Frances E. Willard. They had evidently never heard of Ward Eight.

We passed on, amid apologies, to Tucson. Once more the spectres evoked by Mrs. Flanagan had been laid. Artistically, it was a pity. The canyon made a

perfect setting for a hold-up. As such I recommend it
to the outlaws of Pima County.

As we drove into the city, acquitted of boot-legging, a
wonderful odor stole to our nostrils. We sniffed, looked
at each other and sniffed again. We were entering Tucson on the historic afternoon when sixty thousand dollars
worth of liquor had been poured relentlessly into the
gutters of the old town,—a town which a generation
ago had stood for wild drinking and picturesque lawlessness.

CHAPTER VIII

TUCSON

WHAT school child reading of the Pilgrim's landing, of Montcalm's Defeat, and the Revolutionary War, but thinks he is learning the whole of America's colonial history? Studying from text-books eastern professors wrote about the time when the Mississippi held back the lurking savage, he skips over the brief mention of Coronado and Cortez as of sporadic explorers who kindly lessened home work by changing the map as little as possible. He reads of Independence Hall in Philadelphia, and Faneuil Hall in Boston, and the Old South Church. Yet in the land of Coronado, the uncharted wilderness his mind pictures, rise the white turrets and dome of a Mission beside which the Old South is as ordinary as a country Audrey compared with a lady of St. James' court. Who of his elders can blame him, who pride themselves on their familiarity with the cloisters of San Marcos and Bruges, Chartres and the ruined giant Rheims, and have heard vaguely or not at all, of the pearl set by devout Spaniards against the blue enamel sky of Arizona and dedicated to San Xavier?

As it lies relaxed on the tinted desert carpet, dome and tower so light that they seem great white balloons, kept from floating away into the vivid sky by substantial anchors of buttress and arch, compare it with the neat smugness of our Bulfinch and Georgian meeting-houses in New England. Even at its best, the latter style has

74

the prim daintiness of an exquisite maiden lady, while the Mission is like the Sleeping Beauty, with white arm curved above her head, relaxed and dreaming. Without claiming to speak with authority, I consider San Xavier the loveliest ecclesiastical building in America. Certainly its obscurity should be broken more frequently than now by pilgrimages, its outlines as familiar in school histories as Independence Hall or Washington Crossing the Delaware.

In its fashion this mission personifies a sort of Independence Hall of the first Americans,—the Papagoes, who might be termed Red Quakers. Founded in 1687 by Father Kino, a Jesuit priest of the royal house of Bavaria, the original mission suffered from Indian rebellions, Apache massacres, and the expulsion of the Jesuits. Abandoned for awhile, it fell a century later to the Franciscans, who erected the present building, which represents the almost single-handed conquest by some eighteenth century padre of engineering difficulties which might well baffle a Technology graduate. It became the Rheims of the Papagoes, Christians, in their peculiarly pantheistic fashion, since the advent of Father Kino. Mildest of all Indians, in their whole history they went on the war-path but once,—after hostile Apaches had thrice desecrated their loved San Xavier and murdered its priests. The Apaches never returned.

Nine miles from Tucson, on a wide plain which the Santa Rita mountains guard, the Mission lies cloistered, exquisite souvenir of the Moors and Spaniards, its arched gateway a legacy from Arabia. Little Papago huts of wattled reeds and mud, scarcely different in construction from prehistoric cliff-dwellings, lie scattered over the

plain.   Out in the sunshine, Papagoes in blue overalls
and brilliant bandas mended tools or drove a primitive
plow, and the women caught the wind and the light in
billowing scarves of purple, green and red.   They smiled
broadly and sheepishly at us, proudly exhibiting blinking,
velvet-eyed progeny in wicker cradles, who bore such
good Catholic names as Clara, Juan, Madelina.   Some
women were busy covering reeds with split yucca fiber,
intertwined with the black of the devil's claw, a vicious
curving seed-pod which more than once had clamped
about our feet in our desert travel.   Others baked round
loaves in rude outdoor ovens of mud.   Across the plains,
sheep grazed, and an occasional horse: the omnipresent
mongrel beloved of the Indian snarled and yapped as we
drove to the Mission doorway.

Here we stepped into another world.   An Irish
Mother Superior welcomed us, her soft brogue tempered to the hushed stillness within, and offered us trays
of cold milk.   Hers was the mellow presence which long
ripening in cloisters sometimes,—not always—brings.
Walls four feet thick shut out the yellow sunlight, save
where it fell in dappled patterns on the flags, or filtered
through green vines covering open arches.

The central dome of the mission roofs the nave of the
church.   Inside, it lights the obscurity with a rich gleam
of gold leaf, put on with barbaric lavishness.   Paintings
and frescoes of Biblical stories add to the ornate effect;
painted-faced Holy Families in gauze and lace stare
from their niches unsurprised; two great carved lions of
Castile, brought in sections from Old Spain, guard the
altar treasures.   Rightly did the Jesuits and Franciscans
gage the psychology of their dusky converts.   Never

SAN XAVIER DEL BAC, TUCSON AND THE PAPAGO INDIAN VILLAGE

eliminating the old religion, but grafting to it the vigorous shoots of the new, they made it appeal to the Indian's love of pomp and color. Pictorial representations of the saints bridged the gap between the two languages, and the glitter of the decadent Renaissance style was gilded the brighter to attract the curious minds of the red children. At least two artists of some gifts decorated the nave, for two styles are apparent. One artist was fairly unimaginative and conventional; the other painted with a daintier flourish his flying angels, who float about in their curly ribbons with a Peruginian elegance, hinting too, in their fragility, of the more perfect creatures of Fra Angelico. Certainly, this latter artist had a touch, but who he was or what he did so far from the studios which trained him, I do not think is known.

The Mother Superior led us out of the church and into the courtyard flanked by what were once cells for the resident monks, and are now schoolrooms for young Papagoes, intoning lessons to a sharp-faced nun. At the end of the court a graceful gateway, triple-arched, harked back again to Old Spain, and thence more remotely to Arabia, for it is a copy of the "camel gates," which at sunset closed their middle arch, and left tardily arriving camel trains to crawl through side openings. It is a far cry from Arabia to Arizona, yet there are camels in Arizona, too, according to a creditable account. But that story belongs elsewhere.

Framed through low white arches of the courtyard walls, against which clusters of china berries make brilliant splashes of color, are exquisite pictures of emerald green pastures leading out to white topped crests. Toward sunset these peaks turn rosy, then red; the

somber, barren hills below them become deep purple,
then chilly blue.   Over the plain, mingling with the
tinkle of sheep bells float the silver notes of the chimes
brought from Old Spain, and little by little darkness
falls, and the fluttering veils of the Papago women
vanish from the scene.

Tucson is perhaps the most liveable town in Arizona.
It boasts several good hotels, macadam boulevards, a
railway station so attractively designed and placed it
might be taken for a museum or library, an embryo sub-
way, and a university.   The last may account for an
atmosphere of culture not perhaps remarkable in the
West, yet not always found in a provincial town of the
size.

The University of Arizona is situated in the newer
part of the town.   Its buildings are of classic architecture, well proportioned, their simple, dignified lines suited
to the exuberance of nature surrounding them.   Still
new, its landscape gardening has been happily planned
in a country which aided the gardener rapidly to achieve
his softening effect.   The grounds boast two attractions
Northern colleges must forego, an outdoor swimming
pool and a cactus garden, in which all known varieties of
cactus grown in the state are found.   The University
necessarily lacks some advantages of older colleges, but
it owns a rare collection of Indian basketry and pottery.
The well-known archeologist, Prof. Byron Cummings,
who was the first white man to behold the Rainbow
Bridge in Utah, in winter has the chair of archeology,
and in summer leads classes through the cliff dwellings
and prehistoric ruins which stud the Four Corners of the
United States.

DOORWAY OF SAN XAVIER DEL BAC, TUCSON

The old part of the town, where lived the "first families" who settled the district when the Apaches raided, and the "bad man" frequented saloons, and made shootings and lynchings common in the sixties and seventies, has lost many of its thick-walled, verandahed houses in the face of the builder's fervor for bungalows. The inhabitants who remember picturesque and bloody tales of the frontier days, and even participated in them, are still in hale middle age.

Viewing the electric lights, the neat and charmingly designed bungalows, the tramways and excellent garages, the cretonne lined coupés, Toby and I decided we had discovered the West too late. We had before us only a denatured California, and were, indeed, feelingly reminded of that fact by the increasing numbers of Native Sons we encountered. Some of the benefits long enjoyed by the Golden State have seeped across the boundaries, and Arizona has become canny, and in the health resort zone which embraces Tucson has learned to add in the climate at the top of every bill. But Arizona's boom is but a feeble pipe when a real Native Son begins. Some of these have, for unknown reasons, migrated to Arizona, and whenever such an individual, male or female, saw our sign, after the customary greeting, he opened fire, "On your way to California?"

"No."

Following blank astonishment, "No?"

"No."

Recovery, "Oh,—just come from there?"

"No."

"No?"

"No."

'And you're not *going* to California?"

"No."

"Why aren't you going?"

"Because we want to do this part of the country."

"But there's nothing here but sand. Look here, you can go to California just as well as not. You'll get a climate *there*. You won't have any trouble with the roads, if that is what is troubling you. The roads are wonderful,—nothing like here. You'll find a live state across the border,—only ninety miles by Yuma. A little sand—then good roads all the way."

"Yes, but we don't want good roads. We want to stay in Arizona."

A long pause, "You want to stay in Arizona?"

"Yes."

"But California is only ninety miles away."

"But we like Arizona better."

Wounded incredulity. "Oh, you can't. You've got sand and cactus here,—just a blamed desert. And look at California, the garden spot of the world. Roads like boulevards, scenery, live towns, everything you've got in the East, and a *climate!* Now, I tell you. Here's what you do. I know California like a book, born there, thank God. You let me plan your route. You go to San Diego, work up the coast, see the Missions, Los Angeles, San Francisco,—say, that's a *town,*—and then up to Seattle. You'll have good roads all the way."

"Yes, but we were planning an entirely different trip. Arizona and New Mexico, the Rainbow Bridge, then north to Yellowstone and Glacier Park."

"Well, it's lucky I saw you in time. You go straight to Needles,—you can't miss the road, marked all the way. Good-by and good luck. You'll like California."

Like Jacob with the angel they wrestled with us and would not let us go. After several such encounters, we learned to recognize the Native Son at sight, and when he opened with "Going to California?" we would reply, with the courage of our mendacity, "Just left." It saved us hours daily.

CHAPTER IX

COMPLICATIONS arose when we reached Tucson. We planned to see endless places but most of them, at an altitude of a half mile to a mile and a half, could be reached only by roads still under ten feet of snow. The district ridged by the White Mountains was completely cut off, its unbridged rivers flooded, and its few highways covered by snow-drifts thrice the height of a man. The same conditions prevailed from Flagstaff to Winslow, and while Southern Arizona picked oranges and basked in the sun, the Grand Canyon was in the grip of winter. It became necessary, therefore, to find a ranch in which to hibernate for a month, till Arizona highways became less like the trains in the time table Beatrice Hereford describes, where "those that start don't get there, and those that get there don't start."

Tucson being apparently devoid of "dude" ranches, we decided to move on to the center of the state until we found what we sought. The shorter and more obvious route by the Old Spanish Trail, through Florence to Chandler and Phoenix, we discarded for the "new state highway" to Winkleman and Globe, thence over the Apache Trail to the Roosevelt Dam, and Chandler. Globe maintains all contact with the world by the Apache Trail: in the huge, irregular quadrilateral between Globe and Phoenix, through which the Mescal and Pinal ranges stray, there is no other road. The difficulty of travel in Arizona is not that the state has no roads, as has been unjustly claimed, but that the roads make no pretense of linking together the widely scattered towns.

We had one other reason for taking the Apache Trail besides its widely advertised beauty. Everyone who mentioned it spoke in bated breath of its difficulty, "the steepest and most dangerous road in Arizona,—you two women surely can't mean to go over it alone? It's dangerous even for a *man*."

Whatever inward qualms these remarks evoked, they made us only more curious to try our luck. We had already learned that taken a car-length at a time, no road is as bad as it seems *in toto*, and few situations develop which admit of no solution. As for doing without a man, we found Providence always sent what we needed, in any crisis we could not meet ourselves. In Tucson we found two old friends, Miss Susan and Miss Martha, who shared our brash confidence in ourselves enough to consent to go with us as far as Phoenix.

One can travel north from Phoenix to the Dam, then east to Globe, or reverse the route. Most people consider the Trail more magnificent going north and east, but circumstances forced us to take the opposite course. A month later, we made the reverse journey, so that we had opportunity to judge both for ourselves. It is hard to weigh splendor against splendor. No matter which direction you take, you will be constantly looking back to snatch the glory behind you, but on the whole, if I could travel the Apache Trail but once, I should start from Phoenix.

We left town in a raw, bleak wind which became bleaker as we circled the small hills about Oracle. For fifteen miles we had fine macadam, though occasionally torn with deep chuck-holes. Then we left the made road, and meandered up and down bumpy paths through forests of the finest, most varied cacti we had seen anywhere. Steep slopes were covered with the giant sahuara, standing bolt upright and pointing a stiff arm to heaven, like an uncouth evangelist. Demon cholla forests with their blurred silver gray haze seemed not to belong to this definite earth, but to some vague, dead moon. Among them wavered the long listless fingers of the ocotilla, and the many-eared prickly pear clambered over the sands like some strange sea plant. In this world of unreal beauty, tawny dunes replaced green slopes, and such verdure as appeared was pale yet brilliant, as if lighted by electricity.

Climbing steadily, we passed Winkleman, a little, very German settlement. Nobody had suggested we should find the scenery anything out of the ordinary, though many had said the road was good,—an outright and prodigious mis-statement of fact. One temperate person had mentioned it might be "well worth our while." If that same lady were to meet Christ she would probably describe him as "a very nice man." The scenery was grand; it progressed from grand to majestic, and from majestic to tremendous. The raw wind, with its ensuing flurry of cold rain had died down, and the sun was out. Threading westward into one mountain pass after another, we soon were making our cautious way along a narrow shelf which constantly wound higher and higher above the rushing, muddy Gila River. We had come suddenly upon magnificence minus macadam where we had been led to expect macadam minus magnificence.

Suddenly looking down, I decided the scenery was becoming altogether too grand. Far below, the Gila was a tiny thread, getting tinier every moment. On the very edge of the fast deepening canyon hung the road, with neither fence nor wall between us and eternity, *via* the Gila River. As we climbed, the road narrowed till for a dozen miles no car could have passed us. Regularly it twisted in such hairpin curves that our front tires nearly pinched our back tires as we made the turn. Instead of being graded level, the road rose or fell so steeply in rounding corners that the car's hood completely concealed which way the road twisted. If we went left while the road turned right we should collide with a cliff; if the road turned left and we right, we should be plunged through space, so it behooved us to get our bearings quickly.

Once, fortunately at a wide place, we met a team of four mules. Ignorant of the Arizona law requiring motorist to give animals the inside of the road, we drew up close to the cliff, while the faithful mules went half over the crumbly edge, but kept the wagon safely on the trails. I began to notice a strange vacuum where once had been the pit of my stomach. Ordinarily I cannot step over a manhole without my knees crumpling to paper, and that thread of a stream a mile, or probably only about 500 feet below, gave me an acute attack of "horizontal fever."

At that giddy moment, on the very highest spot, I essayed to turn a sharp corner down grade, where a ledge threw us well over to the edge of the curve, and I found my foot brake would not hold. I tried the emergency. It, too, had given way from the constant strain put on it. We were already in "first," but even so, at that grade our heavy car would coast fifteen or twenty miles an hour. The road ahead switch-backed down, down, down. I calculated we could make two turns safely and that the third would send us spinning over the chasm. I felt my face undergo what novelists call "blanching." I stiffened, and prepared myself—no time to prepare the others—for the wildest and probably the last drive of my life. And then a weak voice from behind called: "Stop the car, please! I feel ill."

Poor Miss Martha had been suffering all day from a sick headache, but had gallantly admired the scenery between whiles. Now, oblivious to scenery, with closed eyes and wan face, she waited for the dreadful motion to cease. I wanted to, but was in no position to obey her reasonable request. As a drowning man sees everything, to my sharp mental vision of the car spinning over and over toward the final crash, I added a picture of poor Miss Martha, bewildered all the way down, and too ill to do anything but wonder *why* the car would not stop. I lost fear in a glow of altruistic sympathy. Then, deciding something had to be done quickly, I ran the "old lady's" nose into a ledge. The left mudguard bent, but we stuck.

"The car's going over!" exclaimed Miss Susan, much surprised.

"No, it isn't," I said, rather crossly. As well as two paper knees permitted, I got out, and explained about the brakes. Relieved that motion had ceased, Miss

Martha sank back blissfully closing her eyes. The others had not realized our danger.

It was evident the brakes must be tightened if we were to reach the bottom of the canyon alive. Neither Toby nor I knew how to tighten brakes, except that in the process one got under the car. Accordingly, as diagnostician, I crawled beneath, and in a few moments found a nut which looked as if it connected with the brake, while Toby, who is exceedingly clever with tools, and something of a contortionist, managed to tighten it. We tried the foot brakes. They held! Never had we known a prouder moment. The incident gave us courage to meet new contingencies, and never again did I experience just that sick feeling of helplessness of a moment before. While Toby was still beneath the wheels, a horn sounded, and another machine climbed around the bend. Miss Susan flagged it with her sweater just in time. Two men emerged, rather startled at the encounter, and asked how they were to pass. As the ascending car, they had the right of way, and unlike the courteous mules, intended to keep it. I could not blame them for not wanting to back down hill,—neither did I. I could not tell whether my knees would ever be "practical" again. The road was little more than ten feet wide, and very crooked. I am usually good at backing, but sometimes I become confused, and turn the wrong way, —and I hated to spoil the view by backing into it. After some prospecting, we discovered a little cubby-hole at the third turn down. At the rate of an inch a minute we reached it. The chauffeur of the other car gave us valuable advice,—never to use our foot brake on mountains, but instead to shut off ignition, shift to first gear,

and if we still descended too fast, use the emergency brake at intervals. If the grade were so steep as to offset all these precautions (as actually happened later, on several occasions) the foot brake could be alternately pressed and released.

With all the Rockies before us, this information gave us back the confidence which we had momentarily lost while we poised brakeless over the Gila. Before reaching home, we were to travel over many such roads, for we motored along the spine of the Rockies from Mexico to Alberta, but never again did "horizontal fever" attack us virulently. This "fine state highway" from Winkleman to Globe proved as dangerous a road as we were to meet, and being the first encountered after the plains of Texas and the deserts of New Mexico, it especially terrified us. A month later we traversed it without a quiver.

Once more into the valley, and into Globe as the lights came out. Globe runs up-hill at the base of a huge, dark mountain, full of gold and copper and other precious metals. Cowboys and bright-robed Apaches still walk the streets. We knew the town was busy and prosperous, but as usual the Arizonans had forgotten to mention its scenic value, which any hotel proprietor back home would have envied. The air, too, blows bracing and keen, and the town's whole atmosphere is brisk — except at the drug-store, where I dropped in to shop for a cake of soap, and spent an hour,—a delicious, gossipy hour. The druggist evidently had a weakness for high-priced soaps which he had indulged lavishly in the seclusion of Globe, more for esthetic pleasure than hope of commercial gain. We were kindred souls, for Toby and I had developed a mania for soap-collecting, and at each new hotel pilfered soap with joy. We discussed the relative merits of French and domestic soaps, of violet and sandalwood, of scented and unscented. He told me the kind his wife used, and as an indirect compliment I bought a cake of it.

And so, to bed, and to dream I had driven the car to the third floor of our hotel, when the proprietor discovered it, and ordered me to take it away. They refused us the elevator and I was forced to bump the great leviathan downstairs, one step at a time. How I labored to keep the unwieldy bulk from getting beyond control! I awoke to find both feet pressed hard against the footboard of the bed.

At the garage next morning we heard more of the dangers of the Apache Trail. Considering nobody had thought the dangers of the Winkleman road important enough to mention, I became extremely dubious that we would reach Roosevelt Dam alive. Still, the weather was charming, blue sky and hot sun. I could not believe the Lord would let anyone die on such a day.

As if the sun were not bright enough, fields of golden stubble made the scene dance with light. A herd of Holsteins lent a dash of black and white, and the far hills across the Gila were pink, mauve, orange, lemon, —any preposterous color but those a normal hill should be.

We were following the trail over which Coronado and his army rode when, incidentally to their search for gold, they made history in 1540. Over this same road, for thousands of years, native Americans, Toltecs, cliff-dwellers, Apaches, friars, and forty-niners, have traveled to satisfy blood-lust and gold-lust, religion, fanaticism, and empire building. Until the Roosevelt Dam let in a flood of tourists, few traveled it except on grim business. The romance of a thousand years of tense emotions experienced by resolute men haunts that lovely sun-flooded valley.

Mormons still follow the Trail, recognizable by their long, greasy beards. One such passed us, driving an ancient Ford,—the very one, I should say, in which Brigham Young came to Utah. It showed faded remnants of three coats of paint, white, blue and black. On the radiator rested a hen coop containing several placid biddies. We tacitly ignored a murmur from Toby about "an eggs-hilarating drive." A dozen children, more or less, sat beside the Mormon. Attached to the Ford was a wagon, drawn by six burros, with a burro colt trotting beside, and atop the wagon, under a canvas roof, a few more women and children. We were too appalled to notice whether the Ford pulled the burros, or the burros pushed the Ford. Following the prairie schooner came a rickety wagon, piled with chairs, stoves and other domestic articles. Last of all came a house. It was, to be sure, a small house, but considering that the car was only working on two cylinders, one could not reasonably expect more.

Later we passed a man on horseback, wearing two sombreros, one atop the other, with a certain jaunty defiance. Whether he did it from ostentation, for warmth, to save space, to keep out moths, or was just moving, we could not guess. Or he may have been a half-crazy prospector, whose type we began to recognize,—old, vague-eyed men with strange beards, speech curiously halting, from long disuse, and slow, timid manners,—riding a burro or rack-of-bones horse up a side trail. In every section of the Rockies one meets these ancient, unwashed optimists, searching in unlikely crannies, more from life-long habit than in the hope of striking it rich. So long have they lived remote from human beings, that if a gold mine suddenly yielded them the long sought fortune and compelled them to return to the world, they would die of homesickness.

When Coronado marched over the Apache Trail, he saw far above him a walled town built in the recessed cliffs, whose protective coloring made it nearly invisible to the casual passerby. The Spaniard, seeking the Seven Cities of Cibola, imagined he had discovered one of their strongholds, but when he rushed up the steep path, more breathless, doubtless in his heavy armor than we four centuries later in our khaki suits, he found the swallow's nest deserted, and the birds flown,—where and for what reason is the great mystery of the Southwest.

So cunningly hidden are these sky parlors that we drove by them without seeing them, and had to inquire their whereabouts at the local postoffice. At Monte Cristo they show you the very window from which the Count did not leap; at Salem any citizen will proudly stop work to point out the hill where the witches were not burned, but the postmistress in a Georgette waist knew of the cliff-dwellings only as a fad of crazy tourists, although she could have walked to them in the time she took to remove her chewing gum before answering us. Out West they have not learned the art of making their ancestors earn an honest penny.

We lunched at the Tonto ruins, and that lunch marks

the beginning of Toby's mania for hoarding bits of broken pottery, charred sticks and other relics of the past. She learned to distinguish between the red and black of the middle ages, the black and white of an earlier era, and the plain thumb-nail of remotest antiquity. She never could resist adding just one more bit of painted clay or obsidian to her knobby collection, and the blue bandana in which she tied them grew steadily larger, until it overflowed into the pockets of the car, and the food box, and after awhile she clinked as she walked, and said "Ouch" when she sat down absent-mindedly.

Leaving the ruins and following the shelf high above the blue lake, we came quite unexpectedly on the dam, not five miles further. It was a surprise to reach our first night's stop with half the dread Trail behind us, and no thrilling escapes from destruction. We learned at the Inn that the worst sixteen miles lay ahead on the road to Fish Creek. Indeed, the Apache Trail, although narrow, full of turns and fairly precipitous in places, proved a far simpler matter than the unadvertised "highway" out of Winkleman, while the scenery itself was hardly lovelier.

Rounding the shoulder of a massive cliff, we swung sharply down hill to a narrow bridge of masonry, the arm holding back the great artificial body of water. In front was the dam, one of the largest in the world, and in difficulty of construction, one of the most interesting to engineers. Yet the flood twice Niagara's height pouring over it, is dwarfed to a mere trickle by the majesty of the cliffs above. To get its full impressiveness you must descend to the bottom of the masonry and look up at the volume pouring over the curved wall, which has made a quarter of a million acres of desert the most fruitful section of this continent. You observe a man walking along the steps which line the concave wall of the dam in close formation, and notice that his shoulder is on a level with the step above. Gradually, isolated from its dwarfing surroundings, the handiwork of Man impresses you. There has been talk of placing near the dam a memorial to Roosevelt, but no fitting memorial could be placed there which would not seem of pigmy significance. The best and most appropriate memorial to the man of deeds is the dam itself, and the fertile and prosperous Salt River Valley below it.

At the Inn built on the borders of the lake we asked for rooms. The innkeeper, a plump and rubicund Irishman, seemed flustered. His eyes swam, and he looked through us and beyond us with a fixed glare. His breath came short and labored—very fragrant.

"Don't hurry me, lady," he replied pettishly to Miss Susan, "can't you see the crowds waiting for rooms? They ain't trying to get in ahead of their turn. *They're* behaving themselves. *They* aint trying to nag the life out of me asking for this and that. *They* aint pushin' and shovin'. Now, lady," fixing a stern eye upon her, and speaking like a man whose patience would outlast any strain, "I'm at my wit's end with all these people. Can't you be reasonable and wait till I git 'round to you?"

As we were the only people in sight, we were forced to conclude he was seeing us in generous quantities. Possibly, too, we were not standing still, but were whirling around in an irritating way. So we waited patiently for an hour or so, while John made frequent trips to the back of the house. As the afternoon shortened, and John's temper with it, the crowd steadily increased.

"Are our rooms ready yet?" I finally asked. His eye wandered past me and lighted upon Miss Susan. He fixed upon her, as a person who had given him much trouble a long time ago.

"What! You here again?" He had a fine exclamatory style. "Lady, you're giving me more trouble than all the rest of 'em put together. Here, Ed," he called a clerk, with great magnanimity, "take 'em. Give 'em a room. Give 'em the hotel. Give 'em *anything* they want. Only get 'em out of my way."

They led us to our tents, where the beds were still unmade. The clerk left, promising to get John to send a chambermaid. We felt less hopeful than he, for as we were banished from his presence we observed him feeling his way, a cautious mile or so at a time, to the far reaches of the kitchen. We made one or two trips to the hotel to induce somebody to make up our beds, keeping Miss Susan well in the background, for the sight of her seemed more than John could bear. But he pounced on her.

"Have you any idea of the troubles of a hotel keeper?" His forbearance by now had become sublime. "*Any* idea? No, lady, I can see you haven't. If you had you'd be a little patient."

Our beds were made, but an hour later we were still without towels and water, while one tent had no lights. The rest of us were thoroughly cowed by this time, but opposition had stiffened little Miss Susan to the point where she would risk being hurled over the dam before she would be brow-beaten. We timidly followed, giving her our physical if not our moral support, while she stated our case, which she did quite simply.

"We've been here some hours, and we still have no towels or electric lights."

"*Be* reasonable. I ask you, lady, one thing, if possible." Heavy sarcasm. "*Be* reasonable. I've got my troubles, same as you have. All the world has its troubles. Now why can't you stand yours with a little patience?"

"I'm sorry for your troubles," said Miss Susan, sympathetically. "But we are paying for towels and electric lights. Why shouldn't you give them to us?"

At this John became violent.

"Lady! Go!" He pointed dramatically to the dam, and the road out into the wilderness beyond. "Go! I don't want you! And never come back again. Lady, if everyone was like you, I'd go crazy. You've been asking for something ever since you struck the place. Why, since you've come here, the help has all come to me and give notice. Now, get out!"

For fear he might carry out the eviction on the spot, and send us on sixteen miles of precipitous darkness, we again retreated. After supper, facing the terrifying prospect of feeling her way to bed, lightless, and with no lock on the door to keep out inebriated landlords or mountain lions, Miss Susan resolved on action. She tiptoed to the dining room, and was in the act of unscrewing a bulb from its socket when John appeared from the vicinity of the kitchen. At sight of his arch enemy thus outraging his hospitality, anger and grief swelled within him. Probably the only thing that kept Miss Susan, dauntless but scared, from being completely annihilated was that he could not decide which one of her to begin on first.

"Lady!" he exclaimed, sorrowfully, as if he could not believe his eyes,—and possibly he could not—"Lady! Off my own dining-room table!"

He reached wobbly but sublime heights of forbearance, his voice filled with reproachful irony.

"Lady, I got one thing to ask you. *Only* one. If you got to take my electric lights,—if you've sunk as low as that, lady,—all I ask is, *don't* take 'em off my dining-room table. I've seen all sorts of people here in my day,—all sorts, but none of them would steal the lights off my dining-room table."

"I have never been so insulted in all my life," exclaimed Miss Susan.

"Lady," said John, swaying as by an invisible breeze, "I am *trying* to be as nice as I know how."

A few scared employes later sought our tents, to apologize for John.

"John is never like this," said one succinctly, "except when he's this way."

"I thought Arizona was a prohibition state," I said, remembering the sheriff of Pima County, "where does he get it?"

Their eyes wandered to the horizon, and remained fixed there.

"Vanilla extract," said one.

The scientifically minded Toby made an excursion to the Inn, and came back with a satisfied sniff.

"It wasn't vanilla," she reported positively.

Upon the hotel porch, we could see John's white

jacketed fat figure mincing up and down before a group of late-comers holding an imaginary skirt in one hand. First he was Miss Susan, red-handed and infamous; then he became himself, majestic yet forbearing.

"Took them right off my dining-room table," we heard him say.

CHAPTER X

THE APACHE TRAIL AND TONTO VALLEY

FEARING the wrath of John, we made a guilty start in the freshness of the next morning. But when we paid our bill and left, John was still heavily under the influence of vanilla, and to Miss Susan's relief, we did not encounter him. Even in bright daylight with no traffic we were an hour and a half driving the sixteen miles to Fish Creek. Salt River Valley became a narrow chasm, dark and gloomy but for the glint of emerald cottonwoods edging the stream at the bottom. A chaotic heap of brilliant-hued peaks filled the valley.

The road was all that had been claimed for it. Had we not been inoculated with horizontal-fever serum on the still more precarious Winkleman trail, we might have fallen over the precipice in sheer giddiness. The natural hazards of a road which skipped from top to bottom of a series of thousand-foot rocks were increased by tipping outward up-hill and around corners, so that frequently we lurched over steep chasms at a far from reassuring angle, while our long wheel-base increased complications. Boulders loosened from the crumbling cliffs above, cluttered the road at the most dangerous turns. A glance ahead at a dizzy drop of several thousand feet, then beyond to a corresponding climb, and still further to dips and swoops exceeding the most breath-taking devices of Coney Island, would make me weak-kneed. But taking the road in a near-sighted way, after one quick glance over switch-backs to make sure we should meet no traffic, and meet-ing each problem in driving as it came abreast the steer-ing wheel, I found the Apache Trail as safe as a church.

We breakfasted under the highest peak of all, at the little Fish Creek inn. Here the scenery resembled the landscapes of impressive grandeur our grandmothers re-ceived for wedding presents, with crags and waterfalls, jungles, mountains and valleys gloomily heaped together in a three foot canvas. Our breakfast was a simple af-fair of stewed fruit, oatmeal, fried ham, fried eggs, bacon, hot biscuits, coffee and griddle cakes. Thus se-curely ballasted, our chance of being toppled off a cliff's edge was materially lessened. Now came the climax of the drive,—the climb to Lookout Point.

Two thousand vertical feet of rock would seem a suf-ficient barrier to turn humanity back into the fastnesses whence it came. But moccasined feet had won to the summit, and motor cars with the power of many cayuses now roar over the same trail, a tortuous mile upward to Lookout Point. Whether this spot was named for its scenic beauty or for a warning, matters not: the name fits. We looked our fill. I cannot describe what we saw. Go and see it for yourself, even at the risk of breaking a neck. The safety of one's neck is always inversely as the beauty of the view.

Miles on jagged miles of mountain tops lay below us. It was not long before we became aware of the extreme unimportance of ourselves and our tiny affairs. The mountains shouted to each other, "GOD IS!"

With a suggestion of Bunyan, we reached Superstition Mountain next, and left it behind. Then the scenery, having had its last triumphant fling of grandeur, settled down to levels of gray and brown. The world which a moment since had stood on its head for joy tumbled flat, and became content with mediocrity.

Five miles more, and the reason for Roosevelt Dam lay before our eyes. Five miles of blistering country, so dry, as a guide said, that "when you spit you can't see where it lands"; a country burnt to a crisp by withering sunshine so intense that shadows, sharp-edged as razor blades, look vermilion purple. Only horned reptiles, poisonous and thorny-backed, can exist here, and plants as ungracious, compelled to hoard their modicum of moisture in iron-clad, spiny armament. And then, a line of de-marcation the width of a street, and the Water-God has turned this colorless ache of heat to emerald green. Thwarted cactus gives way to long rows of poplars and leopard-spotted eucalyptus bordering blue canals. We saw a corner of Southern France where the hills of Provençe edge the fertile plains of Avignon. We were in the famous Salt River Valley, the boast of parched Arizona.

We followed these shady canals into Phoenix, bump-ing over dismally paved roads, and making wide detours where some irrigator greedy for water had flooded the street. After leaving our friends at the station, we returned, sand blowing in our faces, to the San Marcos Hotel at Chandler. Neither town nor hotel has geo-graphic or commercial reasons for existing, but both are examples of one man's patient persistence in a fight with stubborn Nature. Chandler is typical of the whole Val-ley. Sand-besieged from the north, it sets a flame of verdure to meet the devastating onslaught of the desert, blossoming defiantly till the air is saturated with perfume. A contrast to the uncompromising shoe-box fronts of most Western hotels, the San Marcos displayed low plaster arcades hung with swinging plants inviting all the song birds of the valley, cool corridors and carefully planned interiors, and gardens framed by distant lilac mountains. Across from the hotel little shops repeated its design of reposeful Mission. Only on the outskirts of this little town did we meet with the crude unsophistication of the Rockies. Yet before a week passed all this artificial fertility and prettiness palled. It was not Arizona. Beyond the orange and olive groves of the Valley, beyond the blooming roses and the song of the nightingale, and all the daintiness of eastern standards inlaid upon the west we felt the threat of the arid waste circling this little island of fruitfulness. The dam, beneficent as it is, harnesses but does not destroy the desert.

We found ourselves making excursions back to the untrammeled wastes of sand beyond. Once we made a day's excursion to Casa Grande, forty miles away, over the Maricopa reservation.

No spot could look more untouched by human life than this wind-ribbed and desolate palimpsest of sand on which layer on layer of history has been scratched. The old Santa Fe Trail, from armored Spaniard to Wells-Fargo days, ran directly over a corner of ruins since excavated. Before 1700 Father Kino came upon this remote house of the Morning Glow, as the Indians called it, and held mass in its empty rooms for the tribes of the region. Coronado the ubiquitous may have seen it since he speaks of a Great House built by Indians. Even then, the place lay in ruins, and for how much further back?

Nobody knows, and guesses are a millennium apart. It is America's oldest ruin.

We drove home across the desert through a world transfigured. The afternoon sun in that pure air scattered prismatic stains over gray mesquite and sage, and colored the translucent hills in gay pinks and blues. Superstition Mountain loomed clear and cold on our left. But what caught and held our eyes in this pastel land was a riot, a debauch of clear orange-gold. Born overnight of a quick shower and a spring sun, a million deep-centered California poppies spread a fabulous mosaic over the dull earth, fairy gold in a fairy world, alive, ablaze. A sunset was thrown in, and a crescent moon in a Pompadour sky helped us thread our way home through arroyos and over blind trails.

Still in search of a "dood ranch," we trailed all over the Salt River Valley.

Some of the ranches where we sought board and lodging were surrounded by orange groves. The hosts made a point of the privilege allowed guests to pick and eat all the oranges they liked, but at the prices charged we could have procured the same privilege in any hotel in New York. Arizona prices do not, like the ostrich, hide their heads in the sand. The completion of the dam made Salt River Valley realize that the climate she had always possessed, crowned with fruit and flowers, made her California's rival. She began to cultivate oranges, pecans and a professional enthusiasm for herself. One Native Son of Phoenix of whom I was buying post-cards almost sold me a triangular corner of his ranch, at $300 an acre. If it had been irrigated, he said he would have had to charge more. The longer he talked the more eager I was to secure this Paradise whose native milk and honey would keep me in affluence and spare tires the rest of my days. Toby, however, who had been strolling about during the exhortation and had not been splashed by his golden shower of words, advised postponing purchase till we saw the land. We drove out, and looked at it. One thing he had claimed was true:—it *was* triangular. It was frankly desert, but not even pretty desert. Except for a deserted pigsty in the immediate foreground, there was no view. We drove back to Phoenix.

Now Phoenix has paved streets and electric lights and a Chamber of Commerce, a State House and a Governor. But somehow, Phoenix had no charm for us. Phoenix may be Arizona, but it is Arizona denatured. All Salt River Valley seemed denatured. It had taken its boom seriously, and the arch crime of self-consciousness possessed it. For the first time since the Aztecs one can find Arizonans trying to do what other people do, rather than what they dam-please. And it set, oh, so heavily on Phoenix and the Phoenicians and on the Easterners and Californians who had come there to be as western as they dared. Finally we heard of a little ranch away up in the country north of the dam, where we need not dress for dinner, and there we hied us.

As we were leaving, we did find one person in the Valley who was entirely free from the vice of self-consciousness. While I bought gasoline at forty-five cents a gallon in Mesa to save having to pay seventy-five in Payson, she spied me and came up eagerly to pass the time of day.

"Awful hot," she said cordially, fixing calm brown eyes on me.

"Indeed it is," I said.

A worried expression passed over her sweetly creased old face.

"Terrible unseasonable. Hard to know what to do about your winter flannels."

"I changed mine today," I replied.

Her brown eyes again became serene pools.

"Guess I will, too," she answered.

In Boston it would have taken two generations to have reached the subject of winter-flannels. We exchanged no further courtesies, except smiles, and she left looking cooler already.

At a little ranch near Pine, Arizona, northwest of Roosevelt Dam, we hoped to find lodging. Hoped, because a letter from Chandler took a week or more to penetrate to its remoteness, and ours had not long preceded us. Some discussion there had been as to whether the snow would permit us to get through, but we decided to chance it, for spring was daily working in our favor.

We had not gone far from town when the "old lady" without any preliminary groans, stopped short. Cars have a way of doing that, but ours till now had stopped only for external reasons, such as a tire, or a too persuasive mud-hole. Now she stopped as though she needed a rest and intended, willy-nilly, to take one. On such occasions I always open the hood and peer inside, not because it enlightens me or starts the car, but because Toby has not yet learned to regard it as a graceful gesture, merely.

"What is it?" she asked, with the respect I liked to have her employ.

"Either the carburetor or the batteries," I answered expertly.

A man drove by. Our silent motor, and ourselves in the despairing, bewildered attitude common to all in like situation, were the only signal needed, for this was Arizona. A moment before he had seemed in a tearing hurry, but as he pulled up and offered help, he seemed to have all the time in the calendar. He got down in the dust, wrestled with the tools we intelligently handed him at proper intervals, explored the batteries, and struggled to his feet.

"Batteries all right. Ignition."

Four miles from town, with a dead motor! But before we had time to exchange doleful glances, he asked briskly,

"Got a rope?"

We protested at his inconveniencing himself, for we had a fixed scruple that having taken to the road regardless of consequences, we should be willing to take our own medicine and abide by what arrived. But we might have saved our breath. The Samaritans who passed by on our side always answered comfortably as did this latest benefactor.

"What'm *I* here for?"

Thus, with at least an hour's loss, Number 10, or 11, or 12 of the Nicest Men We Ever Met towed us to the nearest ranch, and there telephoned for help. How welcome were the rattletrap ex-racer, and blue-overalled mechanic with a smudge on his left cheek who came to a dashing stop opposite our machine,—the same mechanic we had despised yesterday for forgetting to fill our grease-

cups,—I was tempted to paraphrase Goldsmith, or somebody,

"Garageman, in thine hours of ease
  Uncertain, coy, and hard to please,
But seen too oft, familiar with thy face
  We first endure, then pity, then embrace!"

Smudge and all, we nearly embraced him when he took
apart and put together the whole ignition system, and
came out even.   Presently, at the heart of that tightly
closed metal box, on a tiny point hardly larger than a
needle he discovered a few grains of sand, memento of our
last sandstorm.   Like the blood clot which strikes down
robust men, it had stopped a ton of mechanism from func-
tioning.   Philosophizing thus, we idly watched the me-
chanie put together those intricate parts, little realizing
how useful the experience would prove later.

It was part of the odd luck which from beginning to
end followed us that our breakdown happened before we
had re-entered the isolated Apache Trail, with its break-
neck grades.   Still, our adventure delayed us, until on
entering the pass with its looming mountains and wild
gorges shutting us away from the world, darkness had
closed in around us,—the pitch-black of a wilderness
night.   Ahead lay the famed Fish Creek road, fairly terrifying a week ago when we climbed it in broad daylight.   Now, in the dark, we were to descend this dizzy
corkscrew which dropped a thousand feet in a mile and
a quarter.   One lamp gave only a feeble light, but the
other threw a magnificent steady glare which pierced the
loneliness of that jumble of crags and forests far below

us. Would our brakes hold, and would our nerves obey us? Though I felt cool, I admit to gripping the steering-wheel harder than good driving required. From Toby's direction came a funny noise.

"I just remembered Mother's last words," she explained.

We both laughed, though feebly, at the perennial joke.

Night has the effect of seeming to double distances. At the pinnacle of this crag we paused a second. Below, we looked down vast depths upon the points of lesser pinnacles, jumbled in the valley. There was no bottom to the Pit directly under our headlights. Used to scenery with a bottom to it, however remote, we had rather a prejudice in favor of it. Beyond the radius of our lights we could pierce the blackness only in vague outlines. Then we dropped down, taking each switch-back with caution. The nose of the car swung periodically out over the edge, daring our brakes to go the inch more which meant a mile—downward. One loose rock, of which there were so many, might send us spinning, crashing among the treetops below. But why harrow the reader unnecessarily? It must be evident we reached the bottom in safety. Yet halfway down I was not so sure of the outcome, for a spark of light and a little click, regular and ominous, came from the engine, just when the grade pitched the car head-down. I took the turns with my heart in my mouth. When we reached fairly level ground again we investigated. It was only a loose wire, connecting with the cylinders, but a little longer descend and we might have had a cross circuit, —and trouble.

It was good to have the valley come up to us. It was

very good to see little friendly lights twinkling in the
vast circle of the hills.   The lights meant the Inn, and
our day's journey ended.   The host welcomed us, rather
astonished that two Easterners should have risked that
hill at night.   Had there been any other way we should
have taken it, but no grassy meadows offered where we
could run the car in safety; only empty chasms or perpendicular cliffs.   Once on the road we had to go on.
Then, too, we preferred the hot and appetizing food of
the Inn to our own amateur camp cooking.   Food is a
powerful magnet.

Toward sunset next day we had passed beyond the
lake of cobalt which science had set in the golden circlet
of the desert.   We had left the haunts of motors.   As we
rose from one hilly crest to the next higher, we met only
an occasional prospector, afoot, or an emigrant from
Utah with an old-time prairie schooner and a flock of
burros.   We were on that further branch of the T-shaped
trail named Apache, and later we turned due north, and
left it for mountain ranges of sweeping loveliness.   I
cannot, at the risk of boring, write of mountains without
enthusiasm.   These were on a colossal scale, as befits
the Rockies, but their grandeur did not repel.   They were
homey mountains.   As we traveled upward over the
same kind of shelf-road with which the Winkleman trail
had made us so quickly familiar, we could look down
upon range after range, their blues and ochres melting
together as far as eye could reach.

In a cup of these hills, yet so high it was itself on
a mountain, the road forked sharply, each branch leading straight up a mountain, and each seeming well-nigh
unconguerable.   Below lay a little mining settlement of

half a dozen cabins. At the juncture a sign-board bore the name of the town toward which we were traveling. It was an excellent sign-board, plainly marked. Its only draw-back was that it pointed midway between the two roads, quite impartially. Toby was for taking the right fork, I for the left. We argued hotly but finally Toby won, and we took the right-hand road. Soon the mining camp dropped several hundred feet below, and then became a dot. Ahead, the road circled in a twenty-mile horse-shoe on the inside of a mountain range, seeming to lead miles into the wilderness. I announced that Toby was mistaken.

"The Mormon said to take the right turn," said Toby, standing to her guns.

"And we've taken half a dozen right turns since then," I answered. Now the problem facing us was: To turn a heavy car with a 122 inch wheel-base around on a steep twelve-foot road with a mountain slope on one side and on the other, sheer precipice. Often in nightmares of late I had found myself compelled to drive down Bright Angel Trail at the Grand Canyon, turn at Jacob's Ladder, and ascend,—and the present reality was hardly less terrifying. It turned out later that Toby was right, as she always was when she should have been wrong,—and we could have been spared our acrobatics. But we should have missed Mr. Kelly.

We made the turn. I never want to try it again. A few inches forward, till a yawning gulf lay under our front wheels; then back till we hit a steep bank, then forward, down grade to the edge; brakes, reverse, and the fear of a plunge forward between release of brakes and the catch of the reverse gear. We made half a dozen

maneuvers before we again faced the misleading sign-
post. We passed the mining camp, drove up the left
fork, and bumped against a mountain which refused to be
climbed.

"You see I was right," said Toby smugly.

Before she had finished, a man with a refulgent smile
came running up, thrust into our hands a visiting card
which he took from his wallet, and shaking our hands
enthusiastically said, "Glad to see ye, gurrls. Kelly's
my name. What's yourn? I'm boss of the mine here.
Come on out, and stay to supper. Stay all night. Stay
a week,—the b'ys will be tickled t' death. You can have
my room,—I'll bunk wid the foreman. I'm f'rm Providence, Rhode Island. Been in the Legislat'ur twenty
years. Been a horse jockey, an' an inventor, an' foreman
of a factory. Makin' my everlastin' fortune in this mine
just now, and no stock to sell. Where 'ye from?"

"Boston, now! Well, say, ye're a long ways fr'm
home. Ye'll have to stay, neighbors like that. We got
a big fat cook, two hundred and fifty she weighs, and a
crackerjack with the eats, and she says tell ye she'll never
speak to you agin if ye don't stay to supper."

I looked wistfully at Toby. We had been warned
we might not get through to Pine, because of snow drifts
in the passes, and it was only an hour to dark, over twisting and unknown hill roads, but our recent trapeze work
had left us with an all-gone feeling at the belt. If we did
not eat now we might go hungry till morning. We decided not to renounce the friendship of the two hundred
and fifty pound crackerjack.

Kelly was one of Nature's enthusiasts, but he had un-
derstated concerning his cook, both in weight and pro-

ficiency. All of her three hundred odd pounds billowing and undulating in the bounds of a starched white apron waddled a testimonial to her skill. When Kelly delicately left us under her chaperonage she overflowed with joy.

"Girls, you don't know what a treat it is to see womenfolks. I been here all winter, the only woman in camp, and I could die with homesickness."

We said something appreciative of the beauty of the scenery. She sniffed.

"This? Say, girls, you ought to see God's country!"

"California?" we said intelligently.

"You bet!" answered the Native Daughter. "I s'pose you're headed that way?"

"No,—" weakly,— "we thought we'd see Arizona first."

"Well, girls, it's lucky you met *me*. Now I can lay out a trip for you through California that will knock Arizona silly. There's the Yosemite,—and the Big Trees,—and the climate,—grandest scenery in the world,—and San Francisco. After you reach Needles, you get good roads all the way,—nothing like these. My! To think you'd 'a wasted your time in Arizona if I hadn't met you."

"Yes, indeed. We can't be grateful enough."

The truth, with a little ingenuity, always serves. At this point we were luckily called to supper, cooked early for our convenience. We sat between Mr. Kelly, who leaped lightly from ships to sealing wax, from cabbages to kings in a jovial torrent of brogue, and the engineer of the mine. The latter was an Englishman well past middle age, with a slight cockney accent, apparently self-educated but with the thoroughness only his type achieves. When he spoke in a hesitating, deprecating way, vastly unlike Mr. Kelly's self-assured flood, he exhibited a vast range of information, correct, unlike Mr. Kelly's again, to the last detail. His vague brown eyes, the iris blue-rimmed, cleared and shone with faith when in a matter-of-course way he suddenly spoke of the "spirit world," which it seems was very near to him. Fifty, painfully ugly, shabby middle-class, learned, and on telepathic terms with ghosts, he piqued curiosity, as a man who seemed to have much behind and little before him.

Kelly, on the other hand, was a man of futures, the longer and riskier the better. He was waiting a necessary month or two for the mine to yield him and its owners an immense fortune,—"and no stock to sell." Arizona was "the greatest country in the world," and this pocket of the hills the finest spot in Arizona. The "b'ys" who were expected to be entranced at our advent were the finest in the United States.

"All good b'ys," he proclaimed while, eyes downcast, they shoveled huge knifefuls of beans to conceal their embarrassment, "good b'ys, and refined,—not what you usually get in mining camps. You won't hear them speak a wor'rd before you not fit for ladies."

He was right, there, for they opened not their mouths, except to fill them, while the boldest mumbled a "pass the butter!" Yet, without vanity, I think the company of "ladies" did give them a kind of agonized pleasure. When we left they watched us out of sight.

"An' d'ye know what stopped the war?" continued Kelly, taking a jump we could not quite follow. "Ye thought Wilson did it, didn't ye? He did not. It was copper. Copper did it. And Kelly. I saw how things was goin'—I wint to the Secret'ry of the Treasury, an' I says to him, 'McAdoo,' I says, 'Ye know as well as meself that this war has to stop. An' why? Copper,' I says,——"

The inside story of the armistice we never did learn, for an interruption came in the shape or shapelessness of the Native Daughter bearing a four layer cake, which we hardly finished before the gathering dark warned us to leave. We could barely withstand the pressure to stay overnight, to stay a week, or a month, or better,—"Come and settle. There's land enough; ye can pick y'r spot, and I'll have the b'ys put up a bungalow f'r ye. They'll be tickled to death to do it." As a sop to propriety he added, "Me old woman's coming out next week."

"It's good to see women," said the little engineer as he quietly shook hands. His vague eyes looked more haunted than ever. "It—it gets lonesome here."

"Give my love to California," screamed the cook, taking our destination for granted.

As we gave one last look at those hospitable miners, friendly as dogs who have been locked in an empty house, and a last look over the wonderful landscape rolling below us for miles, we too felt a pang at leaving.

"We'll stop in on our way back," we promised.

Toward dark, we began to encounter snow drifts. The first were easily passed, but as we climbed higher and the night thickened we found each drift a little harder to conquer, though the mild air was hardly tempered with frost.

Toby, a beginner at Galveston, could already manage almost any ordinary road, but not until later did she

become experienced enough for sky-climbing. Consequently I took the canyons, and for two days there had
been little else. By ten, when one of the neat state sign-
posts told us we were but five miles from the Goodfellow
Ranch, our destination, I felt nearly exhausted, nervously and physically. But the home stretch proved worst
of all. It led across a prairie to a descent encourag-
ingly marked "Private road. Dangerous. Take at your
own risk."

Well, to reach our bed that night we had to take it. In
a moment we were nose-diving down another canyon,
which in daylight was only moderately terrifying, but at
night seemed bottomless. It was Fish Creek over again,
with two irritating additions,—one, a slimy, skiddy
adobe road full of holes and strewn with boulders; and
two, a ridiculous baby jack-rabbit, who, frightened by
our headlights, leaped just ahead of us in the ruts. He
would neither hurry nor remove himself. At times his
life seemed directly pitted against ours, yet we could not
bring ourselves to run over his soft little body. It was
the last straw. When the sickening distance down the
canyon lessened, and we saw the cheery lights of the
ranch through the fir trees, I nearly cried with relief.

"Will you come in,—you must be tired," said a pretty
Scotch voice. A little woman held a lantern. "Two
ladies! We saw your lights, but never dreamed you'd
be coming down in the dark. There's many that think
the road none too safe in the day."

Her remark was balm to my chagrin at having let a
jack-rabbit unnerve me. All our lives, it seemed, had
been spent driving down the edge of hair-raising precipices in the dark; to be free of them at last, to enter a

warm, lighted, snug cottage, where a friendly Papago servant led us to the cleanest, most luxurious of beds,—this was heaven.

Natural Bridge can be reached two ways from the world,—south from Flagstaff ninety miles, or by the Apache Trail from Globe or Tucson. The northern road lay under twenty feet of snow, and this while a huge apricot tree,—the oldest in the state,—bloomed pink, and the alfalfa floor of the little canyon was varnished with emerald. Next morning we looked on this budding and blossoming world, hedged in with red cliffs and lapis lazuli hills. A few neat cottages and farm buildings nestled together,—but where was the bridge, large enough we had been told, to hide three or four of the Virginian variety under its arch?

They laughed at our queston. It is the standing joke at the Goodfellow ranch. They pointed to the five acre field of level alfalfa, edged with a prosperous vineyard. "You are on the bridge."

Bewildered, we walked for five minutes to the edge of the little level ranch surrounded by high pinon-covered walls on all sides. Still no bridge. At our feet they showed us a small hole in the ground, a foot deep. Looking through it we saw a steep chasm with a tangle of cactus and trees, and at the very bottom a clear, swift stream.

Unknown years ago some strange explosion had taken place through this tiny vent, creating the powerful arch beneath, which at this point seemed perilously thin, yet supported houses, cattle and men. At a crisis the accidents of Nature, like those of men, crystallize, and thereafter become unalterable. This tiny peep-hole, whim of a casual meeting of gases, would survive a thousand of our descendants. This was only one of a hundred spectacles Arizona was staging at the time. Think what a fuss the San Franciscans made of their little eruption in 1906,—and yet Arizona managed an exposition of fireworks back in the dark ages compared to which San Francisco's was like a wet firecracker. But Arizona showed poor business judgment in letting all her Grand Canyons, natural bridges and volcanoes erupt before the invention of jitneys, railroads, motion pictures and press agents. Naturally her geologic display attracted no attention, and today you can come upon freaks of nature casually anywhere in the state, of which nobody ever heard.

Even Natural Bridge, the widest of its kind in the world, is unknown to most Arizonans; many have only vaguely heard of it or confuse it with the Rainbow Bridge in Utah. Yet it is the strangest jumble of geologic freaks in any equal area, outside of Yellowstone.

Standing under the arch, so broad and irregularly shaped that at no point can it be photographed to show adequately that it is a bridge, you are really on the ground floor of a four-story apartment of Nature's building. The first floor is laid with a tumbling brown stream, flecked with white, and tiled with immense porphyry colored boulders of fantastic shapes. Exotic shrubs of tangly cactus, huge spotted eucalyptus, and firs, and myriads of dainty flowers dress the vestibule. Pools and stone tubs sculptured by Father Time invite,—oh, how they invite to bathe! The floor is speckled and flecked with sunlight which filters under the arch. Great rocks seem to float on the stream, mysteriously lighted, like

GREAT ROCKS SEEM TO FLOAT ON THE STREAM. MYSTERIOUSLY LIGHTED,
LIKE BOCKLIN'S ISLE OF THE DEAD

Böcklin's Island of the Dead. For half a mile you push through stubborn mesquite, wade and leap from rock to stream, finding a picture at every turn.

Then climbing sixty or more perpendicular feet on an amateur ladder, whose stoutness is its only reassuring feature, built by the discoverer of the Bridge, Scotch old Dave Goodfellow, you reach the second floor, devoted to one room apartments hollowed by drippings of age-old streams, and slippery with crusted lime. The cliff is honeycombed with caves in which stalactite and stalagmite meet, resembling twisted cedar trunks. Wolves and coyotes have made their homes here, and even somnolent grizzlies; in the smaller niches on warm spring days one has to take care that one's fingers do not grasp a twining mass of sluggish rattlesnake. In one of these caves the human rattlesnake, Geronimo, hid for a month in the Apache revolt of the nineties, while the United States scouts scoured Arizona to find him, and a story and a half above, the canny Goodfellow hid in his little one-room cabin, each fearing discovery by the other.

Above this floor is a mezzanine with another nest of caverns. Three sets of ladders riveted to a vertical shelf of rock lead you to the most interesting cave of them all, where the fairy tale comes true of the wizard who had to climb a mountain of glass. Toby knows no fear of aerial heights, so I had to pretend not to. A grandnephew of the elder Goodfellow led us where I hope never to return. We entered through a hole just wide enough to admit our bodies, and barely high enough to stand upright in. Then up a grade of 40 per cent over a limestone surface glassy from age-long accumulations of dripping chemicals, we wriggled flat on our backs, with feet braced against the ceiling to prevent our slipping out of the cave. Only a bat could have felt completely nonchalant under such circumstances. Harry Goodfellow worked himself along swiftly and easily, with an extraordinary hitch, hands and feet braced against the ceiling of the cave. After him, less expertly, we came, using his ankles for ladder rungs, and clinging to them frantically. How I prayed, not altruistically, that his ankles were not weak! My imagination took the wrong moment to visualize his grip failing, and his sudden descent out of the cave and over the cliff, with Toby and me each frantically clinging to an ankle. However we made the climb up safely, but going down was worse. I wonder why human nature never remembers, when it climbs to dizzy heights, that the go-down will be dizzier still.

I daresay I should yet be mid-way down that glass-bottomed cave, with feet barnacled to its ceiling, had I not realized how uncomfortable life would be spent in that position. Therefore I slid,—and jumped, hoping the force of my descent would not bounce me out of the narrow entrance into a clump of cactus sixty feet below. What happened to the others at that moment I did not care.

In caves still higher up beneath the bridge we discovered bits of baskets and pottery fashioned by ubiquitous cave-dwellers a thousand years ago. Then turning a corner, we came upon a fairy grotto, a shallow rock-basin filled with shining water; walls covered with moss and glossy maiden hair fern, over which a sparkling cascade fell. All this, built out like a Juliet balcony high over the babbling brook.

NATURAL BRIDGE, PINE, ARIZONA

From here it was only a short scramble back to the ranch-house, the barn, gardens and orchards on floor three, from which a steep canyon road leads to the upper world. Years ago when Dave Goodfellow, hermit and prospector, built his shack here the undergrowth was so wild that a calf who wandered into the brush and died within ten feet of the house was not found till a month after. Now the tangle has been smoothed and planted to alfalfa. Under the huge fruit trees he planted, meanders a brook edged with mint, violets and water-cress. Visitors drop down only occasionally, but they are always sure of good food, a clean bed, and a whole-hearted Scotch wel come. When news finally seeped in to us that spring had melted the snow-packed mountain roads, leaving them dry enough to travel, we departed with regret. "Pa" Good-fellow built us a food box out of two empty gasoline tins, "Ma" Goodfellow gave us a loaf of fresh bread, a jar of apricot preserves, and a wet bag full of water-cress, which provided manna for two hot, dusty days.

Spring had wrought marvels to our thrice traveled Apache Trail. The hills were gay with blue lupin, the color of shadows in that hot land. The valleys blazed with the yellow blossoms of the prickly holly bush, sweeter in odor than jasmine. Dozens of times we stopped to collect the myriad varieties of spring flowers, more prodigal than I have seen anywhere else in the world; poppies, red snap-dragons, Indian paint brush, the blue loco-weed which gives permanent lunacy to the cattle and horses which eat it; little delicate desert blooms like our bluets and grass flowers, shading from blue to white, and daisies of a dozen kinds, yellow, orange, yellow with brown centers, with yellow centers, and giant marguerites.

At the mining camp we stopped for a how-d'y-do with the Kellys. "The old woman," who had arrived from Providence recently, was brought out to meet us. A short, asthmatic and completely suburban lady, the beauties of the lovely scene rolling away to the horizon left her blank. She still panted in short gasps from the terrors of the Apache Trail.

"Awful!" she told us. "Awful! I was so scared I thought I'd die. Straight up and down. Straight up and down. My heart was in my mouth all the trip. I'm homesick. Look at this place,—no stores and no neighbors—not a bit like Providence."

Her dampening presence seemed a little to have affected her husband's effervescence. However, he still had the finest mine in Arizona, and Arizona was the finest state in the Union.

"She'll get used to it by and by," he said. "Horizontal fever,—that's what the old lady's got. Ought to heard her squeal on them turns."

They pressed us to stay over night.

"You ain't heard how I stopped the war," said Kelly.

But we regretfully said we must push on. So, loaded with specimens of ore and good wishes, we sped away.

CHAPTER XI

FRIDAY THE THIRTEENTH

IT was one of those days when everything goes wrong, and it fell on Friday the thirteenth.

Three days earlier, on reaching Globe, we learned we could not take the direct road to Santa Fe without chartering a steamer to ferry us across the untamed Gila. Most roads in Arizona are amphibious; to be ready for all emergencies, a motor traveling in that region of surprises should be equipped with skates, snow-shoes and web-feet. As our chosen road lay under some eight feet of river, we were obliged to make a slight detour of five hundred miles, or half the distance from Boston to Chicago. So we retraced the dizzy Winkleman trail, far less dizzy since we had become indifferent to tight-rope performances, passed through Tucson without attracting attention from the Sheriff of Pima County, and were rewarded for our digression by a sunset drive over the famous Tucson-Bisbee route, where a perfect road, built by convict labor, combined with perfect scenery to make our crossing of the Continental Divide for the dozenth time an event.

There are about as many Continental Divides in the West as beds in which Washington slept in the East. I first crossed the Divide somewhere up in Montana, and thinking it the only one of its kind, I was properly thrilled. But later I met another in Wyoming, and in the Southwest they seemed to crop up everywhere.

We were soon glad chance had sent us over the route
we had discarded when we first entered Arizona.   It was
a mellow, gracious loveliness we passed, looking down
from the top of the world on fields of silvery pampas, on
stretches of velvet-brown grazing country, misted over
with moon-white and sun-yellow poppies, and patches
of wild heliotrope whose intoxicating scent tempted us
to frequent stops.   Then on again to overlook a magnificence of blue and ochre canyons, down which we swooped
and circled into Bisbee.

Many-terraced as a Cornish village, Bisbee straddles
a canyon and climbs two mountains in its effort to ac-
commodate the workers who swarm its tortuous streets,
and spend their days in its huge copper mines.   When Bisbee finds a mountain in its way, down goes the mountain,
carried off by great steam shovels working day and night.
But always beyond, another ring of hills holds her prisoner.   In the town's center lies a tiny, shut-in square into
which streets of various levels trickle.   Here at any day
or any hour, agitators of one sort or another violently
harangue small groups.   There is always at this spot an
air of unexploded tenseness.   No wonder!   Precious
minerals imprisoned by Nature,—machinery fighting
Mother Earth,—labor resisting capital,—conservatism
against lawless radicalism,—greed against greed,—all
braced to hold their own and push the other down; all
pent in by the enclosing hills, and pressed down to the
narrow confines of the little Plaza.   No wonder the
steam from these conflicting forces has at times blown the
lid into the air.

From this Plaza, during the war, gathered the citizens
of Bisbee, and escorted to the Mexican border certain

obstructionists claiming to be striking in the cause of labor. The suddenness of their taking off has been criticized, but its effectiveness was admirable. In the informality of the grim-purposed patriots who acted as body-guards on that dusty march south, one sees the old West, which emerged into law and order through similar bands of exasperated citizens.

Friday the thirteenth, the date of our own exit from that picturesue and turbulent town, opened inauspiciously. A flat tire, incurred overnight, caused an hour's delay at the start. While we breakfasted at the Copper Queen, it again lost courage, and we had no choice but to thump downhill to the garage, near the great Copper Queen mine which daily levels mountains and fills up valleys. But our spare tire was found to be locked, and the key was in one of our seven suitcases. All work ceased till by a miracle of memory we recalled that the key was in a coat pocket, the coat was in a suitcase, the suitcase in the bottom of the trunk,—but where was the trunk key? More delay while we both searched our overflowing handbags,—and nothing embarrasses a woman more than to have half a dozen men watch her futile dives into her handbag. At last it appeared, and in due time, when we had wrestled like born baggage-smashers with the heavy suitcases, opened the bottom one and found the key, repacked the suitcase, put it back, lifted the other four on top, locked the trunk, and replaced the other baggage, we unlocked the spare tire. It did not budge from the rim. Earlier that luckless morning, I had backed into an unexpected telegraph pole, jamming the spare tire braces out of shape. So the garage men went back and forth on futile errands, as garagemen will, picking tools up and dropping them again with an air of satisfied achievement. Finally a young Samson came to the rescue, bending the tire into place with his bare hands, and after that they took only an hour to change the tires. With the sun high in front of us, we drove through the smoke and fumes of the mines, past pretty suburbs, into the open plateau leading to Douglas. We expected to be in Deming that night.

The mountains and canyons of yesterday subsided into a broad plain, with a poplar-bordered canal trickling prettily through it. At noon we sighted Douglas, a city of smoke-stacks simmering in a fog of coal gas. A once-good macadam road wound into an unsightly group of smelters and huge slag heaps,—the usual backdoor entrance of a Western town,—and suddenly reformed into a main street, imposing with buildings so new they looked ill at ease among the old-settler lunch shacks and ex-saloons. Side streets beginning bravely from the new electric light pillars, became disheartened at the second block, and were smothered in sand at the third.

To crown a banal hobby with the height of banality, I have for years amused myself wherever I may be by collecting postcards of Main Street looking South, or North, depending on the location of the public library and the fire station. Every orthodox postcard artist begins with Main Street. An extra charm to Main Street looking South in Douglas lay in its crossing the border and fizzling out into Mexico. Each time we had skirted the border, Mexico had beckoned alluringly, tempting us to discover what lay behind her drop curtain of monotonous blue and brown.

A little band of Mexican Indians, clad in the rainbow,

and making big eyes at the wonders of this gringo metropolis, staged a gaudy prologue. "They say you can't get into Mexico without a passport," mused Toby.

"We might as well find out and be done with it," said I.

A half mile led us to a row of government tents, followed by several buildings,—the first a low, wooden house, the second a neat, almost imposing two-story brick affair. Beyond was a smaller group, which we decided was the Mexican customs-house.

A long man untangled himself from a couple of porch chairs, and sauntered out to the road, as we whizzed past the first cottage. He shouted something and held up his hand, but we failed to catch what he said. A moment later we reached the fine looking brick house. A swarm of dark-complexioned gentlemen speaking an excitable language rushed out and surrounded our car. Toby gave a sigh of satisfaction.

"They said you couldn't get in without a passport," said she.

We were in Mexico. We could gather so much from the dazed attitude of the U. S. official, who stood enveloped in our dust, staring after us, but still more from the flood of questions, increasingly insistent, which came from the bandit's chorus surrounding us. They seemed to be asking for something,—possibly our passports. Looking ahead, Mexico didn't seem worth our while. We saw only bare brown hills, sand and cactus. Perhaps, like Toby's namesake, we had better leave before being kicked out. I displayed our camera.

"Take a picture? Turn round? Go back?" said I in purest Mexican.

The bandit's chorus gathered in an interested if

puzzled group about the camera, and looked as if they were waiting for me to do a trick proving that the hand is quicker than the eye. After a few repetitions, aided by liberal gestures, they got our meaning and laughed, showing dazzling sets of teeth.

"Take *your* pictures?" we added, at this sign of clemency. The Latin in them rejoiced at our tribute to their beauty. Two senoritas coming all the way from the Estados Unidos, passportless, braving the wrath of Carranza entirely because the gringoes were not handsome enough to snap! They straightened their uniforms, and curled their mustaches and flashed their teeth so brilliantly that Toby had to use the smallest diaphragm of her kodak. Before they could unpose themselves, we were back in the United States. They started after, as if to assess us for ransom, or something, but too late.

The U. S. official met us. "Why didn't you stop when I signaled?"

"We didn't see you. We thought the brick building was the United States customs,—it's so much grander than yours."

"Well, you're in luck," he said. "They could a held you there for months, confiscated your baggage, and made things pretty unpleasant generally. They're doing it all the time, under the name of official business. I tell you, I was scared when I saw you go through there."

Grateful to him for taking this humane view rather than arresting us, we said good-by and went our way, exhilarated at having triumphed over the custom departments of two nations in one short hour. It offset the morning's gloom, and the two horrible sandwiches (fried egg) with which Douglas had affronted our digestions.

At three o'clock we reached Rodeo, which means "round-up." We should have been there at ten. The town faced the desert, and seemed permanently depressed at its outlook. It contained a few Mexican shanties, a garage and general store, and a poison-green architectural crime labeled "Rooms," surrounded by a field reeking with dead cattle. Even our Optimist, when he laid out our route, had exclaimed, "If your night's stop is Rodeo, Lord help you!" The next town, Deming, lay a hundred miles beyond, with no settlement between. We looked once at the hotel, bought gas at fifty cents the gallon, and pushed on.

Whether we would reach Deming that night, we had no idea. Nearly a day, as desert travel goes, lay between us and food, drink and shelter. We had an orange apiece, and our folding tent, stove and lantern. We had a guide-book which, to escape a libel suit, I shall call "Keyes' Good Road Book," though it was neither a good road-book nor a good-road book. We had an abounding faith in guardian angels. Lastly, we had Toby's peculiar gift at reading guide-books, whereby she selects a page at random, regardless of our route, telescopes paragraphs together, skips a line here and there, and finishes in another state.

For this reason, as I pointed out with some heat, we took a road which led fourteen jolty miles out of our way. It came out that Toby had been reading the Colorado section. So chastened was she by this misadventure that at the next doubtful corner, where a windmill marked two forks, she kept her nose glued to the page and read with meticulous faithfulness, "Pass wind-mill to the left."

Now the left led through a muddy water-hole, while an

excellent road apparently trailed to the right of the windmill.

"Left?" I inquired, with pointed skepticism, "or
right?"

She peeked again into the guidebook, and answered
firmly, "Left!"

Toby was right for once, but she had chosen the moment to be right when the guidebook was wrong, which
entirely canceled her score. I drove into the chuck-hole,
—and stayed there. The hole was V shaped, two feet
deep at the point, and shelved so steeply that our spare
tires made a barrier against its edge when we tried to
back out. We were following Horace Greeley's advice
literally. We had gone West, and now we were settling
down with the country. We settled to our running board,
then to our hubs, and then over them. It was the more
exasperating because our car was immersed in the only
water hole within a hundred miles.

We got out and surveyed the road to the right. It
proved to be an excellent detour, which a few yards
further joined the left fork. This was the last straw. I
left Toby, who was trying to redeem her criminal rec-
titude by busying herself with the jack, and went out hat-
less into the scorching desert, like a Robert Hichens
heroine. My objective was not Oblivion, but the cross-
roads two miles back, where with luck I might still hail a
passing car.

Though the sun was low, the heat drove down scorch-
ingly. Only the necktie I tied about my forehead saved
me from sunstroke. It was bright green, and must have
made me look like an Apache; I had the consciousness of
being appropriately garbed. At the crossroad half an

hour's wait brought no car to the rescue. Night was too near for anyone with commonsense to start across that uncharted waste. Obviously I could not wait longer, leaving poor Toby to fish disconsolately, as I had last glimpsed her, in the mud. Obviously, too, if I returned nobody would know of our plight, and I should have my four-mile walk for nothing.

Looking aimlessly for help in this dilemma, my eye caught a scrap of a poster on a fence rail, which savagely and in minute pieces, I tore down and scattered to the desert. The poster read, "Keyes' Good Road Book. It Takes You Where You Want to Go."

Heaven knows neither I nor Toby, with all her faults, *wanted* to land in that chuck-hole. After I tore the poster, I wished I had saved it to inscribe a message to the passerby. "Well, take your medicine," thought I. "You have no right to get into any situation you can't get out of. Think of David Balfour and Admirable Crichton and Swiss Family Robinson and Robinson Crusoe. What, for instance, would Robinson Crusoe do?"

Undoubtedly he would have found a way out. I only had to think constructively, putting myself in his place. The thought alone was stimulating. Gifted with omniscience in hydrostatics and mechanics, he would probably have skinned a few dead cattle, with which the desert reeked, made a rope, fastened it about the car's body, looped it over the windmill, and hoisted it free,—and been half way to Deming by this time. As for that copy-cat Mrs. Swiss Family Robinson, she would certainly have produced a pull-me-out from her insufferable work-bag.

How would Crusoe have left a message without pencil

or paper? I knew. Collecting handfuls of large white
stones,—white, because darkness was imminent, I arranged them at the crossroads in letters two feet long,
reading,

2 MI.
WINDMILL
HELP!

I added an arrow to point the direction. And then, to
make sure that my sign was noticed, I placed a few sharp
stones in the ruts. These would probably puncture his
tire, and in looking for the cause, he would observe our
appeal and come to our rescue. It took a long while to
collect enough white stones to make the sign, but when
I had finished I felt much elated, and more kindly toward
Toby for reading the guide book right when she should
have read it wrong. It was cooler walking back, though
my tongue was swollen with thirst. Our canteen had
displayed a leak only yesterday, and we had tossed it into
the sagebrush.

At the windmill I found the car partly jacked up, so
that she careened drunkenly to one side, but her right
dashboard was now above water. Toby's skirt was caked
with mud, and her shoes and stockings plastered with
it. She seemed depressed. She explained she had slipped
trying to balance on a plank, and had fallen in the chuck-
hole.

"This pool is full of dead cattle," she said, dolefully.
"I just put my finger in something's eye."

About to take off shoes and stockings and wade into
the pool, something gave me pause. Gingerly we stood
on the brink, and poked planks where the mud was

thickest, in the forlorn hope of making a stable bottom. Alas, they only sank, and vexed us by protruding on end whenever we tried to back the old lady. We knew the first step was to jack the rear wheels, but while we raised one wheel, the other sank so deep in the mud that we could get neither plank nor jack under it. After many embittered attempts we gave it up, and tried placing the jack under the springs. It worked beautifully; in a few seconds the body of the car was a foot higher, and seemed willing to continue her soaring indefinitely. We took turns jacking; still she rose. We were greatly encouraged. After several minutes Toby said, "The jack's at the top notch,—what shall I do next?"

It was so easy we might have guessed there was a catch somewhere. To our astonishment we discovered that in rising, the body of the car had not taken the wheels with it. Two feet of daylight gaped between mudguard and wheels. A moment more, and the two would have parted company forever. Jacking is easy in theory, or in a garage, but the trouble with the outdoor art is that the car usually lands in a position where it has to be jacked up in order to get planks under it in order to jack it up. "Pou sto," said Archimedes, defining our dilemma succinctly.

New Mexico boasts an inhabitant to every eight square miles, but the member for our district continued to ignore our invasion of his realm. Two fried egg sandwiches, consumed that noon, was—or were—our only sustenance that day. We were so hungry we sounded hollow to the touch. Our mouths felt like flannel, and our throats burned with thirst. Not forty feet away a stream of pure water ran from the windmill. But it ran from a slippery lead pipe which extended a dozen feet over a reservoir. The water was there, but we could not get at it without a plunge bath.   Muddy and weary, we worked on without courage.

At sundown, from one of the other squares appeared the Inhabitant on horseback, driving some cows to our cattle-hole.   He was a youth of sixteen, running mostly to adenoids and Adam's apple, which worked agitatedly at sight of us, but his eyelashes any beauty specialist would envy.   As to his voice, the strain of making it reach across eight miles to the next Inhabitant had exhausted it, or perhaps embarrassment silenced him; we could not get a word out of him till he had watered his cattle and started away.   Then emboldened by having his back safely to us, he shouted that at a house, a "coupla miles southeast," we might find a team,—and vanished into nowhere.

Toby had by this time managed to crawl out on the lead pipe, and after gyrations fascinating to watch, captured a pail of water.   Drinking eagerly, we set out for the house the Inhabitant indicated, with the pail in our hands to guard against future thirst.   Sunset was making transparent the low mountain range skirting our valley, when we left.   The sand filled our shoes, and the persistent "devil's claw," zealous to propagate its kind, clung to our feet with a desperate grip.   Our pail became heavy, but we dared not empty it.   At last we reached the ranch. A half-starved dog sprang out eagerly to meet us.   The house was deserted; there were no teams to pull us out, nor any food to give the poor, famishing beast.   He watched us leave, with a hurt, baffled look in his brown eyes, as if patiently marveling at the inhumanity of man,

From the ranch, we glimpsed another house, a mile further away, and again we started hopefully for it, while a horned moon circled up a pink sky. The desert from a barren, ugly waste was become unbelievably lovely in the transfiguring twilight.

The crescent moon brought us no luck, for we saw it over our left shoulders. It was still Friday the Thirteenth. The second house, even to the hungry dog, duplicated the first. It stood dismantled and deserted. We saw nothing ahead but a ten mile tramp to Rodeo in the dark, the poison green hotel, and "Lord help us!" whatever that meant.

Our flashlight was in the car. To return for it meant three more weary miles. Toby was for risking the road without it, but my sixth sense warned me to return, and I persuaded her to this course. As we crossed the desert the dim shape of our marooned machine loomed up in the dusk. And beside it—

"Another mirage!"

"Where?" asked weary Toby, indifferently. At this moment the wonders of Nature meant nothing to her.

"There seem to be two cars,—I can see them quite plainly."

"There *are* two cars," said Toby, and we ran, the pail slopping water on our feet.

With a broad grin on each face, two men watched us approach. They were young; I judged them thirty and thirty-five. They stopped just short of being armed to the teeth. Each wore a cartridge belt, and they shared two rifles and a revolver. The older and the more moderately arsenaled, looked like a parson. The younger wore a tan beaver sombrero, of the velvety, thirty-dollar kind proclaiming its owner a cow-puncher, an old-timer, a hard boiled egg who doesn't care who knows it. His shirt was of apple-green flannel, his small, high boots festooned with stitching and escalloped with colored leather like a Cuban taxi, his purple neckerchief was knotted with a ring carved from ox-bone, and from his cartridge belt in a carved leather case hung the largest revolver I ever saw. His generous silver spurs were cut in the shape of spades, hearts, diamonds and clubs. Montgomery Ward, Marshall Field and Sears-Roebuck combined never turned out a more indisputable *vachero*. We greeted them with joy; their happy grins told us they would see us through our difficulties. It was nine by the village clock of Rodeo, if they had one, which I doubt. It was not the sort of town which would have a clock, or even an Ingersoll.

"You girls nearly caught us pullin' out," Sears-Roebuck greeted us. "We figured how the feller who owned this car would be cussin' mad, and we was plannin' to stick around to hear his language, an' then we seen women's things in the seat, so we jest had our supper here, while we waited for you."

It never would have happened east of Chicago. They had waited nearly two hours that they might do us the favor of another hour's hard work in setting us on dry land again. They had been "making time" for El Paso, and the delay spoiled a half day for them, but they did not complain. They acted as if persuading our dinosaur from her nest of mud were a most delightful joke,—on us, themselves and the car. They did not regard what they were doing as a favor, but as their sole business and recreation in life. In sheer high spirits, Biron, as he speedily introduced himself,—the giddier of the two in dress and deportment,—whooped, cleared the mud-hole in one leap, and pretended to lassoo the inert machine. The other, smiling benevolently at his antics, went steadily to the serious work of harnessing the car.

Toby made a jesting remark to Biron about the revolver hanging at his belt, not from fear but as a pleasantry. Misunderstanding, he unslung it instantly, and tossed it into his car.

"I don't want that thing," he elaborated, "it gets in my way."

They got to work in earnest, with great speed and skill. Twice the rope which they hitched to their car broke as we turned on our power. Meanwhile the old lady churned herself deeper into the mud, skulls, and shinbones of the pool. After an hour's work, with much racing of the engine, and a Niagara of splashing mud which covered us all from head to foot, she stirred, heaved over on one side, and groaning like seven devils commanded to come out, lumbered to terra firma, looming beside the pert wrecking car like Leviathan dug out with an hook.

After all, it was a glorious Thirteenth. No sensation is more exhilarating than to be rescued from a mud-hole which seemed likely to envelop one for life. Even the slender arc of the young moon, in that clear air, poured a silver flood over the desert, now a mysterious veil of luminous blue. The vibrant heat waves of day had risen and twisted into the thin air, and frosty currents swept and freshened the simmering earth. The elder, a slow-speaking chap from Tucson, gravely filled our radiator from the reservoir, filled his canteen and offered us a drink, and then asked us if we had eaten supper. We bravely fibbed, with hunger gnawing within, not wishing to put ourselves further in their debt. As they prepared to leave I was uncomfortably reminded we had no breakfast for next morning, and no water, owing to our canteenless state. They were our food and drink—and we were letting them depart!

But I wanted to make sure what they would do next. In businesslike fashion they started their car, then bade us a cordial good-by. They made no hint toward continuing our acquaintance, nor asked our plans, and even the merry Biron showed only an impersonal twinkle as he shook hands. So I spoke, choosing between apple jelly for breakfast, and ham, eggs, coffee and impropriety.

"Would you mind if we followed you and camped somewhere near?"

They accepted our company with the same jovial enthusiasm with which they had met us,—Biron I thought a trifle too jovial, but Tucson steady as a Christian Endeavorer. They jumped in their car, took the lead, and in the dark we streaked after their red lantern, over thirty miles of "malpais."

We had been warned of "malpais" in the untrustworthy Keyes, but without knowing what it meant. Several thousand years ago, the tire trust manipulated a geologic cataclysm which strewed millions of needle-pointed granite stones over our road. To drive a newly-tired car over malpais hurts one's sensibilities as much as to stick a safety-pin into a baby, with the difference that the baby recovers. Over chuck-holes, down grades, into arroyos, always over malpais we dashed after their bobbing light, terrified lest a puncture should deprive us of their guardianship. Thirty miles of weariness and mental anguish at the injury we did our springs and tires gave way to relief when the red lantern suddenly turned to the left, and we found ourselves in an open, treeless field. We sank to the ground, worn out with waiting for the "plop" that never sounded.

Save for a waning moon, it was pitch dark. We were on a high tableland, with looming hills completely enclosing us. For the first time, it occurred to me that here we were unarmed, at midnight, fifty miles from a settlement, at the mercy of two men fully armed, whom we had known two hours. What was to prevent them from killing or wounding us, taking our car, and abandoning us in that lonely spot where we should never be found? Or, as the novelist says,—Worse? I could see Toby gripped by the same terror. Chaperoned only by the Continental Divide, with not even a tree to dodge behind if they pointed their arsenal our way, we wondered for a fleeting moment if we had done wisely.

Our neighbors for the night pulled two bedding rolls from their car, threw them on the ground, and announced they had made their camp. An awkward moment followed. We looked for a sheltered place for our tent, but there was none. Seeming to have no other motive than that, lacking a tree, we had to sling our tent-rope over the car, we managed to use the old lady as a discreet chaperone, placing her in front of our tent-door, which we could enter by crawling over the running-board.

With widening smiles they took it all in; took in our efforts to be ladies, took in our folding stove, folding lantern and tiny air pillows. As we put together our folding shovel and proceeded to dig a hip trench, their politeness cracked, and a chuckle oozed out.

"My!" said Tucson, as profanely as that, "you're all fixed up for camping out, aint ye?"

Our tent invited, after our weary day, but an expectant something in our host's manner made us hesitate. Politeness, ordinary gratitude in fact, since we had nothing but our company to offer, seemed to demand that we visit awhile. We sat on a bedding roll; Biron joined us, while the parson-like Tucson took the one nearby.

"Was you ever anyways near to being hung?"

Biron shied a pebble at a cactus as he put this question. All in all, it was as good a conversational opening as the weather,—not so rock-ribbed, perhaps, but with more dramatic possibilities.

"No," I said, "I don't think I ever was. Were you, Toby?"

It was mean of me to ask her. Toby hates to be outdone, or admit her experiences have been incomplete. I saw her agile mind revolving for some adventure in her past that she could bring up as a creditable substitute, but she had never been anywhere near to being hung, and she knew I knew it.

"H'm-m," she said noncommittally, her inflection implying tremendous reserves,—"were you?"

"Onct," replied Biron, "only onet. But if anyone ever tells you he was near hanging, and was brave under the circumstances, don't you believe him. There I was with the rope around my neck, and I a hollerin' and a squealin' like a baby, and beggin' to be let off. There aint no man livin', I'll say, feelin' them pullin' and sawin' away on his neck that aint a goin' to bawl and cry an' beg f'r mercy."

"What was the—occasion—if you don't mind our asking?"

Biron shied another stone at the cactus and missed.

"Well, you see," he raced along, "another feller had stole some horses, an' knowin' how he come by them an' all that, I jest sorter relieved him of them. An' I was a ridin' along toward Mexico when they caught up with me."

"But I thought they no longer hanged people for,—er —for——"

"Horse stealin'? They don't much, but y'see this feller had happened to kill a coupla men gettin' away, and when they seen me with the horses he started off with they natch'ally thought I was the one done it all."

How dark and gloomy looked the encircling hills!

"They got the rope on me, and my feet was off the ground, but I blubbered so hard bimeby they let me off."

He looked at Tucson with a glance that seemed to share a common experience.

"I aint sayin' I didn't do other things they might 'a got me for——"

Tucson nodded, and opened his slow mouth to speak, but the nimbler Biron cut in.

"Oh, I been pretty bad some times. Any feller thirty years old or so, if he gits to thinkin' all the fool things he's done, he's likely to kill himself laughin'."

Tucson nodded gravely. "I reckon——"

"We uster to go down to the border, to them Mexican dances, to have fun with the Mexican girls. They have music an' everthin' an' the greasers sit on one side of the hall and the girls on the other. We'd mix in and take the girls away from the men, an' every time the big bull fiddle give a whoop, we'd take a drink of mescal. Then we'd go shoot up the town. Whenever we'd kill a Mexican, we'd put a notch on our gun, as long as the' was room.   I knowed one feller, Tom Lee by name, knowed him well, they say accounted for five hundred, all in all."

"And didn't you get into trouble with the law?"

"Law?" Biron snorted. "Law? They aint no law against shootin' *dawgs,* is they?"

His seemed a reasonable attitude, demonstrating the superiority of a real American over the contemptible greaser. This excitable mixture of half a dozen inferior and treacherous races turns ugly when our boys, out for a harmless lark where it will do least harm, shoot up his towns and his neighbors, and violate his women. Then the Mexican uses a knife. No decent man uses a knife. And so our border is kept in a state of constant turmoil.

"There aint no harm potting Mexicans," continued Biron, "especially when they get fresh. The Mexican girls aint so bad. Sometimes an American will marry one, but it has to be a pretty low white girl that will marry a greaser."

"That's so. I—" drawled Tucson. He seemed collecting his slower wits for a narration, but Biron rattled on.

"This Lee is out **hidin'** somewhere now, in the mountains,—him and his brother. The sheriff shot at him just as he was ridin' past a glass window, and cut his eye half out so it hung down on his face. But he got away into the canyons, and was ridin' with them on his heels for three days and nights, with his eye like that."

"Then the law *did* try to redress the murder of those five hundred Mexicans."

"I guess *not*. They was after him for committing a crime, and serve him right,—he tried to evade the draft."

"They was two ignorant boys," explained Parson Tucson to me, "raised in the backwoods, who didn't rightly know what the draft was for, or they wouldn't have done it."

The attitude of both men was gravely patriotic. Yet one could see they cherished the idea of the outlawed boys, eighteen and twenty, who could bear with traditional stoicism such unendurable pain. The West clings pathetically to these proofs that its old romantic life is not yet extinct, even though it is but the wriggle which dies at sunset. Stories like those of Biron's are still told with gusto even amid the strangest familiarity with Victrolas,—though the saloon is replaced by the soda fountain, and the only real cowboys are on film, and the hardy tenderfoot now rides so well, shoots so well and knows his West so well that he is an easy mark for the native, only when the latter tries to sell him an oil well, an irrigated ranch, or a prehistoric skull.

We made a move for our tent, but Biron had not finished his thirty years' Odyssey. He had lightly skipped from tales of outlawry to big game, and the dangers of the hunt. He was now among the Mormons, and the subject was deftly moon-lit with sentiment. He was enjoying himself, and he glanced from one to the other of us as he rattled on.

"Up in the Mormon country, I met two Mormon girls, only I didn't know what they was, and was cussin' the Mormons and what I thought of them, when one of them ast me what I thought of Mormon girls, so then I caught on. So I expressed a little of what I thought of *them*, an' we got on fine. She ast me to a dance, an' I said I'd go if I could ride back to my bed in time to get my other pants. But it was a day's trip, an' I couldn't make it. I meant to go back later, to ask some questions of her,—personal ones, I mean,—" he took time to hit the cactus blossom squarely,—"relating to matrimony, if you know what I mean. But I never did get to go back."

Now like most men, the westerner recognizes two kinds of women, but with this distinction;—he permits her to classify herself while he respects her classification. The Merry One seemed to be leading up to a natural transition.

"I don't know nothin' about love. Jest kinder cold, I am, like a stone." He snickered softly.

"Truly?" said Toby, innocently interested. "Why is that?"

He shied a pebble at the long-suffering cactus.

"Jest my nature, I reckon. My French blood. Didn't you know all Frenchmen was marble-hearted?"

Tucson beamed slowly, like a benevolent minister of the gospel.

"Toby," I said, "you have yawned twice in the last five minutes."

Toby never needs to hear the word bed repeated. She got to her feet, sleepily.

"We can't thank you enough for all you've done to-day," I went on in a cordial way. "All through the west we have met with the greatest help and courtesy. People ask us if we're afraid to travel alone, but we always tell them not when we are among westerners."

Tucson beamed, bless his heart, at my model speech, and found tongue. "That's right," he said, leaning toward us earnestly, "There won't nobody hurt you in *this* country."

We shook hands all around. As we were nearing our tent, Biron followed us with something in his hand, which he proffered with the flourish of an eighteenth century marquis.

"Here," he said, "take this." I jumped. It was his ferocious revolver.

"What is this for?" we asked.

"For protection."

"Against what?"

"Against us."

"Oh, no, thank you. We feel quite safe without it," we prevaricated.

"Go ahead and take it," said Biron, politely stubborn.

Here was a dilemma. Could one accept such an offer from one's hosts, even though on their own confession unhonored and unhung horse thieves, light-hearted murderers and easy philanderers? And yet he seemed so sure we should need it.

"Never for that reason," I said, thinking to make a graceful exit from the dilemma, "still if all the stories you have told us of wild animals and outlaws——"

Biron blocked my exit; "You needn't worry about *them*," he chuckled mirthfully, "But you don't know what ructions *we* may raise in the night."

"Better take it," Toby whispered. So we bore our

arms to our tent, where they helped us pass a restless night. When I did not wake in a cold agony from dreaming I had rolled over on the pistol and exploded it, Toby would wake me to warn me against the same fate. I think we would have been happier if we had relied on the honor system. Once a shriek and a roar startled us awake, and a half mile away a Southern Pacific express streamed by like a silver streak. Occasionally a placid snore from Tucson reached us, and once an old white ghost of a horse, her bones making blue shadows in the moonlight, crunched at our tent posts, and fled kicking terrified kicks as I looked out to investigate.

Later sleep came, deep sleep, from which Toby woke me. Toby is brave, but her whisper had a tremolo. "There's a wild animal of some sort, butting against the tent."

I looked out cautiously. "It's a huge bull," I reported. Toby shuddered. A moment later I saw it was only a moderate sized cow, but to impress Toby I did not mention this discovery, as I boldly left the tent and approached the beast. She was chewing with gusto a shapeless mass lying on the ground,—was it a calf? Was she a cannibal among cows, an unnatural mother? She muzzled it, licked it, and tossed it in the air, where against the setting moon her smile of delight was silhouetted like the cow in Mother Goose. I took courage to investigate her new form of caviar,—and found she had chewed our new yellow slicker, in which we wrapped everything which would not go anywhere else, into a slimy, pulpy mass. To her hurt astonishment, she was immediately parted from her find, and went galloping off into the brush. It seemed cruel to break up her midnight revel, but at the rate her new taste was developing we should not have had a tire left by morning.

Before going back to sleep, I looked about me. Long gray shadows drifted over from the low range of black hills which cupped our camp. The air, crisp, and faintly scented with sage, exhilarated me with a sense of wild freedom. Often, in the East, I am awakened by that scent, and am filled with a homesick longing to go back. It is not sage alone, but the thousands of little aromatic plants graying the desert imperceptibly, the odor blown across hills and plains of charred camp fires, bitter and pungent, the strong smell of bacon and sweated leather, all mingled and purified in millions of cubic feet of ether. Two blue-black masses stirred, and a sigh and a chuckle came from our sleeping Galahads. No danger of "ructions" from that quarter now. I went back to our lumpy bed, put the revolver outside the tent, and fastened the flap. A few minutes sped by, and I was startled awake by a gunshot, thunderous in my ears.

Toby and I sat up. It was broad daylight. We peered under the car cautiously. Tucson had built a fire, and a coffee-pot sat atop, which he soberly tended. Biron swanked about in his fleecy chaps, shooting into the air.

"Come alive, girls," he called, tossing a flapjack at us. "Throw that into your sunburned hides."

We obeyed this playboy of our Western world without demur. We had barely eaten since the previous morning. At eight we were off. Our car had no spare tire, two broken spring leaves, and a dustpan which dragged on the ground, loosened by miles of high centers. Our friends were in haste to reach El Paso, so we suggested they leave us, but they refused, and became our body guard as far as Deming, stopping when we did, mending our dustpan with a bit of stolen fence wire, getting water and gas for us at Hachita, a dismal little collection of shanties which Biron regretfully described as "the wickedest town in the United States, before prohibition spoiled it. Yessir, prohibition is what ruined New Mexico."

In the midst of a swirling sand storm we said good-by to our friends and asked their names and addresses in order to send them some photographs we had taken. Biron gave his readily,—"Manchester, N. H., is where I was born, but most of my folks live in Fall River, Mass."

It was not the address we expected from a man who had seen worse deeds than Jesse James. It was out of the picture, somehow. I knew Manchester, N. H., and had met nothing in the town so tough and bad as Biron had described himself, unless it were the sandwiches sold in the Boston and Maine station. When we turned to Tucson for his name, we were prepared to have him give the address of a theological seminary, and again we were surprised. For Tucson hesitated and stammered, and took longer recalling his name than is usually needed. I remembered a remark Biron threw off the night before,—"a man gets to calling himself a lot of different names in this country," and snickered, while Tucson remained grave as a judge. I wondered, if his voluble friend had given him a chance, whether Tucson might have told us something interesting. However, Tucson had just discovered a copper vein on his land, and as this book goes to print may already be a respectable Fifth Avenue millionaire.

As we thanked them and said good-by, Toby said, "We can't be too grateful you saw our sign in the road."

"Sign? What sign?"

"Didn't you see a sign made of white pebbles on the road from Rodeo, asking for help?"

"No, we didn't see no sign. We didn't come from Rodeo. We came the other road,—over the hills."

There it is. No matter how much one does as Robinson Crusoe would have done, the other characters will not play up to their opportunities. Instead of following your footprints cunningly, step by step, they will insist on catching sight of you across lots, completely spoiling the climax. No doubt Crusoe was firm with infringers on his plot. Probably when they came by the wrong road, he refused to be rescued till they had gone back and done the thing properly.

But then, we were very glad to be rescued at all.

CHAPTER XII

WE had trailed spring up from Texas through Arizona, timing our progress so cleverly that it seemed as if we had only to turn our radiator's nose down a desert path for blue lupin and golden poppies to blaze up before us. At last we reached the meeting of the Rockies with the Rio Grande in New Mexico, led by the devious route, sometimes a concrete avenue, but oftener a mere track in the sand, of the old Spanish highway. El Camino Real is the imposing name it bears, suggesting ancient caravans of colonial grandees, and pack-trains bearing treasure from Mexico City to the provincial trading-post of Santa Fé. Even today what sign-posts the road displays bear the letters K T, which from Mexico to Canada stand for King's Trail. The name gave us a little thrill, to be still extant in a government which had supposedly repudiated kings this century and a half.

From San Anton' on, as we left behind us the big mushroom cities of Texas, the country became more and more sparsely settled. The few people we met, mostly small farmers ploughing their fields primitively, bade us a courteous good day in Spanish, for in this country Mexico spills untidily into the United States. We soon forgot altogether that we were in the States. First we came upon a desert country, vast and lonely, with golden sand in place of grass, spiny, stiff-limbed cactus for trees, and strangely colored cliffs of lemon and orange and livid white. After days of this desolation we emerged upon the valley of the Rio Grande where its many tributaries rib the desert as they run from snowy peaks to join its muddy red waters. The air here is crystal keen, warmed by intense sun, cooled by mountain winds, and sweetened by millions of piñons dotting the red hillsides. Lilac and blue mountains ring the valley on both sides, and from them emerald fields of alfalfa, sparkling in the sun, slope down to the old, winding stream. Because its silt is so fertile, one race has succeeded another here —cliff-dwellers, Indian, Spanish, Mexican, and American —and a remnant of each, save the earliest, has clung where living is easy. So we came all along the Rio Grande for a hundred miles to little groups of towns, each allotted to a different race keeping itself to itself, Mexican, American, and Indian.

It was under the deep-blue night sky that we saw our first pueblo town. Out of the plains, it came surprisingly upon us. Solitary meadows with bands of horses grazing upon them, a gleam of light from an adobe inn at a crossroad, a stretch of darkness, strange to our desert-accustomed senses because of the damp breath from the river and snow-capped peaks beyond—then the barking and yelping of many mongrel dogs, and we were at once precipitated into the winding, barnyard-cluttered alleys of Isleta, feeling our way through blind twists and turns, blocked by square, squat gray walls of incredible repose and antiquity, caught in the mesh of a sleeping town. Instantly we had a sense, though no light was struck nor any voice heard through the darkness, of

Isleta awake and alert, quickening to our invasion.

We were already a little awed by our encounter with the Rio Grande. Since twilight and quickly falling night came on, we had crossed and recrossed the sullen brown waters many times, feeling its menacing power, like a great sluggish reptile biding its time, not the less because the suspension bridges above it creaked and swung and rattled under our weight. The mystery of driving after dark in an unfamiliar country sharpened our susceptibilities to outside impressions. We felt the river waiting for us, like a watchful crocodile; a sudden misturn in the shadows, or a missing plank from a bridge, and our vague sensation of half-fear, half-delight, might at any moment be crystallized by disaster. It was a night when something dramatic might fittingly happen, when the stage-setting kept us on the sharp edge of suspense.

The Pueblo Indian, we had heard, differed from other Indians, being gentler and more peaceably inclined than the Northern races. We were not such tenderfeet as to fear violence, scalping, or sudden war-whoops from ochre-smeared savages. But it was our first experience with Indians (the first in our lives, in fact), save those tamed nomads who peddle sweet-grass baskets and predict handsome husbands along the New England beaches. We were a little expectant, a little keyed to apprehension. We knew, as if we had been told, that a hundred or more of this alien race had waked from their sleep, and lay with tightened muscles waiting for the next sound. Increased yelping from the mongrel pack might bring them swarming about our car, and we had no experience in dealing with them; no knowledge of their prejudices or language to trade with. In our haste we circled through the town twice, threading corrals and back yards. Suddenly, the town still tensely silent, we emerged into a shallow plaza. Crossing directly before our lights came a young man, tall and supple, his straight short locks bound with a scarlet fillet, his profile clear and patrician, and over his shoulders a scarlet robe, covering his white cotton trousers. As he passed us, unmoved and stolid, he spoke one word of salutation, and continued on his way across the silent plaza.

Simple as was the incident, the flash of scarlet against the blue-black sky, the dignity and silence of the Indian, made the climax we had been awaiting. Nothing else happened. But it had been a night whose setting was so sharply defined, its premonitions so vibrantly tense with drama, that only that little was needed to carve it on our memory.

We saw the town later, in broad daylight, swept by an unclean sand-storm, pitilessly stripped of romantic atmosphere. But the romance was obscured, not obliterated, for its roots are sunk deep in the past. Isleta has one of the finest built-up estufas of the pueblo towns. It has a thousand inhabitants, whose proximity to the railroad gives them the blessing or curse of the white man's civilization. It has a church, whose ancient adobe flanks have been topped by two wooden bird-cages for steeples, for when the Indian adopts our ideas, his taste is rococo; when he clings to his own art, he shows a native dignity and simplicity. Lastly, Isleta has a ghost, well authenticated, and attested to by a cardinal, an archbishop, a governor, and other dignitaries, to say nothing of Juan Pancho, a man who does not lie. It is probably the oldest ghost in the United States.

About the time of the first Spanish penetration into the Southwest, a friar made his way to the Pueblo country through the hostile tribes to the east. In one of the towns north of Santa Fé, probably Tesuque, he found shelter and a home. The friendly Indians, although keeping him half-prisoner, treated him kindly. He soon gained their respect and affection, as he applied his knowledge of medicine to their physical, and as a priest administered to their spiritual needs, without giving offense to the Pueblos' own beliefs. He seems to have been a gentle and tactful creature, who won his way by the humane Christianity of his daily life. Gradually, as they became better acquainted with him, they admitted him to the inner circle of village life, even to the sacred ceremonies and underground rituals of the kiva. He was taught the significance of their medicine and of their tribal and religious symbols. Almost forgetting his alien blood, they had made him one of themselves on the day, twenty years later, when news came of the approach of armed conquistadores, with Coronado at their head, seeking plunder and the treasures of Cibola the legendary. Whether such treasure existed has never been known. If it did, the secret was closely guarded by the Indians. Perhaps the monk had been made their confidant. At any rate, he knew enough to make certain factions in the tribe regard him as an element of danger, when he should again meet with men of his own race, hostile to the people of his adoption. Would he remain true, thus tempted? It was a question of race against individual loyalty, and one Indian, more fanatic and suspicious than his brothers, cut the Gordian knot of the

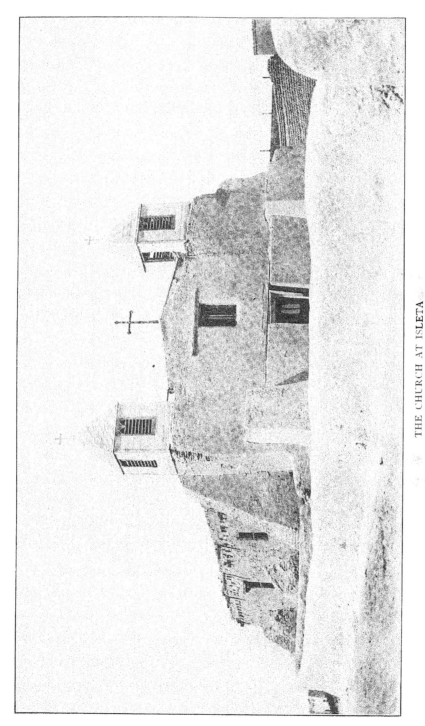

THE CHURCH AT ISLETA

A church, whose ancient adobe flanks have been topped by two wooden bird-cages for steeples

difficulty with a dagger, planted squarely in the back of the God-fearing friar.

The gentle Pueblos, horrified by this act of personal treachery, which they regarded not only as a violation of their sacred laws of hospitality but as a crime against a medicine-man with powerful if strange gods, were in terror lest the approaching Spaniards should hear of the monk's fate and avenge the double crime against their race and religion on the entire village. What the Spaniard could do on such occasions was only too well known to the Pueblo tribes. At nightfall the chiefs of the village placed the body, wrapped only in a sheet, on a litter, which four swift runners carried seventy miles south to Isleta.

There under the dirt floor of the old church, whose walls have since been destroyed and replaced by the present structure, they placed the padre without preparing his body for burial or his soul for resurrection. If they had only said a prayer for him, they might have spared much trouble to their descendants. But they were in a hurry. They buried the corpse deep, six feet before the altar and a little to one side of it, and pressed down the dirt as it had been. The Spaniards came and went, and never learned of the murder.

This prelude to the story came from Juan Pancho, one of the leading citizens of Isleta. The sand-storm which had turned the sky a dingy yellow gave signs of becoming more threatening, and a flat tire incurred as we stopped at his house for directions seemed to make it the part of wisdom to stop overnight in the little town. When we inquired about hotels, he offered us a room in his spotless adobe house, with the hospitality that is instinctive in that part of the country. We found him an unusual man with a keen and beautifully intellectual face. In his youth, he told us, he was graduated from one or two colleges, and then completed his education by setting type for an encyclopedia, after which he returned to his native village and customs. He can speak four languages—Spanish, English, baseball slang, and the Isleta dialect which is his native tongue. When he came home after his sojourn with the white man, he discarded their styles in clothing, and adopted the fine blue broadcloth trousers, closely fitting, the ruffled and pleated white linen shirt which the Indian had adopted from the Spaniard as the dress of civilized ceremony. On his feet he wore henna-stained moccasins, fastened with buttons of Navajo silver. He took pride in his long black hair, as do most Pueblo Indians, and, though he wore it in a chonga knot during business hours, in the relaxation of his comfortable adobe home he loosened it, and delighted in letting it flow free.

His house Mrs. Juan kept neat as wax. They ate from flowered china, with knife and fork, though her bread was baked, delicious and crusty, in the round outdoor ovens her grandmothers used as far back as B. C. or so. She had not shared Juan's experience with the white man's world, except as it motored to the doors of her husband's store to purchase ginger ale or wrought-silver hatbands. But she had her delight, as did Juan, in showing the outside world she could put on or leave off their trappings at whim. She was a good wife, and how she loved Juan! She hung on his every word, and ministered to his taste in cookery, and missed him when he went away to his farms—just like a white woman.

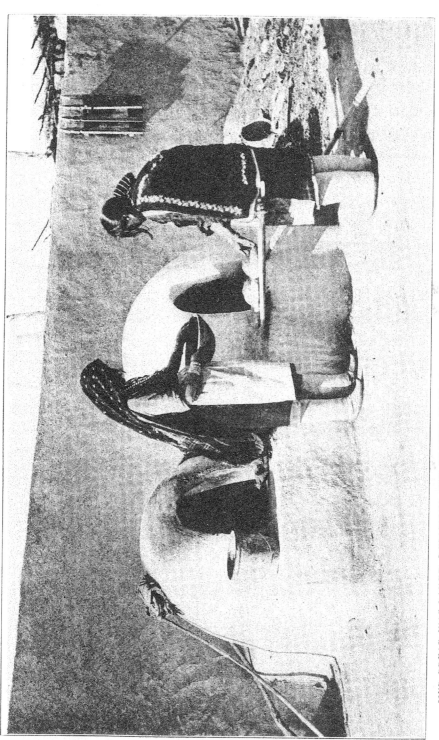

HER BREAD WAS BAKED, DELICIOUS AND CRUSTY, IN THE ROUND OUTDOOR OVENS HER GRANDMOTHERS USED AS FAR BACK AS B. C. OR SO.

Juan's ranch is near the new church, which has stood above the foundations of the older church only a century and a half or less.   It befits his rank as one of the leading citizens of the village that his property should have a prominent location on the bare and sand-swept little plaza.   He loves his home and the life he has returned to.

"I have tried them both—you see I know English?   I can talk books with you, and slang with the drummers that come to the trading-store?   I have ridden in your trains and your motor-cars, and eaten at white men's tables, and bathed in his white bathtubs.   I have tried it all.   I have read your religious books, and know about your good man, Jesus.   Now I have come back to the ways of my people.   Well!   You know me well enough to know I have my reasons.   What is there in your ways for me?   I have tried them all, and now I come back to Great Isleta, where are none of those things you white men must have—and life is full as before.   I have what is inside me—the same in Isleta as anywhere else."

He fastened his piercing eyes on us, a trick he has when he is much in earnest.   Those eyes see a little more than some people's eyes.   To him the aura that is hidden to most of us is a commonplace.   He allows himself to be guided by psychic manifestations to an extent a white man might not understand.   I heard him say of two men, strangers, who came to his ranch: "When they came in, I saw a light about the head of one.   All was white and shining, and I knew I could trust him.   But the other had no light.   It was black around him.   The first man can be my friend—but the other, never!   I do not trust him."

Moonshine?   But the odd thing is that Juan's judgment, so curiously formed, became fully justified by later events. The second man is not yet in jail, but there are people who know enough about him to put him there, if they cared to take the trouble. This trick of seeing the color of a man's soul is not unique with Juan. Many Pueblo Indians share it, as a matter of course, but it is a thing which they take for granted among themselves, and seldom mention.

Mrs. Juan had cleared away the supper dishes, and sat by a corner of the fireside. She had removed from her legs voluminous wrappings of white doeskin, symbol of her high financial rating, and sat openly and complacently admiring her silk-stockinged feet, coquettishly adorned with scarlet Turkish slippers, which she balanced on her toes. Pancho eyed the by-play with affectionate indulgence, and sent a long, slow wink in our direction at this harmless evidence of the eternal feminine. The talk had drifted to tales of wonder, to which we contributed our share as best we could, and now it was Juan's turn. He leaned forward earnestly, his black eyes somber and intense.

"You know me for an honest man? You know people say that Juan Pancho does not lie? You know that when Juan says he will do a thing, he does it, if it ruins him?"

We nodded. The reputation of Juan Pancho was a proverb in Great Isleta.

"Good! Because now, I am going to tell you something that will test your credulity. You will need to remember all you know of my honesty to believe what I tell you now."

We drew forward, and listened while he narrated the

story of the good monk of the time of Coronado, as I have told it in condensed form.

"Well, then! You've been in that church where they buried the monk—six feet from the altar, and a little to one side. Most Indian churches have a dirt floor, but the church of Great Isleta has a plank floor, very heavy. Now I will tell you why.

"The Spaniards came and went, without learning of the padre who slept with the knife wound in his back, under Isleta church. Five years went by, and one day, one of our old men who took care of the church went within, and saw a bulge in the earth, near the altar. It was of the size of a man's body. The bulge stayed there, right over the spot where they had buried the padre, and day after day it grew more noticeable. A year went by, and a crack appeared, the length of a man's body. Two years, three years—and the crack had widened and gaped. It was no use to fill it, to stamp down the dirt —that crack would remain open. Then, twelve years maybe from the death of the padre, the Isletans come into the church one morning, and there on the floor, face up, lies the padre. There is no sign of a crack in the earth—he lies on solid ground, looking as if he had died yesterday. They feel his flesh—it is soft, and gives to the touch of the finger, like the flesh of one whose breath has just flown. They turn him over—the knife wound is fresh, with red blood clotting it. Twelve years he has been dead!

"Well, they called in the elders, and talked it over, and they bury him, and give him another chance to rest in peace. But he does not stay buried. A few years more and the crack shows again, and at the end of twelve years, as before, there he lies on the ground, his body as free from the corruption of natural decay as ever. They bury him again, and after twelve years he is up. All around him lie the bones of Isletans who have died after him. The soil he lies in is the same soil which has turned their flesh to dust and their bones to powder.

"So it goes on, until my own time. I have seen him, twice. There are old men in our village who have seen him half a dozen times, and have helped to bury him. They don't tell of it—it is a thing to keep to oneself—but they know of it. The whole village knows of it, but they don't talk. But the last time he came up we talked it over, and we decided we had enough. This time, if possible, we would make him stay down.

"I saw him—in 1910 or '11 it was—and so did many others. The priest of Isleta saw him. We sent for the governor, and he came and saw. And the archbishop of Santa Fé came, and with him a cardinal who was visiting from Rome itself; they all came. What is more, they drew up a paper, and made two copies, testifying to what they had seen, and signed it. Then they took one copy and placed it with the long-dead padre in a heavy oak coffin, and nailed it down. And the other copy the visiting cardinal took back to Rome to give to the pope. My signature was on it. Then we buried the coffin, deep, and packed the earth hard about it and stamped it down. Then we took planks, two-inch planks, and laid a floor over the entire church, and nailed it down with huge nails. We were resolved that if he came up, he would at least have to work his passage."

"I suppose you've heard the last of him, then?"

Juan leaned forward. His eyes sparkled.

"We hope so. We hope so. But————"

He stood up and faced us.

"You are good enough to say you believe the word of Juan Pancho. But I will not test your credulity too far. You shall judge for yourselves."

Juan took a lantern from a nail, and lighted it.

"Come and see for yourselves!"

We followed him across the deserted plaza, whose squat houses showed dimly gray under a windy, blue-black sky. He unlocked the heavy door with a great key, and entered the church. Feeling our way in the dark, bare interior, we advanced to within six feet of the altar, and he placed the lantern on the floor, where it shed a circle of yellow light among the black shadows. We knelt, and touched the nails. The heads were free of the floor. On them were no tool-marks. No hammer had loosened them. We bent down further, and laying our heads aslant the planks, sighted. In the lantern light, we discerned a slight but unmistakable warp in the timbers, the length and width of a man's body.

In silence we returned to Juan's warm, lighted living-room, where Mrs. Juan still sat by the fire admiring her red slippers. If it is humanly possible, I intend to be in Great Isleta about the year 1923.

CHAPTER XIII

SANTE FÉ AND THE VALLEY OF THE RIO GRANDE

NOWHERE else did we find spring as lovely as at
Santa Fé. Here, a mile and a half above sea
level, was a crystal freshness of atmosphere, through
which filtered a quintessence of the sounds and scents
and colors that make a joyous season of spring even in
downtown New York.

A bit of a surprise it was to find, dozing in the sun like
a New England village, a town important enough to
have given its name to a railroad; to mark the end of
one trail, and be a station on another; to have been the
capital of an ancient Empire of the New World; and
now to be the capital of a state. Yet the world passes
it by, leaving it on a railroad spur high and dry from
transcontinental traffic. So much the worse, then, for the
world; so much the better for Santa Fé. The town does
not owe its personality to its railroad stations and Cham-
bers of Commerce. The peaks guarding its high isolation have looked down upon many changes in its history.
Yet it stays outwardly nearly unaltered; valuing material importance so little that it hides its Capitol down
a grassy side street, while its Plaza still is dominated by
the sturdy old Governor's Palace, where Onate raised
the Spanish flag in the early seventeenth century, and
Kearny replaced it with the American flag in 1846.

The heart of Santa Fé is its Plaza. To its shady

trees, traders tied their horses when they had reached the end of the perilous Santa Fé Trail, glad enough to gain its shelter after being beset by the primitive dangers of hunger, thirst, wild beasts, Indians and robbers. The same Plaza where drowsy Mexicans now rest upon park benches, where processions of burros pass loaded with firewood, where shining automobiles flash by, has witnessed siege and countersiege, scenes of violence and heroism and romance. Richly laden caravans once came galloping into the town, sometimes closely beset by bandits or hostile Apaches, and weary adventurers from the land of Daniel Boone or Washington dismounted, and looked bewildered about them at this gay and alien civilization. Here the Pueblo Indians, in their final revolt, besieged the white settlers, and committed the only violences in their long career of patience, and here the conquering De Vargas finally overcame them, and surrounded by Franciscan monks, offered mass for his victory. Dominating the Plaza is the three century old Governor's Palace, whose walls conceal prehistoric Indian foundations. It is a one-story building running half the length of the square, built in a day when hospitality demanded royal scope. Half inn, half fort, its six-foot thick walls stood for strength as well as coolness, and its mighty doors frequently knew the marks of assault. In modern times, until the beginning of this century it served as residence of the governor of the Territory. In a back room, Lew Wallace is said to have written chapters of Ben Hur.

No question but that the Palace might be made more interesting as a Museum, less a storehouse of half forgotten oddments. It might tell less spasmodically and with greater dignity the story of its successive occupations, from the Royal Governor of Spain to the present time. It creates the impression now of having been forgotten, except as, at intervals, a legacy of antiquities was deposited wholesale, without selection. The exhibits should be pruned, gaps filled, and arranged with better proportion and consecutiveness.

It might well, indeed, take a leaf from the book of the new Museum, built on the same side of the Plaza. Its exterior skilfully assembles various parts of nearby buildings of Pueblo architecture. Its corners copy the towers of Laguna, Taos and Acoma. The warm stucco walls are studded with pinon *vegas,* and the doorways, windows and balconies are of cedar, deep-set in the thick walls. An infant art-gallery, fed from the local Santa Fe and Taos schools, sometimes according to Holt and sometimes on Cubist pickles and doughnuts, does the double service of giving the artist permanent exhibition-rooms, and illustrating local color for the tourist.

I mean no disparagement here against the Santa Fé school, which numbers several names of national reputation. The country cries to be painted in vividest colors; Nature here is in vermilion mood, and man tops her gayety with slouching *insouciance,* sky-blue shirts, and head-bands giving the needful splash of scarlet. Add skies as blue as a spring sun can stipple them, dash across them a blur of pink apricot bloom, bank them against cliffs of red-orange, pure gold where the light strikes it, and grape purple in the shadows, tone with the warm gray of a pueblo clustered about a sky-blue stream, and fringed yellow-green cottonwoods bordering it,—and what artist can paint with sobriety? That a few manage it is to their credit, nor can one wonder that this riot of color goes to the heads of others till their canvasses look like an explosion in a vegetable garden.

Tucked away in another street off the Plaza stands the old Cathedral, begun in 1612. As cathedrals go it is an unimpressive example of the worst period of church architecture: to the usual trappings of its interior is added the barbaric crudity of the Mexican in church art; an art like the French Canadian's, naïve and literal. It must show the bleeding heart much ensanguined, the wounds of Christ fresh with gore, and its doll-faced saints covered with lace and blue satin, like fashion plates of Godey's Ladies. What interests me in this as in other churches of the Southwest is the colossal ironic joke on the Pilgrim Fathers and Puritans, whose contemporary efforts on the stern rock-bound eastern coast were just about offset by the equally earnest efforts of the Spanish padres on the cactus-ridden desert of the west. However, what each bequeathed of value has remained to build a vaster, freer, and perhaps better community than either unwitting opponent previsioned.

Quite Colonial, and oddly reminiscent of New England is the Governor's mansion of today, across from the present Capitol, which like every Capitol in the United States rears a helmet shaped dome. In the houses of this New Mexican government occurs a phenomenon unknown to any other state: two languages are officially spoken, Mexican and English, with an interpreter to make each side intelligible to the other. I do not know whether this bilingual Assembly and Senate produces twice as much verbiage as the usual legislature or whether the two tongues serve as a deterrent to oratory.

New Mexico, it must be remembered, is more Indian and Mexican than American by a proportion of three to one, and includes a sprinkling of negro and Chinese. The Indian lends a touch of the primitive; the Mexican brings Spain into the picture. In doorways painted sky blue or lavender, swarthy women gossip, in mantilla and fringed black shawl. Against a shady wall, in sash and sombrero, all but too lazy to light the inevitable ciga-rette, slouches a Mexican who should be working. On Sundays and fête days, the roads about Sante Fé are splashed with the vivid colors of the girls' frocks,—pinks, purples and scarlet accenting the inevitable black of the women's dress,—as they make their way under fringy cottonwoods to some country alberge. The sound of a jerky accordion usually follows them up the canyon roads.

Mostly the Mexicans are gregarious, keeping to their own quarters in Santa Fé, and their own villages further out in the country, often near an Indian pueblo of the same name, as at Taos and at Tesuque, famed for its grotesque Indian godlets. All about Santa Fé these little adobe towns, Chimayo, Teuchas, Cuamunque, Po-joaque, Espanola, Alcalde and Pecos, lie in some fertile river valley, surrounded by their fruit trees and alfalfa fields. The Mexicans, though indolent, understand truck farming thoroughly. Like their occupations, their rec-reations are primitive. They have their own dances, where the men sit on one side of the room and the girls, giggling and shoving, at the other, until some bold swain sets the ball rolling. Then it does not cease to roll, fast

AGAINST A SHADY WALL, ALL BUT TOO LAZY TO LIGHT THE INEVITABLE
CIGARETTE, SLOUCHES, WHEREVER ONE TURNS, A MEXICAN

and furious, till morning, often ending in some tragic fray, where a knife flashes.

They have their own schools and churches;—and almost always, at the end of the town, a little window-less house which looks like a church. The Americano is unwise who attempts to enter, or even ask questions concerning this building. It is the morado, or brother-hood house, of a secret sect called the Penitentes, who have been described briefly in certain books on this locality, but are almost unknown to the outside world. The sect is entirely Mexican, not Indian, as has fre-quently been misstated. Only a very few Indians have ever become Penitentes, and most of the race hold the idea in abhorrence. Survival of a cult which flourished in Spain four centuries ago, the practice was brought to Old Mexico, of which New Mexico was then a part, by some Franciscans who followed the conquistadores. In Lisbon, in 1801, a procession of flagellants went through the streets. This seems to have been the latest outbreak in Europe, yet in our own United States it stubbornly persists today, despite the utmost the Catholic church can do to discourage this horrible self-torture.

We had the very good fortune to enter Santa Fé during Holy Week. All along our route, through the little Mexican towns bordering the Rio Grande, church bells were ringing, and Mexicans in gala array riding to special services on pintos, burros, or in carts laden with entire families of eight or ten. When we reached our hotel, three miles out, for adequate hotels for some strange reason do not exist in Santa Fe, we were invited to go "Penitente Hunting." The sport is not without its dangers. Strangers who venture too near the mysterious processions have been shot, and only the most fool-hardy would seek to go near the morado.

We learned that while the members are quiescent dur-ing the year, committing whatever laxities of conduct seem good to them, Holy Week heaps on them, voluntarily, the ashes of bitter atonement. On Monday, they gather in their morado, and enter on a week of fasting, ritual, and self-inflicted torture. To a few selected by the high priests of the order is given the honor, from their point of view, of taking upon themselves the sins of all. They endure incredible torments; some lie on beds of cactus the entire week, others wear the deadly *cholla* bound on their backs or inserted under the flesh. Every Penitente bears on his back the mark of the Cross, slit into his skin with deep double gashes at his initiation into the sect. These wounds are re-opened each year. Weak from flogging, with blood raining from their backs till old wounds mingle with the new, eating only food brought to the morado at nightfall by their women, these vicarious sufferers come forth on Good Friday to the culmination of their agony.

Santa Fé was agog with rumors. At one town we heard the penitentes would not leave their morado, re-senting the growing publicity their rites attracted. An-other, further from civilization, was to show a cruci-fixion, with ghastly fidelity even to the piercing of hands and feet,—a fate for which the honored victim begged. Loomis has related this circumstance as a fact, and rumor of the year previous to our arrival gave it con-firmation.

Early Good Friday morning, our party drove in and out the valleys, fording to our hubs streams that yesterday

A MEXICAN MORADO, NEW MEXICO.

The Americano is unwise who attempts to enter or even ask questions concerning this building.

THE MUSEUM OF SANTA FE.

Its corners copy the towers of Laguna, Taos, and Acoma.

were mere trickles, and tomorrow, augmented by melting mountain snows, would be raging torrents. New Mexico has few working bridges. One fords a stream, if it seems sufficiently shallow, or waits a day or week at the nearest hotel for it to subside. Rivers were fast leaving their bounds this morning, but we managed to cross in time to arrive at Alcalde before ceremonies had begun.

Built like most adobe pueblos, Indian and Mexican, about a straggling square, this little village furnished a good vantage for Americans to see and to be observed, —watched with quiet hostility by idling natives. Cross-currents of ill feeling we sensed intangibly; not only did the village as a whole bristle toward us, but it contained two sects of flagellants, and two morados, whose families were fiercely partisan; and in addition these were opposed by the native element of strict Catholics who, obeying the mandates of the Church, frowned on the fanatic religionists. We were warned not to take pictures nor show our cameras, nor to follow the procession too closely. Our presence was barely tolerated, and our innocent attempts to become an inconspicuous part of the landscape met with scowls and uncomplimentary remarks. Perhaps they were justified; the desire to guard one's religious rites from curious eyes is a high instinct, which, no matter how effacingly we "hunted penitentes," we were violating.

The saints in the whitewashed church had been dressed for the occasion in new ribbons and laces. On a low wheeled platform stood a crudely painted figure of Christ, his eyes bandaged with the pathetic purpose of saving him from the sight of the agony to come to his followers. With him were other figures; one I think was Judas, with his bag of silver and mean grimace. Soon from the morado came a short procession of men and boys, weak-kneed and trembling, clad only in cotton drawers and shirts which speedily became ensanguined from wounds made by hidden thorns. They walked with a peculiar swaying motion, as if their knees were broken. Three of them, no more than boys, bore great crosses of foot-square timber, about twenty feet long. The heavy ends dragged on the ground; the cross beams rested on bent backs, on which, the whisper went, were bound the spiky cactus whose every curved needle pressing on the flesh spells torture. Blood ran down their shaky legs, joining blood already crusted. Their faces were hooded.

A band of flagellants followed who as yet played a less active part. At wide intervals over the scorching desert were planted the fourteen stations of the cross, to which the three principals, barefooted, dragged their burdens. At each they rested while the drama of that station was enacted as crudely and literally as an early mystery play. A middle-aged penitente in store clothes, fiercely in earnest, read appropriate passages from the Mexican Bible, stumbling over the pronunciation. Then the procession chanted responses, and the brief respite, if respite it was for the cross-bearers, came to an end. At the proper station, three little black-robed Marys broke from the crowd, and played their tragic part.

We watched in suspense the slow progress, wondering if the martyrs would reach their goal alive. As they neared the fourteenth station, one of the "two thieves" tottered, and had to be supported, half-fainting, the rest of the way. The other two barely managed to finish. Our dread was heightened lest the Mystery be carried to its bitter close.

No printed word could have aroused among its ignorant spectators the tense devoutness inspired by this medieval drama. Religion to many of us has become a denatured philosophy, a long step from this savage brutality. Yet have we any substitute which will so kindle our imagination and idealism that it could school the body to endure gladly even the supreme agony?

During the heat of the day, all was silence within the morado to which the actors had retreated. The sobbing Mexican women who followed the procession vanished with their black veils into their houses, some perhaps to await news of the death or collapse of their men, which not infrequently attends the Holy Week celebrants. Toward dark, over the country side, automobile phares began to converge toward the silent morado. The world outside had taken up "penitente hunting" as a cold-blooded sport. They came openly baiting the penitentes, who angered, refused to appear. Eight, nine, ten, eleven! We left our darkened car, and hid ourselves in the sand dunes near the graveyard, in the dark shadow of a clump of piñons.

We waited with cramped legs, while the blue sky became black, and mysterious shapes loomed up in an unspeakably vast and lonely country. The Flagellants were still sulking. At last, a light across the river flickered, swung, and started down a distant trail, whose route we traced by an occasional lantern glimmer through masses of trees. A sweet, weird wail floated over to us on a gust of wind. It was the *pito,* wild and high-pitched flute, making a most dismal, shivery music. The procession twisted and turned toward the river. We crouched uncomfortably by our sand dunes, not daring to make a sound for fear it might be carried on the clear air. Suddenly came a chant, broken, taken up and dropped by voices too weak to modulate. It sounded unevenly, as spurts of energy forced it from tired throats; loud, then a whisper. The chant continued, with an ominous new sound added; a thud, thud, thud, regular and pitiless, the fall of thongs upon flesh. No outcry came; only the chant and the wail of the *pito* rose louder.

It was a neighboring sect on the way to pay a visit to our morado. Frequently the light was arrested, and the singing stopped. We knew then they were paying their devotions at one of the heaps of stone, rude wayside memorials seen everywhere in this locality, erected by the Mexicans to their dead, some of whom lie in battle-fields of France. Then the chant continued, the thud, painful enough only to hear, and the shuffle of feet, in a sort of weary lockstep. Across the river another light flickered and started. Soon, from our hiding-place high over the valley, we could see half a dozen processions, wending up and down through the hills.

A movement from the direction of our morado, and the *pito* sounded close at hand, accompanied by the uneven creak of a rude cart, filling us with a delightful, terrifying suspense. So close that we could have touched them, passed chanting men, swinging lights. We heard the break of leaden whips on their bare backs, but no groans. It was the procession of the death wagon, on which a skeleton was strapped, a macabre *memento mori* borrowed from the Middle Ages. The gleaming lantern illumined its ribs as it tottered on its seat in grisly semblance of life.

Suddenly a motor drove up aggressively, and halted straight across the path of the death wagon. The *pito* and chanting stopped. A crowd quickly gathered, and angry voices made staccato demands. The car remained insolently unmoved, blocking the penitentes' most private ceremony. The mob was angry beyond bounds at what to the most unsympathetic observer was gross rudeness, but to them was outrageous sacrilege. Pistols were drawn. The increasing numbers of penitentes surrounding the car buzzed like swarming hornets whose nest has been smashed, and who hunt the marauder with vicious intent. Then came a heavy voice from the car, a moment of confusion, and the crowd melted away, muttering but evidently cowed, while the car moved arrogantly forward. Puzzled, we asked for explanations.

"That fellow in the car owns the big store where all those greasers trade. They buy on credit, run in debt, and he takes a mortgage on their ranches or herds of sheep. Some of them owe him two or three thousand. They were all ready to make trouble when they recognized him. He told them he was going to see the show, and if they didn't like it they could pay what they owed him tomorrow. So they slunk off. He is a German."

Echt deutsch!

Barbarous as may be this custom of flagellating, there is devout belief behind it. To the ignorant Mexican stimulated by these annual reminders, it is as if, as is literally true, the torture and anguish had occurred to a neighbor in his home town. The faces of the men and women, even of little children witnessing the penitente rites, showed the reality to them of what to most of us is remote as the legend of Hercules. Faith so beautiful and unusual must command respect no matter what arouses it. Yet in black contrast to it is the political and moral corruption said to accompany this dangerous doctrine of expiation. Being especially saintly because of their endurance test, the penitentes during the rest of the year commit murder, adultery, theft and arson with cheerful abandon. Nobody dares oppose them or revenge their excesses, either from pious veneration, fear, or a knowledge of the uselessness of such a procedure. For the Penitentes are whispered to be potent politically. Membership in the sect is kept secret. Many prominent judges and state politicians are said to be Penitentes. If a fellow member is brought to justice, he gets off lightly or goes scot-free, and strange deaths are predicted for enemies, private or public, of the sect. I was even warned not to write of them, for fear their power should extend beyond the state's borders. Doubtless much of this local fear is exaggerated.

But I predict that what church and legislature have failed to do, the ubiquitous tourist will accomplish. In the more remote hill towns, services still reproduce the incarnadined Passion with all its horrors. Nearer to Santa Fé, the flagellants withdraw closer and closer into their morados. Without an audience to sympathize, pain and torture become less tolerable. No man, however sincere he believes himself, turns Stylites unless his pillar stands in the market place.

Ten miles from this strange Good Friday we passed an equally strange Easter in the Indian pueblo of San Ildefonso, whose many generations of Catholicism do not prevent invoking the gods who have given service even longer than the Christian's deities. They shake well and mix them, somewhat after the fashion of my colored laundress who confessed she always wore a hoodoo charm:—"Of course I'se a good Christian, too, but the Bible says, don't it, the Law'd he'ps them as he'ps they-selves?"

Somewhat in this spirit, Easter Sunday was chosen for the Rain Dance which was to end a long drought. For miles we passed buckboards carrying large Indian families endimancheés with rainbow hues; Indian bucks on little neat-footed ponies, their square-chopped raven hair banded with scarlet or purple, wearing short gay velvet shirts, buttoned with silver shells bartered from the Navajos, white cotton trousers, or the more modern blue overalls, henna-colored moccasins, silver buttoned on their tiny feet. Their necks and waists were loaded with wampum and turquoise-studded silver, their faces rouged.

"Why do you paint your face?" we asked a visiting Santa Domingo dandy.

"Oh, to be na-ice," he replied to our impertinence. "Why don't you paint yours?"

Volumes have been written of the Pueblo Indians' folklore and religion, much of it probably wrong, for the Indian has a habit of telling what he thinks you want to be told, and concealing exactly what he wishes to conceal. His religion is too sacred and intimate to be revealed to the first inquirer. While he has a sense of humor, which some people persist in denying, he is, like most practical jokers, extremely sensitive to ridicule, especially when directed against himself. Always a mystic, he finds his way easily where the Anglo-Saxon

gropes. The common lore of Strange Things, which
he shares with the gypsy, the Hindu, and the Jew, races
to whom he bears a certain physical resemblance, was
his centuries before he adopted clothes. In ordinary
learning he remains a child, albeit a shrewd child, yet his
eyes are open in realms of the unknown. He hears the
rush of mighty winds through the heavens, and is acquainted with the voice of the thunder. He can com-
mune with unseen forces without the trumpery aid of
ouija or the creaky mechanism of science. Though he
can barely add and hardly knows his multiplication tables,
I venture to guess that if the fourth dimension be ever
demonstrated, the Indian will be found to have had a
working knowledge of it, and will accept it as a commonplace to his tribe and his medicine men.

In the Casa Grande ruins is a tiny hole through which
the sun shines the first day it crosses the vernal equinox.
Like the lens of a telescope, this focusses into other tiny
holes in other parts of the building. Why it is there
nobody knows, but it indicates a knowledge of astronomy
which places the prehistoric Pima on equal footing with
modern scientists. Before the Zûni Indians knew a white
race existed, according to Cushing, Powell and the musi-
cian Carlos Troyer, they had evolved the theory of
prismatic rays coming from the sun, and had established
a fixed relation between color and sound tones, anticipat-
ing by some centuries Mr. Henderson and others. Their
medicine men took shells, found in their magic Corn
Mountain, a giant mesa overshadowing the village,
polished them to tissue thinness, and then painted each
shell a pure color, corresponding to the colors of the
prism. One by one they placed these shells over the ear,

nearest the sun. The corresponding color ray from the sun would strike a musical note so powerful that care had to be taken to prevent the ear drum being broken. These absolute color-tones the medicine men noted, and used exclusively in sacred ceremonies, but did not permit their use in secular music. Are the red men more subtly attuned to rhythms of the universe than the superior white race? Has the dirty, half-naked medicine-man somehow found the parent stem of the banyan-tree of life, while we are still digging around its off-shoots?

But this is a long digression from the sunlit plaza, splashed with the scarlet Pendleton blankets and sky-blue jerkins of visiting chiefs, and the pink sateen Mother-Hubbard of the squaw next me, whose too solid flesh was anchored with pounds and pounds of silver and turquoise,—enough to pawn at the trader's for a thousand or two of *bahana* money. To our questions of the symbolism of the dance they made child-like answers: it is to "make rain,"—*mucha agua* (Spanish is the lingua franca of the Pueblo Indian). Babies in every state of dress from a string of wampum up, crowded shyly for our fast melting chocolates; aged crones, half-blind from the too prevalent trachoma, hospitably invited us into their neat white-washed living rooms, or offered us chairs at their doorways. Doors were wide open; the town kept open house. It gave us an opportunity to see their houses without prying. Our first reaction was surprise at their universal ship-shapeness. We saw dirt floors, on which two or three pallets were folded in neat rows, or in the grander houses, a white enamel bed with one sheet only, and a lace counterpane; a crucifix and two or three portraits of saints on the walls, next a gayly flowered cover of some seed catalogue; a rafter hung with rugs, clothing, and strings of wampum and silver; slings in which the beds are suspended at night, and a blackened stone fireplace in the corner. And nearly always, a blooming plant in a tin can on the wide windowsill, and a lilac bush just outside.

Houses are strategically situated in a Pueblo village to permit of every one knowing everything which goes on. If a dog barks, or a stranger takes a snap-shot without toll, twenty women are at their doors shouting malediction. There can be no secrets,—gossip screamed cat-a-corners across a plaza with a face at every door and window and the roofs thronged loses much of its piquancy.

But before the dance a certain decorum prevailed. This Rain dance, we were told, was especially sacred. Then, whooping and performing monkey antics, two strange figures, mostly naked except for some horizontal stripes painted with grease paint on their legs and bodies, leaped down the outside stairway of the priesthouse. Horns adorned their heads, and a tail apiece eked out their scanty costume. They turned somersaults, seized women by the waist and waltzed with them, hit each other playfully over the head with sticks, rushed into houses, and came out with pails of food, whereat they squatted in the plaza, and ate with simulated gusto. They were the *koshari,* or delight-makers,—the hereditary clowns who open the dance ceremonies. Like the ancient Lords of Misrule, they are king for the day, and all must obey their fantastic whims. They are licensed plunderers, privileged to rush into any house, which must be left open, and run off with anything which takes their

KOSHAR   RAIN DANCE. SAN YLDEFONSO

TAOS WOMAN.

SANTA DOM NGO WOMAN.

fancy. Possibly because the *koshari* availed themselves too enthusiastically of this part of their priestly office, it is now the custom to set out food for them, to which they are supposed to confine themselves.

One *koshari* was tottering and blind, steering himself with a cane, and the brusque aid of his companion, a fat young rascal who would have been funny in any language. He, poor soul, no longer amusing, contented himself with rushing about on his withered legs, and uttering feeble yelps in concert with his colleague. The dancers followed, all young men,—some in their teens, —and began a solemn march around the village preceding the dance. Necklaces of evergreen wreaths comprised their costume from the waist up, two eagle feathers topped their hair, short white hand-woven skirts reached to the knee, with an occasional fox skin hanging behind, and at the side red, white and green tassels of wool. The limbs and bodies were painted; at the ankles tortoise shells rattled, and gourds in their hands shook with silvery precision. In moccasins edged with skunk fur, they stamped in light, unvarying rhythm, first on one foot, then the other, wheeling in sudden gusts, not together, but in a long rhythmic swell so accurately timed to undulate down the line that each foot was lifted a fraction higher than the one in front. They sang quietly, with the same shuddering little accent their gourds and feet maintained, at intervals stressing a note sharply, in absolute accord. Two women, young and comely, in the heavy black squaw dress and white doeskin leggins of the Pueblo woman, squatted midway before the line of lithe dancers, and beat, beat all through the day on their drums, while all through the day, lightly, sharply, the moccasined feet were planted and lifted, with a snap and re-bound as if legs and rippling bodies covered not sinews, but springs of finely tempered steel, timed to hair trigger exactness. Their lean faces wore an intent look, hardly heeding the antics of the *koshari* who gamboled around them, standing on their heads, tumbling, shouting, and pulling each other's tails like monkeys. About evergreen trees planted in the center, they pivoted to all four points of the compass. The dance varied little. The song, the tombés, the shivery gourds and shells, the syncopated beat of each tireless foot on the earth became a background to the color and picnic movement of the village, drowsy in the sunshine, steaming with the odors of people, dogs, jerked beef, cedar smoke and buckskin, whiffs of lilac, fresh willow, snowy sprays of wild pear, and a wet breeze from the Rio Grande.

Because rain in that parched country is literally life, the Indians hold this rain dance too sacred to admit as participants any women save the two who beat the drums. "Tomorrow," said the fat young *koshari,* "nice dance. We dance with the girls then."

I dare not claim any authority for the interpretation of the costumes of the Rain Dance. Several natives of the pueblo, including quiet-eyed Juan, the governor, gave us various versions which did not tally in every particular. We had learned that an Indian's meaning of a lie, which he is fairly scrupulous in avoiding, does not include the answers to questions touching his cherished customs and the private code of his race. The evergreen, all agreed, stood for fertility or verdure; the eagle feathers, with their white and black tips, for the black and white

AN YLDEFO   O

of slashing rain and lowering clouds; the yellow fox-skins represented the yellow of ripe corn; the red and green tassels at the waist the flowers and grass of spring; the white tassels, snow or hail. The symbolism of the thunder clouds was repeated in the black and white of the skunk fur moccasins; the gourds echoed the swish of rain, and the drum-beats the rumble of the thunder; the tortoise shell rattles at the ankle meant either rain and wind, or were a symbol, like the shell necklaces most of them wore, of the ocean, which all desert tribes especially revere, as the Father of all Waters.

During the dance the fat and impudent *koshari* honored me with a command,—"You take me and my chum for a ride?" Fat and very naked, covered with melting grease paint, and ferocious in horns and tail, he was not the sort of companion I would have chosen for a motor drive, but a refusal might have prompted him to expel us from the village. On a fête day, the lightest word of a *koshari* is law. He clambered in, and moved over to make room for his chum, a loathsome and mangy old fellow, with rheumy, sightless eyes, whose proximity filled me with disgust. Tottering with age and excitement, his first move was to clutch the steering wheel, and when I had disengaged his claws, he grasped the lever with an iron grip. Meanwhile, thirteen brown babies, some of whom had been bathed as recently as last year, climbed into the tonneau. We whirled around and around the plaza, the children shouting, dogs barking, the fat *koshari* bowing like visiting royalty to the cheering spectators, uttering shrieks in my ear to take me off guard, kicking his heels in the air, or sliding to the floor as a too-daring visitor tried to snap his picture, while *koshari* senior occasionally seized the levers and threw us into reverse, nearly stripping the gears.

A curious people! Childishly admiring of the white man's automobiles, radium watches and canned foods, and gravely contemptuous of his civilized codes, morals and spiritual insight; unsanitary in daily life, yet with rituals of hospital cleanliness; believing in charms and "medicine," yet with a knowledge of herbs, and mental therapy beyond our own; introducing buffoonery into their religious services, yet with a reverence for religion uncomprehended by the white man; unable to persuade the government to give him citizen rights,—but easily able to persuade the Lord to send him rain! For, two days after the dance, rain came in abundance in sheets, torrents and cataracts, after a drought which had lasted months. The Hopi snake dance they say never fails to bring rain. Other rain dances about Santa Fé have the same result. Is it coincidence,—or has the Indian a weather sense beyond ours;—or does he look the Deity more squarely and unflinchingly in the eye when he makes his demands? Jacob wrestled with his angel. The Indian *knows* his prayers will bring rain. And however obtained, his percentage of correct answers seems higher than the white man's.

A week later, when the town of San Felipe gave a "corn dance," we found another instance of the thoroughness with which the Pueblo jumbles his religions. Through the old white plaza, dazzling with color, dividing its lively crowds impartially between the lemonade stand at one end, and the draped altar at the other, we made our way to the old church which looks through an avenue of blossoming cottonwood on to a gentle blue and green landscape picked out by the meanderings of the Rio Grande. Meanwhile the dance in the Plaza had begun. Almost within sight of the stamping, chanting rows of Squash and Turtle clans, the men naked to the waist with long hair flowing, the women's black-clad bodies and bare arms swaying, the congregation slipped in to the cool interior of the church, and, dressed in the gorgeous clothes and jewels they wore to honor their native gods, listened respectfully to a visiting Bishop, and knelt in prayer with accustomed reverence. They saw no incongruity in it, and neither do I, so long as good Christians throw spilled salt over their left shoulder, or wish on the moon. Yet it made a delightful contrast,—the little brown boys in their white robes intoning with the nasality of altar boys the world over, plus the Indian's special brand of nasality; the quiet attention of the drifting congregation, and outside, the noise, color and sunshine; the bands of giddy bucks sprawling on painted ponies, the cool lovely valley beyond, and at its heart, the power which brought all these elements together,—sluggish old Rio Grande, taking its time on its everlasting journey to the Gulf.

Within a short radius of Santa Fé, one can trace all the successive steps in the history of the Pueblo Indian. We go furthest back at Rito de los Frijoles, where a glance half way up a perpendicular cliff reveals black spots of pin-head size. An arduous climb up rough ladders and steps notched in crumbling yellow tufa shows these holes as large caverns hollowed by water under the shelving roof of the soft rock, and built up with a masonry which today would easily command ten dollars a day and a forty-eight hour week. "The Cloud City,

Acoma," on the Arizona road is built atop a high mesa, facing the still higher Enchanted Mesa, now peopled only by troubled ghosts. Doubtless the first Indians to advance from cave dwellings to mesas felt as emancipated as the first New Englander who left the old homestead for a modern apartment-house. Further east the rock-bastioned villages of the Hopis still carry on the customs of their kin, if not their ancestors. At Taos and Laguna the timid Pueblos finally ventured down to the ground, but retained the style of the mesas and cliff dwellings, of terraced receding houses, several stories high. The final and most modern adaptation are the one-story, squat little adobe houses of the river pueblos, whose dwellers have shaken off entirely the ancestral fear, and raise corn and alfalfa, melons and apricots on the rich irrigated soil.

The journey to Frijoles is worth risking a fall over precipices as one dashes over switchbacks of incomparable dizziness on roadbeds of unsanctified roughness. From Buckman, if the bridge is not washed away by the floods, like most bridges about Santa Fe, the ascent starts to the neat little, green little Rito de los Frijoles, —Bean Valley is its unpoetical English. No motorist should undertake this trip with his own car unless he thinks quickly, knows his machine thoroughly, and is inoculated against "horizontal fever." The road climbs past orange hills up blue distances, through warmly scented forests of scrub pinon, with a vista of the river far below. At the top the car must be abandoned, for nothing wider than a mule can manage the descent into the canyon.

A precipitous and dusty trail drops to a refreshing

CAVE DWELLINGS IN THE PUMICE WALLS OF CANYON DE LOS FRIJOLES, SANTA FE

little valley, long and narrow, grown with shady pines, and watered by a brook which was probably the *raison d'etre* for the city so many ages silent as the sphinx and dead as Pompeii. In a beautiful semi-circle, so symmetrical and tiny seen from above that it looks like a fantastic design etched on the valley floor, lie the ruined walls of a city whose people were the first families of North America. It is hard to believe this peacefully remote valley ever echoed the noise of playing children, of gossiping women and barking dogs. The dark-skinned Jamshyd who ruled here left speechless stone walls to crumble under the tread of the wild ass, and whether drought, pestilence or murder drove him and his race forth, forsaking their habitations to the eternal echoes, nobody knows. He was timid, or he would not have plastered his houses like swallows' nests in the cliff, or huddled them together in this remote canyon, walled in against more aggressive tribes. He was agricultural, for traces of his gardens, dust these centuries, may be found. Shard heaps of pottery designed in the red and black pattern that dates them as from one to two thousand years old, and arrowheads of black obsidian prove he knew the same arts as the Southwestern Indian of today. Each tribal unit, then as now, had its kiva, or underground ceremonial chamber with the altar stone placed exactly as in every kiva in Utah, Colorado or Arizona.

Parenthetically, the kiva may have retained its popularity through the sunshiny ages because it offered the men of the tribe a complete refuge from their women-folk. Once down the ladder, they need not pull it after them, for custom forbade and still forbids a squaw of any modesty from acting as if the *kiva* were within a hundred miles of her. Once inside, the men folk are at liberty to whittle their prayer sticks, gossip, swap stories, and follow whatever rituals men indulge in when alone. It is as bad form for a pueblo woman to invade the kiva as for us to enter a men's club,—with the difference that no kiva had a ladies' night. Besides furnishing shelter to the henpecked Benedicts, the kiva became a sort of Y. M. C. A. for the young bucks. In ancient times the bachelors of the tribe slept together in the kiva, their food being left outside the entrance. This very wise provision greatly protected the morals of the young people, forced to live in very close juxtaposition.

On the ridge opposite the caves of Frijoles lies an unexplored region believed to be the summer home of the race who lived here so secretly and vanished so mysteriously. In a few years the excavator may discover among the shard heaps at the top of this canyon the reason for the exodus, but at present more is known about lost Atlantis than these ruins in our "rawest" and newest corner of the States.

One need not thrill to the prehistoric, however, to enjoy Santa Fé, especially when the apricots blur the flaming green valley with a rosy mist. All trails from the sleepy little town lead to the perpetual snows of the hills through scented forests of pine, past roaring streams. A good horse will clamber up the bed of a waterfall, leap fallen logs, pick his way, when the forest becomes too tangled, over the slippery boulders of the river, canter over ground too rough for a high-school horse to walk upon, and bring his rider out to the top of some high ridge, where crests of blue notch against crests of paler and paler blue, without end.

Near enough to Santa Fé to be reached in a day by motor and somewhat longer by pack-train, lies the enchanting valley locally called "The Pecos." One mounts the piñon-scented red trail, studded with spring flowers, to the heights above, where to breathe the air of dew and fire is to acquire the zip of a two year old colt and the serenity of a seraph. In this least known corner of our country, the Pecos is the least traveled district, known only to a few ranchmen, and old guides with tall, "straight" stories, and short, twisted legs,—mighty hunters who have wrestled barehanded with bears, and stabbed mountain lions with their penknives. Sportsmen are only beginning to know what the streams of the Pecos produce in trout, and its wilderness in big game. Given a good horse, a good guide, good "grub" and a comfortable bedding roll, a month free from entangling alliances with business, and the Pecos provides sound sleep, mighty appetites, and air two miles high, so different from the heavy vapor breathed by the city-dweller that it deserves a name of its own.

Nobody can stay long in Santa Fé, without becoming aware of the Rio Grande's influence on the dwellers in its valley. It furnishes not only their livelihood, but little daily happenings, "So and So's car got stuck crossing at Espanola, and had to stay in the river two days,"—"The river rose and tore down the bridge at Buckman, and they say there will be two more bridges down by night." —"You can't get out at Pojoaque, this week" But to see the river in its magnificence, one should drive over the canyon of the Rio Grande, following along the precipitous road to Taos.

The day we started for Taos, rain invoked by the prayerful Pueblos had reduced the road-bed to a sticky red plaster which more than once slid our car gently toward the edge and a drop of a hundred feet or more. Like the foolish virgins we were, we had forgotten our chains. To put on the brakes would invite a skid; not to do so meant a plunge over the bank. The road, like an afterthought, clung for dear life to the edge of a series of hills, now dipping like a swallow to the river bed, then after the usual chuck-hole at the bottom, rising in dizzy turns to the top of the next hill, unwinding before us sometimes for miles. Steep cliffs, and narrow gorges at times shut us completely from the world. Far below, the river frothed turbulently.

Occasionally as we took a turn, a bit of bank caved in with us, and left one wheel treading air. On sharp curves a long wheel base is a great disadvantage. The earth is liable to crumble where rain has softened it in gullies, and one must learn to keep close enough to the inside edge in turning to prevent the back wheels from skimming the precipice, and yet not drive the front wheels into the inside bank. Add to this a surface of slick mud on which the car slides helplessly, heavy ruts and frequent boulders, steep graded curves with gullies at the bottom, and it will seem less surprising that the mail driver who takes his own car and his life over this road twice a week to Santa Fé receives about three times the wage of a Harvard professor.

A few miles before reaching Taos we left the canyon and came out on a broad plain. The first sight of Taos takes one's breath,—it is so alien to America. Ancient of days, it suggests Jerusalem or some village still more remote in civilization. Houses terraced to five and even seven stories are banked against purple mountains, thirteen thousand feet in the air. A little stream winds to the walls of the village, dividing it in two. On the banks women wash clothes, and men draw primitive carts to the water, or gallop over the plain like Arabs in the flowing white robes characteristic to Taos. The roofs of the square plaster houses, terraced one above the other, are peopled with naked babies. Women wrapped in shawls of virgin blue or scarlet outlined against the sky, again suggest the Orient. Constantly in these Pueblos one is reminded of the Far East and it is easy to believe these Indians of the Southwest, of sleek round yellow cheek and almond eyes are of Mongolian stock. The Grand Canyon old-timer, William Bass, tells of seeing a distinguished Chinese visitor talk with ease to some Navajos of the Painted desert, who, he reported, used a rough Chinese dialect. In the Shoshone country, I myself saw Indians enter a Chinese restaurant, and converse with the slant-eyed proprietor. When I asked whether they were speaking Shoshone or Chinese, I was told that they used a sort of *lingua franca,* and had no difficulty in understanding each other. Oriental or not, the origins of Taos are clouded with antiquity.

Coronado was the first Aryan to visit this ancient pueblo, and we, to date, were the last. The same gentle courtesy met us both. We were given the freedom of the village, invited into the houses, and allowed to climb to the roof-tops, with the governor's pretty little daughter as our guide. Taos, like all pueblos, has a republican form of government, and a communal life which works out very peaceably. Annually the two candidates for governor run a foot-race, one from each division of the town, and the political race is indeed to the swift. Perhaps they get as good governors by that method as by our own.

Taos, like all Gaul, is divided into tres partes, quarum unam the Cubists incolunt. No place could be more ideal for an artist's colony, with scenery unsurpassed, air clear and sparkling, living inexpensive, picturesque models to be had cheaply, and little adobe houses simply asking to become studios. San Geronimo de Taos, on the Pueblo Creek belongs to the Indians. Ranchos de Taos, where a fine old mission church, bulwarked with slanting plaster buttresses has stood since 1778, at the lower end of the straggling town, is given over to Mexicans. The middle section, once famous as the home town of Kit Carson, proclaims by its blue and lavender doorways, mission bells, fretted balconies and latticed windows, the wave of self-consciousness that had inundated American Taos. But it has its own charm and adapts itself admirably to the native dwellings. Kit Carson's old home, facing a magnificent view over the river, has become a sumptuous studio; and scaling down from that to the most humble loft over a stable, every available nook in the town is commandeered by artists, where every style of art is produced from canvasses out-niggling Meissonier to the giddy posters of the post-post-impressionists. Regardless of results, they are lucky artists who have the pleasant life and brisk ozone

ARTIST'S STUDIO IN TAOS, NEW MEXICO.
No place could be more ideal for an artist colony.

CORONADO WAS THE FIRST WHITE MAN TO VISIT THIS ANCIENT PUEBLO
AT TAOS, NEW MEXICO

of Santa Fé in the winter, enjoy the picturesque Indian dances in spring and fall, and in summer paint and loaf in the purple glory of the Taos mountains, cooled by frosty air blowing from the two and a half mile snow line.

CHAPTER XIV

SAYING GOOD-BY TO BILL

AS the spring sun daily pushed the snow line higher up toward the peaks of the Sangre de Cristo, and the time approached when we must leave Santa Fé, Toby and I grew sad at heart. We knew we must begin to think of saying good-by to Bill.

For Bill was Santa Fé's most remarkable institution. He was surgeon general to all maimed cars in a radius of twenty miles. We had encountered mechanics competent but dishonest, and mechanics honest but incompetent, and were to meet every other variety,—careless, sloppy, slow, stupid, and criminally negligent, but to Bill belongs the distinction of being the most honest, competent and intelligent mechanic we met in eleven thousand miles of garage-men. Hence he shall have a chapter to himself.

When we discovered Bill, we permitted ourselves the luxury of a complete overhauling, and he, after one keen non-committal glance at our mud-caked veteran, silently shifted his gum, wheeled the car on to the turntable, got under it and stayed there two weeks. Three months of mud, sand, and water had not crippled the valiant "old lady," but had dented her figure, and left her with a hacking cough. Her dustpan had been discarded, shred by shred, three spring leaves had snapped, the gear chain, of whose existence I learned for the first time, rattled; the baking sun had shrunk the rear wheels so that they oozed oil, the batteries needed recharging, the ignition had not been the same since the adventure of the mud-hole, and there were other suspected complications. Besides which, all the tires flapped in the breeze, cut to sheds by frozen adobe ruts, and a few tire rims had become bent out of shape. A thrifty garageman could have made the job last a year.

Now Bill had two signs which every good mechanic I ever knew bears,—a calm manner, and prominent jawbones. Whenever, during our hobo-ing we drove into a garage and were greeted by a man with a grease smudge over his right eye, and a lower jaw which suggested an indignant wisdom tooth, we learned to say confidently and without further parley, "Look the car over, and do anything you think best." It was infallible. Nor was our confidence in Bill's jaw-bone misplaced, for at the fortnight's end, Bill rolled her out of the garage, shining, sleek and groomed, purring like a tiger cat, quiet, rhythmic and bursting with unused power. He had taken off the wheels, removed the cylinder heads, repaired the ignition, put in new gear chains and spark plugs, adjusted the carburetor to the last fraction, loosened the steering wheel, removed the old lady's wheeze entirely, and done the thousand and one things we had repeatedly paid other garagemen to do and they had left undone. He had finished in record time, and my eye, long practised in the agony of computing the waste motions of mechanics, had noted Bill's sure accuracy and unhurried speed. Not content with this much, he sent in a reasonable bill, in which he failed to add in the date or charge us for time of his which other people had wasted. In

fact, nobody dared waste Bill's time. Over his work-
bench hung a sign, "Keep out. Regardless of your personality, this means YOU!" We took a trial spin, up a
cork-screw and nearly vertical hill, the local bogey, and
made it on high. I thanked Bill almost with tears, for
being a gentleman and a mechanic.

"I always claim," answered Bill, modestly, "that a
man aint got no right to take other people's money, unless
he gives 'em something in return. When I'm on a job,
I try to do my best work, and I don't figure to charge no
more than it's worth."

Ah, Bill! If every garageman in this free country
adopted your code, what a motorist's Paradise this might
be! Almost weeping we said good-by to Bill that day
—our last but one, we thought, in Santa Fé. We would
have liked to take him with us, or at least to have
found him awaiting us at each night's stop, and Bill
was gallant enough to say he would like to go.

With two friends, we had planned an excursion to
Chimayo, where in the Mexican half of the town are
made soft, hand-woven rugs, famous the world over.
On the way, we stopped at Pojoaque, for the purpose of
seeing the old road-house made famous by old M. Boquet
of fragrant memory, when Santa Fé was an army post,
and officers rode out to lively supper parties here. A
tangled orchard and flower garden, a well renowned for
its pure water, and the quaint little Spanish widow of M.
Boquet are all that is left of what was once a ship-shape
inn where people loved to stop. The rest is cobwebs and
rubbish. But any spot where gaiety has been enhanced
by good food is always haunted by memories of former
charm.

At the sleepy Indian pueblo of Nambé, now fast diminishing, we forded a trickle of a stream, hardly wide enough to notice, which sported down from the hills. Then out into a sandy waste, surrounded by red buttes, we drove. And then we drove no further. On a hilltop the car gently ceased to move, even as it had done outside of Chandler. For a hot hour we examined and experimented, till we finally fastened the guilt on the ignition. We were ten miles from everywhere, and which were the shorter ten miles we were not exactly sure. Like the hypothetical donkey, starving between two bales of hay, we wasted time debating in which direction to go for help. An Indian riding by on a scalded looking pony we interrogated, but like all of his race, the more he was questioned the less he contributed. Much against his will, we rented his pony, and while the man of our party rode bareback to Pojoaque and the nearest telephone, we coaxed the pony's owner from his sulks with sandwiches. Would that we had saved them for ourselves!

Two hours later, Bill rattled up, in a car shabby as a shoemaker's child's shoes, and as disreputable as the proverbial minister's son. Remembering our premature farewell, he grinned, lifted the hood of the car, nosed about for a moment, called sharply to his ten-year-old assistant for tools, and in two minutes the engine was running. Smiling just as cheerfully as if his farewell appearance had not cost us twenty dollars, Bill started his car, and wished us good luck.

"I wish we could take you with us, Bill," I said.

"I sure wish I could go," said Bill.

"Well, good-by, Bill."

"Good-by, and over the top," said Bill, driving off.

"I hate to say good-by to Bill," said Toby and I, to each other.

Thus delayed, it was twilight when we reached the old Sanctuario, famous as the Lourdes of America. Inside, its whitewashed walls displayed crutches and other implements of illness, as witness to the cures effected by the shrine. The interior as of most Mexican churches, was filled with faded paper flowers and tawdry gilt pictures of saints. Outside, twin towers and a graceful balcony, and a walled churchyard shaded by giant cottonwoods gave the church a distinction apart from all its miracles. At a brook nearby, a majestic, black-shawled Mexican madonna filled her *olla,* mildly cursing us that the fee we gave for opening the gate was no larger, lest we should realize it had been too large.

Across the plaza stood a fine example of a built-up kiva or *estufa,* and nearby we dared a glance, in passing, at a morado. But we had come to see and perhaps buy rugs,—those wooly, soft blankets at which the heart of the collector leaps. During the day, however, the Santa Cruz, which divides Mexican from Indian Chimayo, had risen from the melting of snows in the mountains, and we could only feast our eyes on the lovely hill-lined valley, with its greens and mauves, its cobalt hills and blossoming apricots. There was positively no way to cross. I remembered that Bill said he too had been delayed at Pojoaque by swollen streams. But the idea of hurrying home did not occur to us, as it might have to a native. We communicated our interest in rugs to little Indian boys and handsome swart Mexicans, who stripped the floors and beds of their great-grandparents, learning that we sought antiques. We soon had a choice of the greasiest and most tattered rugs the town afforded, but nothing worth purchasing. We were on the wrong side of the river, and out of luck. Relinquishing the idea of seeing rug-weaving in process, we at last turned homeward, with a new moon menacing us over our left shoulder.

Passing through a beautiful little canyon, over a road which tossed us like a catboat in a nor'easter, we again came, at dusk, to sleeping Nambé, and the brink of the stream. Toby, who was driving, plunged boldly in, without preliminary reconnoitre. We afterward agreed that here she made a tactical error. The trickle of the morning, had risen to our hubs. To make matters worse, the stream ran one way, and the ford another. We all hurled directions at the unhappy Toby.

"Keep down stream!"

"Follow the ford!"

"Back up!"

"Go ahead,—*go ahead!*"

Toby hesitated. Now in crossing a swift stream, to hesitate is to lose. The car struck the current mid-stream, the water dashed up and killed the engine, and the "old lady" became a Baptist in regular standing. Toby saw she was in for it, I could tell by the guilty look of the back of her neck. She tried frantically to reverse, but no response came from the submerged engine.

"Toby," I cried in anguish, "start her, quick!" And then I regret to say I lapsed into profanity, exclaiming, "Oh, devil, devil, darn!"

In a moment, everyone was standing on the seats, and climbing thence to the mudguard. Our cameras, coats, pocketbooks, and the remains of some lettuce sandwiches floated or sank according to their specific gravity. I plunged my arm down to the elbow, and brought up two ruined cameras, and a purse which a week later was still wet. Meanwhile the others had climbed from the mudguard to the radiator, fortunately half out of water, and thence jumped ashore. Before I could follow suit, the water had risen to the back seat, and I scrambled ashore soaked to the knees. We were on the wrong side of the stream from Nambé, and the river was too deep for wading. Finally the man of the party risked his life, or at least the high boots which were the joy of his life, and reached the opposite shore, where lay the pueblo. After a long interval he returned with two Indians who led a team of horses across.

Trained as I have said poor Lo, or Pueb-Lo, to make a bad pun, is in matters of the spirit, in mechanics he has not the sense of a backward child of three years. These two attached a weak rope to the car, where it would have the least pulling power and the greatest strain, drove the horses off at a wrong angle,—and broke the rope. For two hours, with greatest good nature and patience, they alternately attached chains and broke them until we had exhausted the hardware of the entire town. It was now long after midnight. Having reached the point where we hoped the car would sink entirely and save us further effort, we accepted the Indian's offer of two beds for the ladies and a shakedown for the man, and went weary and supperless to bed. Toby and I were used to going supperless to bed, but it was hard on our two friends to whom we had meant to give a pleasant day.

As we entered the bedroom into which the Indian proudly ushered us, I exclaimed "Toby!" The room contained two large beds, a piano between them, some fearful crayon portraits of Nambé's older settlers, and a scarlet Navajo rug. Nothing remarkable about the room, except that the piano and the two lace-covered beds denoted we were being entertained by pueblo aristocracy. But on that morning, being one of those people who do not start the day right until they have unloaded their dreams on some victim, I had compelled Toby to listen to the dream which had held me prisoner the previous night. In it, we had started off into the desert with the "old lady," and traveled until we found ourselves in a sea of sand. Then, for some reason not clear when I woke, we abandoned the car, and set out afoot over wastes of sand, in which we sank to our ankles. All day we walked, and at night exhausted, found shelter in a crude building. Presently, the men in our party returned to say they had found beds for the women, but must themselves sleep on the ground. Then they led us into a room. And in this room were two beds, a piano, some crayon portraits with gimcrack ornaments on the wall, and on the floor a brilliant crimson rug. The arrangement of the furniture in the real and the dream world was identical. In my dream I also had a vivid consciousness of going to a strange and uncomfortable bed, tired and hungry. Now a psychoanalyst once told me that science does not admit the prophetic dream as orthodox. Yet our little excursion, ending so disastrously, had not been planned till after I told my dream to Toby. My own firm belief is that our guardian angels were violating the Guardian Angels' Labor Union Laws, working overtime to send us a warning. Would we had taken it!

This night, however, our dreams were broken. Indians are the most hospitable people in the world, especially the Pueblos, long trained to gracious Spanish customs. These simple hosts of ours had made us free of all they possessed. We could not properly blame them if their possessions made free with us. Their hospitality was all right; just what one would expect from the Indian,—grave and dignified. But their Committee of Reception was a shade too effusive. They came more than half-way to meet us. Perhaps in retribution for her imprudent dash into the river, its members confined most of their welcome to Toby, with whom I shared one bed. She woke me up out of a sound sleep to ask me to feel a lump over her left eye.

"I would rather not," I said, feeling rather cold toward Toby just then. "I prefer not to call attention to myself. Would you mind moving a little further away?"

"I must say you're sympathetic," sniffed Toby.

"If you had looked before you leaped, you wouldn't be needing my sympathy."

It was our first tiff. A moment later she jumped up as if in anguish of spirit.

"I can't stand this any longer," she said, referring not to our quarrel, but to a more tangible affliction, which we afterward named Nambitis,—with the accent on the penult,—"I'm going to sleep on the floor."

"Perhaps it would be as well," I answered.

Toby made herself a nice bed on the adobe floor with old coats and rugs, and we went to rest,—at least ninety-five out of a possible hundred of us did. For some reason we sprang gladly out of bed next morning, to find that our hosts had taken the trouble to prepare us a liberal breakfast.   The lump over Toby's left eye had spread, giving her a leering expression, but otherwise she was again her cheerful self.   The rest of the party suggested it was hardly tactful for her to show herself wearing such an obvious reproach to our hosts on her countenance, and advised her to forego breakfast.   Toby rebelled.   She replied that she had only eaten two sandwiches since the previous morning, and was faint from loss of blood, and was going to have her breakfast, lump or no lump.   Toby is like Phil May's little boy,— she "do make a Gawd out of her stummick."   I on the contrary can go two or three days without regular food, with no effect except on my temper.   So we all sat down to a breakfast neatly served on flowered china, of food which looked like white man's food, but was so highly over-sugared and under-salted that we had difficulty in eating it.

Our host informed us the river had been steadily rising all night.   He doubted whether we should see any signs of our car.   His doubts confirmed a dream which had troubled me all night, wherein I had waked, gone to the river, and found the old lady completely covered by the turgid flood.   I dreaded to investigate, for when one dreams true, dreams are no light matter.   Somewhat fortified by breakfast, we went to view the wreck.   With mingled relief and despair, we found my dream only about 80 per cent true.   The radiator, nearest to shore, lay half exposed.   The car sagged drunkenly on one side. The tonneau was completely under water, but we could still see the upper half of the back windows.

While others rode eight miles to telephone, we stood on the bank, breathlessly watching to see whether the water line on those windows rose or fell. The Indians told us the river would surely rise a little, as the snow began to melt. But Noah, looking down upon fellow sufferers, must have interceded for us. Inch by inch, the windows came into full view. The worst would not happen. A chance remained that Bill could rescue us before the river rose again. Bill was our rainbow, our dove of promise, our Ararat.

An hour later, he rattled up to the opposite bank, threw us a sympathetic grin, and got to work. It was a pleasure to watch Bill work. It is a pleasure to watch anyone work provided one has no share in it oneself, but some people weary one by puttering. I could watch Bill on the hardest kind of job, and feel fresh and fairly rested when he finished. He always knew beforehand what he intended to do, and did it deliberately and easily. He first drove two stakes into the ground, some distance apart, attached a double pulley to them, and to the front bar of the car, the only part not under water, and he and his assistants pulled gradually and patiently till from across the river we could see the sweat stand out on their brows. In ten minutes, we were astonished to see the half drowned giant move slightly. Hope rose as the river fell. Bill took another reef in his trousers and the pulley, then another and another, and at last the old lady groaned, left her watery bed, shook herself, and clambered up on dry land.

We crossed on horseback to the other side and waited with a sick internal feeling, while Bill removed the wheels and examined the damage.

THE CAR SAGGED DRUNKENLY ON ONE SIDE.

FORDING A RIVER NEAR SANTA FE

Crossing fords, to our hubs, which yesterday were mere trickles and to-morrow would be raging torrents

ON THE WAY TO GALLUP

Jack and all sank in the soft quicksand beneath the weight of the car.

"Everything seems all right,—no harm done," remarked Toby, with hasty cheerfulness, emerging from the taciturnity resulting from one closed eye and a general atmospheric depression among the rest of us. Her remark showed that she now expected to assume her usual place in society.

"If anything," I answered bitterly, "the car is improved by its bath."

The poor old wreck stood sagging heavily on one spring, two wheels off, the cushions water-logged, and a foot of mud and sand on the tonneau floor and encrusting the gears. Maps, tools, wraps, chains, tires and the sickly remains of our lunch made a sodden salad, liberally mixed with Rio Grande silt. Sticks and floating refuse had caught in the hubs and springs, and refused to be dislodged. A junk man would have offered us a pair of broken scissors and a 1908 alarm clock for her as she stood, and demanded cash and express prepaid. I think Toby gathered that my intent was sarcasm, for she relapsed into comparative silence, while in deep gloom we watched Bill scoop grit out of the gears. I braced myself to ask a question.

"Can you save her, Bill?"

"Well," Bill cast a keen blue eye at the remains, "the battery's probably ruined, and the springs will have to be taken apart and the rust emoried off, and the mud cleaned out of the carburetor and engine, and the springs rehung, and if any sand has got into the bearin's you'll never be through with the damage, and the cushions are probably done for,—life's soaked out of them.'

As Bill spoke, the Rainbow Bridge, for which we had planned to start in a few days, became a rainbow indeed, but not of hope.   The Grand Canyon, the Hopi villages, Havasupai Canyon, Yellowstone, Glacier Park!   Their red cliffs and purple distances shimmered before our eyes as dear, lost visions, and faded, to be replaced by a heap of junk scattered in a lone arroyo, and two desolate female figures standing on the Albuquerque platform, waiting for the through train east.

"Well, Bill, will you make us an offer for her as she stands?"

Bill squinted at her, and shook his head, "Don't think I'd better, ma'am."

The day shone brilliant blue and gold, and the valley of cottonwood sparkled like emeralds, but all seemed black to us.   Toby looked almost as guilty as she deserved to look, and that, though unusual and satisfactory, was but a minor consolation.

"Too bad," said Bill, sympathetically, "that you didn't sound the river before you tried to cross."

"It was indeed," I said, without looking at anyone.

"I didn't hear *you* suggest stopping," said Toby.   One would have thought she would be too crushed to reply after Bill's remark, but you never can tell about Toby.

We watched Bill methodically and quickly replace the wheels, shovel out the sand and mud, put the tools in place, wipe the cushions, and put his foot on the starter, the last as perfunctorily as a doctor holds a mirror to the nostrils of a particularly dead corpse.   Instantly, the wonderful old lady broke into a quiet, steady purr!   A cheer rose from the watchers on the river bank, in which ten little Indian boys joined, and Toby and I embraced and forgave each other.

We did not say good-by to Bill.   We had a rendezvous

with Bill at the garage for the following morning. Fearful lest the engine stop her welcome throb, we jumped into the car, and drove the sixteen miles home, up steep hills and down, under our own power. Fate had one last vicious jab in store for us. Five minutes after starting, a thunder cloud burst, and rained on us till we turned into our driveway, when it ceased as suddenly as it started.

What was left of the car, I backed out of the garage next morning. Toby stood on the running board, and directed me how to avoid a low hanging apricot tree, her eye and her spirits as cocky as ever.

"All clear!" she called. I backed, and crashed into the tree. A splintering, sickening noise followed. The top of the car, the only part which had previously escaped injury, showed beautiful jagged rents and the broken end of a rod bursting through the cloth.

For three days, Toby discoursed on photography, sunsets, burros, geology and Pima baskets, but nobody could have guessed from anything she said that automobiles had yet been invented. At last she gave me a chance.

"In driving over a desert road with sharp turns," she said confidently, "the thing is to——"

"Toby!" It was too good an opening. "As a chauffeur, you make a perfect gondolier."

Bill presented us at the end of a week with a sadder but wiser car, a little wheezy and water-logged, but still game. When we steered it out of the garage which had become our second home in Santa Fe, we did not say good-by to Bill. We couldn't afford to. On reaching Albuquerque safely, we sent him a postcard.

"Dear Bill:—The car went beautifully. We wish we could take you with us!"

CHAPTER XV

LAGUNA AND ACOMA

IN spite of Toby's making the slight error of driving fourteen miles with the emergency brake on, we seemed to have placed misadventure behind us for a brief season at least. We coasted the twenty-three switch backs of La Bajada hill, now an old story, and returned for the night to the Harvey hotel at Albuquerque, where the transcontinental traveler gets his first notion of Western heat, and wonders if he is in any danger from the aborigines selling pottery on the railroad platforms, and speculates as to whether the legs of the squaws can possibly fill the thick buckskin leggins they parade in so nonchalantly. If it is his first visit West, he little realizes how Harveyized these picturesque creatures have become, and he snatches eagerly at what he thinks may be his last chance to pick up some curios. The pottery, from the village of Acoma, is genuine, though of a tourist quality. The white doeskin legs are also genuine, although many pueblo women have ceased to wear them except to meet the twelve o'clock. They always inspire in me an awed respect, worn under the burning sun with such *sang froid*. The explanation for this indifference to discomfort lies in the fact that a lady's social prominence is gaged by the number of doeskin wrappers she displays, as the Breton peasant is measured by her heavy petticoats, and a Maori belle by her tattooing: *il faut souffrir pour être belle*.

The Indians furnished the most entertaining spectacle of modern, prosperous Albuquerque, whose solid virtues intrigue the hobo but little. We took advantage of her porcelain bathtubs, and then hastened on into a more primitive region, which became wilder and wilder as we neared the Arizona boundaries. Only two little adventures befell; neither had a proper climax. A two day old lamb, wobbly and frightened, had lost its mother, and wandered bleating pitifully from one sheep to another, who treated it with cold disdain. It finally approached our car as if it had at last reached its goal; but asking for nourishment, it received gasoline, and seeking woolly shelter, it was startled by metal walls. Piteously weak and terrified, the thumping of its heart visibly stirring its coat, it fled away in distress, with us at its frail little heels. Yet run our fastest, we could not catch it, though we tried every subterfuge. We baa-ed as if we were its mother, and it approached cautiously, to scamper off when our hands shot out to catch it. Poor little fool! It had not the courage to trust us, though it longed to, and after a hot and weary hour, we had to leave it to starve. As we started off, another car shot past us, challengingly, its very tail light twinkling insolence. A dark and handsome face leered back at us, with a full-lipped, sinister smile. At the next settlement, where we stopped to buy food, this half-breed Mephisto was there lounging against the counter, and looking at us with the look that is like a nudge. When we left, he swaggered after, and kept his car for some miles close behind ours. The country was so wild that we saw a coyote sneaking through the sage, and not long after, a wildcat disappeared into a clump of piñon. Beyond the orange cliffs we saw in the distance, we could expect no human assistance, and it was uncomfortably near nightfall. Then, to our relief, the road branched, one fork leading to a silver mine. Our Mexican shot into it, giving us a parting grimace. Slight enough, this was our first and last encounter with that particular sort of danger.

At sunset we came to Laguna, ancient and gray as the rocks on which it sprawled, its church tower picked out against a golden sky. This is the first Kersian pueblo met going from east to west. Ancient as it seems, it is the offspring of the parent pueblo of Acoma, which itself descended from an older town situated on the Enchanted Mesa. "Laguna" seems a sad misnomer for this waste of sand and rock. But years ago, what is now desert was a country made fertile by a great lake. When a dissension arose in old Acoma, as frequently happened among these "peaceful" Indians, the dissatisfied members of the tribe left Acoma, and settled near the lake. Here they stayed from habit long after the lake had dried and its green shores became barren sand-heaps, until the new town became as weather-beaten as its parent. This is why, unlike most pueblos, Laguna and Acoma share the same dialect.

Laguna, built on a solid ledge of mother rock, attracts attention by the notched beauty of its skyline. It is entertainingly terraced on irregular streets, forced to conform to the shape of its rock foundation. A ramble about town brings unexpected vistas. You start on what seems to be the street, trail along after a shock haired little savage in unbuttoned frock, and suddenly find yourself in a barnyard, gazing with a flea bitten burro upon the intimacies of Pueblo family life on the roof of the

PUEBLO WOMEN GRINDING CORN IN METATE BINS.
The women are the millers who grind the varied colored corn In lava bins.

PUEBLO WOMAN WRAPPING DEER-SKIN LEGGINS.
A lady's social prominence is gauged by the thickness of doeskin wrappers she displays.

house next door. Through the village come sounds of the leisurely tasks of the evening. The mellow, throaty boom of the tombé, and syncopated rhythm of the corn-grinding song come from the open doors, framed in the warm glow of firelight. A dead coyote, waiting to be dressed, hangs by the tail from a *vega*. Children play in the streets. The shifting hills of shimmering sand, moonlight silver in the frosted air of morning, and golden at noon, turn from rose to violet. Above the village rise pencilled lines of smoke from ancient fireplaces. Towering above everything stands the white mass of the old mission, with a gleaming cross of gold cutting sharply against the glory of the west.

Laguna owns no hotel, so Toby and I sought out the missionary, whose ruddy, white-haired countenance and stalwart frame bespoke his Vermont origin, and whose hospitality bore the hearty flavor of Green Mountain farmhouses. At something less than what is called a pittance, he had worked for years among the Indians of the pueblo, and at the nearby tubercular sanitarium for government Indians. He seemed to feel no superiority over his charges, and showed none of the complacent cant and proselyting zeal which distinguishes too many reservation missionaries. He had retained with delightful fidelity the spirit of the small community pastor working on terms of equality with his flock,—raising the mortgage, furnishing the church parlor, encouraging the Sewing Circle exactly as he would have done back in Vermont. As he told us of his work the yellow waste and glaring sunshine, squat 'dobe houses and alien brown figures faded, and we seemed to see a white spire with gilded weathervane, and cottages with green blinds; we smelled lilacs and ginger cookies, and walked in a lane of flaming maples.

"The work is slow here," he said. "One needs patience. Yet looking back over the years results are gratifying. Gratifying. Souls who walked in darkness have been won to Christ. Only last night, I attended the bedside of a dear sister,—the oldest person I believe in the state. Her years number one hundred and twenty-six. She confessed her faith and will die in Christ."

"Have you had many conversions?" we asked.

"Well,—as numbers go,—not so many. Perhaps forty, possibly more. They will go back to their own ways. Yet they are a splendid people to work with,—a delightful people. I have many real friends among them. The parish is slowly improving. We have paid off the mortgage, and are now putting an addition on the church. The men have erected the frame, and when the ladies of the parish finish planting, they will put the plaster on the walls."

Thus imperceptibly had the good man merged New Mexico with New England. At the village school next morning we saw another phase of the white man's standards grafted upon the red man. The teacher, a Pueblo Indian woman and a graduate of Carlisle, wife of a white man in the neighborhood, in spotless print dress and apron was showing twenty little Indians the locality of Asia Minor. They were neat and shining and flatteringly thrilled by the presence of visitors.

"And now," said their beaming teacher, when we had heard their bashful recitations, "you must hear the children sing."

We heard them. The difficulty would have been to

avoid hearing them. Bursting with delight, each of the twenty opened their mouths to fullest capacity, and twenty throats emitted siren tones,—not the sirens of the Rhineland, but of a steel foundry. They began on "Come, Little Birdie, Come," though it is doubtful if anything less courageous than a bald-headed eagle would have dared respond to the invitation. Toby clutched me, and I her, and thus we kept each other from bolting out of the door. We even managed a frozen smile of approbation as we listened to the discordant roar, like the voices of many hucksters, which issued from their mouths. A white child would have warped his throat permanently after such effort, but these roly-poly babies finished in better condition than they began.

"I am going to let them sing one more song," said the teacher when we rose hastily. "They don't have visitors every day."

They sang "Flow Gently, Sweet Afton," and if Sweet Afton had been Niagara it would have wakened Mary less than the stertorous warning which bellowed from that schoolroom. Then a dozen brown hands waved in the air, and a clamor arose for other bits of their repertoire to be heard. Teacher was smilingly indulgent, proud of her pupils and anxious to give them and the visitors a good time. So we were treated to Old Black Joe, and Juanita, and other sad ditties, which never seemed sadder than now.

"And now you must show these ladies you are all good Americans," said the teacher. We all stood and sang the Star Spangled Banner. The children showed individuality; they did not keep slavishly to one key. Each child started on the one that suited him best, and held it

regardless of the others.   By the time they were well
started, every note in the scale was represented, including most of the half notes.   Our patriotism ended in a
dismal polychromatic howl, and the sudden silence which
followed nearly deafened us.   We had forgotten there
was such a thing as silence.

What a pity the government does not encourage the
Indian to cultivate his own arts, instead of these alien and
uncomprehended arts of the white man!   In his ceremonial dances, he is lithe, graceful, and expressive; when
he tries the one-step and waltz he is clumsy and ludicrous.   His voice, strident, discordant and badly-placed
when he attempts second-rate "civilized" music, booms
out mellow and full-throated, perfectly placed in the
nasal cavity, when he sings Indian melodies whose tan-
talizing syncopations, difficult modulations, and finely
balanced tempo he manages with precision.   His music fits
his surroundings.   To hear it chanted in a wide and lonely
desert scene, to watch its savage, untamed vigor move
feet and bodies to a climax of ecstatic emotion, until it
breaks all bounds and produces the passion it is supposed
to symbolize is to understand what music meant to the
world, before it was tamed and harnessed and had its
teeth extracted.   To wean the Indian of this means of
self-expression, and nurse him on puerile, anaemic melodies,—it is stupid beyond words, and unfortunately, it is
of a piece with the follies and stupidities our government
usually exhibits in its dealings with its hapless wards.   If
I seemed to laugh it was not at those enthusiastic brown
babies, rejoicing in their ability to produce civilized dis-
cords, but at the pernicious system which teaches them
to be ignorant in two languages.

We finally left the strains of patriotism behind us, as we drove across the level plain to Acoma. Two tracks in a waste of sand made the road to the Sky City. A day sooner, or a day later, the wind would shift the fine grained beach sand, left there by some long vanished ocean, and block the road with drifted heaps; today, by the aid of our guide Solomon's shovel, we were just able to plough through it.

Dotting the lonely landscape, flocks of white sheep and shaggy goats were tended by Indian boys with bows and arrows. They fitted the pastoral scene; for a thousand years, perhaps, the ancestors of these same flocks were watched over by the ancestors of these boys in blue overalls. Suddenly to our left, rising from the flat plain, we saw blocked against the sky a shimmering tower of soft blue and gold, seeming too evanescent for solid rock. Its sheer walls thrust upward like the shattered plinth of a giant's castle from a base of crumbling tufa, in itself a small mountain. It was the mesa of Old Acoma, called by the Indians the Enchanted Mesa.

I believe that two Harvard students of archæology once reached the summit of this perpendicular rock, by means of a rope ladder shot to the top. But no white man by himself has for centuries gained a foothold on its splintered walls. Yet once, from legend borne out by bits of broken pottery and household utensils found at the base of the mesa, a large and flourishing Indian village lived on its summit in safety from marauders. A stairway of rock, half splintered away from the main rock was the only means of access to the village. A similar stairway may be seen today in the Second Mesa of the Hopi villages.

Up these stairs, old women toiled with filled *ollas* on their heads, and little boys and men clambered down them to work in the fields below. It is their ghosts the Indians fear to meet between sunset and sunrise. For one day, while the men were absent plowing or tending their herds, a bolt of lightning struck the stairway and in a moment it lay the same crumbling heap of splintered rock one sees today at the base of the mesa. To envision the horrors that followed imagine a sudden catastrophe destroying all stairways and elevators in the Flatiron building, while the men were away at lunch, and the stenographers left stranded on the top floor. The case of Old Acoma was even more pitiful, for those left on the top were old men, helpless from age, women and babies. They lived, ghastly fear and despair alternating with hope as long as their supply of corn stored in the barren rock held out,—perhaps a month, perhaps longer. Then one by one they died, while their men on the plain below tried frantically to reach them, and at last gave up hope. No wonder that when the towering mass which is their monument fades from blue and gold to grayish purple, the Indians turn their ponies' heads far to one side, and make a loop rather than be found in its neighborhood.

Across the plateau a few miles from the Enchanted Mesa stands another mesa, longer and lower than the other, reached from the ground by several paths. Here the survivors transferred their shattered lives, built a village like the old one, and in time became the ancestors of the present Acomans. While we drove toward it, listening to the story our guide told of that early tragedy in his exact Carlisle English, we nearly added three

ACOMA, NEW MEXICO.

Dotting the lonely landscape flocks of white sheep and shaggy goats were tended by Indian boys with bows and arrows.

BURROS LADEN WITH FIRE-WOOD, SANTA FE, NEW MEXICO.

more ghosts to those already haunting the plain. Ahead of us the road had caved in over night, as roads have a way of doing in this country, leaving a yawning canyon thirty feet deep, toward which we sped at twenty miles an hour. Our brakes stopped us at the edge. I hastened to back, and make a side detour around the chasm, where in time our tracks would become the road, until some other freshet should eat into and undermine the porous ground. Roads in New Mexico are here today and gone tomorrow, cut off in their flower by a washout or a sandstorm, or simply collapsing because they weary of standing up. A miss is always as good as a mile, and our close escape was worth singling out from a dozen others only because of its dramatic reminder of what happened in the dim past from almost the same cause, on that magnificent rock. Both the Enchanted Mesa and the gaping hole behind us pointed out the uncertainty of life, which seemed so eternal in that brilliant spring sunshine.

Less dominating than the haunted mesa, New Acoma, which is, by the way, the oldest continuously inhabited town in the United States, reveals its towering proportions only at closer range. To view it best, it should be approached from the direction of Acomita. It stands 357 feet above the floor of the desert. Under its buttressed cliffs, a sheep corral and a few herder's huts help to measure its great height. In the lee of the rock we left the car to the mercy of a group of slightly hostile women filling their waterjars at the scum-covered spring. The Acomans are not noted for pretty manners or lavish hospitality. Probably if a second bolt of lightning were to approach Acoma, a committee from the Governor would refuse it admittance unless it paid a fee of five dollars. It is said that since the San Diego Exposition, when the Acomans acquired an inflated idea of the cash value of their picturesqueness, tourist gold must accompany tourist glances at their persons, their pottery, their village, their children, and even the steep, hard trail up to their little stronghold.

We thought we had almost earned the freedom of the town by our toilsome climb, first over a young mountain of pure sea sand in which we sank ankle deep, and then hand over hand up a steep ledge of rock, where ancient grooves were worn for fingers and toes to cling to. Centuries of soft shod feet had hollowed these footholds, and centuries of women and men had carried food and water and building materials over this wearisome trail. Yet the Acoman may be right in demanding toll. He has gone to infinite trouble through generations of hard labor to perfect the little stronghold where he preserves his precious individuality. The giant beams in his old church, the mud bricks and stone slabs for his houses, the last dressed sheep and load of groceries, the very dirt that covers his dead were brought to the summit on the backs of his tribe. Acoma to the native is not an insignificant village of savages, but by treaty with the United States an independent nation; proud of its past, serenely confident of its future. It is almost as large as Monte Carlo, or the little republic of Andorra; with the assertive touchiness which so often goes with diminutive size, both in people and nations. Being a nation, why should it not have the same right to say who shall enter its gates, and under what conditions, as the United States; that parvenu republic surrounding it?

Nevertheless the Acoman is not popular, even among

AT THE FOOT OF THE TRAIL, ACOMA.
(Enchanted Mesa in middle distance)
Less dominating than the haunted Mesa, New Acoma reveals its towering proportions
only on nearer approach.

THE ENCHANTED MESA, ACOMA, NEW MEXICO.
A shimmering tower of blue and gold, seeming too evanescent for solid rock.

Indians of other villages. Though neighboring towns, Laguna and Acoma always have swords drawn. The Acoman has a wide reputation for being surly and inhospitable, and I am willing to admit he does his best to live up to that reputation.

Many tourists have made the journey across the desert, and the climb to the mesa's top, only to be turned back or admitted at exorbitant fees. Luck was with us. We arrived on a day when the governor and all the men of the village were at work in the fields of Acomita, and only the women and children, as on the fateful day when the Enchanted Mesa was struck, remained in the village. Our guide, being from Laguna, spoke the dialect of the Acomans, and proved a doughty aid. Hardly had our heads shown above the rocky stairs when the gray landscape was suddenly peopled by women and children; the children clad in one gingham garment, or, if of tender age, in nothing save the proverbial string of beads, for even the smile was missing from their faces. Most of the women, short-skirted, with brilliant floating scarves on their heads, carried babies slung in knotted shawls. Their clamor at sight of Toby's camera required no knowledge of Acomese to be recognized as vituperative. They seemed as anxious to be photographed as a burglar is to have his thumb-prints taken. They were in fact so uncomplimentary that we recalled uneasily the Spanish monk who visited the town to make converts, and was hustled down to the plain by the short trail. No tourist uses this trail if he can help himself. It leads off the walled edge of the graveyard into space for three hundred odd feet, and ends on the rocks below. With great presence of mind the monk made a parachute of his flowing skirts, and alighted unhurt on the desert. Wearing khaki breeches, we closed the camera regretfully.

An Indian's prejudice against the camera arises logically from his theological belief that nature abhors a duplicate. With keenest powers of observation, he has noted that no two trees, no two leaves, no animals, even no blades of grass are exactly alike. Hence, when he makes a rug, a basket or an *olla*, he never duplicates it absolutely. Therefore he fears the camera's facsimile of Nature. If he allows himself to be photographed, he believes that something of himself passes into the black box, and thereafter his soul is halved of its power. If he afterward falls sick, undergoes misfortune or dies, he attributes it to this sin against an inexorable law of Nature. It all sounds childishly crude, yet a much respected man named Plato held a somewhat similar belief.

The difference between Plato and the Pueblo Indians lies less in their theology than in the ease with which a piece of silver changes its effectiveness. Among the river Pueblos, we could manufacture free-thinkers for a quarter apiece, but at Acoma, the process threatened to be as expensive as a papal dispensation. We appeased their gods by putting away our camera, but having satisfied the Church, we still had to deal with the State. The boldest and fattest citizeness of the Sky City, girt round with a sash of Kelly green, triumphantly produced a paper. Contrary to her manifest expectation, it did not shrivel us. It was written in sprawly Spanish on the reverse of a grocer's bill, and even at present prices no grocer's bill could intimidate us; we had seen too many of them. Solomon deciphered it as a command *in absentia* from the

Governor to pay five dollars a head or decamp at once.

Meanwhile the women, from ten years up, had brought us offerings—at a price—of pottery, in the making of which the Acomans excel all other tribes. Seeing a chance for a strategic compromise, through our faithful and secretly sympathetic Solomon, we announced we would either buy their pottery or pay the governor's toll, but we would not do both. We succeeded in maintaining an aspect of firm resolve, and after many minutes of debate, or what sounded like debate in any tongue, they wisely concluded that what was theirs was their own, and what was the governor's was something else entirely. We instantly compounded a crime against the State, and acquired many barbaric and gorgeously designed *ollas*.

We were now permitted to wander freely about the village, though the women after they sold their pottery retired to their houses and kept the doors closed. At the head of the village near where the trail enters, stands the old stone church, forbidding and bare as a Yorkshire hillside, built of giant timbers and small stones wedged hard together. It has stood there, looking off over the cliff, since 1699. Its ungracious front, unsoftened by ornament and eloquent of gruelling labor, fits the hard little village. Its really magnificent proportions tell a story of incredible effort; no wonder it looks proudly down on the desert from the height which it has conquered. Each timber, some large enough to make a burden for fifty men, each rock, each fastening and bolt, came up the trail we had taken nearly an hour to climb, on the shoulders of a little people hardly more than five feet tall. It is the only Indian mission I can remember built entirely of stone slabs, due perhaps to the difficulty of carrying up mud and water in sufficient quantities for the great eight foot thick walls and giant towers.

Between the church facade and the parapet which over-looks the desert is a crowded graveyard, containing in deep layers the bones of many generations of Acomans. Even the soil in which they rest was brought from the plain to form a bed over the mother rock of the mesa. Each year the level of the graveyard comes a trifle nearer the top of the parapet. Bits of pottery clutter the surface of the graveyard, not accidentally, as we at first imagined, but due to the Indian custom of placing choice ollas at the head and feet of the dead, to accompany them on their long journey. It is a bleak God's Acre: not a tree shades the bare surface. The four winds of heaven sweep it mercilessly, and the hot sun beats down on it. Yet a few feet beyond it becomes glorious, "with the glory of God, whose light is like unto a stone most precious, even like a jasper stone, clear as crystal." For the desert below is not a waste of sand, arid and monotonous, but a filtered radiance of light broken into pure color. Those who know only the beauty of green fields and blue waters cannot vision the unreal and heavenly splendor we saw from the Acoma churchyard, as convincing to the inner self as if Earth, that old and dusty thought of God, dissolved before our eyes and crystallized again into a song of light and color, as it was at the beginning.

Acoma, different as it was, reminded me oddly of the New England nature. At its heart lay a spiritual beauty, —this intense beauty of the desert,—and wrapped about it a shell of hard, chill unloveliness. The three little streets, dribbling off to the edge of the rock, had no wel-come for us. Its houses, two and three tiered, slabbed

A STREET IN ACOMA, NEW MEXICO
A flock of ducks splashed in a rainpool in the middle of the road.

THE ACOMA MISSION, NEW MEXICO.
At the head of the village stands the old stone church, built with giant timbers.

with flint instead of the more pleasing adobe, closed tight to our approach. The windows were mean and tiny, made before the era of glass, of translucent slabs of mica, roughly set in the walls. The houses, bleak and blackened, were roughly masoned of the same flint-like stone as the church. The few interiors we saw were barely furnished; a few bowls on the dirt floor, a lava corn bin,—nothing more. A flock of ducks splashed in a rainpool in the middle of the road; a mangy mongrel yapped at us, and women on the housetops scolded whenever Toby ventured to produce her camera. With their colored veils, red skirts and bright sashes they gave the village its only animation, as they brought out more and more bits of pottery to tempt us, carrying it carelessly on their heads down the ladders of the houses.

Solomon, the only man in sight, took every opportunity to efface himself whenever the bargaining raised a cross-ruff of feeling. He even ducked around a corner when a very stout lady, having sold us all her pottery, again brought up the subject of our paying five dollars admission. We appeased her by offering her a bribe to carry our purchases down to the car. While we were still halfway down, lifting our feet laboriously from the heavy sand, we saw her, a tiny round dot, with the *ollas* balanced above her floating turquoise scarf, stepping blithely and lightly over the desert floor.

"What a pity we couldn't get any pictures," I said to Toby, as we raced a thunder-cloud back to Laguna.

"H'm!" said Toby. "I took a roll of pictures while you kept them busy selling pottery. I got a beauty of the fat woman who made such a fuss. I must say it would be an improvement if half of *her* passed into the camera."

CHAPTER XVI

THE GRAND CANYON AND THE HAVASUPAI CANYON

A GLITTERING day, cool and sweet. Long shadows slanted through the scented Coconino Forest. The Gothic silences of the woods were clean of underbrush as an English park. Endless rows of pines had dropped thick mats of needles on the perfect road, so that our wheels made no sound. Beside these pines of northern Arizona our greener New England varieties seem mere scrubs. Then, unexpectedly, we passed the forest boundaries. Driving a few rods along the open road, we had our first sight of the Canyon at Grand View Point, with the sun setting over its amethyst chasm.

Years before, stepping directly from an eastern train, like most tourists I had seen the Canyon as my first stunned inkling of the extraordinary scale on which an extravagant Creator planned the West. This time, Toby and I had the disadvantage of coming newly to it after being sated with the heaped magnificence of the Rockies. Would its vastness shrink? Would it still take our breath away? I don't know why people want their breath taken away. In the end, they usually put up a valiant fight to keep it, but at other times, they constantly seek new ways to have it snatched from them. But we need not have worried about the Grand Canyon. It is big enough and old enough to take care of itself. It could drink up Niagara in one thirsty sip, and swallow Mt. Washington in a mouthful. It could lose Boston at one end, and New York at the other, and five Singer buildings piled atop each other would not show above the rim.

Not that I mean to attempt a description of the Canyon. To date, millions have tried it, from the lady who called it pretty, to the gentleman who pronounced it a wonderful place to drop used safety razor blades. They all failed. The best description of the Grand Canyon is in one sentence, and was uttered by an author who had never bought a post-card in El Tovar. "What is man, that Thou art mindful of him!"

As I cannot leave blank pages where the Canyon should be given its due, I must be content with skimming along its rim, and dipping here and there down among its mountain tops, like the abashed little birds that plunge twitteringly into its silences. It is so great a pity that most of those who "see" the Canyon do not see it at all. They arrive one morning, and depart the next. They walk a few rods along its edge at El Tovar, visit the Hopi house, and hear the Kolb Brothers lecture. If adventurous, they don overalls or divided skirts, mount a velvet-faced burro who seems afflicted with a melancholy desire to end his tourist-harassed existence by a side-step over Bright Angel. They speak afterward with bated breath—the tourists, not the burros—of the terrors of a trail which is a boulevard compared to some in the Canyon. The first moment, it is true, is trying, when it drops away so steeply that the burro's ears run parallel with the Colorado, but after several switchbacks they point heavenward again, until Jacob's Ladder is reached. Few trails in the West are so well graded and mended, and walled on the outside to prevent accident. Being cen-

trally situated, the Bright Angel gives an open vista of the
length and breadth of the Canyon where the coloring is
most brilliant and mountain shapes oddly fantastic. It is
an excellent beginning, but only a beginning after all.

There are so many ways to "do" the Canyon, that vast
labyrinth that could not be "done" in a thousand years!
The best way of all is to take a guide and disappear beneath the rim, following new trails and old down to the
level of the pyramidal peaks, to the plateau midway between rim and river, then wind in and out of the myriad
of small hilly formations clustering about these great
promontories which spread out from the mainland like
fingers from a hand. The river, a tiny red line when
seen from the top, froths and tumbles into an angry torrent half a mile wide. Its roar, with that of its tributaries, never is out of one's consciousness, echoing upon
the sounding board of hundreds of narrow chasms. It is
remarkable how soon the world fades into complete oblivion, and this rock-bound solitude is the only existence
which seems real. I once spent ten days on the plateau.
At the end of a week I had forgotten the names of my
most intimate friends, and on the ninth day I spent several minutes trying to recall my own name. I was so
insignificant a part of those terrific silences, to have a
name hardly seemed worth while. One could forget a
great sorrow here within a month. If I had to die within
a stated time, I should want to spend the interval within
the red walls of the Grand Canyon, the transition to
eternity would be so gradual.

All along the plateau there are by-trails and half-
trails and old trails where immense herds of wild burros
congregate, and the bleached bones of their ancestors lie

N THE GRAND CANYON OF THE COLORADO.

A NAVAJO MA D ON A PAINTED PONY.

thick on the ground. Not an hour's ride from the Bright Angel Trail is hidden one of the prettiest spots on earth. A little side path which few take leads from it around a great porphyry-colored cliff. Here we made camp after a dry, burning trip, our horses reeking with lather, and gasping with thirst. We rode along a little stream choked with cotton wood saplings.

"Ride ahead," ordered our sympathetic guide, who had a sense of the dramatic common to most of his profession. He wanted to give us the pleasure of discovering for ourselves. In a moment we came upon it, amazed. Gone was the arid Golgotha we had been struggling through. The stream had widened just where a rocky shelf dropped down to shelter it with a high wall. Low-growing trees and shrubs on the other side left an opening only wide enough to penetrate, and we suddenly entered a miniature grotto which seemed more the work of a landscape artist than of nature. The rock and shrubs enclosed completely a green pool, wide and deep enough to swim in. The water was cold and clear, its bottom fringed with thick velvety moss. The trees met overhead so densely that the sky showed only in tiny flecks on an emerald surface vivified by the reflection of sunlit leaves. The curved rock hiding the pool on three sides was covered arm-deep from top to bottom with maidenhair fern, and sprinkled through this hanging garden were the bright scarlet blossoms of the Indian paintbrush. As a crowning delight three little white cascades trickled through this greenery into the pool. A nymph would want to bathe here. We were not nymphs, but the weather was hot, the guide discreet and the pool so hidden it could not be seen ten feet away.

We camped gratefully over-night here. When Indians were plentiful in the Canyon this was one of their
favorite camps. Around the corner of the ledge, we came
upon some dry caves showing traces of former habitation. In a little stone oven they may have built I saw
the dusty tail of a rattler flicker and disappear among
the warm ashes of our fire. The refreshed horses
munched all night on the luxuriant grass, sometimes coming perilously near to stepping on our sleeping-bags.
Toby woke me at dawn. "Look!" One hundred asses
were ·circled about, gazing fascinated at us. When we
moved they galloped to the four winds.

From Bass Camp, kept by William Bass, one of the
pioneer guides of the Canyon, it is twenty odd miles by
an uncertain wagon trail to Hilltop, for which we started
the next morning. Very few of those thousands who visit
Grand Canyon yearly even know of the existence of
Havasupai Canyon, whose starting point is Hilltop.
Fewer visit it. Within its high, pink walls is a narrow,
fertile valley, watered by a light blue ribbon of water,—
the Land of the Sky Blue water, celebrated in the popular song by Cadman, the home of a little known and
very neglected tribe of Indians, the Havasupai. Havasupai means literally Children of the Blue Water. It is a
fairy vale, with grottoes and limestone caverns, seven
cataracts, three of them higher than Niagara, jungles of
cacti, mines of silver and lead, springs running now
above, now beneath the earth's surface, groves of tropical and semi-tropical fruit, in a summer climate as moist
and warm as the interior of a hothouse.

We reached this heaven over an unimproved trail so
nearly vertical that had it been any steeper our heads

THE LAND OF THE SKY-BLUE WATER, HAVASUPAI CANYON, ARIZONA

would have preceded our feet. Sometimes our horses balked, and had to be pulled forward by the bridle, the more nervous becoming panicky, and trying to turn back. It takes a bad trail to make a Western broncho do that. Frequently we had to dismount, and avoiding their hoofs, urge them to leap obstructing boulders. Except for the usual mesquite and sage, the trail was barren of vegetation, and the sun found us out and scourged us. Old travelers will speak of Havasupai Canyon as the hottest resort in this world, with even odds on the next. We rejoiced when, an hour later, we rested under a jutting ledge of cliffs where springs called Topocoba made a malodorous pool which had been fouled by many wild horses. Trees and overhanging rocks gave us moderate relief from the burning sun. We reclined, panting, while the horses' packs were loosened and they made friends with a band of Indian horses which roam the Canyon.

This oasis is one of the last links in the story of the Mountain Meadows Massacre, the horror of the fifties. Few know that when John Lee escaped by what afterward was named Lee's Ferry into the Grand Canyon, and thence by some devious route then known only to himself, and even now known to very few, to this refuge, he subsisted here for nearly two years on what he could shoot and trap while Federal officers scoured Utah for him. He found a rich vein of lead which is still unworked, and by melting ore from it traded it to the Navajos for ammunition. He finally worked his way back to Lee's Ferry, where he was recognized and captured. I was told that he was a relative,—I believe an uncle,—of Gen. Robert E. Lee.

We looked up, on reaching the bottom of the trail, to

find Hilltop almost directly overhead, or so it seemed. The descent at this part of the canyon actually measures about 2600 feet, and a plumb line dropped from a horizontal one drawn over the precipice for 42 rods would strike the bottom of the trail. Every bit of merchandise reaching the little village of the Havasupai must be carried on mule-back down this helter-skelter mass of boulders and winding ledges. Once an enterprising superintendent (of whom the Havasupai have had all too few) tried to import a melodeon for the benefit of the church services he instituted for the Indians. It reached the bottom, but it was too entangled with burro bones and twisted wires to be of any use except as a curiosity.

To reach the village, one follows the winding river bed for several miles between cliffs of beautifully colored sandstone, flame, pink or purple as the light plays on it. Some of these walls stand nearly a thousand feet high. The river, nearly dry now, and occasionally disappearing underground, had been a torrent in the spring, as we saw from the black water marks high over our heads. During the winter, the Indians are obliged to live in caves halfway up these walls, while the river inundates their villages, carrying away their flimsy willow houses on its tide. Some Havasupai take to Hilltop for the winter. Then when the river returns to its banks in spring and the Havasupai climb down from their chilly caves, the valley becomes a little Paradise, luxuriant and secret. The little pale blue stream is bordered all along its course with beds of watercress a dozen feet deep, sharpened deliciously by the lime water in which it grows. The bleak and thorny mesquite is transformed by masses of feathery leaves, and its heavily pollened yellow catkins fill the nar-

HORSEMAN IN HAVASUPAI CANYON, ARIZONA

The small dark spot on the edge of the floor of the canyon is the Horseman, giving
an idea of the scale

row valley with a scent like lilies and willow sap. The willows native to this region wear slenderer leaves than our home trees, and are festooned with fragrant lavender flowers, shaped like doll orchids. Never have I seen such lavishness of cactus in bloom. The prickly pear creeps with its giant claws across the sand, its red blossoms giving place to rows of unsightly purple bulbs, which later in the year make good eating.

We gathered armfuls of the watercress, our first bit of green food in weeks, for the West lives mainly by virtue of the can-opener, and has yet to discover the value of vitamines. Our horses splashed to their knees in the cooling stream. From time to time a sharp turn in the canyon displayed long vistas from lateral canyons, ending in far-off mountains which may have been part of the Father of all Canyons. Frequently the river dropped underground, as rivers do here, taking all the spring verdure with it, and reappeared again to make a veritable Happy Valley, the like of which few ever see on this earth.

Narrow at the entrance, it widens to an oval surrounded by thousand-foot walls glowing with color, its floor of new alfalfa shining like green enamel. Giant shady cottonwoods line the river and the lazy road meandering beside it along the valley. A deep blue sky, nearly hidden by sun-flecked leaves, arches over rose-red cliffs. Before the agency, women, with stolid dark faces and head-dresses made of four brilliant handkerchiefs sewn together into a long scarf, gathered, chattering with excitement at sight of the white women, making simple friendly overtures, offering us yellow plums, and giggling good-naturedly at our riding breeches. They themselves wore calico skirts billowing to the ground, in a style popular in the eighties.

The agent hospitably put his house at our disposal, though he was preparing to leave soon for another post. He was a homesick man. Life in Paradise is bad for the civilized. He and his wife were the only white people in the canyon, and he admitted that at times the Indians were too much with him;—while we were there, in fact, they camped all day on his lawn. And since all that he uses must be packed down the trail, he was obliged to dispense with most unessentials and many essentials. It must be admitted, too, that this reservation has been usually neglected by the Indian Commissioners, which makes life hard both for the agent and the tribe.

Though this natural garden has long harbored various tribes, the length of the Havasupais' tenancy and origin is uncertain. They are possible akin to the Wallapis and Yumas. Their history tells of a slow drifting northward from the Tonto basin, then the San Francisco peaks, and later, the Grand Canyon. Their skin is intensely brown, almost mulatto, their short, black hair in ill-kempt thatches. Having long known bitter poverty, they lack the beautiful silver trappings of their northern neighbors. The tribe has dwindled to a few hundred people. For years they had to travel more than a hundred miles to a government physician; consequently tubercular ulcers, trachoma and other revolting diseases ravaged the tribe, leaving the fortunate survivors so unbeautiful to behold, and unpleasant to live among that reservation agents, often inferior themselves, treated them with scant sympathy or open contempt. The men are fair farmers, and the women rival the Pomos in bas-

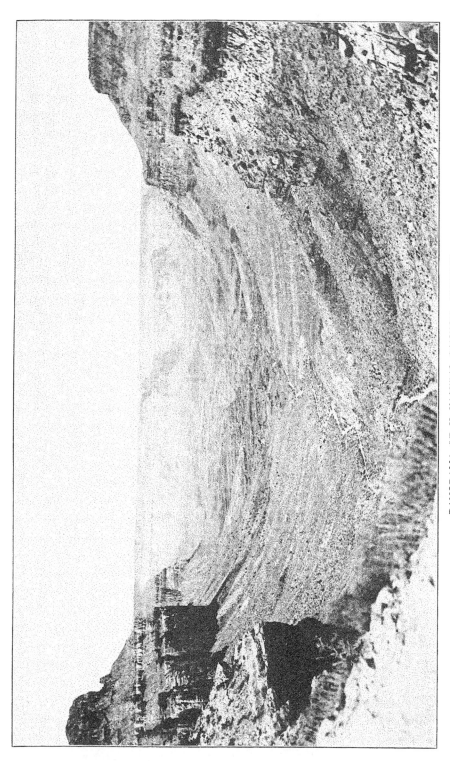

PANORAMA OF H VASUPAI CANYON. ARIZONA.

ketry, but their remoteness prevents their making a living thereby. Their lovely valley is too narrow for the sheep grazing of the Navajos, and no oil wells have made them millionaires, like the Cherokees. With the winter floods, their life becomes meager and rheumatic. The government seems to assume that the unimportant handful, so inconveniently remote, is likely to die out soon,—so why trouble about them?

Visitors are so rare that we were the centre of an admiring group on the agent's lawn. Havasupai from nine months to ninety years freely commented on our every move. They imitated us as we ate apricots, and imitated us as we threw away the pits. The chief's wife, a bride from the Wallapi, centered her fascinated gaze on Toby, and nearly sent that young lady into hysterics by faithfully repeating every word and inflection she uttered.

Though of the sincerest flattery, this mimicry finally palled, and we made our way to what we had been told was a secluded nook of the river, where we might bathe unmolested. Seclusion was essential, as we had to bathe as the small boy does, sans clothes and sans reproche. We found the nook, the river shaded by dense osiers, but its shore bordering the main street of the village. Several Havasupai rode by our swimming hole, and we ducked, in danger, like some of Toby's films, of overexposure. Their heads turned as gentlemen's naturally would in such circumstances,—or, not to be ambiguous, —away. These Havasupai, though dirty and unread, were gentlemen, according to the definition of a certain Pullman porter I once met.

Being about to descend from an upper berth on a

crowded sleeper I had inquired of the porter if the berth below was occupied.

"Yas'm," the porter replied. "A man, lady. But he's a gen'lman. He's turned his face to the wall. An' now he is a shuttin' his eyes. Take youah time, lady."

I relate our adventure, not to flaunt our brazen conduct —the valley registered one hundred odd in the twilight, and you would have done as we did,—but to illustrate the rightness of certain Indian instincts, not confined to these few Havasupai.

It was the following day, when we explored the lower Cataract canyon, that we had our supreme experience in bathing, the bath of baths, before which Susanna's, Marat's, Anna Held's, Montezuma's, Hadrian's, Messalina's, Diana's and other famous ablutions were as naught. Our ride took us into the lower village, past the prim board houses the government erects and the Indians refuse to inhabit, to the clusters of thatched mud and reed huts which they prefer. The chief of the tribe sat before his dwelling, his family about him to the third and fourth generation, including his new Wallapi wife. We bought baskets from him, prompting him to call "Hanegou" after us.

"What does 'Hanegou' mean?" asked Toby.

"It means 'fine,' 'all right,' 'how do you do' or 'good-by'," answered the guide.

It seemed a convenient sort of word, as it has several lesser meanings as well. As we rode along I amused myself by inventing a conversation in Havasupai, quite a long imaginary conversation between two Havasu bucks. It is remarkable how quickly I can pick up a language.

1st. Havasu. "Hanegou?" (How do you do?)

2d. Havasu. "Hanegou." (How do *you* do?)

1st. Hav. "Hanegou." (Fine.)

2d. Hav. "How are crops?" (In Havasupai, of course).

1st. Hav. "Hanegou." (All right.)

2d. Hav. "Hanegou!" (Fine!)

1st. Hav. "Hanegou." (Well, good-by.)

2d. Hav. "Hanegou!" (Good-by, yourself!)

Then the two would pass on, each no doubt thinking of the other, "What a card that fellow is—always getting off some new wheeze!"

Before the chief's Hanegous had died away, we were riding through an enchanting glade, half forest, half orchard. Golden, luscious apricots hung so low that we picked handfuls as we rode under the trees. Then the tangle of half-tropical growth grew thicker, till the whole red-walled valley was a mass of feathery verdure. It opened suddenly upon the river at a broad quiet ford, through which the horses splashed eagerly.

"Look back," said the guide. Over our shoulders we saw a sight that alone would have repaid us for our two days' ride. Framed by the green jungle, a delicate exquisite white waterfall high above us fell into a series of rocky basins, with the water from these making smaller shadows and rapids until it reached the ford. They were the Navajo Falls, which in a country less prodigal of wonders would have a reputation all to themselves.

As we continued up and down through the thicket, a veritable flight of stone steps too steep for descending on horseback dismounted us, and again quite casually we looked to our right, and saw falls twice the height of

Niagara. But Niagara cannot display the same background of vivid cliffs, long canyon vistas, tangled and
matted with tropical trees and vines, nor its perfect pool
of aquamarine. But to name a waterfall Bridal Veil
is like naming a Smith offspring John.

Mooney's Fall, the third and grandest of all in this
rare canyon, was more appropriately named, though
whether in reverence or irreverence is hard to judge.
For this was doubly Mooney's Fall. Mooney was a prospector, intent on investigating some of the rich veins of
lead, gold and silver still unexplored in this canyon. In
descending a cliff sheer enough to daunt anyone but an
old prospector, he lost his hold. His skeleton was found
months later by our own guide, William Bass, at the
foot of the falls now bearing his name. Sheer precipices lead to the pool at the base of the cascade, and to
reach it, we left our horses and entered a limestone tunnel
ingeniously worked in and out the soft rock, and thus
threading our way finally reached the bottom, and stood
exulting in the suddenly cool air, electric with white spray,
falling into the great pool below. Like the caves through
which we crawled, the cliff behind the falls was of red
limestone, not solid rock but like carved lace, or rather,
like the Japanese wave symbol, which seemed to have
frozen eternally when at its crest. And this was covered
with ferns and moss and bright flowers, while blue birds
flashing over the pool in flocks were singing their joy at
reaching this cool haven.

Here was our bath de luxe. I am sure no king or
courtesan ever found one more nearly perfect. While
the guides explored another canyon, we swam to our
hearts' content, cool for the first time in days. The white

MOONEY'S FALL, HAVASUPAI CANYON, ARIZONA.

lime bottom gave the pool a jewel clearness. Though it came to our shoulders it looked only a few inches deep. Spray-drenched, we swam as near as we dared to the great cascade, which set the pool dancing in eternal waves. When we finished our swim we were invigorated as if a dozen masseuses had spent the day over us.

Our last night in this Eden known only to a few brown Adams and Eves, when the heat became too intense for sleep indoors, I took a blanket and spread it under the trees. The full moon made the little valley more of a Paradise than ever. I lay and watched the light climb the massive cliffs that wall in the canyon entrance, till it reached the two grotesquely shaped pillars surmounting either cliff. The Havasupai have a legend concerning these monoliths, so oddly perched that they command oversight of the whole village. They are not really rocks, but gods,—the tutelary gods of the tribe. One the Havasupai call the Old Lady, while the other is naturally the Old Man. For centuries they have guarded their people. Yes, but the breath of scandal touches even gods, —and even gods of stone. For one morning, years ago, a chief of the tribe rose unusually early,—and saw,—don't let it go any further, although I had it very straight,—he saw the Old Man returning hastily to his rock. At four o'clock in the morning, mind you! Easy enough to guess where he'd been.

But I fell asleep watching, and when I awoke the Old Man and Old Lady were still sedately on their pillars. Well, that was a long while ago, after all, and gods will be gods.

CHAPTER XVII

FROM WILLIAMS TO FORT APACHE

WILLIAMS," said the Old-Timer to us, as he directed us to that progressive but uninteresting little town, "when I first came west was a typical shoot-'em-up town, with thirty-six saloons;—thirty of them in tents," he added emphatically, as if this made a climax of inquity, I remarked later to Toby.

"The drinking, I suppose, was more intense," she replied.

"Owing to more frequent drafts," I retaliated.

Williams, set in a sea of white dust, looked both modern and harmless, as if to make up for its youthful wild oats by a humdrum middle-age. Numerous drug-stores had replaced its three dozen saloons, and a Sabbath calm reigned on its dusty streets. We bought gasoline, and went on, not over-pleased with Williams. We felt it did not live up to its early rakishness. But appearances count for very little after all. Not five minutes later, a small man driving a small car, with a large blond woman beside him, approached and signaled us. We saw he was excited, and she, though normally florid, was the color of an uncooked pie.

My prophetic soul caused me to say, "Shall we stop? It may be a hold-up," when he called, "Stop! stop! We've just been held up, a mile back."

"When?"

"Five minutes ago." We had spent those same five minutes buying gasoline at Williams. "Canst work in the ground so fast?" I apostrophised our guardian angels. The woman broke in shrilly. "Two masked men with revolvers stood by the road. They took everything we had, then made for the woods."

"Did you lose much?"

"Nine dollars," said the little man. "If I'd had more they'd got it."

When the shaken couple left, we debated whether to go ahead. Perhaps the masked pair awaited us in the road beyond. Finally deciding they would be no more anxious to meet us than we them, we hid our valuables, I in my hat and Toby under the floor. Before we finished, a Ford approached driven by two men of villainous appearance enhanced by a week's beard, and criminal looking red shirts. Seeing us they wavered, slowed down and seemed about to stop beside us, then changed their minds and dashed past, looking at us searchingly. Their peculiar conduct and unprepossessing features made us certain that they were the thieves. Our long expected bandits had come, and had passed us for a little man in a flivver with nine dollars. We were to a certain extent relieved, I must confess. Still, when you go west adventuring, your friends expect you to be held up by outlaws, and you hate to disappoint them with an anti-climax.

When we reported the incident at "Flag," the Flagstaffians seemed wounded in their municipal pride. Nothing of that sort, they said, had happened for years, and asked if we had visited the Observatory. Flagstaff is no longer a frontier town. I bought a hat there which was afterward admired in Boston, if that signifies anything.

The town is best known for its observatory, which we drove up a beautiful winding hill to view, and found it looked like any other observatory. There are some cliff dwellings overlooking a pretty little green ravine, called Walnut Canyon. Dominating all Flagstaff the crescent of cold San Francisco peaks looks benignly over half Arizona, lovely in their bold and serene silhouette.

On the road between Holbrook and St. Johns, as we journeyed toward Apacheland, we stopped a few hours in the petrified forests whose fallen trunks line the road for miles. Whatever turned them to stone, at the same time burned the heart out of the surrounding country. Leprous looking erosions, sulphur colored and sickly white, make the only break in an absolutely flat landscape. An unbending road stretches miles without a change in its monotony, choking in alkali dust and twisting sandstorms. Beyond is the painted desert—bad lands which, but for the ethereal sunset colors tinting butte and mesa with unearthly glory, would be as unspeakably desolate as the rest. The forest itself lies fallen in an alkali plain. Uncountable tons of these giant fragments, waist-high, perfeet to the last detail in the grain of the wood, the roughness of the bark, knot-holes and little twigs, cover the ground. The strange stone, which polishes like glass and cuts like diamonds, is nearly semi-precious, yet in this vicinity houses are paved with the blocks. We passed over a bridge whose foundation was a giant petrified tree. It was depressing, these acres and acres of stone trees, frozen in the height of their glory by the cruel Medusa, Nature. I felt the same pensive kinship of mortality with these trees one feels at Pompeii with the huddled, lava-encrusted bodies clutching their treasures.

"I wonder what petrified these here trees?" exclaimed a voice behind us. We turned. If I had not known the trees were petrified before her arrival I might have held her responsible. As she stood, she might easily have turned a whole continent to stone. She might have posed for Avoirdupois, minus the poise. She wore, in addition to her figure, a gayly striped silk sweater, high-heeled French slippers, silk stockings, a jockey cap and over-alls. Overalls, like boudoir caps and kimonos in Pull-mans, are the approved hiking costume of the new West for both sexes. Unfortunately, there was more of her to wear overalls than there were overalls to wear.

We had seen many of her kind, always touring the country in a little rattly car, out for a good time, careless of looks, dressed in a motley of overalls, sunbonnets, middy blouses, regardless of age or former condition of dignity, sometimes driving, and sometimes delegating the task to a little man crowded up against the wheel;—there is never more than one man to a carful of women and children. We were now in the heart of the sage-brush tourist belt, where motoring is not the sport of the wealthy, but the necessity of the poor. With bedding rolls and battered suitcases strapped to running boards; canteens, tents, chuck-boxes and the children's beds tied on with ropes wherever ropes will go; loaded inside with babies, dogs and Pater and Materfamilias, and outside with boastful, not to say sneering banners; these little cars serve for transportation, freight-van, restaurant and hotel. Bought second or third hand, they rattle the family off on vacations or business, and at the journey's end are sold third or fourth-hand. At night no garage or hotel for them, but a corner, a secluded corner if they arrive early enough, in the municipal parking grounds. Here with frank gregariousness they exchange confidences with other sage-brush tourists, while Paterfamilias mends the dubious tires and tinkers with the weak spark plug, and Materfamilias cooks supper over an open fire. Then they drape a tent or a mere canvas over the car, take a lantern inside, and one by one undress, blissfully ignorant that their silhouettes are shamelessly outlined on the canvas. As these municipal camps were a bit too noisy for people who loved sleep as did Toby and I, we usually sought the open country, but we loved to walk through the grounds, and enjoy their sociability. The rich **and** haughty, we thought, would not be half so bored with travel if they earned their delights as these sage-brushers do. Fords have replaced prairie schooners, and Indians are less interested in one's scalp than one's pocketbook, yet overland travel still furnishes adventure, as any one of the tow-heads we met from El Paso to Gallup will tell their grandchildren fifty years hence. But you must leave behind limousine and liveried chauffeur, forswear palace hotels, and get out and rub elbows with folks. The real sage-brush tourists care nothing for "side." Proudly flaunting their atrocious banners, they patch their tires **to** the last ribbon, and wash their dirty babies in public.

Occasionally there are exceptions to these happy-go-lucky pioneers. One such family we met at the very ebb of their fortunes. They were migrating to Texas, and midway, their hoodless ramshackle engine, tires, and pump had collapsed like the one horse shay. We filled their canteen, which had also leaked dry, pumped their tires with our engine, and offered what road advice we could, with the remains of our lunch. At last, after repeated cranking the man got the wheezy engine started, and the woman, like Despair in a calico wrapper, leaned forward and took up her task of holding down the engine with her hand, protected by a black stocking. Poor shiftless folk, wherever they settled eventually, it is fairly certain their luck did not improve.

We were bound by easy stages for a long-sought goal, a seductive and elusive province of which even native Arizonans knew little. Yet it was the little they told which enticed us.

"I've not been myself to the White Mountains," one old-timer after another would say, "but I've always heard how they are the prettiest part of the state. Everything in the world you'd want,—mountains, rivers, a world of running water, trout that fight to get on your bare hook, big game, mountain lions and such. I've always aimed to go sometime."

Our "sometime" had come, after long waiting for the twelve-foot snows to melt which covered the road till May. Through pretty, little irrigated towns high in the hills, we reached at sunset a district far different from the burnt aridity we passed at noon. Lakes were linked to each other under green hills like ours at home. We looked across ridges and long irrigated pastures, and rode through fields blue with iris, and groves of gummy pines and the hugest white birches I ever saw. The roads were next to impossible. We bumped violently over annoying thank-you-marms past Cooley's ranch, former home of an officer who married an Apache woman, and whose sons now own half the beautiful valley, and have built a lumber camp that is fast converting these forests into history. At ten o'clock of a full and weary day, we reached the reservation of the White River Apaches, situated on the lovely river of that name. A few miles below, where the river forks between rolling hills, is a cavalry station, relic of the days when the Apache was the terror of Arizona.

We had to beg Uncle Sam once more to put us up for the night. Not too gracious—rather grumpily, in fact,—he granted permission, notwithstanding that in that remote and innless region, his is the only resort travelers have, and the one to which they are always directed. They pay a stipulated sum for lodging and for meals;—nevertheless the average government agency is not the most hospitable place in the world.

Only a few Indians were visible next morning on the reservation. A crowd of men hung round the village store at Fort Apache, or loafed under the trees in the square. A pretty girl on horseback smiled at us, conscious that her necklace of brass bells and celluloid mirrors made her the best dressed debutante in Apacheland. A very intelligent lad directed us to the trout stream where we hoped to see the trout fight for the privilege of landing on our bare hooks. The Apaches are roundheaded Indians, rather sullen we were told, with staring round eyes, more stocky than the lithe Navajo, better able to account for themselves than the Papagoes; though in the past of ceaseless warfare, it has been give and take, the Apaches losing as often as the other tribes. In a land teeming with fish and game, they have become lazy, and the beautiful craftwork for which the tribe was formerly noted is seldom attempted by the younger generation. Their industry does not compare with that of the Hopis, who are constantly weaving baskets, baking pot-

A TROUT STREAM IN THE WHITE MOUNTAINS, ARIZONA

tery, or wresting meager crops from the land. Being the last tribe to take the warpath, not so many years ago, they are closely watched against another outbreak.

Bright and early we drove up the river fork, until what road there was ceased, and became a flight of steps, and our progress was made in standing jumps. The old lady outdid herself, and when her nose bumped against rocks too abrupt to ride over, actually gathered herself together like a hunter, and leaped over them. At last when the hilly trail began to cave in on the outer side, we abandoned the car and walked a mile farther to our camp, near a cottage whose owners were away.

It was a beautiful glade we had selected for camp, so peaceful and remote that we seemed at the earth's end. The White Mountains were indeed all they had been painted. Sunny fields leading to distant peaks, a glade with dimpling brown brooks, fallen logs, tiny cascades, baby whirlpools, sunlit shadows tempting to trout, a green tangle of summer overhead, and the delicious tang of pine-sweetened mountain air, ought to please the most exacting. We lacked only the trout, for, relying on their abundance, we had traveled light for food. Flecks of white in the brook showed this abundance no empty promise. Occasionally a shining body leaped in the air and splashed back into the brown water. Not the fourteen pound monsters of the northern lakes, these, but little brook trout, of a hand's length, meltingly sweet to the taste. Our mouths already watered. Untangling our tackle, we started to dig for worms. We had been presented with a pailful of bait, but in the excitement of getting off had left it at the reservation.

The sun was just low enough to fleck the river with

warm pools and shady eddies. Soon Toby exclaimed
with pleasure, the pleasure finding a worm gives only
when one intends to fish. She had bisected a fat, tempting rascal, assuring one trout, at least. When the sun
was an hour lower, and it was getting a trifle chilly for
fish to bite well, I unearthed another, a long, anæmic,
dyspeptic victim, which gave us renewed courage. Either
worms were scarce or trout fishers had dug them all. We
decided to give it up, and fish with what we had.

It took much less time to get rid of our worms than
it did to find them. Undoubtedly the trout fought to get
on our hooks, but by the same token they fought still
faster to get off again. We doled out Mutt and Jeff, as
we dubbed our treasures, inchmeal to the rapacious brutes,
but we were not proof against their popularity.

"This is the last piece," I said to Toby. And, of
course, when she dropped it into the water, there came a
timid tug, and a rush. Victorious Toby pulled out a
trout, and threw him back in disgust. He was all of two
inches long.

It was four and after when we returned to our trenches
and started digging again. Then a splash, and through
the speckled shade a cavalry officer came riding. We
called after him.

"Any worms in this place?"

"Any what?" His horse was carrying him further
downstream.

"Wor-rums?"

His voice came faintly back,—"Dig near the water."
We dug near the water for another half hour. Then we
gave it up, and hot and discouraged made for the empty
cabin on the hill, hoping someone might have returned

and could advise us. The house, though open, and invitingly adorned with beautiful Apache baskets, a rarity since the Apaches became too lazy to make them, was as empty as before. The tinkle of the telephone which suddenly sounded, emphasized its loneliness.

Toby and I had the same idea, but always more active, she had the receiver down while I was crossing the room.

A forest ranger twenty miles away was making his accustomed round by 'phone, tracing the spread of a forest fire whose smoke we could dimly see.

"Hello!" he said, "Hello!"

"Hello," replied a female voice, in cultured Cambridge tones. "Where do you dig for worms?"

But a forest ranger learns to be surprised at nothing. Instantly his reply came back, "Look under the stones at the river's edge."

"Thank you," said Toby, hanging up the receiver.

Thanks to his advice, before sundown we caught a dozen dainty brook trout, beauties all, which, when dipped in cracker crumbs and lemon juice, and fried in butter over hot coals, were as good as they were beautiful.

It was the first time I ever fished by telephone.

CHAPTER XVIII

THE LAND OF THE HOPIS

IN starting for Hopiland, that little island set in the ocean of the Navajo's country, we had anything but a definite idea whether we should arrive at our destination, but we hoped for the best. We were used by now to steering our craft by desert signs, as a navigator steers his ship. The desert continually impresses one with its resemblance to the sea,—opalescent, glittering in the sun, its sands ribbed as by waves; sky and horizon meeting in unbroken monotony, and mesas floating on its surface like purple islands. We were dazed by its vast distances and always changing beauty. We made for great promontories looming up in a sea of sand; tacked and veered to the next landmark; skirted reefs of rock; and looked for windmills, arroyos and buttes to guide us as a mariner does for lighthouses and buoys. For us who had always known the restriction of well-marked, prim highways, it was a keen pleasure to rely on our newly awakened primitive faculties. For the first time we sensed the reality of expressions that the protected artificiality of cities had made valueless before. For the first time water was not a commodity which inevitably flows when a tap is turned; but the difference between life and death. Old Bible phrases became real in their vivid poetry. "Cattle upon a thousand hills,"—we passed them every day. "The shadow of a great rock in a weary land"

244

we learned to avail ourselves of from the pitiless heat with deep gratitude. For a brief time, we had become as pastoral and elemental as David or Jacob.

Keams Canyon we reached at sundown,—a tiny, jagged little place, oddly charming, with hills packed behind it and a few government buildings striding the canyon. In that easy-going land, those who directed us had taken for granted that we should be looked after, regardless or perhaps because of the fact that Hopiland has neither hotel nor boarding house in its confines. The traveler must camp or depend on private hospitality, which is not, probably because of frequent abuse, as ungrudging as it is reported to be. We could have camped, but desert touring is exhausting, and by nightfall we seldom had strength left to attempt it. We were dog-weary from the heat and bad roads, but no hospitable door opened to us, as we had been assured they would. The agent was away, and we were directed from house to house, no inmate wanting us himself, but each thinking his neighbor might. At last a man more solicitous than the rest thought the minister might take us in. And he did, most cordially.

Here and there on the reservations we heard talk among traders and old settlers against the missionaries; —they were officious, or lazy, or ignorant of Indian psychology, or bigoted. Yet by far the finest hospitality we met on Indian reservations was from missionaries, and altogether we gained a general impression that they were mainly disinterested and sincere. Their work is far from remunerative, and they are resigned to constant discouragement.

After serving us with supper, the missionary invited us

to a prayer meeting in his parlor.   Four Indians and two
babies comprised the prayer meeting.   Slicked up and
awkward, their faces shining with soap, they proved once
more that clothes make the man.   An Indian who is terrifying and dignified in beaded buckskin is only stolid in
overalls and necktie.   To the tune of a parlor melodeon
they dismally sang "Brighten Up the Corner Where You
Are," though it was obvious from their expressions and
the wails of the babies that if it were left to them the
Corner would stay just as it Was.   I could not help wondering, with all respect to the sincerity of our host, what
advantage there was in offering Billy Sunday's elemen-
tary twaddle to a people whose language is so subtle that
a verb paradigm often has 1500 forms.   But surely, when
the Indian is taught to discard his own arts and crafts and
culture, let us give him substitutes of an equally high
standard from our viewpoint.   Pater might pass over his
head, but Poor Richard would not, for his homely commonsense would find an echo in the Indian's own native
philosophy.   Probably the most valuable thing the missionary and his wife had to offer they thought the least
of,—their warm friendliness and human interest in each
convert and backslider, their folksy neighborliness with
red people, and the unconscious example of their straight-
forward lives.

   Keams Canyon is only eleven miles from the first mesa,
and our car was soon climbing dunes of sand toward
the base of the long, bold mesa on which Walpi is built.
From below we could hardly discern the tiny villages
perched on the cliff, so perfectly were the buildings fused
with the gray rock itself, both in color and mass.   Even
the black specks which marked the position of doors and

windows seemed like natural crevices in the rock. Mont St. Michel is the only other place I know where architecture is so completely one with its foundations.

As we climbed to Polacca, the Indian hamlet at the base of Walpi, the ruts became so deep that at the last we were buried to the hubs. A dozen little Indians, giggling and shy like boys the world over, ran to help us push, but their help was of little value. All our questions, though they are taught English at school, passed over their heads, and their replies were limited to "Yes" or "No," shouted so hoarsely that we jumped involuntarily whenever they spoke. For an hour we chopped brush in the broiling sun, backed and shifted gears till the wheels caught at last, and we plunged up hill to the trader's. He told us we were the first of a dozen cars stalled there that week to extricate ourselves.

The village seemed deserted as we passed through. Finally we met with a red-haired man with a vague chin who advised us to camp near the spring, to which he promised to direct us.

"Everybody in town seems to have gone to the next mesa," commented Toby.

"They have," said he, while a sheepish expression came over his aimless face. "They're holding an inquiry into a white man's fighting an Indian. You can't lay a finger on these Hopis, they baby them so. Fact is," he said in a burst of confidence, "I'm the man that did it. A buck called me something I wouldn't stand from no one, so I jest lit into him. I was goin' to kill him, but I kinder changed my mind,—and slapped him instead."

He looked as if his mind would make such changes. He went on with much violence of expression to give his

opinion of the white settlers on the reservations, especially the missionaries,—"they stay here so long they git
all dried up, and jest nachally hate themselves and everybody else."

His annoyance against the world was so large that we
made haste to leave him. It was too hot to champion
anyone's grievances, and his seemed dubious. I felt
sorry for the Indians who had to deal with him. Indian
reservations, as we saw them, always seemed to harbor
a certain proportion of white vultures who were not calculated to increase the Indian's gratitude or respect for
the Great Father, and some of them, unhappily, were in
government employ.

We engaged a little boy to act as our guide to the
villages on the mesa in which he lived, who thought more,
we afterward discovered, of getting a ride in an automobile,—the delight of all Indians—than of his duties
as guide. Not many white drivers, I dare say, have been
up that rocky and primitive road which leads to the
ancient village of Walpi. The natives told us we could
do it, so we started. Two roads led to the wagon trail.
Our little guide, who was as tongue-tied as most Indian
children, was for directing us toward one, when a fat
woman, hung with jewels, and clad in a cerise wrapper,
leaned over a fence and argued the point with him. Polacca sees more strangers than any other Hopi village,
owing to its position, and the importance of the snake
dance which takes place there every September, yet visitors were rare enough for us and our car to be objects of
interest. So we followed her advice and took the other
road, and a few rods further, came to a dead stop in the
deep beach sand which surrounds the town. It was only

the third or fourth time it had happened, so that we did not despair, though we did not relish the thought of another half hour's digging and shoving under the burning, sickening heat of the desert sun. Our guide took the inevitable quarter hour for reflection common to Indians, then he summoned his juvenile playmates, and they cut bush for us, and tramped it into the bad places until we were able to go on sooner than we expected. We branched on to a road, roughly paved with great rocks, and rutted by the cart wheels of three centuries, like the dead streets of Pompeii. The nose of the car began to point skyward, and climbed up, up, while the desert dropped away from us. To go over that road once is an experience, but I should not care to repeat it often. It wound up the side of the mesa, with sometimes a low parapet to keep us from dropping off, and sometimes nothing at all. A boulder now and then or rough ledge cropping across the road would tilt the old lady at an uncomfortable angle. Heights and climbs over dangerous switchbacks had become commonplaces of travel by now, and we had gained confidence from learning the tremendous flexibility of which a motor car is capable. We were willing, without taking credit for extraordinary courage, to undertake almost any road wide enough for our tracks. People who confine their driving to perfect boulevards and city roads have no idea of the exhilarating game motoring really is. My wrists were like iron, and I had developed a grip in my fingers it would have taken years to acquire otherwise. No grade seemed too steep for the "old lady,"—how we relied on her pulling power! Much of the climb we accomplished on high, though at the final grade, where she fairly stood on end, we shifted to low. And at last we were in the street of Walpi, looking down on a blue-gray sea several hundred feet below us, and surrounded by a group of interested natives, who with great presence of mind had filled their hands with pottery to sell.

What is commonly called Walpi is really three towns, Walpi, Sichomovi, and a Tewa village called Hano. The people in the last village, which is the first as you enter the towns from the road, have little traffic with the Walpi people, but the division line is well nigh invisible between Sichomovi and Hano. Beyond the second town the mesa narrows, and over a slender tongue of rock, part of which has fallen away in recent years during a severe storm, we looked across to the most interesting village of Walpi.

Against an intense blue sky it blocked its irregular outline high above the delicate desert, with gnarled sticks of ladders angling out from the solid mass of buildings. The crazy but fascinating stone houses merging into one another, now swallowing up the road and later disgorging it, made with their warm sandstone color an effective background for the people who came and went in the streets, or sat in the doorways in silver and scarlet. The housetops were lively with children and women in native costume, or, more comfortably and less picturesquely in the ginghams and plaid shawls beloved of Indians. The squat houses, the women bending their necks to great water jars, the desert, all suggested a new-world Palestine.

Compared with Walpi, the first two villages are neat and tidy, their interiors whitewashed clean, and little pots of flowers almost invariably on the window sills.

THE VILLAGE OF WALPI.

OLDEST HOUSE IN WALPI.

The Indian love of flowers impressed us everywhere. House after house we entered, to receive a soft smile of welcome from the old grandfather squatted on the floor dangling a naked brown baby, or from the grandmother, busy with a bowl of clay which she shaped and painted with quick fingers, while she talked to us through her English-speaking daughter.

In these Hopi houses, ropes of dark crimson jerked beef buzzing with flies fill the hot room with a fragrance loved only by the Indians; strings of wampum, worth sometimes two horses and a burro, rugs, native woven and of the gaudy Pendleton variety, coats, overalls, dried herbs and peppers hang from convenient beams. In another corner, in the older houses, is a row of two or three metate bins, for grinding corn, with a smooth round stone lying beside it. If one arrives during the season, he can witness the corn grinding ceremony. A Pueblo woman, loaded with beads and silver, stands behind each bin, which is filled with varied colored grains. In the corner an old man sits, beating the tombé in rhythmical strokes and singing the Song of the Corn Grinders, to which the women bend back and forth in perfect time, rubbing their flat stones over the corn. No man except the singer of the ceremonial song can be present in the room while this grinding is in process. To violate this rule is a grave offense.

Most of the houses have a small Mexican fireplace in the corner. At the side of some rooms is a loom with a half finished rug on it, but this is becoming a rare sight. The Hopis, who originally were expert weavers and taught their art to the Navajos, gradually relinquished it to the Navajos, who were able to get a superior quality of wool.   Now the Hopis trade their baskets and pottery to the Navajos for their rugs, or buy the less beautiful but more gaudy commercial rugs from traders.

Being a native of Hano, our little guide hesitated to take us into Walpi.   It was evident that no great love was lost between the two villages, for a reason we learned later, so we preceded him across the uneven, narrow tongue of rock which led to the tip of the mesa.   The late afternoon sun lighted the stony pile with glory, and cast rich, violet shadows the length of the houses. It was almost impossible to disentangle the stairs of one house from the roof of another.   Stairways terraced into the mortar of the houses led to roofs, and ladders pointed still higher.

Somehow Walpi reminded me of the little hill town of Grasse, and the old parts of San Remo, on the Riviera. There was the same tolerance toward live stock in the narrow, unevenly paved streets; there were the same outside stairways, and roofed-in alleys and houses tumbling on each other, and looking into each other's mouths; the same defiant position on the height, watchful of enemies, the same warm stucco and brightly painted door ways.   Even the dark, velvety eyed children bore out the resemblance to Italy, as they slouched against a wall, as Italians love to do.   A small army of children in one or less garments was watching us from the parapets; we pointed the camera at them, and snapped.   When the film was developed only one child remained,—the rest had ducked.

We met with less hospitality in Walpi than in the other two villages on the mesa.   Doors were tightly closed, for the most part.   A few inhabitants, mostly old women, let their curiosity overcome their pride, and called out to us. One woman was baking pottery in an oven edging the lane which was Walpi's Main Street. She had buried it, and was raking sheep-dung over it to insure its being burned the peculiar reddish brown which the Hopis prefer in their pottery. A tiny burro wandered about at will, and the usual array of dogs yapped at us. At the great rock, the most conspicuous identifying mark in Walpi, which bisects the narrow street, and is so shaped that in a Northern country it would have to be called Thor's Anvil, my eye was attracted by little sticks bound with feathers in the crevices of the rock. I pulled one out, and asked our guide what they were.

"Don't know," he shouted, in the tone he used when speaking to us, perhaps thinking it more official. His face was stolid and stupid. Of course he knew. They were, as we afterward learned, the prayer sticks used in the Hopi ceremonies for rain.

Across from Walpi, looking west over the desert, is a low long mesa. There the Indian youths go to hunt wild eaglets, to be used in the Snake Dance ceremonies. We saw a group of men, Indians and white, clustered with great interest about a rough box made of wooden slabs. As we came nearer, curious, we saw them jump quickly back, wary and respectful. A young eagle, with a heavy chain on one ankle, angry and ruffled stood at bay, its eyes gleaming red, its beak wide open and the feathers on its neck standing straight out. It was not a creature to tamper with, even chained as it was. Never have I seen anything so angry in my life. It was the embodiment of Fury, of rage that, silent and impotent as it was, stays with me ever now. How far we Easterners have traveled from the life that was a commonplace to our ancestors! Here was the creature so native to our country that its likeness is on our national coin, yet outside a zoo it was the first eagle I had seen. I only recognized it as an eagle because its feather-trousered legs looked so like the St. Gaudens designs.

Between the little painted prayer sticks in the big rock at Walpi, the long mesa on the horizon, and the captured fighting creature in the cage at Polacca, is an interesting connection. Rain, rain, is always the prayer on every desert Indian's lips. When the spring freshets are finished, and the land lies exhausted under the metallic glow of an August sun, life itself hinges on breaking the drought. Because the eagle is the bird which reaches nearest to Heaven, and hence is most apt to carry his prayer to the gods, the Hopis make excursions to that distant mesa where eagle's nests are still found, and bring back a young eagle. This they keep in captivity until the time approaches for the Snake Dance, which is really a dance for rain, the snake being the ancestor god of the Walpi people. Then they kill the eaglet, not by a gun or an axe, but without shedding its blood, they gently stroke its neck until it is numb and in a stupor. Then they wring its neck, and pluck out the downy feathers to wing their prayer sticks to the gods above.

Inextricably woven with the legends of the Hopi, and especially those inhabiting Walpi, is the Snake myth, which began when a chief's son living north of the Grand Canyon decided to learn where the Colorado River went. His father put him in a box, and thus he reached the ocean, where the Spider Woman (the wise-woman of Hopi mythology) made him acquainted with a strange

YOUNG EAGLET CAPTURED FOR USE IN THE HOPI SNAKE-DANCE CEREMONIES

island people who could change at will into snakes. Passing through all the various tests imposed on him, with the help of the Spider Woman, the young man was given a bride from the Snake people. They wandered until they came finally to the foot of Walpi, and here the Snake woman gave birth to many children, all snakes. Some of these bit the Hopi children; therefore the chief's son and his wife returned all the snake offspring to her people. On their return the Walpi folk permitted them to live on top of the mesa, and after that time the woman's children took human form, and were the ancestors of the Snake clan today.

The Hopi were originally migratory people moving slowly down to their present home from the north. Probably the cliff dwellings in Colorado and the southern Utah country, and certainly in the Canyon du Chelly, were built by them. After Walpi had been settled, other tribes came to Sichomovi. Meanwhile the Spanish monks had discovered Tusayan, and had thoroughly disciplined and intimidated the unhappy people. Like the parent who gives his son a thrashing, they did it for the Hopi's good, but their methods were tactless. Great beams a foot thick and twenty long may today be seen in the old houses in Walpi, which these sullen Hopis dragged from San Francisco mountains a hundred miles away, under the lash of the zealous monks. The Walpis seem to have a morose nature, which one observes today in their attitude toward visitors. Perhaps the regime of the Spaniards cured them forever of hospitality. They joined enthusiastically in the rebellion of 1680. When every Spaniard was killed, the Walpis went back contentedly to their reactionary ways.

The Hano people are of the Tewa tribes, some of whom still live near Santa Fé. On the invitation of the Walpi, they migrated to Tusayan, but the Walpi treated them abominably, refusing to share their water with them, or to allow them on their mesa. When the Hano asked for food, the Walpi women poured burning porridge on their hands. When the Hano helped defeat the Utes they were allowed to build the third village on top of the mesa. They still speak a different tongue from the Walpi, though they lived for centuries within a quarter of a mile of them. The reason is interesting, if true.

"When the Hano first came, the Walpi said, 'Let us spit in your mouths and you will learn our tongue,' and to this the Hano consented. When the Hano moved to the mesa they said to the Walpi, 'Let us spit in *your* mouths, that you may learn *our* tongue,' but the Walpi refused, saying it would make them vomit. Since then, all the Hano can talk Hopi, and none of the Hopis can talk Hano."

However that may be, our little guide was uneasy when we crossed into Walpi, and exchanged no words with its inhabitants, who as they passed gave him uncordial looks.

As we left Walpi, it was almost twilight. It had been a burning hot day, but the coolness of evening at high altitude had settled on the sizzling rock. Shadows that in midday had actually been, not purple, but deep crimson, had lengthened and become cool blue-gray. We carefully steered our car, loaded with Hopi pottery, down the rocky and uneven wagon trail. At times, the ledges projected so high in the road that we heard an unpleasant scraping noise of loosening underpinnings. We used our

SECOND MESA, HOPI RESERVATION.

A HOTAVILLA SYBIL.

brake constantly, and braked with our engine at the steepest turns. At last we reached the sandy stretch at the bottom, and with the advantage of a downgrade, managed to get through it safely.

Still below us and as far as eyes could view, we were surrounded by the desert. Now, as the sun sank lower, and the shadows increased, it was no longer a dazzle of gold and silver, as at noonday. All the colors in the world had melted and fused together, a wonderful rose glow tinged rocks and sky alike. Distant, purple mesas floated on the surface of the desert. The sun was a golden ball tracing its path to the horizon. A sea-mist of bluish gray hung over the desert, and undulating waves carried out the semblance of the ocean. The great rock of Walpi seemed like the prow of a ship, or a promontory against which the waves beat. Here in the crowded East, it is hard to write down the satisfying emotion the tremendous vastness created in us. In this world of rocks and sand, something infinitely satisfied us who had been used to green trees and shut in spaces all our lives. We did not want to go back; the desert was all we needed.

CHAPTER XIX

THE FOUR CORNERS

FORTY-SECOND street and Broadway is probably the most crowded spot in the United States. The least crowded is this region of the Four Corners, where Utah, Colorado, New Mexico and Arizona come together. Almost as primeval as when Adam and Eve were bride and groom, it fits no accepted standards; too vast and too lonely for the taste of many, too arid and glaring with sunshine to be called beautiful in a conventional sense, it differs from the ordinary "landscape" as Michelangelo from Meissonier. Here, in a radius of seventy-five miles are a collection of wonders strange enough to belong to another planet. The Navajo and Piute possess this land. Southeast is Zuni with its highly civilized people. Southwest are the Grand Canyon, the Havasupai Canyon, the desert promontories of the Hopis and the petrified forests. Northeast is Mesa Verde National Park. Silence-haunted Canyon du Chelley lies on the edge of Arizona, and just over the line in Utah is a land of weird and mighty freaks, monoliths, erosions, tip-tilted boulders a thousand feet high, and natural bridges, of which the greatest is the Rainbow Bridge.

It was the lure of the Rainbow Bridge that had gathered our party together in the immaculate dining-room of El Navajo at Gallup, one morning in late May. We already felt a certain distinction bestowed on us by our quest. Not eighty white people since the world began had viewed that massive arch, one among whom, named Theodore Roosevelt, had written most respectfully of the difficulties of the trail. There were six of us, who had originally met and planned our trip in Santa Fé; the guide, Toby, and I, a brother and sister from Ohio named Murray and Martha, and the Golfer, a man of indestructible good-nature.

"Did you get my balls?" inquired the last named, as he stepped from the train.

"Did you bring your clubs?" I asked, simultaneously.

The questions arose from a pact made in Santa Fé. Now few are free from the vanity of wishing to do some feat nobody has yet accomplished. Without it, Columbus would not have discovered America, Cook and Peary would not have raced to the North Pole, Blondin crossed Niagara on a tight-rope nor Wilson invented the League of Nations. Ours was a simpler ambition than any of these, having its origin in the Golfer's passion for improving his drive at all times and places. We had hoped, at Santa Fé, to be the first white women to visit the Bridge, having heard a rumor that none had yet done so, but our guide disillusioned us; several women had forestalled us.

"I wish we might be the first to do something," said Toby, who in fancy had seen herself in a Joan of Arc attitude planting the blue and white flag of Massachusetts on the pinnacle of the Bridge.

"We might put a golf ball over it," I suggested, watching the Golfer polish his brassie. "I don't believe that's been done."

"Guess it hasn't," laughed the guide. "Wait till you see the Bridge."

"Won't do any harm to try," said the Golfer.

Then Murray and the Golfer and the guide began discussing whether a golf ball could or couldn't be driven over the arch. The guide bet it couldn't, and to make things interesting, we took him up. The Golfer modestly deprecated his skill, but thenceforth he was observed practising his drive on every occasion.

We were to drive to Kayenta, and take horses from that point to the Bridge, a hundred miles further on. While the guide packed the car, we took in the sights of Gallup. Thriving though unlovely, facing the dust of the desert, it has a stronger flavor of the old West than most railroad towns, for roads from remote regions converge into its Main Street. Old settlers from all four states rattle in over the dusty trails, no longer on horses, but in the row-boat of the desert, a Ford. They gather at the Harvey lunch-room, and see the latest movies. The Santa Fé thunders by with its load of eastern tourists. Gentle-eyed Zunis wander in from their reservation to the south. Occasionally cowboys in blue shirts and stitched boots ride in, or a soldier in khaki from the Fort. The shops are hung with the silver every Navajo knows how to fashion from Mexican dollars. We saw a group of fat chiefs decked in their best, their henna faces etched with canny lines, fingering and appraising the chunks of solid turquoise and wampum chains on each other's necks as a group of dowagers would compare their diamonds.

We started at noon, our faithful car sagging like a dachshund under a thousand pounds of bedding, tents, food and suitcases, in addition to six passengers,—a load which was a terrific test on these roads. As we left Gallup, passing the "Haystacks" and other oddly shaped landmarks, the road became an apology, and later an insult. High centres scraped the bottom of the weighted car, so that our spare tires acted as a brake, and had to be removed and placed inside, to form an uncomfortable tangle with our legs, wraps and baggage. But in spite of cramped positions we were hilarious, knowing we had actually started on this long-planned adventure, and that before us were eighteen days of companionship, with unknown tests of our endurance, our tempers and possibly our courage, riding hard, sleeping hard, living a roofless existence, without benefit of laundry.

An arid place in the scorching sunlight of lunch-time, the desert toward late afternoon became a dream of pastels, isolated mesas floating above its surface in rosy lilac, its floor golden, washed with warm rose and henna tones, with shadows of a misty blue, under a radiance of reflected sunset light.

When the color faded, mesas and buttes stood out sharp and black. The desert was no longer a pastel but a charcoal sketch. As vision disappeared our sense of smell was heightened. Freshened in night dew after a parched day, a million tiny flowers seemed concentrated into a penetrating essence, with the aromatic sage strongest of all. Our headlights pierced a gloom miles long. It was ten hours before we reached the twinkle of Chin Lee lights, where we were glad to find shelter and beds.

On the next day we averaged exactly nine miles an hour in the eighty miles to Kayenta. In a jolty handwriting I find my auto-log for that day, "Rotten road.

High centres, deep arroyos, many ditches. Sand. Part of road like painted desert."

It was a treacherous country to drive in. There were no maps, no sign-posts. Most of the day we met only Navajos, speaking no English. From the few white men we met, we would get some such instructions: "Bear northwest a ways, follow the creek till it forks; a way down on the lower fork you pass a mesa, then bear east, then west." This over a distance of eighty miles! It was worse than Texas, where we were expected to get our bearings by Uncle Henry!

Sometimes our course was deflected by a swollen river, or the wind had buried our tracks with sand. Sometimes the settlement we sought to guide us would be completely hidden by a dip in conformation of the country. Sometimes a mirage brought under our very noses a group of buildings really miles away, with a river between us. Occasionally a vicious chuck-hole jarred our engine to a standstill. Once our guide lost his bearings, and for nearly thirty miles we skipped lightly cross-country, taking pot-luck with the mesas and washes and sage thickets we encountered, finding our way only by a range of hills on our west.

I have always wondered what would have happened if Toby and I had attempted that journey alone, as we first intended. This Navajo desert was the wildest, most unfrequented district we saw from Galveston to Boston. Only a Dunsany could give an idea of its loneliness, its menace, its weird beauty. Our guide had the western sense for general direction, and had been to Kayenta before, yet even he lost his bearings once. To us, it was a tiny spot easily obscured by the tremendous wastes on all sides. Yet I should like to know if Toby and I could have managed it alone.

Something about the country, and in the swart faces of the supple Navajos on horseback, their flowing locks banded with scarlet, reminded me of old pictures of Thibetan plains and the fierce Mongolian horsemen with broad cheek-bones, slant eyes and piercing gaze. Kayenta is a gateway, like Thibet, to the Unknown. It is a frontier, perhaps the last real frontier in the States. Only Piutes and Navajos brave the stupendous Beyond.

Backed up against oddly-shaped monoliths and orange buttes are half a dozen small adobe houses, among them the vine-covered house and store of John Wetherell, the most famous citizen of Four Corners. A thousand sheep fill the air with bleatings like the tin horns of a thousand picnickers, as they are driven in from pasture by a little Navajo maid on a painted pony, her rope around her saddle horn. A stocky Indian in leather chaps gallops down to the corral, driving two score horses before him. Wagons come creaking in, laden with great bags of wool. A trader from the Hopi country or Chin Le rattles in to spend a few days on business, or stay the night in the hospitable adobe house. Government officials, visiting or stationed here, saunter in to chat or get information. Groups of Navajos bask in the sun. Every passing, every stir of life on the great expanse, is an event to be talked over from many angles.

At the Wetherell's, we found homeliness, a bountiful table, and marvel of marvel, the bath-tub furthest from an express office in the States. A few miles further north, all traces of civilization drop out of sight, and you are living the Day after Creation.

John Wetherell, though supple as a lank cowpuncher and fifty years young, is already an "old-timer." Henry Ford put him and his kind, as fine as this country ever bred, into the past generation, overnight. In this youth, he and his brothers rode down an unknown canyon hunting strayed cattle, and discovered the cliff dwellings of Mesa Verde, now the best known of all. From that moment, discovering cliff dwellings became a passion with the Wetherells. Shard heaps yielded up their treasures to them, and lonely canyons disclosed human swallow's nests hitherto uncharted by the government. From Colorado, John Wetherell moved to Kayenta, where he gained the confidence of the Navajo as few white men have ever done.

In this achievement—and a difficult one, for the Navajo is a wary soul,—he was greatly helped by Mrs. Wetherell, who possesses an almost uncanny understanding and sympathy for the Navajo that make her a more trustworthy Indian student than many an ethnologist learned in the past, but little versed in Indian nature. She speaks their tongue like a native, and has their confidence as they seldom give it to any of the white race. They have entrusted to her secrets of their tribe, and because she keeps their secrets, they reveal others to her.

When the "flu" swept across the desert, it was particularly virulent among the Southwest Indians. They died like flies in their hogans, in carts on the road, and beside their flocks. Babies hardly able to talk were found, the only living members of their family. An appalling number of the tribe was lost. Government medical aid, never too adequate on an Indian reservation, could not cope with the overwhelming attack. Missionaries forgot creeds and dogma, and fought with lysol and antiseptic gauze. The "medicine men" shut the doors of the hogans, built fires to smoke out the bad spirits, filled the air with noises and generally made medicine more deadly to the patient than to the devils that possessed them. Mrs. Wetherell and her family hardly slept, but rode back and forth through the reservation, nursing, substituting disinfectants and fresh air for "medicine," took filthy and dying patients to her own home till it became a hospital, and prepared the dead for burial.

Parenthetically, from this epidemic comes a piquant example of the way fact can always be bent to substantiate creed. Soon after the "flu" had reaped its harvest, a fatal distemper struck the horses and cattle on the reservation. Following the human epidemic, it was cumulatively disastrous. But the Navajo could explain it. In the old days, when a chief or warrior died, his favorite horse was buried beside him, so that he might ride properly mounted into the happy hunting ground. To the Indian mind it was only logical that when the influenza swept away hundreds of men, as many horses should go with them to Paradise.

When the United States entered the world war, Mrs. Wetherell saddled her horse, put food and a bedding roll on a pack-mule, and went far into the interior of the reservation, wherever a settlement of Navajos could be found. Most of them had never heard of the war. She told them of the government's need for their help, till she aroused them from indifference to a patriotism the more touching because as a race they had little reason for gratitude toward a too-paternal government. Out of their flocks they promised each a sheep,—no mean gift

at the war price. When the "flu" epidemic interrupted
her work, she had already raised $3000 among a people
as far from the Hindenburg line, psychologically, as the
Eskimos or Patagonians.

To this lady of snapping black eyes and animated
laugh came rumors from her friends the Navajos of an
arch, so sacred that no religious Indian dared ride under
it without first uttering the prayer specially designed for
that occasion, handed down from one generation to the
next. No white man, presumably, had reached the Rainbow Arch, a day and a half beyond the sacred Navajo
mountain, whose thunder peak dominates the country
even to the Great Canyon. The location was told her
by a Navajo, and the first expedition, led by a Navajo,
with Mr. Wetherell as guide, reached Nonnezosche Boco
(Bridge Canyon) in August, 1909. The party consisted
of Prof. Byron Cummings, then of Utah, now of Arizona University, Mr. Douglas, of the government
Federal Survey, James Rogerson, and Neil Judd, of the
Smithsonian Institute, the restorer of the cliff ruins of
Beta-Takin.

Already a controversy over who really "discovered"
the Rainbow Bridge has been waged, and zestfully con-
tested. To Douglas went the official recognition, with
the privilege of naming the arch, upon his own claim.
Prof. Cummings, while giving Douglas the official right
as discoverer, is the first white man who saw the bridge.

Our own party, the sixteenth to visit the Bridge since
its discovery, waited a day at Kayenta while we equipped.
Our letters had not arrived in time to announce our
coming, and the horses were still at Oljeto, at winter
pasturage, and had to be driven down. Saddles needed

mending and food and bedding had to be collected. While the guides worked, we lay in the cool of the Wetherell's grassy lawn,—the only grass in a hundred miles,—or bargained for Navajo "dead pawn" silver in the trading store. The Navajo is a thriftless spender, and against the day when he can liquidate his debts by selling his flocks, he pawns his cherished turquoises and wampum. By a government law, he is given a period of grace to redeem his heirlooms, after which time they go to the trader, who may not sell them for more than he paid the Indian, plus a small percentage.

We took clandestine snapshots of the timid Indians, who lost their timidity when we were the focus of their curious eyes and guttural comments. Indian speech is always called guttural; the Navajo tongue really deserves the adjective. The Navajo not only swallows his words, but sounds as if he did not like the taste of them. They had a favorite trick of looking our party over, while one of them expressed in a few well chosen consonants a category of our defects, which set the observers into guffaws and shrieks of laughter. Yet they say the Indian has no sense of humor.

One old crone in a garnet velvet jacket sat in the doorway of the store, and with contempt looked us three women over in our khaki riding breeches and coats. Then she sneered in Navajo through her missing front teeth, "Do these women think they are men?"

We had forgotten the warning given us at Chin Le to wear skirts, so as not to outrage the Navajo sense of modesty. This in a land where suffrage never needed an Anthony amendment,—where the son, from antiquity, has taken his mother's name, where the man does the indoor task of weaving while the woman devotes herself to the larger business of tending flocks, and property becomes the woman's at marriage, so that when she divorces her husband, as she may for any or no reason at a moment's warning, he is obliged to walk out of his —I mean her—hogan, wearing only what he had on his wedding morn. So far as I could learn, the man has only one privilege,—that after marriage, he must never see his mother-in-law. "Nas-ja1" they cry ("Become an owl;" i. e., look blind) when the two are in danger of meeting.

Yet this old crone, who had so many privileges, gave us and our outrageous costumes such a look as Queen Victoria might have given Salome at the close of her dance of the seven veils. Wearing the breeks in spirit, she could make a point of forswearing them in the flesh.

The handsome Navajo lads who slouched over the huge bags of wool before the trading store were more tolerant. The boldest let us photograph them, giggling as they posed, and were pleased when we admired the exquisite turquoise and silver bracelets on their brown arms. They were lithe and full of sinewy strength and steely grace, lounging in their gay velvet jackets and chaparrals.

And all through the day, regardless of the burning-glass heat of the sun, Murray and the Golfer, to the delight and amusement of the whole post, red and white, patiently improved their drive by lofting over the wind-mill which Roosevelt had instituted for the Navajos. Three brown children on horseback acted as caddies. Mr. Wetherell quizzically watched a shot go wild over the seventy foot windmill.

"Think you're going to put a ball over the Bridge?"

"I'm going to try to," said the Golfer modestly.

He chuckled. "Wait till you see it, young fellow."

In answer, the Golfer sent up a ball that clove the heavens in twain. And then the entire population of Kayenta spent the rest of the day on their knees, hunting in the sage-brush.

CHAPTER XX

RAINBOW BRIDGE

IT was as exciting as a well-fought football game to watch the horses, when at last they straggled down from Oljeto, to be cajoled and subsequently roped. Having spent the winter away from humans, they had forgotten our self-willed ways, and developed wills of their own. Though bony from a hard winter, they had plenty of fight left in their mud-caked hides. We all sat on the corral fence and joyfully watched a Navajo herder tobogganned over rocks and cactus, at the end of a taut rope, while an old white horse, pink from a bath in the creek, looked over his shoulder and laughed, as he kept the rope humming. The Navajo must have thanked fate for his leather chaps, which smoked with the friction. The horses were a gamble. Our unexpected **arrival** left no time for them to be fed and hardened for the trip. We had to take them as they were. From the fence we made bids for our choice. Our amateur judgments were received with respectful attention. Toby wanted a little horse with flat sides and an easy trot. I asked for the biggest horse they had, knowing from former experience that on a long, hard trip a big horse is less likely to tire, and a long trot is easier on the rider. Martha wanted a pony with a lope, but, speechless with disgust, was given a little white mule called Annie. She broke off a branch of yucca blossom for a whip, and with

270

this held upright and her demure look, she reminded us of the popular picture of the Holy Child riding to Jerusalem.

At about four in the afternoon,—an outrageous hour, —we started across a long draw and over flat lands, not especially interesting, except for the wealth of wild flowers beneath us. Our party was imposing, with our two guides and two helpers. Our five pack horses ambled discontentedly along as pack animals will do, as if they had a grudge against somebody and meant when the opportunity came to release it. Our Navajo who looked after the horses was named Hostein Chee, which is to say, Red Man. He was not so named for his race, but because, for some mysterious reason that may or may not have involved Mrs. Hostein Chee in malicious gossip, like Sally in the cowboy ballad he "had a baby, and the baby had red hair."

Hostein Chee rode his horse like a centaur. His riding costume was moccasins, overalls, an old sack coat, and a mangy fur cap with a band of quarters and dimes, his most cherished possession. He wore an armlet of turquoise and mellow carved silver. The Navajos of former days used these ornaments on their left wrist to steady their arrows as they aimed them at Utes or Apaches, but those they make today with raised designs and encrusted gems are only for display.

Once we passed a small camp of Navajos, and at a word from Mr. Wetherell, Hostein Chee rode off, and a quarter of an hour later rejoined us with a dressed sheep hanging to his saddle horn. A sharp knife is slung from the belt of all Navajo shepherdesses, and their dexterity in handling it is marvellous.

Ahead of us the pack horses jogged reluctantly, as if they knew they were in for it. The trail we were to make has the reputation of being difficult if not dangerous in its rough footing, widely separated camps and lack of water. Yet the beginning was uneventful enough. For a dozen miles we wound through Marsh Pass, with the typical desert scenery of hot, burnt plains, rolling hills and low cliffs, and dry river beds. Then we turned at right angles into Segi, or Lake Canyon, winding east to west between bright pink sandstone bluffs, outlined in whimsical shapes against a clear gold sky. The green, grassy valley abounded in the sweet flowers of the desert, a strange contrast to the bare, stark and forbidding rocks hemming it in.

We persuaded our horses to a trot, for we still had miles to go. At twilight, when the heat suddenly changed to a frosty cool, we turned into a side canyon whose narrow walls rose higher as we progressed. The horses slipped and tumbled in the dark. Unexpectedly, Toby and I found ourselves struggling alone up a path which became more precarious every minute. Our horses finally refused to advance, and dismounting, we saw that we had mistaken for a trail a blind shelf of the bank high above the stream. The ledge narrowed till there was scarcely room to turn around; the horses' feet slipped among the loose boulders. We could see little but the blazing stars overhead. We could hear nothing; our party had ridden far ahead without missing us. At last a faint call drifted to us, and soon a guide appeared to our rescue. Turning down the stream-bed we made our way after him to camp, a mile further, where the others were already dismounted, and the pack unloaded.

Tired and ravenous, we rested on our saddles while the horses strayed off, munching the fine, sweet grass. If Mr. Wetherell was tired he showed no sign, though since morning he had been busy. While the other men unpacked bedding and arranged camp, he dug a deep pit, placing burning logs within. The pit finished, he buried the mutton that a few hours ago was a happy sheep, and covered it lightly. Before we could believe it possible, it was cooked. Steaming and crisp it was sliced and distributed, and the mutton which had been a sheep became as rapidly a remnant.

The day had been sultry, but we were glad now of the roaring fire. It sent a glare on the face of the red cliffs on the opposite bank, not unlike El Capitan of Yosemite in contour. We looked and forgot them again, to look again and be surprised to see them in place of the sky. Not till we threw our heads far back could we see their edge. The pleasant sound of the little stream came incessantly from below. His silver glittering in the firelight, Hostein Chee sat smoking a cigarette, like a Buddha breathing incense. I went to him, and tried to bargain my Ingersoll wrist-watch for his armlet. I let him hear it tick.

"Wah-Wah-Tay-See, Little Firefly," I said, in the Indian language of the poet, pointing out the radium hands. "Light me with your little candle. I give you this?"

Hostein Chee accepted it with a child-like smile.

"And you give me this?" I said, touching his armlet.

"No good," said Hostein Chee, drawing back in alarm. But I had difficulty in getting my watch back. Each night of the trip thereafter, we went through the same game, the Red Man accepting my watch with gratification, but showing the same surprised obstinacy when I tried to take the armlet, and polite regret at having to return my watch. In the end, he lost the name bestowed on him by a derisive community, and became Wah-Wah-Tay-See for the rest of the trip.

Sleep that night was more romantically staged than under ordinary circumstances. The cold, glacial tang of high altitude nipped us pleasantly. The cliffs shut us in, not forbiddingly but protectingly. The firelight was cozy and homelike. We made a little oasis of human companionship in this wide primeval solitude, but our spirits were high enough not to feel our isolation. Rather, we had an increased elation and sense of freedom. What myriads of people, jostling each other every day, never get more than a few feet away from their kind! We had a sense of courage toward life new to us all. The mere fact of our remoteness helped us shake off layers and layers of other people's personality, which we had falsely regarded as our own and showed us new selves undreamed of. We laugh, at the movies, at the frequency with which the hero goes "out there, away from all this" to "find himself." Yet I think everyone should, once in a while, leave routine and safety behind, with water that runs from faucets, beds under roofs, and food coming daily from baker and grocer, and policemen on every corner. Too much security stales the best in us.

It seemed the middle of the night when we were wakened by the sound of galloping hoofs. From our tent window, we saw the morning sky painting an orange band against the cliffs, and Hostein Chee driving the outfit up the ravine. On his pony's saddle hung the carcass of a second sheep, for from today we were to leave fresh meat behind us. Even the Navajos and Piutes seldom wander far into this hinterland of nowhere. We snatched a few minutes more of sleep, guiltily, while through our door came sounds of preparation for breakfast. We shivered and piled on more coats. At last the crackle of the fire promised warmth; we crawled out, washed in the stream, and found breakfast ready and the packers impatiently waiting for tents and gunnysacks.

"Look," said somebody, pointing. Mr. Wetherell smiled. To our right, sheltering us with its six hundred feet of red wall rose a cliff, curved half-way up like an inverted bowl, and blackened with streaks where water had once run. The same water had carved the bowl, and had it worked awhile longer it would have bored through the cliff and made a natural bridge. As it was, it formed a simple but perfect shelter for a large cliff city, so completely the color of the cliff that but for the black window holes, we should never have found them for ourselves.

With all the joy of discoverers we speedily climbed the precipitous bank to the narrow shelf on which the ancient city was built. Strung together on their precarious ledge like beads on a necklace were rows of rooms, compared to which a kitchenette in a New York apartment would be spacious. Above them were second and third stories, the ceilings long ago fallen, and only a few decayed piñon *vegas* to show where they had been. On one building the tumbled masonry exposed a framework of willow wattles. A thousand years before, perhaps, some Indian had cut the saplings fresh from the brook where we had just bathed. The great stone slabs of the altars and the cedar beams must have been dragged up from below,—a stupendous work of patient human ants. In the fine, crumbly floor dust, we found innumerable bits of pottery, painted in the early red, black and white, and fragments of the still earlier thumb-nail. Toby tirelessly collected armfuls of them, and tied them in bandana handkerchiefs. The place had hardly been excavated. We pawed the dust, each believing we might discover some souvenir the Smithsonian would envy us, and ethnologists refer to wistfully in their reports, yet somehow, we did not. But many interesting things came to light, feathers twisted together into ropes, obsidian arrow-heads, sticks notched by a stone adze, grinding stones such as the Hopis use today, and the altar stones found in each apartment. No wonder their builders worshipped, living so near Heaven.

These ruins, called Beta-Takin, or "Hillside House" were well named. Above was only the deep blue sky, framed in the smooth red arch that roofed these swallows' nests. Below were steep slopes of crumbling sandstone, the glowing flowers near the river, and beyond, castellated peaks of bold outline. I climbed with caution to the furthest tip of the crescent town, and my traitor knees began to crumple like paper. I had suddenly begun to wonder, at the wrong moment, whether any cliff dwelling babies had ever fallen over that edge.

Hostein Chee was finishing his last diamond hitch when we returned to camp. Our horses were changed; some who yesterday had been mere pack animals were promoted to the rank of saddle horses. The Golfer had drawn a powerful black mule, and had mounted him jauntily. The Golfer was new to horses, but anyone could ride a mule. Just then, as he bent to adjust a stirrup, the familiar jingle of the departing pack and the music of Hostein Chee's alien profanity came to those long ears. Forgetting his recent rise in station, the mule leaped eagerly forward to join his mates. Briar and bush did not stop the pair; they tore downhill over boulders and through thickets. Young alders slapped the Golfer in the face, but he hung on until the mule, in despair at seeing demure Annie trot out of his vision, took the stream at a leap. At that moment, those who were ahead say that the black mule caught up with Annie.

The Golfer had lost interest in the amorous pursuit, and was sitting up picking the cactus thorns out of himself when we arrived.

"What happened?" we asked, in the way people will ask questions.

"I'd thought I'd get off," answered the Golfer.

But thereafter, he and the black mule became firm, if not fast companions.

The gorge we had passed through in the dark we retraced to find full of color. Great aspens bordered the heights, while the river bed was full of flowers. As we came to the opening the canyon broadened, and the reddish cliffs became higher and took on strange shapes of beasts and humans. A whole herd of elephants carved in the sandstone seemed guarding the entrance into Segi canyon, meticulously complete, even to white tusks, wrinkled trunks and little eyes, as if these had been the freehand plans the Creator of elephants had sketched on the wall before he began to work them out according to blue-print.

We worked through and across Segi canyon until we stood on a ledge of rock, and looked over miles of rose, purple and stormy blue, toward corrugated walls high enough to fence in the world. And then began a descent of two hours, while the sun blazed up in this shadeless waste of rocks. We scrambled over boulders bigger than our horses, dragging the reluctant animals after us on the rein, ready to dodge quickly if they slipped. A few lizards glided under cover as we advanced, the only living creatures in sight, though from the heights came occasionally the melancholy story of a ring-dove or a hoot-owl. The trail clung to sheer walls, its switchbacks rougher and at times far steeper than the Grand Canyon trails. Since its discovery ten years ago, little has been done to improve it, necessarily, because of its extreme length and the fact that it is not situated in a national park. For these reasons, it will probably never lose its primitive wildness.

We lunched under a few spreading junipers, where water in muddy rock basins was to be found. The sun was low when we started again, for in that country it does not pay to ride through the heat of mid-day. The region, broken no longer by gigantic canyons, softened to a dull monotony of sage and rolling hills. Camp was already made, when at evening we rode into a small, semi-enclosed valley at a short distance from a second cliff-town, under an arched recess of rock high above us. While the men unpacked, Martha, Toby and I found a tiny pool yielding a basin full of water, but ice-cold, it soothed our weary bodies wonderfully. About all we need for our physical selves in this world is a bath after dust and heat, food after hunger, sleep after weariness,

NAVAJO MOUNTAIN FROM THE MOUTH OF SEGI CANYON.

A herd of elephants carved in sandstone guarded the entrance to Segi Canyon.

warmth after cold, and freedom from worry,—and camp
life completely satisfies for a time, because these simple
desires are both intensely stimulated and gratified. Our
campfire warmed the chill night air, and gave us an hour's
relaxation and gayety. But sleep could not be held off
long, and at nine, we all retired to our tents under a
thicket of junipers.

These cliff dwellings yielded Toby magnificent specimens. Behind camp lay a small hill mostly of pottery
fragments. She attacked it and single handed soon reduced it to a hummock. The bandana would hold no
more, and her sweater and pea jacket bulged at the
pockets, and when I opened our pack I found crumbled
pottery mingling with our toothbrushes.

The next day brought us into more dramatic scenery.
Once more we toiled up and up through an unimaginably
vast and lonely country, whose barrenness of rock and
sage was softened by a wilderness of flowers, of new and
strange varieties. The cactus blossoms, most brilliant
and fragile of desert flowers, with the texture of the
poppy and the outline of the wild rose, ranged from the
most subtle tones of golden brown, tea rose color and
faded reds to flaming, uncompromising rainbow hues.
We passed a bush with white waxen flowers like apple
blossoms, called Fendler's Rod, and another with mahogany branches, smooth to feel, with fragrant yellow
bloom; blue larkspur in profusion, the Indian paintbrush in every shade from scarlet through pink and cerise
to orange and yellow. Wild hyacinths began to appear
in the cooler, tenderer shades of early spring, and a new
flower, very lovely, called penstaces, in pink and purple.

The mariposa lily of southern Arizona appeared here as waxy cream and twice as large as we had ever seen it.

Once out of Piute Canyon, we camped at the Tanks, a series of waterholes worn in a dry river bed of solid rock. A group of piñons sheltered our camp, but before the tents were fairly up a downpour of rain drove us wet and uncomfortable to huddle together in one tent. The horses slanted into the driving storm with drooping heads and limp haunches. Saddles and provisions were hastily covered with Navajo rugs. Through it all Hostein Chee in overalls and drenched sack coat moved about his business with neither joy nor sorrow. He showed no animation until over the great roaring fire our supper was cooked, and he could once more, with bland and innocent smile shake the bag of sugar into his coffee, murmuring "Sooga."

The sheep killed by the Navajos had not died in vain. Again it formed the staple of our meal. With each appearance it seemed to lose some of its resiliency. Mutton, most unimaginative of meats, with the rain drizzling on it was less inviting than ever. Nor was it improved by being set down on the ground, where a shower of sand was unwittingly shaken into it by each person who went to the fire to fill his tin plate. Still we chewed on, and in the end besides the exercise, got a little nourishment. We did not care; we wanted to eat, and get back to our tents out of the downpour. It was one of those days all campers know and enjoy—afterward.

I woke toward morning and peered through the tent window to see dawn banding the windy sky. Against its dramatic light, stood Hostein Chee, the Red Man, beside a campfire blazing shoulder high. His body slanting back, his face frozen to exalted calm, he gazed fixedly at the glory of the sky. His inscrutable nature seemed touched and wakened. I called softly to Toby.

"Look—he is saying a prayer to the dawn!"

We looked reverently. The white men were sleeping, but the Indian kept his vigil. He raised both arms above his head, removed his hat,—and scratched vigorously. This done, he repeated the process wherever he felt the need. Toby's awed interest turned to mirth, mainly at my expense. Yet even engaged in so primitive a gesture as scratching, Wah-Wah invested it with the stately grace we noticed in his every move. Though I knew I should not, I watched him make his toilet, fascinated. He removed the trousers he slept in, and in which we daily saw him accoutred, revealing (I had turned away in the interim) an under pair, similarly tailored, of a large black and red checked flannel. He scratched thoroughly, took off his vest, scratched, and then dressed. Then he blew his nose as Adam and Eve must have, and shouted "De-jlss-je!"

That, as nearly as I can spell it, is the only Navajo any of us managed to learn. Mr. Wetherell so frequently addressed Hostein this way that we thought it was his name, and called him by it, even after we learned that it meant "Light a fire" The little jest always brought a silent smile to the face of the Navajo, and he would mimic our mimicry. We christened an unnamed canyon for him De-jiss-je Boco, where we lunched at noon, and cached part of the pack till the return trip. Here was a delicious stream, running between sandstone rocks, into which horses and all put our heads and drank. The sun steamed upon the land of rocks until the heat made us droop, and our horses, poor beasts, were rapidly wearing down from the trail. Only piñons, with hardy roots gripping the red wastes of rock, and thorny cactus, grew in this vast echo-land. Rocks! I could not have believed there were so many in the universe. It looked like the Pit out of which the gods had taken material to build the world, or the abyss where they threw the remnants afterward.

For the first time we saw purple sage, whose scent is indescribably sweet. This rare variety is found only in this region. Its leaf is dark green and differently shaped from ordinary sage. We were nearing great Navajo, whose bare stark head topped all other hills from Mt. Henry in Utah to the San Francisco peaks in the south. Soon we were in the lee of it, climbing beside it, but closer and closer to its heights.

De-jiss-je looked at the cloudless sky, and suggested it might rain. To my surprise the others agreed. The sky was velvet blue and the air as dry and sparkling as ever. Yet we had hardly rounded the shoulder of Navajo when thick, broken clouds shrouded it in terrible grandeur, and the wind swirled them against that rocky mass. The storm broke immediately in wildest fury, and we saw the giant in its proper surroundings, storm wrapped and terrible. I never saw a more majestic storm in more titanic setting. Low waves of prairie, stretching for miles, were broken here and there into strange monoliths and grotesque needles, around which the lightning played sharp and short as a whip snapping, —rose-colored, deep green. The sky turned purple-blue, cut and slashed by gashes of blinding white. Grayed by

RAINBOW BRIDGE TRAIL
Near Navajo Mountain, whose bare, stark head topped all other hills.

sheets of rain, the red rocks took on a sulphurous look. Far off to our right a rainbow canyon opened, almost as vast and quite as brilliant as the Grand Canyon of Colorado, reaching to the horizon.

Though the storm cracked above our heads, it was too beautiful and too awful to fear. We whipped on our slickers. In a second they were drenched, and streams were running to our saddles and soaking us. Toby, protecting her camera with one hand, and her person from the banging of a bag of pottery, wearing the slicker the cow had chewed short, was quickly drenched, and rode in dejected silence. Ahead, the helper, whose thin shirt streamed rivers, shouted in glee, and drove on the stumbling pack-beasts with variegated profanity. The guides took the onslaught of the storm unmoved, dripping like male Naiads. Sometimes the thunder smashed so near it seemed as if our horses had been struck, sometimes it cracked on the cliffs beside us.

The scenery became increasingly dramatic. We were out of the piñon, and riding through nothing but granite and sandstone. An hour passed, while we huddled uncomfortably, fearing to move lest a rivulet find a new and hitherto unwet channel on our bodies. Then as suddenly as it began the storm ceased, and just in time, for we were nearing the crux of the trail,—Bald Rock. Even Roosevelt described this pass as dangerous. The storm had increased the danger. Five minutes more of rain, and the rocks would have been too slippery to cross; as it was, we barely kept our footing.

Bald Rock is a huge dome of solid granite, bordering a precipice several hundred feet deep, overlooking tangled and twisted crags. Crossing it was like crossing the surface of an inverted bowl. Worn smooth by erosion, the only semblance of foothold it offered was a seam a few inches wide near the edge. With the dome polished by rain, it was not easy to keep both footing and nerve. Our tendency was to move cautiously, when the safest way was at a jog trot, though the mental hazard of the drop at the edge made the latter course hard. Even the bronchos shared our caution. We naturally had dismounted, though the intrepid Hostein Chee rode his horse part way across. The horses dug their hoofs in hard, and even then they slipped and scrambled about helplessly. One balked, and another fell several feet. For a moment it looked as if his bones would be left to whiten in the chasm below, but goaded by the Navajo he regained his feet, and, trembling, crossed safely

Beyond came a still worse spot,—a narrow ledge, with cliffs on one side shouldering one toward the edge. Here the horses were halted until blankets and armfuls of grass could be placed along the slanting ledge. In all, we were half an hour passing Bald Rock. Though this is the worst bit of trail on the way to the Bridge, and enough to give one a little thrill, there is nothing to dread under ordinary conditions. Nevertheless, I should not like to cross Bald Rock after dark.

To our left, beyond masses of smooth, marvelously contorted sandstone rose white cliffs, seared and ghostly, and beyond them, far reaches of mountain, with Navajo king of all. Clouds and mist encircled its slopes, but the peak rose clear above them into a thunderous sky. We kept the grand old mountain in sight for several miles, then dipped into a small and lovely valley, full of flowers and watered by a winding stream. This was

CROSSING BALD ROCK, ON RAINBOW BRIDGE TRAIL.
The worst bit of trail on the way to the bridge

Surprise Valley, famous in the movies as the scene of a thrilling tale of a man and woman walled in for years by one boulder pushed to block the only entrance. It is a pity to spoil the thrill, but I could not see how any one boulder, however large, could block all exit from this valley. Nevertheless its seclusion and unexpectedness make it a delight. The inevitable cliffs surround it in a red circle, and once within, a stranger could look for hours for the trail out.

Thus far, the trail had been not only beautiful, but climacteric, and from this point to the great arch it was entirely outside one's experience. We had to recreate our sense of proportions to fit the gigantic land. I felt as if I had been shipwrecked on the moon. We who started feeling fairly important and self-satisfied and had become daily more insignificant, were mere specks in a landscape carved out by giants,—a landscape of sculptors, done by some Rodin of the gods, who had massed and hurled mountains of rock about, twisted them in a thousand fantastic figures, as if they had been mere handfuls of clay. Against the prodigious canyons down which our tired beasts slowly carried us, we were too small to be seen. Nonnezoche Boco,—"Rainbow Canyon," in the Navajo, —brought us into an ever narrowing pass with terra-cotta walls rising thousands of feet on every side, and a turbulent stream, much interrupted by boulders, at the bottom. Sometimes we threaded the valley floor, and sometimes mounted to a shelf along the edge. Finally, when it seemed impossible for Nature to reserve any climax for us, we looked to the left,—and saw an anticlimax. We had been straining our eyes straight ahead, each eager for the first sight of the Bridge, the mammoth bridge, highest in the world. As we crossed the canyon, looking down its length we saw a toy arch nestled among the smooth cliffs, like a mouse among elephants.

Not till we had wound down the trail overlooking the river and leading under the bridge, not till we dismounted under the buttresses of the arch, and saw that they themselves were young hills did we get an idea of its majesty. Our Navajo walked around it, for no good Navajo will pass under the sacred arch unless he knows the prayer suitable to this occasion. We followed Hostein Chee, and camped on a slope on the other side. From this angle the bridge appeared stupendous, towering above cliffs really much higher, but seeming less by the perspective. Unlike so many of Nature's freaks, it required no imagination to make it look like an arch. Symmetrical and rhythmic of outline, with its massive buttresses in beautiful proportion to the rest, it spans the San Juan, which, cutting through the narrow canyon, curves about to form deep pools into which we lost no time in plunging, after our hot and nearly bathless journey.

Whoever called it a bridge misnamed it, for it bridges nothing. Before seeing it we had ambitions to climb to the top, and walk across, and while I daresay we should all have gone if any one of us had insisted on attempting it, we may have been secretly relieved that nobody insisted too hard. It means a stiff climb negotiated with ropes, up an adjacent cliff. From the level top of this cliff one works around to a monument rock near the southwest end of the arch where a single piñon grows from a niche. A rope is swung from the cliff above, fastened in the piñon, and over a twenty-foot gap, at a height of three hundred feet and more above the rock-strewn

RAINBOW BRIDGE UTAH.

river, one jumps to the shelving arch of the bridge. Returning is even worse than going—I believe only eight people have ever mounted the bridge.

The Golfer meanwhile had reached the tee of his ambitions, with two dozen balls and his trusty brassie. We came on him at the edge of the tumbled river, casting a doubtful eye up the rough slopes and crag-strewn course.

"Bunkered, by gosh," we heard him say.

"If you don't mind a little climb," said the guide, "I think we can fix you all right."

Accordingly we stuffed our pockets with golf-balls, while the Golfer tied the remainder to his waist, and began to climb one of the smooth cliffs to the right of the arch, with the understanding that whoever had good courage might go on to the top of the bridge. The last lap of the climb brought us to a ledge which went sheer in the air for about twenty feet (it seemed like two hundred), without visible means of support. But nothing daunts an Old-Timer. Ours twirled his rope, lassoed an overhanging shrub at the top of the ledge, and shinnied up like a cat, twisted it twice about the shrubs and then around his wrists, and one by one, each according to his nature,—but not like a cat,—we followed.

Toby, who is a reincarnated mountain goat, scrambled up with careless abandon. Murray took it without comment. Martha, suddenly stricken with horizontal fever, was yanked up bodily. When it came to my turn, I got halfway up without trouble, but there the thought struck me that Mr. Wetherell was a dreadfully peaked man to be the only thing between me and the San Juan river. I wished that he had sat still in his youth long enough to fatten up a bit. I called to him to sit heavy, and he called back to straighten my knees and keep away from the cliff. My knees, however, will not straighten on high; instead they vibrate excitably. As for throwing my body voluntarily out from that friendly cliff,—the only bit of mother earth, though at a peculiar angle, within several hundred feet,—it hardly seemed sensible. I did not wait to reach the top to decide that it was too hot to climb to the bridge, and I think the others went through a similar mental process, for when I thankfully was pulled over the edge, I heard several people say, "Awfully hot, isn't it? Pretty hot to go much further?"

The Golfer was the last and heaviest to come up the rope. Halfway up, his arms shot out wildly, and I heard a gasp of horror, and far below, plop, plop, saw one hard rubber ball after another leap as the chamois from crag to crag, and join the river below. He had tied the box of balls insecurely, it seemed. For the moment we could hardly have felt worse if it had been the Golfer himself. A baker's dozen went where no caddy could find them. From our pockets we collected eleven balls, with which to perform the deed which had brought us toilfully through these perils.

We could see only the keystone of the Bridge from the summit of our cliff, but its surface offered a good approach. Murray took the first drive. His ball made a magnificent arc, grazed the top of the Bridge, seemed to hesitate a moment, then fell on the near side. Then came the Golfer's turn. He approached it several times, but something seemed wrong. He cast a look in our direction. We had been frivolously talking. He drove, but the ball glanced to one side and disappeared.

Better luck," he said, passing the club to Murray. But Murray had no better luck, and the two alternated until it seemed as if the San Juan must be choked with golf balls.

"It's an easy drive. Any duffer could do it," said the Golfer impatiently. Apparently there was something about the drive more difficult than it looked. Perspective was lost in the clear air, and the jumble of rocks before us seemed closer than they were. With only two balls remaining, the Golfer again took his turn, after several brilliant failures on both sides. Once more he turned a majestic glance toward us. A bee had crawled down my back, and Martha was removing it, but after that glance we let the bee stay where he was. A hushed silence fell on our little group at this historic moment. Since Adam and Eve, we were the first group of people ever gathered together in this lonely, inaccessible spot for the purpose of driving a golf-ball over the Rainbow Bridge. No cheers came from the assemblage as the Golfer addressed the ball innumerable times, and at last raised his brassie and drove.

"Keep your eye on the ball," said someone. We did so, and our several eyes soared toward the arch, struck the rock towering beside the bridge, and ricochetted over the far side. Technically, though by a fluke, we had the ball over. I say we, because we all worked as hard as the Golfer and Murray. Murray refused the last ball, and just because he didn't have to, the Golfer drove this easily and surely over. We had achieved our purpose. We were the first to put a golf ball over Rainbow Bridge, not a great contribution to history or science, but giving us a certain hilarious satisfaction. It is not so easy to be first at anything in these days, when everything has been tried already. Toby who once stigmatized the ambition as "cheap," crossed her fingers as the Golfer launched his last ball, and photographed him in the act for the benefit of posterity. Our Old-Timer, another scoffer, later spent an hour hunting the triumphal ball, and on retrieving it from the river bank, begged it for a souvenir. Anyone who doubts the authenticity of our feat may see the ball at Kayenta today. And even Hostein Chee, alias Wah-Wah, alias De-jiss-je, salvaged a half-dozen of the lost balls, and was seen patiently hacking away at them with the Golfer's best brassie. And he was remarkably good at it, too.

The campfire, built that night under the sweeping black arch, seemed like home amid the looming cliffs and monoliths. The air was full of that strangest, most arresting odor in the desert,—the smell of fresh, running water.

I lay awake for hours, watching the stars wheel over the curve of the arch. It was not surprising that the Navajos held this spot in superstitious reverence, as the haunt of gods. We were all, I think, in a state of suspended attention, waiting for something to happen which never did happen. Soon the moon, startlingly brilliant in the high air, circled over to the wall topping the southwest side of the bridge, and upon this lofty screen the arch was reproduced in silhouette. Why this should have seemed the last touch to the strange beauty of the place I do not know, but when I waked Toby to watch it, we lay there, almost holding our breath, until the shadow had made its arc down the side of the cliff and disappeared.

After a week's travel to reach the Bridge, to turn homeward instantly seemed ridiculous. The first day took us a weary twenty-five miles back to De-jiss-je Camp, prodding our exhausted animals every step of the way, till we too were exhausted. We intended to circle back through Utah, crossing Piute and Nakis Canyons at the upper end and touching the lower edge of the Monument country. Always a wearing trip, ours to the Bridge and back was more than usually so, because our unexpected arrival at Kayenta had given no chance to get the horses in condition. Tired animals mean forced camps, irregular and scanty meals, and consequently less sleep and more fatigue,—a vicious circle.

We ate the last of the mutton that night. Tough and sandy and gristly it proved, but the stew from it was fairly delicious. When the meal ended, Wah-Wah borrowed a needle and thread, and smilingly announced to our circle that he intended to mend his outer garments. Without further ceremony, he pulled his shirt and trousers off, leaving only his checkerboard underdrawers. Pleased at the concentration of interest, which he attributed to his skill at sewing, he beamed upon us all. "Disgusting old heathen," said Martha.

But Hostein Chee was not without friends. Next morning with a show of great enthusiasm an old Navajo rode up, greeted him, and thereafter, either lured by Red Man's companionship or hope of a free lunch thrice daily made himself just useful enough to be permitted to follow our camp. Fat and venerable, with flowing shirt and gray hair tied in a chignon, and hung with jewelry he looked so like an old woman that we dubbed him Aunt Mary. His manners were no better than poor

Hostein Chee's, but his manner was superb. Under his outer trousers, which flapped loose, he wore bed ticking, which served him for napkin, handkerchief, and towel, with princely dignity employed. Between the two Navajos our stock of sugar ran very low. He did us a good turn, however, by riding off to a nearby Ute camp and obtaining fresh horses. All those we had started with had succumbed. Not only Martha, but all of us were glad to exchange mounts for the tough little mules which had carried the packs in and were now willing to carry us out of Nonnezoche Boco. Toby bestrode Annie, who from being despised and rejected of all was now the prize. She never wandered, kept at an even pace, and never missed the trail. Annie is one of the few people in the world who could find her way to the bridge and back without a guide.

Another day brought us to the borders of Utah and Arizona. The Rainbow Bridge belongs to Utah, a day over the line. Piute Canyon crosses both states. We had passed it in Arizona and were now to cross it in Utah. But both states claim the glory of owning the most magnificent territory in the Union. If the Grand Canyon were more tremendous than any one thing we saw in these three days' march, still it has not the cumulative effect of grandeur piled upon grandeur. Since the discovery of the Bridge in 1909 its discoverers and an increasing number of people who have seen this country have advocated making it a National Park. It is certain no park we now have could rival its stupendous uniqueness.

Canyon after canyon opened before us, painted in the distance with every hue imaginable. Piute Canyon was buff and pink; Copper canyon, following soon after, a gorgeous blaze of rich red and deep blue tones. Then came a succession of three smaller canyons each turned a different hue by the sun, the distance and the substance of the rock. We ascended and descended in the blazing heat, until it seemed as if all life had been a going up and a coming down. Toward sunset on the ninth day, a trail overlooking a long narrow valley ended abruptly in a pass cut through solid boulders which we could barely ride through. Beyond, unexpectedly, a broad vista of the Monument country spread like a vision of the promised land. Isolated cliffs pointed the valley, in every grotesque form. Rocks as high as Cleopatra's Needle and the arch of Napoleon, and similarly shaped; new world sphinxes, organ rocks, trumpeting angels, shapes of beasts and men had been carved here in past ages by the freaks of wind and water. One of the busiest corners of the earth ages ago and now the loneliest and most desolate, its beauty was like a woman's who had survived every passion, and lives in retrospect.

El Capitan, rising alone from the yellow sands, sailed before us like a full-rigged ship from sunset to the next morning, when we rode our last eighteen miles to Kayenta. The sight of it, and the orange dunes beyond spurred us all. Spontaneously we broke into a twelve mile canter. The little white mule Annie who had finally fallen to me, kept her freshness and speed and general pluckiness. She out-distanced them all by a length. We made a ludicrous picture as we came flying over the rocks and dunes and desert, shouting and galloping. Even the pack beasts, worn to bone since they departed from the corral, smelled Kayenta, and there was no stopping them. Navajos rode out to join us, leaving their herd of a thousand sheep to cross our path at their peril. We arrived not half an hour after the Indian messenger, sent ahead to tell of our coming.

How civilized the remote little trading post seemed! How ultra-æsthetic to eat at a table with napkins and table linen, food passed by a neat Navajo maid! What throngs of people inhabited Kayenta,—more than we had met altogether in ten days! We bathed who had not seen water, we feasted and relaxed, and bought Navajo necklaces in the store. To our surprise the same old women we had left behind us were still alive and scarcely grayer or more toothless; we had not been away for years, as had seemed from our isolation in the still canyons where all sense of time disappeared and we lived in eternity along with the rocks and sky.

That evening, as we sat on wool bags heaped high near the post, a group of young Navajos came and announced they wished to welcome our return with a serenade. They grouped in a circle, very bashful at our applause, and while one held a lantern, began to sing their ancient tribal songs. I shall never forget the weird setting of rolling hills of orange sand, and moonlighted red cliffs behind the circle of their dark figures. Lightly swaying to the music, they began a savage chanting, with rhythmically placed falsetto yelps and guttural shouts. Their voices had real beauty, and the music suited their surroundings. They started with a mild song of hunting or love, but soon they were singing war songs. Our blood stirred to an echo of something we knew many lives ago. The lantern light made a wilder, wider arc; the shouts became more fierce; the group swayed faster

MONUMENT COUNTRY, RAINBOW TRAIL.
Isolated cliffs pointed the valley in every grotesque form.

RAINBOW BRIDGE TRAIL.

and swung into a wide ellipse. Worked upon by the hypnotism of their war-music, they locked arms about each other in tight grip; for the moment they were ages away from Carlisle. The blackness, the orange hills, the swinging light, the shouts, the listening stillness of the desert,—that will always be Kayenta for me.

CHAPTER XXI

THE CANYON DE CHELLEY

WE had been pulled out of difficulties by donkeys, men, autos and pulleys. It remained for Kayenta to show us a new way out. When a terrific thank-you-marm jolted off our power, our late host's daughter rode out on her stout cow-pony, roped us, so to speak, and started forward as though she intended to tow us. The knowing horse, who had seen thousands of steers act as the old lady was doing now, treated the car with equal contempt, and braced her feet. It was thirty-horse to one-horse power, but the better animal won. We slid forward in gear, jolting our power on again as we moved ahead.

Sluggish after two week's hard exercise, we were late in getting started for Chin Le. Thunderous clouds were already blackening the afternoon sky. They greatly increased the desert's beauty, making it majestic beyond words. Soon the storm burst, and silver sheets of rain obliterated everything but the distant red hills. We were in the middle of a flat plain with landmarks more or less like any other landmarks. By twilight we were traveling through thick, red mud, and by dark the mud had disappeared beneath an inland lake. The road was not. We only knew we kept to it, in some miraculous fashion, because we continued slowly to progress. Halfway to Chin Le we stopped in the dark at a little trader's post,

bought gasoline at seventy-five cents a gallon, and continued our splashing. All we could see between two lines
of hills was water. We lost the road for a moment, got
into a deep draw, and when we emerged from our bath,
the generating system was no more.

Around us was blackness, with a few distant mesas
outlined through the slashing rain. The men got out,
and examined the machinery, while Toby and I stayed
within, enjoying the luxury of a breakdown which neces-
sitated no exertion on our part. They returned covered
with mud halfway to the knees. The guide volunteered
to walk to Chin Le for help. It might be five or ten
miles. We promised, rather unnecessarily, not to move
till he returned. He took our one electric torch, and
vanished into the blackest night I ever saw. A forlorn
feeling settled over us. We had no light, little food and
no guide, and no present means of transportation. If
our guide fell into some new-born raging torrent, not
one of us knew the way back.

In five minutes we were all asleep. We were awakened
hours later by a voice that meant business, shouting
"Stop! Who's there?"

Murray's round, red face loomed above the front seat
like the rising moon.

"Who's there?" The Golfer took up the challenge.

We in the back seat trembled. Whoever was there
had us at his mercy. We were entirely unarmed. Nobody answered, and in a few minutes we regained enough
courage to ask questions in bated whispers.

"What did you see, Murray?"

"The burglar," said Murray, looking bewildered.

Then it dawned on us he had been having a nightmare, and we all breathed again.

"What time is it?" someone asked.

"One o'clock." We looked at each other. The guide had been gone four hours.

"Had we better hunt for him?" asked Murray.

"Where could we go?" asked the Golfer.

That seemed to settle·all question of action. We repacked ourselves and I made myself more comfortable by removing a suitcase from my left foot, and Toby's specimens from the back of my neck, and soon we were asleep again. It seemed heartless, not knowing the guide's fate, but I suppose we reasoned we could face tragedy better if we had our sleep out. So quiet followed. We awoke through the night only to complain of a paralyzed foot or arm, and demand our share of the car and covers. A strange informality prevailed, as must when five people, each aggressively bent on obtaining his proper amount of rest, occupy one touring car all night.

At four, a hideous noise awoke us. Murray had fallen on the horn, and had brought forth sound. It took us a moment to realize this meant the return of our power. We were free to go ahead. But with north, south, east and west completely disguised as an inland sea, we thought it discreet to wait till sunrise. We no longer hoped for the guide's return, and gloomily looked for a sad ending to our trip.

The sunrise, when it came, was worth waiting for. Fresh-washed and glowing, the holiday colors of the hills came out from the mediocre buffs and grays of the desert, and the primrose sky slowly became gilded with

ENTRANCE TO THE CANYON DE CHELLEY

glory. As nothing exceeds the weariness of the desert at noon, so nothing compares with its freshness, its revelation of beauty, at dawn. Each mesa was outlined in gold. Waves of color, each melting into the next, flushed the prairie and sky. We forgot the tedium of the night in this splendor of morning.

We motored slowly through all this glory,—our car having started on the first trial,—through seven miles of mud, but Chin Le had apparently been swallowed up by the deluge. The mesas took on an unfamiliar aspect, and we concluded that hidden by some gully, we had gone beyond our destination. A red-banded Navajo on a pinto rode up curiously when we called him. He was the only soul on the vast horizon, and he understood no English, and appeared slow in comprehending our Navajo. Waving his hand vaguely in the direction from which we came, he repeated one word.

"Ishklish!"

"If we only knew what ishklish meant we should be all right," said Toby hopefully.

"Not ishklish,—slicklish," corrected the Golfer who had made quite a specialty of Navajo, and who could pronounce, "De-jiss-je" better than any of us. "Slicklish! I know I've heard that word before."

"Ishklish! Slicklish," we repeated with bent brows, in Gilbertian chorus. "We've heard that word before. We're *sure* we've heard that word before."

"Ishklish!" assented the Navajo.

The Golfer pursued his philological meditations to a triumphant end.

"Slicklish means matches!" he announced.

His discovery did not impress us as he expected.

"Why should he come up to a party of motorists at five in the morning to say 'matches'?" we asked.

"Because he wants a cigarette," answered our linguist. "As it is a marked discourtesy among Indians to offer a cigarette without matches, he takes the more subtle way of begging a smoke by asking for matches. Slicklish!"

"Ishklish!" nodded the Navajo. Apparently he could keep on like that forever.

Pulling out his cigarette case, the Golfer gave the Indian a handful with a match. The latter gave us a radiant smile, and rode away.

"You see that's what he meant."

Murray often put his finger on the point. "What good does that do us?" he asked.

Following the Navajo's vague gestures, we came at last within sight of the long government buildings of Chin Le. But between them and us an arroyo lay, no longer the puddle we had splashed through on our way to Kayenta, but four feet of red torrent which had already cut down the soft banks into miniature cliffs, and completely barred our crossing. We shuddered when we saw it, and thought how easy it would be for a man to slip over these slippery banks in the dark. Now seriously concerned at the guide's failure to appear, the two men started off to find if possible a ford they might safely attempt, while we got out the coffee pot, and built a tiny fire of twigs, the only fuel in sight. The matches were wet, the sugar melted, and the can-opener lost. By the time we managed to get the coffee boiling we saw a two horse team crossing the stream, with the trader and the missing guide on the front seat.

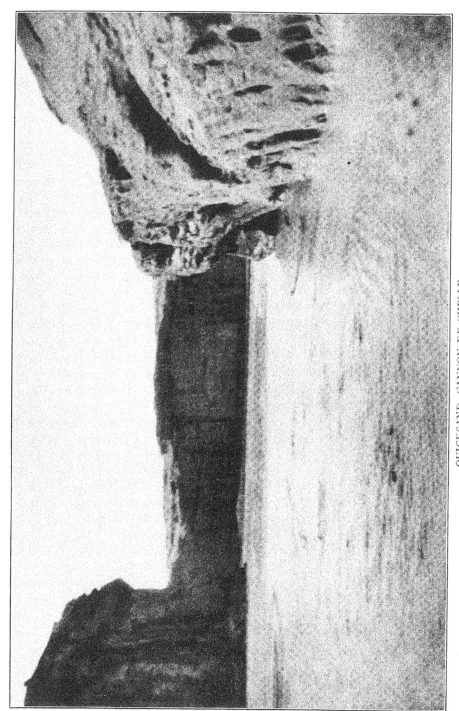

QUICKSAND; CANYON DE CHELLE

"Where did you spend the night?" we asked, much relieved to see him alive.

"In bed, at Mr. Stagg's," he answered. He explained that he had reached Chin Le safely, and had taken a wagon out to find us, but failing to do so, had gone back to bed. He started out in the morning just in time to save Murray·and the Golfer from a cold swim.

Leaving the car until the flood should abate, we piled our belongings and ourselves into the wagon, and started across the muddy stream. The water rose to the hubs, then to the horses' shoulders. One stepped in a hole, almost disappearing, and nearly carrying the wagon with him, but at last we crossed safely, and reached Stagg's in time for breakfast. We told the adventures of the night, ending with our encounter with the Navajo.

"What does ishklish mean?" we asked.

"You mean slicklish," corrected the Golfer.

"Ishklish? Slicklish?" said Mr. Stagg. "Oh, **you** mean ushklush."

"Well, what does ushklush mean?"

"Why, ushklush means mud."

It is, I think, the best name for mud that could be invented, especially the Navajo mud we had ushklushed through since dawn.

We were all unprepared for the Canyon de Chelley when we came upon it, a few hours later. The entrance is the sort all such places should have, casual, yet dramatic,—hiding one moment what it reveals with telling effect the next. The rolling plain apparently spread for miles without variation; nothing unusual, sand and bleak dunes, sage and piñon, and behind, against buff hills, the rather ugly government buildings, schools, hospitals, and like substitutes for freedom that we give the Indian. We rode a few steps down a natural rocky incline, and a wall opened, as it did for Aladdin, and through the aperture of these gate-like cliffs we saw the beginning of a narrow valley, grassy and fertile, bordering a river imprisoned for life between continuous walls, smooth, dark red, varying in height from three hundred to three thousand feet, and as unbroken as if some giant had sliced them with his sword. We rode through this embodiment of Dead Man's Gulch, and came a few feet beyond on the canyon of whose beauty we had heard from afar.

Canyon de Chelley is a dry river bed, with banks a thousand feet or more in the air. In winter and early spring the water brims up to the solid walls hemming it in on all sides, leaving no foothold for horse or man. As it recedes, towards summer, it leaves broad strips of beaches and fertile little green nooks under the shadow of the cliffs, with the river meandering in the middle. Yet lovely as it is, it has a Lorelei charm. Its yellow sands, when not thoroughly dry, are treacherous,—quicksand of the worst sort.

With our outfit we had a large wagon, which our driver turned too quickly over a new cut-bank. In an instant, the wagon toppled on two wheels, and we had a vision of Toby and Martha flying through the air, followed by bedding, cameras and supplies. Fortunately they barely escaped the overturning wagon, which followed them, and landed unhurt. Before we could reach them the contents of the wagon were entirely covered by the sucking sand. Had it been spring, when the pull

NEAR THE ENTRANCE OF CANYON DE CHELLEY, ARIZONA
Canyon de Chelley is a river bed with banks a thousand feet or more in air.

of the quicksand is more vigorous, we should not have been able to recover them.

Those of us who were on horseback followed the edge of the stream, sometimes acting as guide for the wagon, sometimes following in its slow wake. We galloped ahead, on the hard sands, level and smooth for miles, or splashed to our horses' knees in the deeper parts of the stream, or edged them more cautiously through quicksands, of which there still remained more than a trace. They sank to the ankles, and each hoof left a little swirling, sucking well, which quickly filled with water. But only one spot seemed at all dangerous.

The river was constantly turning and twisting upon itself, looking back over its shoulder through gateways of sheer cliffs, smooth as if someone had frosted them with chocolate icing. In the narrow space between them a little Paradise of shade and sunlight, grass and blossoming fruit trees, ran like a parti-colored ribbon. The Navajos have planted peach trees in this fertile strip. Graceful cottonwoods make an emerald shelter, and brooks branch into the central stream. The river spreads out in great shallows at will, with rank grass growing knee-high at its edge. Rocks like cathedrals stand guardian at every turn, so close together sometimes that the sky is held prisoner in a wedge of blue.

Patches of rough gardens cut into the flowered banks gave us our first intimation that the Paradise sheltered an Adam and an Eve. Then we saw wattled huts of willow, the summer hogans of Navajos, airier and more graceful than their mud plastered winter huts. On turning a corner where the receding river had already left a long, fertile island, we came on an encampment of these brightly dressed, alert Arabs, with their keen faces and winged poise. Horses and sheep were pastured near, and under the trees several women had erected frames on which were stretched half-finished rugs. Others, in their full gathered skirts with gay flounces, rode their horses to water as easily as if they wore breeches and puttees. Under the cliffs they looked like tiny dots. This canyon is the favorite summer resort of neighboring Indians, and no wonder. Here for a pleasant season they can forget the arid wastes of the desert in their apricot orchards, and grow without travail their corn and beans and melons.

We had scarcely left this gypsy encampment before we saw mute evidence that the place had been beloved of more than one generation of Indians. Nearly at the top of a rock clustered a few cliff houses, mere crannies in the wall, and all along that unbroken cliff were little, scared shelters, no bigger than mousetraps, watching with scared eyes as no doubt their inmates did long ago, the approaches to their stronghold. Tradition has it that the architects of these houses were ancestors of the Hopis, driven here partly by enemies, partly by drought, but also by the inspiration of their medicine men. It is not strange these empty nests should be arresting sights, dating back to the antiquity when the Hopis could turn into snakes, and the king's son and his snake bride followed the star which led them to Walpi. They may have inhabited the very eyrie we saw. A tiny, bridal apartment it was, so inaccessible at the top of this slab of rock that only a snake could climb to it. Surely no entirely human feet would dare venture those heights.

We were struck by the many isolated dwellings we

CLIFF-DWELLINGS, CANYON DE CHELLEY, ARIZONA

came upon. Unlike the extensive cities at Beta-Takin, at Walnut Canyon, and Mesa Verde, these must have been intended for single families. Between the various groups is a distance sometimes of a half mile, sometimes a mile. The largest and by far the most impressive group in the canyon is Casa Blanca, the White House of some ancient dignitary occupying a commanding position looking far down the valley in both directions. The river cuts deep and narrow here, with shallow islands between. Above it by twenty feet is a bank where crumbling walls, painted with prehistoric pictographs of birds and animals, stand under the shadow of Casa Blanca. The rock is blood red when the sun strikes it, and purple in the shadow. Seventy feet up, the whitewashed walls of this ancient mansion are startlingly, romantically prominent, looking fresh enough to have been painted yesterday.

How the former dwellers reached Casa Blanca is a puzzle. They must have had the aid of ladders and niches in the rock. Today it is completely inaccessible, except to Douglas Fairbanks, who once bounded lightly up its side. A day's ride down the left fork, overlooking a vale meant for stately pleasure domes, is the Cave of the Mummies. This community of cliff dwellings is so called because one startled explorer found in it seven mummies, in perfect preservation. The cave can be reached by diligent climbing, and aside from all interest in things past, the view down that graceful, twisting valley is worth losing many hours of breath.

We camped that night under a red monolith big enough to bury a nation beneath it. The beauty of that scene is past my exhausted powers of description. The campfire and the river, the smooth cliffs penetrating the black sky with such strength and suavity, were the same essentials as we found at the Rainbow Bridge, yet with all the difference in the world. Grandeur was here, but not the rugged hurly-burly of Titans which overwhelmed and dwarfed us there. Where the San Juan tumbles and froths, and bursts over boulders, struggling and tumultuous, the de Chelley river glides peacefully, widening about pretty shallows and quiet islands. In Nonnezoshe Boco, the rocks are tortured into strange shapes, twisted and wrung like wet clay; here they are planed smooth and not tossed about helter-skelter, but rhythmically repeating the pattern of the stream.

The essential quality of the Canyon de Chelley is not its grandeur, I think, but its rhythm, and the opposite may be said of the Bridge. Those who have seen only de Chelley might well challenge this statement, for a river walled in its entire length by cliffs a quarter to a half mile high can hardly be called less than tremendous. But following as it does the meanderings of a whimsical stream, none of the continuous pictures it makes lacks graceful composition. Here one could spend pleasant months, loafing in those little groves by the river's brim. Now the Rainbow Trail could never be called pleasant. It is ferocious, forbidding, terrible, desolate, vast,—with relieving oases of garden and stream, but it does not invite to loaf. It is an arduous and exacting pilgrimage. It does not smile, like de Chelley, nor remind one of the gracious and stately landscapes of Claude Lorraine.

Perhaps a better climax would have been gained by seeing the Canyon de Chelley first, and progressing to the

CASA BLANCA, CANYON DE CHELLEY, ARIZONA
The rock is blood red when the sun strikes it, and purple in the shadow.

Bridge, as we should have done had de Chelley not been flooded when we stopped on our way to Kayenta. But anticlimax or not, we loved the rest and relaxation after our strenuous adventure. It was like entering Heaven and finding it unexpectedly gay.

CHAPTER XXII

NORTH OF GALLUP

I CAN still, by shutting my eyes, see thousands of vistas,—little twisting roads clinging tightly to cliffs, tangles of cactus, gray cliff dwellings, pregnant with the haunting sense of life fled recently, deserts ablaze overnight with golden poppies and blue lupin, forests of giant pines backed by blue mountains, snow-peaked; long views of green valleys with cottonwood-bordered streams, miles of silver pampas grass, neat rows of ugly new bungalows in uncompromising sunlight, older wooden shacks with false fronts, dry prairies white with the skeletons of cattle, copper colored canyons dropping from underfoot far into the depths of earth, water-holes with thousands of moving sheep; spiky, waxen yuccas against a night sky;—all this is the West, but inseparable from these mental visions come pungent odors so sharp that I can almost smell them now.

I cannot hope to reproduce the charm and joy of our wanderings, despite mishaps and disasters, because the freshness of mountain altitudes will not drift from the leaves of this book, nor the perfume of sunshine on resin, of miles of mountain flowers, nor the scent of desert dust, dry and untainted by man, the sharp smell of camps,—bacon cooking, wet canvas, horse blankets and leather;—bitter-sweet sage, sweet to the nostril and keen to the tongue, nor the tang of new-cut lumber, frosty nights, and fresh-water lakes, glacier cooled; the reek of an Indian village, redolent of doe-skin and dried meats hanging in the sun;—I am homesick for them! And so is everyone who has found good hunting northwest of the Rio Grande.

We again found ourselves on the old Spanish Trail, which leads into Utah through Farmington and a bit of Colorado. Most of the way it was desert, a wicked collection of chuck-holes, high centers, tree-roots, gullies and sand drifts. This was a district once highly respected and avoided, for a few miles further north lay the four state boundaries. Men who find proximity to a state line convenient were twice as well suited with the Four Corners, reckoning arithmetically,—or four times, geometrically. Its convenience probably increased by the same ratio their abandoned character over other abandoned characters who had only two states in which to play hop-scotch with the sheriff. No doubt most of these professional outlaws have disappeared, picked off by the law's revenge, or by private feud. We should have liked to explore this region further, but sundown was too near for this to be a judicious act, and while we were not always discreet, we were at times.

In late afternoon we looked ahead of us, and saw in this sea of sand two schooners with purple sails full rigged, rosy lighted by the setting sun. They tilted gracefully on a northerly course, the nearer one seeming to loom as high above the other as a sloop above a little catboat. No other landmark lifted above the long horizon save the low hills on our west which at Canyon de Chelley had been east of us. Only when we traveled five, ten, fifteen miles did we realize the magnitude of

these giant ships of rock, made so light by the reflection
of sand and sun that the sails seemed cut out of amethyst
tissue rather than carved of granite.   When we passed
the first rock, which had seemed so high, it took its
proper place, and it became the catboat, while the real
Shiprock, we saw, far excelled the other in size and
in its likeness to a ship.   With the afterglow, the desert
became gray and the ship golden, with purple edged sails.
At dark the desert became blue-black, and the ship
melted into a gossamer mist, looming higher as we neared
it.   It must be five or six hundred feet high, and so
precipitous that nobody has ever scaled its outspread
wings, though the Human Fly came from New York for
the purpose, and returned defeated.

As we went on in this intensely lonely country, out of
the darkness came an odor that a moment before had
not been, resembling jasmine or syringa, but fresher than
either.   We stopped the car, expecting to find ourselves
in the midst of a garden.   But all around was only greasewood and sage, sage and greasewood.   The twigs we
plucked to smell broke off brittle in our hands.   We
drove on, much perplexed.

Just before we reached the town of Shiprock, the air
lifted with a new freshness.   We sniffed, and raised our
heads as horses do.   We were reminded of home.   It
was water!   We had not smelled water for two dry days.
In an instant we were rolling down shady avenues, and
saw lights reflected on a river, and crossed into a town
so dense with green grass and arched trees and roses in
bloom that it seemed like some old place in New England.   Then the mysterious odor, stronger and of unearthly sweetness, came again.   It blew from a field of

alfalfa in bloom, with the night dew distilling its heavenly freshness. We must have been several miles away when its perfume first reached us in the desert.

A car halted in the road before the superintendent's house,—for Shiprock is a Navajo agency,—and as we stopped, a man and his wife exchanged names and destinations with us in the darkness. They were from California, going to Yellowstone. When we told them our home town they said the usual thing. We discussed plans for the night. They had none, neither had we. It was nearly midnight.

"That's the agent's house," he said, pointing to the only light in town, "but they won't take you there. We just asked. The lady's all alone, but she might give you directions for a hotel."

As we went toward the house, an Indian policeman in uniform shadowed us, wearing the kind of helmet the police used to wear in Boston and rural plays. He seemed to alternate between a desire to protect us against Shiprock, and Shiprock against us, his grave manner signifying he would do justice to both parties.

The agent's wife directed us to a hotel, which she refused to indorse, and when we left, she called after us, —"You aren't alone?"

"Yes," I answered, "all alone, ever since we left Boston." And then, to save time, "We're a long ways from *home.*"

"I don't know what accommodations you'd find at the hotel," she said. "You'd better stay here. Being alone, I didn't want to take in any men, but I'd be glad to have **your** company."

"Did you find a hotel?" asked the kind man in the road, as we returned for our baggage.

"Yes,—here," we said, "not having a man with us."

"You have the luck," he answered, and his wife groaned, and asked him as wives will, what good it did her to have him along.

Our kind hostess gave us a pleasant room, and carte blanche to the icebox, for I believe we had no supper that night. It may have been partly our kind reception, but not entirely so, that made Shiprock seem, when we inspected it next day, one of the most attractive and sensibly conducted agencies we had visited. It is beautifully situated where our old friend the San Juan river joins another stream, and turns the desert into the greenest of farm lands. Roses bloomed about each neat, white-picketed house, big trees shaded the road, and the lawns were like velvet. Happy looking Navajo children in middy blouses played about the schoolyards or splashed in the big swimming pool devoted exclusively to them. The teachers and agents whom we met lacked that attitude of contempt for their charges we had sometimes observed in other Indian schools. I have heard teachers who could hardly speak without butchering the President's English sneer at their Indian charges for reverting to their own tongue.

The day of our stay on the reservation an interesting event took place. Once a year the government requires all Navajos to bring in their sheep to be dipped in a strong solution of lye and tobacco, to prevent vermin and disease. In the early morning the air was filled with a thousand bleatings. The dust rose thick from countless hoofs driven to the sheep-dip. The dip was situ-

NAVAJO SHEEP-DIPPING AT SHIPROCK

Fat Navajo squaws pulled the unhappy beasts to the trough by the horns

ated against great yellow buttes, and in the distance the ship rock sailed in lilac light. Fat Navajo squaws with their jewels tied to their belt for safe keeping pulled the unhappy beasts to the trough by the horns, where they completely submerged them, with the aid of an Indian wielding a two-pronged staff.

"Get in and help," said an old squaw to me. Accordingly I grasped a rough horn, and discovered it took strength and some skill to keep the animals from being trampled, as they went down the trough. Once a tremendous chatter arose, as a result of the squaws counting their sheep and finding one missing. The poor creature was discovered, crushed and bleeding at the bottom of the runway. Immediately he was fished out, and borne off by two women whom I followed to watch. One held the carcass, while the other pulled from her woven belt a long, glittering knife. In twenty minutes the sheep was skinned, dressed and cut into neat chops and loins, and the incident was closed. The women are ✓ sole owners and custodians of the sheep-herds. The gathering that day would have rejoiced the heart of any feminist. With one old hag I noticed a beautiful little Navajo child dressed in the usual velvet jacket, flowing skirt and silver ornaments. Two lumps of turquoise were strung in her ears. Her eyes, like her skin, were golden brown and her hair bright yellow. Her unusual complexion added to her beauty made her a pet of the entire village, and the idol of her old grandmother. If she was an Albino, the lack of pigment took a more becoming form than among the Hopis.

Mesa Verde National Park is only a short day's run from Shiprock. It took us into the edge of Colorado, a beautiful, loveable state, endowed with sense, mountains, good roads and every kind of natural blessing. It has a flavor all its own; more mellow than the states of the West coast, less prim than those on its eastern borders. Our way led between two mountain ranges, one in Utah, the other in Colorado, with a long sweep of prairies curling like waves at their base. We passed a corner of the Ute country, and saw at a spring a group of those gaily dressed, rather sullen people, ample bodied and round headed. Each tribe differs from the others, and these bore a look more like the Northern tribes than those we had already met.

As the Colorado mountains came nearer, I remembered the words of a fellow traveler, spoken on the slippery drive to Taos, New Mexico, which had haunted me ever since.

"This is steep enough, but wait till you climb Mesa Verde. The engineer cut a road straight up the mountain to the top, with as few switchbacks and as little grading as he could. It is so narrow that you have to telephone your arrival when you reach the base of the hill, and they shut off all downward traffic till you report at the Park."

We were both by this time inured to horizontal fever, and could steer quite debonairly within an inch of a thousand foot drop, but we "figured," as they say out West, that we had about reached our limit, and if we were to encounter anything more vertiginous, something *might* happen. I don't say we dreaded Mesa Verde, but I will admit we speculated over our prospects.

"Heavens! Do they expect us to climb *that?*" exclaimed Toby when we sighted the beginning of the

twenty-six mile road to the Park. A mountain stood on
its hind legs before us, and pawed the air. The white
gash of road leading uncompromisingly up its side
showed us all too well what to expect. At the summit, a
naked erosion rose like Gibraltar for a hundred feet
from its green setting. Whether we should have to conquer that bit of masonry we did not know, but if we had
to, I knew our chances were not good. I clung to the
story I had heard of a one-armed girl who had driven a
Ford to the top, and then collapsed. We ought to do at
least as well, we reasoned, reserving the right to collapse
on arrival. At the base of the hill I telephoned the superintendent of the Park, at a switchboard by the roadside,
as commanded by placard.

"Come ahead, and 'phone at the top," he said. His
voice was most matter-of-fact. From that moment, anti-
climax reigned. Roads are never as bad as report makes
them, and this besides being far less narrow than many
mountain passes we had been through, was beautifully
graded on the turns, and in excellent condition. We
passed several steep ravines at curves,—one where a
car had overturned the week previous,—but none was as
bad as we had been led to expect. Thanks to the sane
regulation making it a one way road we had nothing to
fear from traffic. Valleys, blue and red with a magnificent sweep of flowers, dropped down, down, and new
mountains rose from unexpected coverts. We circled the
one we were on, pausing at the summit for the view
over the emerald slopes far below. We reached the base
of our Gibraltar, but saw on nearer approach that we
could no more have climbed it then we could climb Washington Monument on the outside. Instead we rounded

it, and dipped up and down another hillside, overlooking an eastern valley. Here the road was delightfully planned so that we could look far ahead over our course, and coast or climb without fearing the next turn. Well named is the Park, so surprisingly green after the desert. In an hour and three-quarters we had covered the twenty-six miles to the inn. This, we were told by the stage drivers, was fairly near record time.

We met a man soon after our arrival, to whom we mentioned that we had recently come from the Rainbow Bridge.

"Oh," said he, "were you in the party where the mule threw the man off into the cactus?"

News travels like that in the West.

Mesa Verde is what is called a three days' park. One could easily spend three weeks or three months there with profit or delight, camping in its delicious forests and riding over its mountainsides. But in three days all that is to be seen of cliff dwellings and prehistoric ruins can be inspected without hurry, unless of course one is an archæologist. Here are most elaborate ruins, carefully restored, whose many kivas indicate a prosperous and flourishing community. Long canyons, thickly wooded and enameled with wild-flowers are lined on both sides with these airy villages. A small museum of articles found in excavating, displayed in the main house, greatly aids the mere amateur.

We were fortunate in having a guide who knew his park like a book. Forsaking routine paths and steps, he hoisted us up and down the paths,—mere niches they were,—worn in the solid wall by those agile Indians. It seems certain that at that time no cliff-mothers in-

CLIFF–DWELLINGS, MESA VERDE PARK, COLORADO
Here are most elaborate ruins, carefully restored

dulged in the embonpoint affected by so many of their descendants. An inch too much of girdle in the right,— or the wrong,—place, would have sent them hurtling down into the canyon, as they climbed those sheer walls. Being one of the oldest known cliff communities, Mesa Verde is much more carefully restored than those we saw in the Canyon de Chelley and in Segi Canyon. More accessible and compact than other ruins, Mesa Verde combines the historic,—or prehistoric,—interest with the needs of vacation seekers who wish a few luxuries with their cliff dwellings. Although the hotel is of the simplest sort, it is well run. Those who wish to camp may do so by obtaining a permit. Tent houses are provided as a compromise between camping and hotel life for those who want to feel they are roughing it, but prefer a floor and a mattress between them and the insect world.

We entered the Mormon country not long after we left Mesa Verde and turned north again into Utah. Here once more we had desert, villainous prairie roads, utter loneliness, with vista of foothills of the Rockies guarding our route. We drove hard and camped where midnight found us, or, too weary to spread our tent, went still further to the next one of the miserably equipped towns in rural Utah, where we had the benefit of rickety bedsprings and stifling bedrooms. It was cherry time, and each warm day we blessed Brigham Young for his foresight in encouraging the growth of fruit trees. The Mormons were the earliest in the West to understand the use of irrigation. Their villages, slatternly as to buildings, nestle in lanes and avenues of poplar and cottonwood, and their gardens bear all manner of fruit. They are good providers, too, in this rural desert, and at noon sharp, when we stopped doubtfully at some unpainted shack, bearing the sign Café, we were astonished at the abundance of wholesome country food spread on the long table. We sat among a group of overalled men, who ate in silence, except for the sounds of mastication.

"Help yourself, Brother Smith. Brother Thacher, you aint eatin' today," the ample goddess who presided over the stove in the corner of the room would encourage her patrons. At the close of the meal, whether we had consumed one or six helpings of the cheese, the meat pie, the ham, the raspberries and stoned cherries with rich country cream in quart pitchers, the apple pie and chocolate cake, we wiped our fingers on napkins well used to such treatment, paid our "six bits" and departed, our parting "Good-day" being answered with caution.

Through such country, uninhabited for long stretches, we were driving one evening, hoping to reach Green River forty miles north. Though with filial respect we often remembered the last injunction of Toby's parent, we were frequently obliged to postpone fulfilling it till a more convenient occasion. Tonight we had to choose between making a barren camp in open prairie and pushing on to the nearest hotel. A dry camp made after dark represents the height of discomfort, so we chose the alternative. Our route lay over a waste of sand,—that portion of the desert which claims central Utah. For several miles we followed the wretched little prairie tracks, but finally, to our great joy, we struck into a broad state road in perfect condition, raised above the floor of the desert by several feet. We made marvelous speed.

Who would have expected to find a boulevard in the heart of rural Utah?

Whoever would, was doomed to speedy disappointment. Our boulevard seemed to lack continuity; several times we were forced to forsake it and make detours back over the trails. Soon our highway, which was leveled an easy grade above the desert, began to rise in the air, until in the pitch dark it assumed an alarmingly dizzy elevation. About the same time the marks of traffic faded. We passed through a morass of crushed stone, and thence into thick sand, over which we skidded alarmingly toward the edge of the bank. Perhaps we were eighteen or twenty feet above the desert, but when we veered for the edge, it semed like a hundred. The heavy sand clung to our wheels, making progress hard and skidding easy. We passed through a cut with heavy banks on both sides, and in front a black shadow.

"Why, where's the road?" exclaimed Toby

There was none. We were left high and dry, with a sandhill on both sides, steep banks dropping down among rocks and gullies to the desert, a yawning hole in front with a precipitous drop of twenty feet, and two feet of leeway, in which to turn our car. We backed cautiously down the side, and struck a boulder. We turned forward a few inches, and came upon a heap of sand. Toby got out, and directed our maneuvers, inch by inch. Finally we had the car broadside to the jumping-off place, and there we stuck, tilted at a crazy angle, one headlight almost directly above the other. In the heavy, untracked sand we could not move an inch.

"Well," I said bitterly, "here we spend the night. Twelve miles from nowhere!"

At that four men with a lantern sprang up from no-where.

"How kind of you to come," we said to the men, assuming they were there to rescue, not to rob.

"We saw your headlights," answered the one who held the lantern, "and from the way they were slanted we concluded you was in trouble and we might as well come over. We're working on the new state road, and this is as far as it's got. Our camp's just over there, and Green River's twelve miles further."

Backing and filling, with their four brawny shoulders to the wheels, we soon got the car out of the sand heap and turned about, but the deep sand was crowned so high that for a stretch we skidded along at so sharp an angle that only the tug of the sand kept us from turning turtle. Our friends put us on our way, going a half mile out of their own to do so.

The sleepy clerk at Green River was locking the hotel up for the night as we stopped before his door.

"My, you're in luck," said he. "If the midnight train hadn't been late this hotel would have been closed up tight."

Such incidents, happening almost daily, began to give us a reckless faith in our luck, or our guardian angels, or the special Providence said to look after certain types of people, whichever you may choose to call it. Ministering angels of the first calibre had perfected their system to give instant service day or night. They thought nothing of letting us run dry of gasoline on a road where all morning we had not passed a single car, and sending us within five minutes a truck carrying a barrel of the useful fluid. They delighted in letting us drive a bit too fast down a narrow canyon, where a blowout from our ragged tires would have mingled our bones forever with the "old lady's," arriving scatheless at the bottom simultaneously with a blowout which dragged us, standing, across the road.   Once a Ford, driven by inexpert and slightly befuddled Elks, crashed into us on a narrow bridge, with no results beyond a bent canteen.   When we broke four spring leaves at dusk in a lonesome hamlet, they placed across the street an expert German blacksmith of the old school, who did not object to night hours, and who forged us new springs which finally outwore the car.   By happy mistake, they took us down pleasant by-paths less fortunate tourists who went by Bluebook never knew.   Altogether, they were a firm of remarkable reliability, and if I knew their address I should publish it.   But they preferred to do good anonymously.

I think it was they who directed us through the Shoshone reservation on the very day of the year when the tribe held its important ceremony, the Sun Dance.   We reached Fort Hall, the Shoshone agency, one morning, and were told casually of a dance being held on the reservation, not a mile out of our way.   When we reached it a magnificent Indian, the first we had seen who could be called a red man, (for the Southern Indians are brown and ochre colored), barred our path on horseback.   He knew his cerise sateen shirt was becoming, even without the purple necktie he wore.   It gave him confidence to demand an entrance fee of $2.00—an entirely impromptu idea inspired by our eagerness.   The more I see of Lo the Poor Indian the more I am convinced that he is poor only for lack of opportunity to exercise his talents.   However, the dance was worth the money,—far more than some other barefoot dances I have seen.

It had begun when we arrived on the scene, in fact, it had been going on for two days. Crowds of women, some dressed in long plaid shawls and high moccasins, others in starched muslins and straw hats; bright-eyed papooses slung on their mother's backs in beautiful white doeskin cradles; majestic chiefs six feet tall and more in high pointed Stetsons, with long robes of cotton sheeting, giddily dyed, wrapped about them, circled about the dancers, who were partly screened from spectators by the green branches seen in so many Indian dances. These Shoshones are the Indians on the penny. Grave, surly giants with copper skin, coarse jet hair and high cheek bones, powerful, with a hint of ugliness, they were another race from the laughing brown tribes of the south. They frowned upon our camera, and finally forbade us, in no uncertain manner, to use it. Even the insouciant Toby paled and hastily stuffed her camera in her coat as a big chief made a threatening lunge at it. That is why all our photographs of the Shoshones are taken from the rear.

Old women trotted to and fro constantly with bunches of sweet grass and herbs, which they laid on the ground beside the resting dancers, who used them to dry and refresh their exhausted bodies. A group of old men in the corner beat the tom-tom, squatting to their task like gnomes. The dancers, naked to the waist, wore a short apron-like garment of calico or blanket below. Their bodies, old and young, were lithe and stringy,— hardly a fat man among them. They showed much ex-

SHOSHONES AT SUN DANCE, FORT HALL, IDAHO

All our photographs of the Shoshones are taken from the rear

haustion,—as much perhaps on this second day of the dance as white men not in training would after half an hour of similar exercise. Many of them were past middle age. One was white-haired and wrinkled, but with magnificent muscles on his bare chest and arms. They alternately rested and danced in groups, so that the dancing was continuous. Running at a jog trot to a great tree in the center, decorated with elk horns and a green branch, they touched this tree with reverent obeisances and a wild upward movement of body and head, then carried their hand from it, as if transferring its vitality to their knees, their breasts and their heads. For the three days and nights the dance was to last, they would neither eat nor drink.

"What does it mean?" I asked a very modern lady, dressed in flowered organdy. She smiled a superior smile, evidently holding no longer with the gods of her ancestors.

"It's a dance they think will make well sick people. I do not know,—some foolishness, I guess."

A tall chief with a pipe in his mouth, wearing a scarlet shawl, fanned himself with a lady's fan of black spangles and gauze, and as he fanned he frowned at us, muttering at our levity in talking during the sacred ceremonies. He only needed a rose behind his ear to make a gaunt Carmen of him, temper and all. His eyes fell menacingly on Toby's camera, which she had been fingering, and Toby-wise she turned and sauntered off as if she hadn't seen him, though I imagine her knees shook.

From the not too friendly Indians we could get no further information of the meaning of the dance, but later I discovered we had been fortunate enough to witness the

Sun Dance. During the winter, when sickness falls upon a relative, some Indian will vow to organize this dance, if health should return to the sick one. The whole tribe comes to take part or to witness the dance. The participants refrain from food or drink for three days, sustained to their exertion by marvelous nervous energy and real religious fervor. Before the government forbade the practise it was their custom to cut slits in their breasts on the third day of the dance, and insert rawhide ropes, which they tied to the tree, throwing themselves back and forth regardless of the torture, until the rawhide broke through the flesh.

After the adobe huts and hogans of the Pueblos and Navajos, we were delighted by the symmetrical snow-white tepee of the Shoshone, who have made not only an art but a ceremony of tepee building. Two poles are first placed on the ground, butts together. Then two poles of equal length are placed in a reversed position. A rope of pine tree fibre is then woven in and out, over and under the four poles near the top, knotted securely, with long ends hanging. The old custom prescribed laying out the camp in half moon shape, each doorway facing the point where the sun first appears on the horizon, shifting with the season. The camp's location determined, the squaws raise the poles slowly, singing the song of the tepee pole, so timed that it comes to an end with the upright position of the pole. Two women then raise the tent covering, lacing it with carved and polished twigs. Two smoke flaps above the entrance, held in place by other poles, are moved as the wind varies, to draw the smoke rising within the tent. No habitation is more knowingly and simply devised than the tepees,

A SHOSHONE TEEPEE, FORT HALL, IDAHO

which are both warm and well ventilated even in winter. It is only when the Indians are transplanted to the white man's houses that they close doors and windows, light great fires, and soon become soft, and fall easy victims of the white plague.

The Shoshone chiefs made no objection as Toby snapped a beautiful tepee with an Indian pony tethered near, but when she smoothly circled it upon an interested group of gaudy giants, one of them, an Isaiah in a white robe, touched her on the arm.

"Move on, damn quick," he said.

So we did.

CHAPTER XXIII

ON NATIONAL PARKS AND GUIDES

NOTHING fit to print can be said of the Yellowstone Trail, advertised by various and sundry people as a "good road all the way," with the freedom people take with other people's axles. Here and there are smooth patches, but they failed to atone for the viciousness of the greater part of the route from Salt Lake City to the Park. Some of it was merely annoying, but there were places where we had to keep our wits about us every moment, and had we met another car, so narrow and tortuous and hilly were the last few miles, we should have come to an eternal deadlock. We had for consolation a view of some lovely lakes grown about with great pines, and in the open stretches, a long view of the great sawtoothed Tetons sheltering Jackson's Hole, that region beloved of Jesse James before he encountered the "dirty little coward who shot Mr. Howard." All the sinister Robin Hoods of the West once knew the supreme advantage of Jackson's Hole as a place of temporary withdrawal from the world when it became too much with them. Now it is infested only by the "dude" sportsman, who has discovered its loveliness without as yet spoiling it. A tempting sign-post pointed an entrance to this paradise of mountains and lakes, but we had been warned that the road there was far worse than the one we came over, which was impossible, so we gritted our teeth, and went on to the Park.

I shall not attempt a description of Yellowstone Park, for the same reason that I dodged the Grand Canyon, and because its bears, mudholes, geysers, sulphur basins, lakes, Wiley camps, falls and dam, its famous parti-colored canyon, its busses and Old Faithful were well known to thousands long before I was born.

Yellowstone used to be known less attractively among the Indians by the name of Stinking Waters. The park is still circled by a roundabout trail, made by superstitious tribes, who refused to approach this haunt of devils. No-body who has stood on the seething ground of Norris Basin, and watched its manifold evil spirits, hardly tethered, burst forth and sullenly subside can fail to sym-pathize with the untutored savage's reaction. If we had not been taught a smattering of chemistry and geology, we should undoubtedly feel as he did, and even in spite of scientific explanations, the place seemed too personally malevolent to be comfortable. Think of a God-fearing and devil-respecting mind to whom science was unknown, looking on the terrors, the inexplicable manifestations this Park contains for the first time!

I for one, who rap on wood and walk around ladders, would have ridden a long way to avoid those powerful spirits. Yet some Indians boldly hunted and trapped in what was once a most happy hunting ground. The overland course of the buffalo lay through this Park, and wherever the buffalo was, the Indian was sure to follow. Yellowstone was the refuge of Chief Joseph, of the Nez Perces, in his resistance against Howard and United States troops.

Everyone ought to see Yellowstone at least once. No-where else are so many extraordinary freaks in so con-

venient and beautiful a setting. The freaks leave you as
bewildered as the Whatisit's used to, in the sideshows of
your youth. Before the last paint pot and boiling spring
are investigated, the average tourist is in a state of bewildered resentment at Nature for putting it over on him
so frequently. Besides, his feet ache, and he is stiff
from climbing in and out that yellow bus.

Everyone ought to see Yellowstone at least twice. The
second time he will forget the freaks and geysers and
busses running on schedule, and go if possible in his own
car, with his own horse, or on his own feet. He will take
his time on the Cody Trail, now I believe, a part of the
Park but until recently outside its limits. Here he will
see what is perhaps the most glorious natural scenery in
Yellowstone, great pointed needles rising from gigantic
cliffs, deep ravines, and endless forests, pretty little inter-
vales and ideal camping and fishing nooks. Or further in,
beyond Mt. Washburn and the Tower Falls where comparatively few go, he will find deep groves and gorgeous
mountain scenery. Beyond Yellowstone Lake he can
penetrate to the benign Tetons walling the Park to the
southeast. He can take his own "grub" and horses, and
lose sight of hotels and schedules for a month, if he likes.
He is not required, as at Glacier, to hire a guide if he
wishes to camp. Yellowstone's chief charm to me is not
so much its beauty nor its wonders as that it is, pre-
eminently, the People's Park. Founded the earliest of
any national park, when outdoor life was more of a
novelty than it is today, and far less organized a sport,
it follows a *laisser aller* course. And the people ap-
preciate and make use of it. Whole families camp from
one end to the other of the Park, using its open-air

CAMPING NEAR YELLOWSTONE PARK

ovens to cook the fish which they catch in its lakes and streams. They know far more of its charm than the tourists who buy their five-day excursions from the railroads, and don't move a hand to feed or convey themselves from the time they enter at Gardiner to the time they leave at Cody.

I have had experience both ways, once as a personally conducted tourist and once as a human being. With our own car we covered the sight-seeing far more easily and quickly than by bus, with the advantage of being able to linger as long as we pleased over the fascinating mudholes blub-blubbing restfully by a tardily performing geyser, or in some out-of-the-way forest where the tripper never drags his dusty feet. Cars herd together in enticing groves, and their owners exchange destinations and food and confidences about their offspring with an unsuspiciousness lacking at the big hotels. Toby and I proved the efficacy of the old adage about the early bird catching the worm, one morning when we camped near the Great Falls. Our wide-awake neighbors from the wide-awake West got up and caught the worms, then caught the fish, while their slug-abed Eastern neighbors lay in their tents till the sun was high. When we emerged, they presented us with their surplus of four large trout, crisply fried in cornmeal and still piping hot. The early bird has my sincere endorsement every time, so long as I do not have to be one.

Still I think some improvements could be made in Yellowstone. I never go there without getting completely exhausted chasing geysers,—rushing from one which should have spouted but didn't, in time to reach the other end of the Park just too late to see another go off, only to miss a magnificent eruption somewhere else. Or else I arrive, to learn that some geyser which managed to keep its mouth shut for a decade went off with a bang just yesterday, and another rare one is scheduled for the week after I leave.

They really need a good young efficiency engineer to rearrange the schedule of geysers according to location, so that one could progress easily and naturally from one to the other. One first class geyser should perform every day. Then the bears ought to be organized. You are always meeting someone who just saw the cutest little black cub down the road, but when you hurry back he has departed. So with the grizzlies; they never come out to feed on the tempting hotel garbage the evenings you are in the neighborhood. Only Old Faithful keeps up her performances every two hours, as if she realized that without her sense of responsibility and system the Park would go all to pieces. But you can't work a willing geyser to death, which is what is happening to Old Faithful. They ought to arrange to have some geyser with an easy schedule,—say the one which goes off every twenty years,—stop loafing on the job, and give Old Faithful a much deserved vacation.

Having "done" Yellowstone far more comfortably with the car in three days than we could have in six without it, we left on the fourth day for Glacier. The road improved vastly as we entered Montana. Both the Red and Yellowstone Trails were well made and kept in excellent condition. We skimmed over a beautiful country. Bold and free hills, soft brown in color and the texture of velours spread below us. The road curved just enough for combined beauty and safety, and was well

GRAND CANYON, YELLOWSTONE PARK.

marked most of the way. We mistakenly chose the shorter route to Glacier Park entrance, instead of taking the more roundabout but far more beautiful drive through Kalispell. It is a mistake most motorists make sooner or later, in the fever to save time. But to compensate we had a glimpse of Browning, half Canadian, its streets full of Indians, half-breeds and cowboys dressed almost as gayly as the redmen and their squaws. Some garage helper there made the usual mistake of saying "left" and pointing right, with the result that our prairie road suddenly vanished and we were left in the midst of a ploughed track which had not yet fulfilled its intention of becoming a road. For the next twelve miles to the Park we went through wild gyrations, now leaping stumps, now dropping a clear two feet or more, or tilting above a deep furrow or a tangle of roots. Once more we marveled at the enduring powers of the staunch old lady.

Glacier Park is not primarily a motorist's park, as is Yellowstone. An excellent highway runs outside the Park along the range of bold peaks that guard the Blackfeet reservation, and an interior road connects the entrance with St. Mary's Lake and Many Glaciers, the radiating point for most of the trail rides. To run a machine past these barriers of solid peaks would be nearly impossible, yet there are still extensions of the mileage of motoring roads which can and probably will be made. Tourists with their own cars can do as we did, cover what roads are already accessible, then leave their car at Many Glaciers. There they can take the many trail trips, either afoot or on horseback, over the glorious passes from which the whole world may be seen; climb ridges and cross mountain brooks, ice cold from melting glaciers; or look down from Gunsight or Grinnell or Mt. Henry into passes where chain after chain of exquisite lakes lie half a mile below.

Nowhere else have I seen such a wilderness of various kinds of beauty, dizzy ravines and dainty nooks, peaks and precipices with a hundred feet of snow and unmelted ice packed about them, and the other side of the mountain glowing with dog-tooth violets, or blue with acres of forget-me-nots. Fuzzy white-topped Indian plumes border the snow. Icebergs float on lakes just beyond them. Mountain goats make white specks far up a wall of granite, and deer cross one's path in the lowlands, which are a tangle of vines and flowers in the midst of pine forests. Over a narrow ridge dividing two valleys, each linking lakes till they fade into the blue of hill and sky, we ride to an idyllic pasture surrounded by mountain peaks, for nowhere in the Park, again unlike Yellowstone, can you go without being in the shadow of some benign giant. There is, as the parched Arizonans say, "a world of water,"—little trickles of streams far up toward the sky, melting from æon-old glaciers which freeze again above them; roaring swashbuckling rivers and cascades, such as you see near Going-to-the-Sun, and the double falls of Two Medicine; placid sun-flecked little pools, reflecting only the woods, broad lakes black as night, mirroring every ripple and stir above them, lakes so cold you freeze before you can wade out far enough to swim, yet full of trout; and belting the whole park, a chain of long lakes and quiet rivers.

The center of the Park is the corral in front of the big hotel at Many Glaciers, where Lake McDermott mirrors a dozen mountains. From this point trails radiate in all

GLACIER PARK, MONTANA.
You can go nowhere in the park without being in the shadow of some benign giant

directions, varying in length from three hours to three days.

Nature is nowhere more fresh and delightful than when seen from the trails of Glacier Park,—and as for human nature! I don't know which is more engrossing, —the tourist or the guides. Personally I lean toward the guides, for the subtler flavor of personality is theirs. They can be unconsciously funny without being ridiculous, which the tourist cannot be. And they have an element of romance, real or carelessly cultivated, which no tourist has to any other tourist. What each thinks of the other you hear expressed now and then.

"You mightn't think it, but some of those chaps are pretty bright," said a lecturer of a Middle Western circuit to me, as he tried to mount his horse from the right.

"They sent us over that trail with a dozen empties and twenty head of tourists," I heard one guide tell another, with an unconsciousness that cut deep.

Every morning at eight the riderless horses come galloping down the road to Many Glaciers, urged on by a guide whose feelings, judging by his riding, seem to be at a boiling point. In a half hour the tourists straggle out, some in formal riding clothes, some in very informal ones, and some dressed as they think the West expects every man to dress. The assembled guides with wary glances "take stock" of their day's "outfit,"—always a gamble. With uncanny instinct they sort the experienced riders from the "doods" and lead each to his appropriate mount. These indifferent looking, lean, swarthy men sit huddled on the corral rail, and exchange quiet monosyllables which would mean nothing to the "dood" if he could overhear. With their tabloid lingo they could talk about you to your face,—though most of them are too well-mannered,—and from their gravely courteous words you would never suspect it. Guides are past masters of overtones. Their wit is seldom gay and robust,—always gently ironic.

I saw a very stout lady go through the Great Adventure of mounting, plunging forward violently and throwing her right leg forward over the pommel. It was a masterly effort which her guide watched with impassive face, encouraging her at the finish with a gently whispered, "Fine, lady! And next time I bet you could do it even better by throwing your leg backwards."

He was the same one who soothed a nervous and inexperienced rider who dreaded the terrors of Swiftcurrent Pass.

"Now, lady, just hang your reins over the horn, and leave it to the horse."

"Heavens," she replied, " will he go down that terrible trail all alone?"

"Oh, no, lady. He'll take you right along with him."

There is always one tourist whose tardiness holds up the party, and one morning it chanced I was that one. The guide—it was Bill—handed me my reins and adjusted my stirrups with a with-holding air. As we rode up Gunsight, I heard him humming a little tune. A word now and then whetted my curiosity.

"What are you singing, Bill?" All guides have monosyllabic names, as Ed, Mike, Jack, Cal, and Tex.

Very impersonally Bill repeated the song in a cracked tenor:

"I wrangled my horses, was feelin' fine,
Couldn't git my doods up till half past nine.
I didn't cuss, and I didn't yell,
But we lit up the trail like a bat out of hell."

"A very nice song, Bill. Did you compose it yourself?"

"No, ma'am. It's just a song."

They have a way of taking their revenge, neat and
bloodless, but your head comes off in their hand just the
same. Bill had a honeymoon couple going to Sperry, and
taking a dislike to the groom, whom he thought "too
fresh," he placed him at the tail of the queue, and the
bride, who was pretty, behind himself. The sight of
Bill chatting gaily with his bride of a day, and his bride
chatting gaily with Bill, became more than the groom
could bear, and in spite of resentful glances from those he
edged past on the narrow trail, he worked his way patiently up to a position behind the bride, only to receive
a cold glare from Bill, and the words, "Against the rules
of the Park to change places in line, Mister." Bill was
not usually so punctilious about Park rules, but the groom
did not know this, and suffered Bill to dismount and lead
his horse back to the rear, after which he returned to
his conversation with the pretty bride. This play continued throughout the day with no change of expression or
loss of patience on the part of Bill. Glacier Park is no
place to go on a honeymoon.

At Glacier, society has no distinctions, but it has three
divisions,—excluding, of course, the Blackfeet Indians to
whom the Park originally belonged. They are the
"doods," the guides, and the "hash-slingers." Each

guide, as he slants lop-sidedly over a mile deep cut-bank keeps a pleased eye on some lithe figure in the neatest of boots and Norfolk coats, whom he has picked for his "dood girl." He favors her with a drink from his canteen, long anecdotes about his "hoss," or if he is hard hit and she is a good rider, with offers of a ride on his "top-hoss." But when he has helped his tourists dismount, limping and sore at the foot of a twenty mile descent, he gallops his string of "empties" to the corral, and in half an hour is seen roping some dainty maiden in Swiss costume,—playing his tinkling notes on the Eternal Triangle.

When they do cast an eye in your direction it is something to remember. There was Tex,—or was his name Sam?—who took us up to Iceberg. He never looked back at us, nor showed any of the kittenishness common to the male at such moments, but every five minutes issued a solitary sentence, impersonal and, like a jigsaw puzzle, meaningless until put together.

"I never had no girl."

We turned three switchbacks.

"Don't suppose no girl would ever look at me."

Five minutes passed. He looked over the ears of his roan top-horse.

"I got a little hoss home I gentled. She was a wild hoss, and only me could ride her. But I rode her good."

He stopped to lengthen a tourist's stirrups, and mounted again.

"I got a silver-mounted bridle cost $500 when it was new. I bought it cheap. Has one of those here monograms on it, J. W. and two silver hearts."

"Are they your initials?"

BLACKFEET INDIANS AT GLACIER PARK MONTANA

"No, ma'am. They stood for something else—George Washington maybe.'

A pause. "I taught that little pony of mine to do tricks."

A momentous pause. "If I had a girl I liked real good, I'd give her that hoss and saddle."

We had nearly reached the top of the trail.

"I'd kinder like an Eastern girl that could ride a hoss good."

And then the approach direct.

"Onct I had a diamond neck pin. I aint got it now. I pawned it. But I got a picter of myself wearin' that pin you could have."

That night, he sauntered to the hotel, and leaned against the door, and looked at the moon, which was full.

"A great night," he said. And a pause. "One of these here nights when a feller just feels like———"

I thought he had stopped, but sometime later he resumed, still regarding the moon.

"Like kinder spoonin'."

But it takes a moon to bring out the softer side of the guide nature, and they waste little time in thoughts of "kinder spoonin'" when they have a party on a difficult trail. There they are nurse-maids, advisers and grooms, entertainers and disciplinarians, all in an outwardly casual manner. As they swing in their saddles up the trail, what they are thinking has much to do with whom they are guiding. We saw all kinds of "doods" while at Glacier, and some would have driven me mad, but I never yet saw a guide lose his temper.

"Honest," confided Johnson,—Johnson is an old

timer who limps from an ancient quarrel with a grizzly, and wears overalls and twisted braces and humps together in the saddle,—"honest, there's some of them you couldn't suit not if you had the prettiest pair of wings ever was."

There was the gentleman who appeared in very loud chaps and bandana and showed his knowledge of western life, regardless of the fact that Toby's horse and mine just behind him were showing a tendency to buck, by shouting, "Hi-yi" and bringing down his Stetson with a bang on the neck of the spiritless hack the guides had sardonically bestowed on him.

There was the fond mother who held up the whole party to Logan Pass while she pleaded with her twelve-year-old son to wear one of her veils to keep off the flies. Poor little chap! His red face showed the tortures he endured, and the guide turned away and pretended not to hear.

There was the old lady and her spinster daughter from Philadelphia who took a special camping trip high into the mountains where crystal streams start from their parent glaciers, and insisted on the guide boiling every drop of water before they would drink it. And when they left they sent all the saddle bags to be dry cleaned, thereby ruining them.

There was also Mr. Legion, who had never been on a horse before, who complained all the twenty-six miles up and down hill that his stirrups were too long, and too short, that his horse wouldn't go, and that he jolted when he trotted, that the saddle was too hard and that the guide went so fast nobody could keep up with him. It was Mrs. Legion who got dizzy at the steep places and stopped the procession on the worst switchback while she got off and walked, or insisted on taking her eight-year-old child along, and then frightened both the child and herself into hysteria when they gazed down on those lake-threaded valleys straight beneath them.

There was the lady who took a walk up a tangled mountain-side to pick flowers, and got lost and kept the whole outfit hunting for her an entire night.

But there were many as well who were good-natured and good sports, whether they had little or much experience in riding and roughing it,—many who acquired here a life-long habit for outdoors.

Having seen all these sorts and conditions of "doods," we tried not to be vain when Bill introduced us to his friend Curly in these words. The fact that Bill had visited Lewis', the only place in the Park where there was a saloon, had no effect on our pride, for Bill had tightly kept his opinion to himself, heretofore, and *in vino veritas.*

"Girls," he said from his horse, his dignity not a whit impaired because of the purple neck-handkerchief pinned to his Stetson, because "the boys said I didn't look quite wild enough,"—— "Girls, this is Curly. Curly, this is the girls. You'll like them, Curly, they aint helpless!"

Praise is as sweet to me as to most, but those words of Bill's, even with the evidence of the bandana, meant more than the wildest flattery.

Of all the "dood-wranglers" in the Park, Bill was possessed of the most whimsical personality. He had been our guide several summers ago, the year the draft bill was passed. Bill always spoke in a slow drawl, his words, unhurried and ceaseless, forming into an unconscious

blank verse frequently at odd variance with their import.
Could Edgar Lee Masters do better than this?

"I had a legacy from my uncle,
The only one in the fam'ly had money.
They quarreled over the will.
When I got my share
It was just eighty dollars.
I bought me a saddle with it,
Then I got gamblin',——
Pawned the saddle,
Tore up the tickets
And throwed them away."

"I was never in jail but onct," he told us, rather surprised at his own restraint, "and then I was drunk. I was
feelin' fine,—rode my hoss on the sidewalk, shot off my
gun and got ten days. Was you ever drunk? No?
Well, beer's all right if you want a drink, but if you
want to get drunk, try champagne. You take it one day,
and rense out your mouth the next, and you're as drunk
as you were the night before."

When the draft came, no high sentiments of patriotism
flowed in vers libre from Bill's lips.

"There's places in the Grand Canyon I know of where
I reckon I could hide out, and no draft officer could find
me till the war was over," he declared. "I'd rather be a
live coward than a dead hero any day."

But he went, and of course was drafted into the in-
fantry, he who saddled his horse to cross the street, and
who had said earnestly, "Girls, if you want to make a
cow-puncher sore, set him afoot." Like several other
of his "doods" who had witnessed the tragedy of his
being drafted, when he went about with lugubrious fore-

bodings and refused to be cheered, I sent him a sweater, and received promptly a letter of thanks.

"I thought everybody had forgotten me, judging by my feelings. I am the worst disgusted cowboy that ever existed. Existed is right at the present. This is no life for a cowboy that has been used to doing as he pleases. Here you do as they please. They keep me walking all day long. They ball me out, and make me like it. I dassent fight and they wont let me leave. Say —what complexion is butter? I aint seen any sense I left Glacier. I've eat macaroni till I look like a Dago and canned sammin till I dassent cover up my head at night for fear I would smell my own breath. If this training camp don't kill me there will be no chance for the Germans, but I'd sooner a German would get me than die by inches in this here sheep corral."

When Toby and I reached the Park, I inquired for Bill from one of his buddies who was a guide that year, and learned that his fortunes had mended from this peak of depression. He had been transferred to the remount department, and when a mule broke his arm his home-sickness departed, and he was filled with content. He even clamored to be sent over to "scalp a few Huns."

"He did things anyone else would be court-martialed for," his buddy related, "but Bill always had an alibi. When we were ordered out on a hike, Bill would go along, taking pains to march on the outside. When we came to a culvert, he would drop over the edge, hide awhile and go back to his bunk for the day. They never did find him out.

"The mud was a foot deep in the corral, and once when Bill was roping a mule, the mule got away, dragging

Bill after. He splashed in, and when we see him again he was mud all over. And mad. The air was blue. He rushed into the Major's office just as he was. The Major was a stiff old bird every one else was afraid of. But not Bill.

"'Look at me,' he sputtered. 'Look at me!' And then he swore some more. 'Look at this new uniform!'

"'What do you mean,' says the Major, drawing himself up and gettin' red in the face. 'Are you drunk?'

"'No,' says Bill, very innocent, 'do I have to be drunk to talk to you?'

"But he got his new uniform. Any of the rest of us would have been stood up against a wall at sunrise. Another time a consignment of shoes came in that was meant for a race of giants. None of us could wear them. Bill was awful proud of his feet, too. He swore he would get a pair to fit. So he put his on, and went to see the Major.

"'Look at these shoes,' he says.

"'They look all right to me,' says the Major. 'Seems like a pretty good fit.'

"'Yes, but see here,' says Bill. And he took off the shoes, and there was his other shoes underneath. He got a pair that fit, right away. Nobody else did."

Such initiative otherwise applied might well make a captain of industry of him, were it not that Bill is typical of his kind, his creed "for to admire an' for to see, for to behold this world so wide." Free and foot loose they will be, rejecting the bondage of routine that makes of a resourceful man, as they all are, a captain of industry. The world is their playground, not their schoolroom. Independent they will be of discipline.

"Aren't you afraid of losing your job?" we asked a guide who confided some act of insubordination.

"Well, I *come* here looking for a job," he answered.

As Bill put it, in his rhythmic way,—"The Lord put me on earth to eat and sleep and ride the ponies, and I ain't figurin' on doin' nothin' else."

And he finished, "There's just three things in the world I care about,—my hawss, and my rope and my hat."

The genius of the west lies, I think, in its power of objectiveness. The east is subjective. When an easterner tells a story, he locates himself emotionally with much concern. He may be vague as to time and place, but you know his moods and impressions with subtle exactness. Every westerner I ever knew begins his first sentence of a story with his location and objective. Then he adds dates and follows with an anecdote of bare facts, untinged by his emotions. His audience fills in the chinks with what he does not say. For example, a guide, telling of a trip, might say——

"I was headed north over Eagle Pass with an outfit of geologists in a northwest storm. The animals had just come in from winter feedin' the day before. My top-hawss had went lame on me, and I had to borrow a cayuse from an Indian. I had a pack outfit of burros and was drivin' three empties that give out on us. We was short of grub, and twenty miles to make to the trader's. The dudes had wore setfasts on their hawsses, and when I ast them could they kinder trot along, the ladies would hit their saddles with a little whip and say 'gittap, hawsie.' "

Only bald facts are told in that narrative, mainly unin-

telligible unless you know what the facts connote. Told
to a fellow guide they bring forth nods of silent sympathy. Many experiences of the same sort help him to
see the huddled, inexpert figures of saddle-sore dudes,
some clad piecemeal, some in the extreme of appropriate-
ness. He knows the exasperating slowness of horses
drained of the last ounce of endurance. He, too, has
tried to urge on a miscellaneous collection of tired
horses, burros and dudes, all wandering in different directions, at differing gaits. He knows the self-respecting
guide's chagrin at losing the pride of his life,—his top-
horse, and he knows the condition of Indian cayuses at the
end of winter. He has felt unutterable disgust at having
to ride a hack. He knows the necessity of keeping patient
and courteous under irritation, and the responsibility of
getting his party of tenderfeet over a bad divide in a
storm with night coming and food scarce, when a slight
mishap may accumulate more serious disasters. He knows
how weary burros wander in circles so persistently that the
most patient guide,—and all guides are patient, they have
to be,—wants to murder them brutally. And the sickening
scrape of girths on raw, bleeding sores, requiring tender
care after treatment of weeks. He knows every party has
its foolish, ineffectual members who tire the first mile out,
and after that sink into limp dejection, remarking plain-
tively and often, "This horse is no good," as they give
him a light flick which hits leather or saddle roll, but
never the horse, and kick at him without touching him.
And geologists! One or two, he knows, can ride and
camp and are as good as the guides, but others will want
to stop the outfit on the worst spot in the trail, and nearly

TWO MEDICINE LAKE, GLACIER PARK, MONTANA.

WRANGLING HORSES, GLACIER PARK, MONTANA

cause a stampede gathering rocks which the guide must secure to the already overweighty pack.

But see how much longer it takes a story Eastern fashion. Once you have the key to the Westerner's narrative, you get the vividness of these compressed facts. If you have not, he might as well be talking Sanscrit as colloquial English of one and two syllables. You listen and wonder what has happened to your mind: you seem to understand everything he is saying, yet you understand nothing.

CHAPTER XXIV

THE NAIL-FILE AND THE CHIPPEWA

AT Many Glaciers they advised us to visit the lovely Waterton Lakes lying in the Canadian extension of Glacier Park.

"There's only one bad place,—north of Babb. It's flooded for some miles, but all you have to do is climb the canal bank, and run along the top."

As people were always advising us to undertake some form of acrobatics, we stored the canal bank in the back of our minds, and started for Babb and Canada.

Babb proved as short of population as of syllables. We went the length of the town, and encountered only one building,—the postoffice and store. That its populace was treated more generously in the matter of syllables we discovered by idly reading the mailing list of Blackfeet citizens, pasted on the wall. Among Babb's most prominent residents are Killfirst Stingy, Mary Earrings, Susie Swimsunder, Ada Calflooking, Cecile Weaselwoman, Xavier Billetdoux, Joe Scabbyrobe, Alex Biglodgepole and Josephine Underotter Owlchild.

I have been told that many Indian tribes name a child from the greatest event in the life of its oldest living relative. When the child reaches maturity, he earns a name for himself by some characteristic achievement, goaded to it, no doubt, by the horrors of his given name. Thus by a glance at the census lists we are able to read

346

past history, and compare the amorous agitations of Xavier Billetdoux' granddaddy with the bucolic and serene existence of Ada Calflooking's great-aunt. Not a bad way of checking up one's ancestry against one's own worth. If we followed the same system, Cornelius Rowed Washington across the Delaware might be rechristened C. Shimmyfoot, while Adolph Foreclosedthewidow'smortgage might earn the nobler surname of Endowsahospital. It is really a remarkable system of shorthand autobiography, enabling a complete stranger to tell whether one belongs to a good family going downhill, or a poor one coming uphill, or a mediocre at a standstill. How many a near Theda Bara who would like to be named Cecile Weaselwoman would have to be content as Mary Ear-rings. How many a purse-proud Biglodgepole would have to confess his grandfather was named Scabbyrobe. Perhaps this is the reason we leave such nomenclature to the heathen Indian.

Reflecting thus, Toby and I amused ourselves with renaming ourselves and our friends, until we reached a place where some altruistic citizen had inundated the road in order to irrigate his patch of land. Here we were supposed to take to the top of the canal, but the bank was high, narrow and shaly. It looked too much like a conspiracy against both us and the canal, so we disregarded our advice and skirted the open land. By leaving the road altogether and keeping to the hills we avoided most of the bog, and got through the rest with a little maneuvering. A mile further we learned that the canal bank had given way under a car the previous day, and carried car and occupants into the water.

The beautiful Flathead Mountains had faded away

behind us, leaving a prairie country of no charm, dry and burnt. At the border, as at Mexico, we found our little customhouse less formal and more shabby than our neighbor's, but at both we received clearance and courteous treatment. When we said we came from Massachusetts, the Canadian agent sighed.

"Massachusetts! What do you see in a God-forsaken hole like this to tempt you from such a state? I wish I could go there,—or anywhere away from this place.".

Everywhere we heard the same refrain. Three years of killing drought had scorched the treeless plains to a cinder. The wheat, promise and hope of Alberta, had failed, and immigrants who had gone there expecting to return to the old country in a few years with a fortune, were so completely ruined they could neither go back nor forward, but saw dismal years of stagnation before them.

There are more cheerful places than Alberta in which to face bankruptcy. So near the border, this part of Canada is half American,—American with a cockney accent. But it is newer and rawer than our own west by a decade or two, with less taste apparent, less prosperity, more squalid shiftlessness. The section through which we drove had been mainly conquered by the Mormons, driven into Canada when the United States was most inhospitable to their sect. They in turn have converted many of the immigrants from the old country. The church or tithe lands make sharp contrast in their prosperity, their thousands of sleek, blooded cattle and irrigated fields to the forlorn little settlements of individuals. As every Mormon pays a tenth of all he has to his church it is easy to understand this contrast.

In our six months of travel we had driven over the

reservations of the Papago, Pima and Maricopa, the Apache, Hopi, Havasupai, Navajo, Ute, Piute, Pueblo, Shoshone, Blackfeet and Flatheads. We were now on the Blood Indian reservation, though we saw few inhabitants. Those we saw were red-skinned and tall, resembling the other Northern tribes. The country grew less inhabited. We met no other cars and few people. Fifty miles north of Browning, our last town, we came to a lumber camp, and seven miles further our car quietly ceased to move, and rested in peace on a hillside.

Since its wetting in Nambe creek, the ignition had been prone to such sudden stops and starts. From past experience we knew that the ignition system must be completely taken apart, exposing its innermost parts to the daylight. All I knew about it was summed up in my brother's parting advice, "Never monkey with your ignition." All Toby knew was that Bill of Santa Fé had taken it apart, done something to it, put it together again, and it ran. So we decided to follow Bill's procedure as far as we could, and began by taking it apart. That went very well until we discovered some covetous person had removed all the tiny tools used in operating on this part of the engine, leaving us only a monkey wrench and a large pair of pincers. Toby nearly stood on her head trying to unscrew very little screws with the big wrench, and progressed but slowly, as she had to change her entire position with each quarter turn.

After about an hour we had every nut and screw in the forward part of the engine in rows on the running board. My task was to take the parts as Toby unscrewed them, and lay them neatly from left to right, so that we should know in what order to replace them. Then I glanced at the remains which Toby had succeeded in uncovering.

"The distributor needs cleaning," I said expertly, thereby greatly impressing Toby. I remembered Bill had said the same thing, but for the life of me I couldn't remember what the distributor was. By opening the cock of our tank, and holding a tin cup beneath, catching a drop at a time we managed in another hour to get enough gasoline to bathe the affected parts, as druggist's directions say.

So far, not a hitch. And then a little wire flapped before our eyes which seemingly had no connection with any other part. Toby thought it belonged in one place, and for the sake of argument, I held out for another, but neither of us was sure enough to make a point of our opinion. Meanwhile the car could not start until this wire was hitched to something, yet we dared not risk a short-circuit by connecting it to the wrong screw. So we stood still in the hot, dusty road and waited for something to turn up.

"I have a hunch, Toby," I said, "that when we really give up and go for help, the old lady will begin running again."

"Then you'd better start at once," said Toby.

"No, it won't be as simple as that. We shall have to work for what we get."

At this moment a Ford containing four men drew up and stopped. We explained our trouble.

"You took it apart without knowing how to put it together again?" said one of them. They exchanged glances which said "How like a woman!"

"When we took it apart," answered Toby with

hauteur, "we knew how to put it together again, but so many things have happened in the meantime that the exact process has slipped our minds. But if you will explain the principles of this ignition system to us I think we can manage."

The man muttered something about a Ford not having one, and drove on. Like most men, he was willing to stay as long as he could appear in a superior light, but no longer.

Though they were poor consolation, the horizon looked very lonely after they left. Later in the afternoon, two Indian boys with fish-poles over their shoulders sauntered by. Having exhausted our combined knowledge we had decided to give up and telephone to the nearest garage. I hastened to them, not knowing when we should again see a human soul.

"How far away is the nearest garage?" I asked them.

The younger boy giggled, but the older answered in very good, soft-spoken English, "At Browning, fifty miles away.'

A hundred dollars for towing, and days of delay! I caught at a straw.

"Is there by any chance an electrician back at the lumber camp?"

"No, ma'am."

Then noticing my despair, he added diffidently, "I studied electricity at Carlisle. Perhaps I can help you."

Our guardian angels fluttered so near we could almost see their wings. Here was Albert Gray, for so he was hight, transplanted from his Chippewa reservation for a two days' visit to his Blood cousins, for the sole purpose of rescuing us from our latest predicament. Efficiency and economy must have been the watchword of those ministering spirits of ours, for not only did they send the only electrician within fifty miles, but then sent one whose knowledge, combined with our own, was just sufficient.   I do not believe Albert really knew a fuse from a switchbox, but he did remember one essential we had forgotten,—that the points should be a sixteenth of an inch apart.   But without tools he said he could do nothing. So we proffered a nail-file, by happy inspiration, with which he ground the points.   We screwed together all the parts, connected the mysterious wire by a counting-out rime, and turned the engine.   Nothing moved.

I turned my back on the exasperating car, and started to walk the seven miles back to the lumber camp.   Then, on remembering my hunch it seemed as if all conditions were now fulfilled, so I returned, put my foot on the starter,—and the engine hummed.   And until we reached Boston again, it never ceased to hum.

A prouder moment neither Toby nor I ever had, when by grace of a Chippewa and a nail-file we monkeyed with our ignition fifty miles from a garage,—and conquered it.

I shall always remember slow spoken, polite Albert Gray.   Like Lucy of the same sur-name, he made oh, the difference to me!

The good looking garage helper at Cardston met us with a beaming smile.

"I've filled your radiator," he said, "and your canteen, and put in oil and gas, and I've infatuated all your tires."

It was this same delightful Mr. Malaprop of whom

we inquired, discussing various automobiles, "Do you like the Marmon?"

"I'm not one myself," he answered cautiously, "but my father-in-law is, and I get on pretty good with him."

Through his connections-in-law he obtained for us the privilege of seeing the interior of the new Mormon Temple, which is to rival Salt Lake's. Our unfailing luck had brought us here at the only interval when Gentiles are allowed to enter a Mormon church, after completion and before its dedication. This little town of not more than five thousand inhabitants, surrounded by the brown, parched prairie, is dominated by a million dollar edifice, far more beautiful than the parent Temple in Utah, and magnificent enough for any city. A perfect creation in itself, fitted like the Temple of Solomon with matched marble and granite brought from the ends of the earth, it looks strangely out of keeping with the bare shacks and ugly little frontier shanties surrounding it. Its architecture was modified from Aztec designs. The young Salt Lake Mormons whose plans won the award in competition with many renowned architects achieved an arrestingly original building of massive dignity and grace, managing at the same time to conform to the exacting requirements of Mormon symbolism. No two rooms are built on the same level, but rise in a gradual ascent to the roof, from which one may look miles over the rolling plains of Alberta. This requirement, which must have caused the designers and builders much anguish, is meant to symbolize the soul's ascent from a gross and carnal to a spiritual life. The ground floor has many dressing-rooms where those who "work for the dead" change from street clothes to the garments prescribed by Mormon ritual. Above are rooms paneled in the most costly woods,—Circassian walnut, tulip-wood, mahogany and rosewood,—for the use of the church officials, and beyond these, larger rooms called "Earth," "Purgatory," "Heaven," decorated with beautiful mural paintings with appropriate scenes. "Earth" held great attractions for me, with its frieze of jungle beasts threading their way through gnarled forests,—an able and artistic piece of work, done by Prof. Evans of Salt Lake. The stout little Cockney Mormon who accompanied the Bishop and ourselves through the Temple gave us this information, though from his lips it sounded like "Prof. Heavens, of the Heart Department." We passed on from Earth to the assembly room in the center of the Temple, a magnificent chamber with an altar, where services are held and marriages performed.

"Here, if you wish," the Bishop said, "you can be sealed to eternity."

Toby who had all along, I think, expected to be pounced on as a possible plural wife backed away from the altar, but the Bishop was speaking impersonally. He explained that any Mormon happy in his present matrimonial venture (I use the singular, as polygamy is now illegal both in Canada and the United States) may extend that happiness to eternity, and insure getting the same wife in Heaven by this ceremony. He himself had been sealed,—"the children sitting on each side of us in their white robes,"—the ceremonial garment,—and was secure in the belief that his family happiness would continue after death.

We broached with some hesitation the subject of poly-

A MORMON IRRIGATED VILLAGE.

THE "MILLION DOLLAR" MORMON TEMPLE AT CARDSTON, ALBERTA, CANADA.

gamy. The Bishop readily took it up, declaring polygamy entirely abolished.

"Even at its height, not more than three per cent of our men had plural wives," he said.

"As few as that?"

"Yes."

"Then since the majority never sanctioned it, the Church has abolished it, and you yourself never practised it, I suppose you consider it wrong?"

"Oh, no—I shouldn't call it wrong. Why, it was the best advertising we could possibly have had. People heard of the Mormons all over the world, and began talking about them,—all because of polygamy. I don't suppose we should ever have become so prosperous and powerful without the free advertising it gave us. It enabled us to extend our faith to all corners of the earth. While each church has its parish, bishops, elders and presidents, our system is so complete that in three hours the Head of the church can communicate a mandate to the furthest missionary in Japan or India."

"But it wasn't very *good* advertising, perhaps?"

"Any advertising is good advertising, so long as it gets people talking."

The way to Waterton Lakes, several hours from Cardston, lay through the tithe lands of the Church,—a mile north, a mile west, and so on, with the monotonous regularity of section roads. Then suddenly emerging from the barren country, we found ourselves again in the Rockies. We motored past a chain of glassy mountain lakes, each one full to the brim with trout, so we had been told. The air sparkled; late July here in the north had the tang of autumn through the golden sun. Forests of pine edged the shores of the lakes. The same sharply notched peaks we had known at Glacier Park guarded their solitude. This park, under the care of the Canadian government, lies in the hinterland of Glacier. Over its ranges a pack train can make its way in a few days from one park to the other, and a still quicker route is by the intermittent motorboat which carries passengers back and forth during the summer. By road it takes a day or more of rough prairie traveling. With much the same type of scenery as Glacier Park, though perhaps less dramatic, Waterton Lakes should be far more widely visited than they are. These two lovely parks, naturally a continuation of each other, should and could be easily linked more closely together.

At present the accommodations of Waterton Lakes are far inferior to those of Glacier. A few ex-saloons (Alberta "went dry") offer sandwiches and near beer, but the gaudy paper decorations on the walls, covered with flies, and the inevitable assortment of toothpicks, catsup and dirty cruets on the soiled cloths, are successful destroyers of appetite. I was told that the railroad which had developed Glacier Park so intelligently, building the few necessary hotels with dignity and charm, offered to extend the developments to Waterton Lakes, but that Canada, fearing her tourists would thereby be diverted into the "States," jealously refused the offer. A short-sighted decision, certainly, for the flood of tourists coming from the States would have been far greater than that turned in the other direction.

Toby and I pitched our little tent on a delightful pebbled beach, planning to stay several days, if the fishing were as good as it had been reported. But after a fruitless—or fishless—afternoon of dangling our lines in the water, with no profit except the sight of the hills which guarded the blue sparkle, we returned to our tent at sunset with no prospect of food. We had depended too rashly upon our skill at angling. Hunger can take all the joy out of scenery.

To tell the truth, sleeping in a tent and cooking our own meals had somewhat lost their charms. We preferred a lumpy bed in a stuffy room to a hard bed on the ground; and second-rate meals served at a table someone else had taken the trouble to prepare to third-rate meals prepared with greater trouble by ourselves. As we looked wearily at each other, each hoping the other would offer to make the beds and "rustle" for food, we suddenly realized that we were homesick. We had roughed it enough, and the flesh pots beckoned.

"Let's go back to Cardston," I said.

"Let's," said Toby, gladly.

And on all that beauty of pure woods and clear sunset we turned and fled to civilization. Fifth-rate civilization it might be, in a province as crude and unlovely as was any part of our own West in the roaring eighties. For the first time in six months we had our backs to the setting sun, the sun which had dazzled our eyes every afternoon since we left the boat at Galveston. We were leaving the great, free West, "where a man can be a ' man, and a woman can be a woman," and we were going —home!

CHAPTER XXV

HOMEWARD HOBOES

AT Santa Fé we had a worn tire retreaded. "It may last you a thousand miles," said the honest dealer. At the end of the thousand miles, the tire was in ribbons. We put it on the forward wheel and favored it all we could. In another thousand miles the canvas showed through the tread. Time went on, and a complete new set of tires went to the junk-heap, but the old retread still flaunted its tattered streamers. More than once, when both spare tires had collapsed, it carried us safely over long, desolate stretches. At last, when it had gone five or six thousand miles we ceased to worry. The conviction came to my prophetic soul that it would take us home. And it did. It took us to Toby's door, and went flat as I turned into my own driveway. Thus did our guardian angels stay with us, like the guide's mule, to the end.

Like tired horses whose heads are turned homeward, our pace accelerated steadily as we moved east. Each day we put two hundred miles or more behind us. Montana, brown and parched like all the West, yet magnificent in the tremendous proportions of its mountains and valleys, we left with regret. We followed the Great Northern to the bleak town of Havre, then dropped south to the perfidious Yellowstone Trail. Bits of the road were unexpectedly good; for the first time since

Houston the old lady's skirts hummed in the breeze. We unwillingly put hundreds of gophers to death. The roads here were honeycombed with their nests, and as we bore down on them they poked their silly heads up to be sacrificed or ran under our wheels by the gross. We learned to dread them, for each gopher-hole meant a sharp little jolt to the car, by which more than one spring-leaf was snapped.

For several days we trailed forest fires. The whole state was so tindery that a lighted match might sweep it clear. Puffs of blue-white smoke blurred the sharp outlines of the mountains and the air was warm with an acrid, smoky haze. Sometimes we passed newly charred forests with little tongues of flame still leaping at their edges, and once we barely crossed before a smouldering fire swept down a hillside and crossed the road where we had been a moment earlier. The people we met were in a state of passive depression after the ruin of the wheat at this last blow to their bank accounts. Some blamed the I. W. W. for the fires, but most of them spoke of this possibility with the caution one pins a scandal to an ugly neighbor in a small town.

Montana's cities were also at the mercy of the I. W. W. The usual strikes were agitating at Butte, and at the two leading hotels of Great Falls, both perfectly appointed, every waiter had gone on strike, and the cafeterias were doing a rushing business. The chambermaids followed suit next day. Yet we liked Great Falls, and the kindred cities of Montana, sharp-edged, clearly focussed little towns, brisk and new, frankly ashamed of their un-Rexalled past, and making plans to build a skyscraper a week—in the future.

Miles City and Roundup,—what visions of frontier
life they conjured up! And how little they fulfilled these
visions! The former used to be and still is the scene of
great horse fairs and the center of horse-trading Montana, a fact brought home to us by the manifold horse-
shoe nails that punctured our tires in this district. But
as we saw no chaparraled rough-riders swaggering in the
streets of Round-up, so we saw no horses in Miles City.
It may be that once or twice yearly these towns revert to
old customs, and their streets glow with the color of
former years, but otherwise they are more concerned with
their future than their past, and are trying as fast as
possible to wipe out all traits that distinguish them from
every other thriving city.

Of this very section we drove through, back in the
eighties Theodore Roosevelt wrote, "In its present form
stock-raising on the plains is doomed and can hardly outlast the century. The great free ranches with their barbarous, picturesque and curiously fascinating surroundings, mark a primitive stage of existence as surely as do
the great tracts of primeval forests, and like the latter
must pass away before the onward march of our people;
and we who have felt the charm of the life, and have
exulted in its abounding vigor and its bold, restless freedom, will not only regret its passing for our own sakes,
but must also feel real sorrow that those who come after
us are not to see, as we have seen, what is perhaps the
pleasantest, healthiest, and most exciting phase of
American existence."

We came into the town of Medora on the Little Mis-
souri, after the hills had flattened out into the endless
plains of North Dakota. On a cutbank dominating the

river at its bend a great gloomy house frowns. Here the French Marquis de Mores once lived like a seigneur of the glorious Louis, in crude, patriarchal magnificence. Even in his lifetime he was a legend in this simple Dakotan village. But a greater legend centres in a large signboard opposite which tells that Roosevelt once ranched near by,—a matter of pride to all Medorans. Of this town in the eighties he wrote, "Medora has more than its full share of shooting and stabbing affrays, horse stealing and cattle-lifting. But the time for such things is passing away."

As we read the sign, a lanky Dakotan hovered near, and volunteered much information in a sing-song voice which seemed characteristic of the locality. "Right here at this bend," he said, "they're talking about putting up one of these here equesterian statutes of Teddy, mounted on horseback."

Being averse to stopping, we suggested that he ride to the village and tell us what he had to tell.

"Yes'm," he continued swinging to the running board without ceasing to talk. "In this here town interesting things has happened. But as interesting as ever happened is coming off tomorrow, and if you was a writer of books,"—a hit in the dark on his part—"I could tell you something to write down. For there's some of the richest men in this town, prominent men with good businesses,"—his voice took on an edge of strong feeling and I sensed something personal in his excitement,—"who has been found out to be part of a gang that has been stealing cattle wholesale, and shipping them to K. C. There's a fat, fleshy, portly man that's said to have stole 1200 head himself. And they've been getting rich on it for years, and would 'a kept on years more only one of the gang, an outsider, got caught, and is turning state's evidence. There'll be some excitement when they begin to make arrests. You'd better stay over, and see some doings aint been seen in a long time."

But we could not stay,—the Drang nach Osten was too strong for us. And a half-finished story sometimes is more alluring than one with the edges nicely bound. Yet I should like to have heard the reason for the note of personal grievance that shook the lanky stranger's voice when he spoke of the righteous vengeance about to fall on the cattle thieves.

We were not tempted to linger in North Dakota. No shade, no variety, no charm, nothing but wheat, wheat, wheat;—ruined crops left to bake in the glaring sun. Great grain elevators, community-owned, made the only vertical lines in the landscape. The rest was flat, and to us stale and unprofitable; colorless save for the faintly rainbow-tinted Bad Lands. What little individuality the state had was crude and dreary, reeking of Townleyism. With its wheat, its per capita wealth, and its beyond-the-minute legislation I have been told it is one of the most prosperous states of the Union. It may be. I know some people like South Dakota,—virtuous, prosperous, solid, yet with no shade trees, no bosky nooks, no charm. I leave their presence as quickly as we left Dakota to the companionship of its galvanized iron elevators. We sympathized with an old man who chatted with us when one of our frequent punctures halted us in a forsaken little hamlet. In fact, it was hardly a hamlet; it was more like a hamlet with the hamlet left out. We commented on the drought.

"I suppose you're used to it?"

"Me? I guess not! I don't belong here. Where I come from they've got a perfect climate all year round."

"California?" we asked wearily.

"Tacoma."

"But I've heard it's always raining in Tacoma."

"So it does. Rains every day of the year. There's a climate for you. Hope I get back to it some day, but," he shook his head sadly, "I don't know."

"Can't you sell out?"

"Don't own anything. Just here on a visit. Came here expecting to stay a couple a weeks, and been here three years and nine months."

"That almost sounds as if you like the place."

'Naw. Came on to bury my mother-in-law, and what do you know!" His sense of grievance mounted to indignation. "She ain't died yet!"

As we talked to the aged man whose faith in human nature had been so bitterly shattered by this perfidy in a near relative, he pointed to the lad who was mending our tire.

"That fellow went through the war from start to finish," he said. "Got decorated three times."

We looked at the desolate fields and the one forlorn main street, and wondered how a hero who had known the tenseness of war and the civilized beauty of France could endure to return to the bleak stupidity of the town.

"Where were you stationed in France?" we asked him.

"Well, I was everywhere,—in the Argonne, at Belleau Woods and Chattoo Thierry, and all them places."

"It must have been exciting."

"Well, it was pretty hot."

"Do tell us more about it."

"Well it was pretty hot,—pretty hot."

"Did you like France?"

"France?" His eyes kindled as they swept the bare prairie,—"Believe me, I was glad to get back where there's something doing. Mud,—that's what France was, —nothin' but mud!"

The tire he repaired gave out before evening, but we forgave him. Not every puncture can be patched by a hero of Belleau Wood. Besides, it was our twelfth that week, and one more or less had become a matter of indifference.

At Bismarck mine host met us at the sidewalk with, "Where's the Mister?"

"There *is* no Mister," answered Toby, to whom that question was a red rag. "We are alone."

What he said next is memorable only because we were soon to hear it for the last time, and its refrain already had a pensive note of reminiscence. But that we dared go so far from home Misterless raised his opinion of us to dizzy heights, and after personally escorting us to the garage, where he made a eulogistic speech in which we figured as intimate friends for whom any service rendered would be a personal favor to him, he gave us the best room his house afforded. Though cozy it was not the best house in town. We had long avoided exclusive hotels. Hardened by ten thousand miles of vagabondage, we had become completely indifferent to appearances, and wore our grimy khaki and dusty boots with the greatest disregard of the opinion of others either had ever attained. While Toby packed each morning, it was my duty to attend to the car, and to this fact I could boast the trimmer appearance of the two. When the tank was filled, I usually sprayed what gasolene remained in the hose over my clothes where they looked worst, but Toby was so far sunk in lassitude that she scorned such primping. Her suit was a collection of souvenirs of delightful hours. A smudge on the left knee recalled where she rested her tin plate in the Canyon de Chelley. Down the front a stain showed where Hostein Chee had upset a cup of coffee. Her elbows were coated with a paste of grease and dirt from innumerable tires, and minor spots checkerboarded her from chin to knee. As a precaution, when we had to stay at a first class hotel, I usually left Toby outside while I registered. Though the clerk never looked favorably upon me, he would give me a room, usually on the fourteenth floor if they went that high. Then, before he could see Toby I would smuggle her hurriedly across to the elevator. Sometimes she refused to be hurried, but examined postcards and magazines on the way, indifferent to the amazed, immaculate eyes turned toward us.

"I always maintain," she contended when I remonstrated with her, "that a person is well dressed if all her clothes are of the same sort, no matter what sort they are."

"In that case," I said, "you are undoubtedly well-dressed."

Secure in this consciousness, Toby sat down in the lobby of our Bismarck hotel with two dozen postcards which she proceeded to address to her sisters and her cousins and her aunts. As she warmed to her work, she gradually spread out until the cards covered the desk. A fellow lodger watched her, and finally rose and stood beside her, curiosity gleaming from his eyes and reflecting in his gold teeth which glittered as he spoke.

"Say! If you're going east"—he thrust a handful of business cards in her hands as he spoke—"maybe you'd just as lief distribute some of my cards with your own, as you go along."

Something I recognized as Cantabrigian, but he did not, in Toby's expression made him add propitiatingly, "Of course I'd expect to do the same for you. What's *your* line,—postcards?"

When what remained of him had thawed out sufficiently to fade away I ventured to look at his cards. They read, "Portable Plumbing and Bath Fixings."

"According to your theory," I consoled Toby, "in presenting a convincing and consistent appearance as a lady drummer for postcards and plumbing, you are well dressed. Therefore the poor man was only paying you a compliment——"

"He was fresh," said Toby. "Just fresh."

Only as we were leaving Dakota did we see a touch of homeliness,—in Fargo, a green, cozy place, full of neat, comfortable homes. As we crossed the state line here into Minnesota, instantly a change appeared. The air became moist and unirritating. Meadows and leafy forests, such as we have in New England, dozens of black, quiet lakes and little, sparkling streams, long wheat fields shaded by boundary rows of oaks, with six-horse teams harvesting grain flashed by us. Flock upon flock of red-winged and jet black blackbirds and wild ducks flashed from the reedy pools, whirring into the woods. We would have liked leisure to camp on the shores of some secluded pond until the spirit moved us on.

We saw something more in Minnesota than her black-birds and lakes and pretty woods and fields, her macadam roads and beautiful twin cities, frowning at each other from the high banks of the Mississippi. We saw the West fade, and give place to the East. The easy-going, slap-dash, restless, generous, tolerant, gossipy, plastic, helpful, jealous West was departing, not to reappear even sporadically. In its place we began to encounter caution, neatness, method, the feeling for property and the fear of strangers, that we were brought up with. We were clicking back into the groove of precedent and established order, no stronger, if as strong, on the Eastern seaboard than here. We could almost put our finger on the very town along the Red Trail where we noticed the transition. It was not Miles City nor Glendive,—Montana is still entirely western; it was not Bismarck nor the bleak little town of Casselton, west of Fargo. Probably it was Fargo that we should have marked for the pivotal town. At least the slight struggle a few villages beyond made to suggest the old, beloved West was soon quenched by the encroaching East. Some call the West Seattle, others Syracuse, N. Y., but I believe that Fargo very nearly marks the division. Grazing, sheep and cattle-raising increasingly lost place to the industries, city-building and manufactures, from this point eastward until they disappeared altogether.

Our last experience with what for lack of a neater phrase I have called western chivalry, occurred at a charming little town named St. Cloud, near Minneapolis. Our fourteenth and last puncture was changed and mended for us at an up-to-the-second garage. When we inquired what we owed we received a smile and the answer, "No charge for ladies."

"But you worked half an hour."

"Glad to do it. Come again when you have a puncture, and we'll charge you the same."

From this point till we reached home, we met with respectful treatment, but no suggestion that we belonged to a sex to whom special privileges must be accorded. That is what old-fashioned people used to say would happen when women had the vote. Yet we were leaving the pioneer suffrage states, and entering the anti's last stand.

Wisconsin surely is not the West, though we found it a fruitful, welcoming state anyone would be glad to live in. We got an impression of rolling fields, in brilliant patchwork of varying grains, like a glorified bedquilt spread under the sun; elms and summer haze, and a tangle of shade by the road; lazy, prosperous farmsteads, fat Dutch cattle, silver-green tobacco crops. The predominant impression was of gold and blue,—stacked wheat against the sky. Madison, into which we rolled one Sunday morning, presents an unhurried and stately best to the tourist, who sees it unprejudiced by miles of slatternly outskirts. He comes quickly to the Capitol, which is as it should be, the logical center of the town. Flanked by dignified University buildings set in green gardens, the State House stands in grounds planned to set off its perfect proportions. Without making it an object, we had seen many state Capitols,—Arizona's, New Mexico's, Utah's, Montana's, North Dakota's, Minnesota's—and some were imposing and some merely distressing. All, whatever their shortcomings, had a dome, as if it were a requirement of the Federal Constitution that whether it has honesty, dignity, grace or proportion, a state building must have a dome. In poor Boston, the dome has nearly disappeared under an attack of elephantiasis affecting the main body, as if someone had given the State House an overdose of yeast and set it in a warm place after forgetting to put any "risings" in the dome. Santa Fé's is modest and pretty enough. Salt Lake's is impressive and cold and very fine, but leaves one with no more of a taste for Capitols than before seeing it. Helena's is atrocious,—a bombastic dome overtopping a puny body, and Arizona's is so like all the others I cannot recall it in any respect. But Wisconsin's has charm and beauty, dignity and proportion, —all that an architect strives and usually fails to get in one building. Most capitols leave one unimpressed, but this is so satisfying and inspiring one wonders how its corridors can send forth such unpromising statesmen.

Our homeward journey seemed nearly ended before we reached Chicago. Driving over these perfectly kept roads of the middle west furnished no new experience. We decided to shorten the remaining interval still further by taking the Detroit boat to Buffalo. When we suddenly made this decision we had less than two days to make the 340 miles,—time enough, except for the state of our tires, which resembled that mid-Victorian neurasthenic Sweet Alice Ben Bolt. They collapsed if you gave them a smile, and blew out at fear of a frown. No longer in the belt of chivalry, we toiled over obstreperous rims, warped and bent from drought and flood, while able bodied men sailed by, and the only speech we had from them was an occasional jeering, "Hello, girls!"

Thus we knew we were fast returning to civilization. As we made out our bill of lading at Detroit we heard for the last time, "Well, you are a long ways from home." After that we felt we had already completed our period of vagabondage.

But the fates were not to let us finish tamely. The last act of our drama began when our rear tire gave way, and lost us two hours while we waited for repairs, just out of Chicago. The eastern entrance to Chicago, with its unsightly, factory-pocked marshes is cheerless enough even under blue skies. But a soggy downpour only made us shiver and hurry on. Chicago was well enough, as cities go, but the middle west did not hold us, having neither the courtesy of the South, the wide beauty of the West nor the self-respecting antiquity of the East. Yet here and there in the open country of Illinois, with its broad golden wheat fields, tall elms, and its homelike blue haze softening distant woods, a bit of English Warwickshire peeped out at us.

The drizzle soon settled into a steady downpour. All day we slushed over glistening macadam and through the heavy mud of section roads. Night fell early under the gloom of the rain while we were still many miles from the end of our day's stint. We decided to go as long as we could, or we never should reach Detroit in time. Camping was out of the question,—Illinois was too civilized for it to be safe procedure. So in deference to the solemn midwestern habit of laying out their country like a checkerboard, we paced so many miles east, so many miles south.

We left tracks in three states that day, the Yellowstone Trail dipping unexpectedly into Indiana, seen too late and briefly to leave any impression but of an excellent cafeteria at South Bend. Some time after dark, our sense of direction took a nose dive, and was permanently injured. At half-past eight we reckoned the miles, and knew there was to be no rest for the weary if we were to reach Detroit next day. Hopelessly lost by now, confused by many arguments, backings and turnings, we knocked, somewhere in Indiana, at a Hoosier door, and an old man in his stocking feet came out, calling lovingly, "That you, dear?" We almost wished we were his dear, and might rest in the yellow glow of his parlor instead of pushing on in the dark. We were several miles off our bearings in both directions it seemed. He told us off nine turns to the east and four to the north to straighten us out, and we went on into the night and the storm. We had gone out into the night and storm so often that no heroine of melodrama could tell us anything about either. But being by this time completely disorientated, instead of traveling nine east and four north, as they say in the easy vernacular of the midwest, we went instead nine west and four south, and came out at a lonely crossroads, the kind at which a murderer might appropriately be buried. Our arithmetic was quite unequal to adding and subtracting our mistakes. Seeing a house with one light burning, I reached its door to ask directions. There, unashamed, through the lighted window, a lady sat in her nightdress, braiding her hair. I backed away, not wishing to embarrass her. It was not as if I were one of the neighbors, whom she seemed not to mind. A dismal quarter of a mile away, another light gleamed. I walked to it. An old woman cautiously put her head out of the door. She too was in an honest flannel nightie, and I concluded that the mid-west wears its nightgear unabashed.   My sudden appearance, and especially the fact of my inquiring for a great city like Detroit, was not reassuring to her.   She asked suspiciously if I were alone and at my answer, exclaimed, "Aint you afraid?"

Her question gave me genuine amazement.   I had forgotten that in the eastern section of our country people are afraid of each other, and I had grown so far away from it that I laughed and said, "Not in the least." She seemed to think this marvelous.   A motherly old soul, her sympathy struggled hard with her fear that I was bent on forcing a violent entrance into her house, but finally the baser suspicions won and she shut the door firmly on me until she could confer with "Pa."   He, being bolder, came openly to the porch in his,—was it pajamas or nightshirt?—I can hardly say, because not to embarrass him I only looked past his snowy beard and into his nice blue eyes.   He directed us.   We were to go seven north and thirteen west.

For half an hour the sleepy Toby and I wrestled with the problem of where we now were, how far from our starting point, from our destination, from our last checking up,—till we feared for our reason.   Like a ballad refrain, we went seven miles south and thirteen west, —but instead of a town met a pine forest.   So, a few miles more or less meaning nothing to us, we threw in several to the north and a couple east, with the same unpromising result.   At the rate we were going, I expected to reach either the Gulf of Mexico or the Pacific Ocean by morning.

Once we heard the whirr of a mighty engine over our

heads,—some belated airman, lost like ourselves doubtless in the rain above us. If anything could have made
us feel lonelier than we had, it would have been this
evidence of an unseen neighbor who shared the night
and the storm with us.

We came to another house. I stopped the car.
Neither of us moved. "I went last time," I said point-
edly.

"Huh-yah-yah," protested Toby, but I did not yield,
because I had fallen asleep. She wearily tottered out to
the house, and brought back a Hoosier farmer with her,
who fastened his suspenders as he came.

"You're some out of your way," he said, unnecessarily,
"but five east and eight south you'll find a small hotel
where you can spend the night."

"Is it all right?" I asked dubiously.

"Well," he considered, "being a neighbor, I don't like
to say. You might like it better at Orland, seven miles
further."

We decided on Orland and slushed along in mud so
thick we could hardly hold the wheel stiff. Suddenly
we heard an ominous sound,—a steady thump, thump,
thump. I got out in the downpour and looked at the tires.
They were hard. I peered at the engine. It purred with
a mighty purr. So I climbed in again, and we started
hopefully; again came the heavy thumping, a sound fit
to rack a car into bits. However, as the engine still func-
tioned we decided to go as long as we could, though the
noise struck terror to our hearts. We were too weary
and wet to wallow in the mud and dark, investigating
engine troubles. I drove cautiously, and after what
seemed hours we reached Orland. The thumping now

had become violent, but we didn't care. A roof and a bed were practically within our grasp.

It was a neat little town with white buildings and shady trees. Had we been motoring through on a sunny afternoon we might have said, "What a sweet place!" But we were too tired for æsthetic appreciation. Across the street was a large, comfortable white hotel, with broad hospitable porch. We hastened to rap on the door.

After a quarter of an hour, we ceased to hasten, but we continued to knock intermittently. Then Toby blew the horn as viciously as she knew how. The silent town seemed to recoil from our rude noise and gather the bed quilts closer about it. But no response came from the hotel. From the second floor came sounds of slumbering. Becoming expert we counted three people asleep. The three snores dwindled to two snores and a cough, after our experiment with the horn, and later diminished to a cough and two voices, speaking in whispers. We wanted to call out that we knew they were awake, and why didn't they come down and let us in, but we knew they had no intention of stirring. We were in a state of enraged helplessness. We rapped until it was quite apparent the hotel was resolved not to establish a dangerous precedent by admitting strangers after midnight. Then we gave up. But Orland owed us a bed and if we could we were going to exact it. We felt as if it were a duel between the town and ourselves.

Our last knock brought a head from a little room over the store next door, and a woman's voice called, "Who is it?"

"Two ladies from Boston," we answered, guilefully using the magic words which in happier climes had brought cheerful repartee and prompt sustenance. We did not get the expected reaction, but her tone was apprehensive, if kind, when she asked, "What do you want?"

We told her, though she might have guessed.

"Knock again," she said. "There's someone there. They ought to hear you."

"They hear us all right," we said, loud enough for the cough and two voices not to miss, "but they won't let us in. Do you know of any place where we can go?"

"I'd take you in here," said the voice,—the only sign of hospitality we had from Orland that night,—"but my husband and I have one room, and the children the other."

Even standing on an alien sidewalk at two-thirty A. M. in the rain we felt less forlorn now that we had someone to talk to. A male rumble made a quartette of our trio, which after a discussion, she reported.

"*He* says you might try Uncle Ollie's." Her voice implied she thought the suggestion barren.

I dared not let her see we didn't know Uncle Ollie for fear it might prejudice this suspicious hamlet against us. So I queried cautiously, "Now, just where does he live?" as if it had only slipped my mind for the moment.

"Go down the road a piece and turn west,—it's the second house. But I dunno whether you'll be able to wake him. He's kinder deaf."

We thanked her, and said goodnight and she wished us good luck. We bumped the damaged old lady down the main street, her thumpings making such a racket that we expected the constable to arrest us any moment for disturbing the peace. We had, however, no intention of trying Uncle Ollie's.

A half mile further, within a pretty white cottage set shyly from the road, we saw a light burning. This was so unusual for Orland that we invaded the premises with new hope. Toby being again comatose, I waded wearily to the door and knocked. A frightened girl's voice answered, and its owner appeared at the door. I shall always think of Indiana and Michigan as a succession of old and young standing on doorsteps in their nightgowns.

"Who is it?" called a voice from an inner room.

"Two women want a place to spend the night, gran'-maw," answered the girl.

"Well, don't you let 'em in here," answered gran'maw.

"No, I don't know of any place," the girl translated gran'maw to us, shutting the door.

"Of all churlish towns!" we said, left on the doorstep. But it was not a just criticism. We had simply crossed the line where west is east, where a stranger is perforce a suspicious character. Back in New England would *we* have let in two strange women after midnight? Their asking to come in would have been proof presumptive they were either criminal or crazy.

Our duel lost we drew up the old lady in a gutter under some dripping elms, and lay down to a belated sleep among the baggage,—Toby in one seat, I in another. In a twinkling we sat up, refreshed, to broad daylight and a shining morning sky. Our first thought was to search for the car's internal injuries, fearing greatly they might prevent us going further. There were none. Two tumors the size of a large potato on our front tire revealed the cause of the noise. The marvel was that the tire had not collapsed as a finishing touch to last night's dismal story. Luck, in its peculiar way, was again with us.

While we changed to our last spare tire, Toby straightened up for a moment, and suddenly broke into a bitter, sardonic laugh. "Will you look at that!" she said, pointing overhead.

Directly above our patient car a large, brightly painted sign flapped energetically in the clearing breeze. It read, in letters a yard high, "Welcome to Orland!"

Made in the USA
Middletown, DE
05 May 2018